MALCHUS ONE EAR

✠ ✠ ✠

A Novel

R. Gordon Zyne

iUniverse books may be ordered through booksellers or by contacting:

iUniverse
1663 Liberty Drive
Bloomington, IN 47403
www.iuniverse.com
1-800-Authors (1-800-288-4677)

Because of the dynamic nature of the Internet, any Web addresses or links contained in this book may have changed since publication and may no longer be valid. The views expressed in this work are solely those of the author and do not necessarily reflect the views of the publisher, and the publisher hereby disclaims any responsibility for them.

ISBN: 978-1-4502-0774-4 (sc)
ISBN: 978-1-4502-0776-8 (dj)
ISBN: 978-1-4502-0775-1 (ebook)

Library of Congress Control Number: 2010901523

Printed in the United States of America

iUniverse rev. date: 02/23/2010

Then Simon Peter, who had a sword, drew it, struck the high priest's slave, and cut off his right ear. The slave's name was Malchus. But Jesus said, "No more of this!" And He touched his ear and healed him.

Luke 22:50–51 and John 18:10–11

PROLOGUE

✠ ✠ ✠

A YOUNG WOMAN CONCEIVED AND GAVE BIRTH to a son. When she saw that he was very small and deformed, she hid him three months in a paper sack and kept him in the dark cellar of her tenement. When she could hide him no longer, she took a garbage can and filled it with newspapers and a tin of evaporated milk. She put the child in the garbage can and placed it among the flotsam on the bank of the East River. His sister stood at a distance to see what would happen to him.

The daughter of the commissioner of sanitation came down to gaze upon the river and to weep for its lost beauty. She saw the garbage can among the floating debris and filth and sent her assistant to retrieve it. When she opened the garbage can, she saw the child. He cried and she took pity on him. He was a special child like none who had ever been seen upon the earth. The commissioner's daughter took the child, nursed it, and delivered it to the sanctuary of Bellevue Hospital. They named him Malchus, because he only had one ear, and then forgot about him for thirty years.

CHAPTER 1

⊹ ⊹ ⊹

MALCHUS ONE EAR LOOKED AT HIS REFLECTION in the mirror of a subway restroom in Manhattan. He sighed, adjusted his hat, and returned to the platform to wait for the next train. When the train arrived, he ran to the front end of the first car and stuck his face against the window so he could gaze down the dark tunnel. Malchus often spoke with angels who entered the subway trains in Manhattan on their way to the Bronx.

Malchus pressed his nose against the glass window. His floppy hat covered a large hydrocephalic water-filled head. His delicate translucent hands were like those of a tiny tree frog clutching the glass on the inside wall of an aquarium. His lips pressed against the filthy glass and he appeared to be making love to the door at the front end of the car. He hoped that the motorman wouldn't see him, and he dreaded arguing with the transit cops as they tried to arrest him for lewd behavior. He'd point to the signs on the wall and yell in his own defense, "I'm not spitting!" When he was arrested, they'd keep him locked up for the night and then call a psychiatric social worker who would check his medication and then send him on his way.

Malchus knew the New York City subway system well and memorized the maze of routes and stations. He could smell the difference between upper Manhattan and the Bronx while traveling at forty miles per hour beneath the Harlem River. He asked strangers on the platforms for spare change, and he waited for his messiah who would, he claimed, arrive on a train from Coney Island.

In a vision, a prophet had once instructed him to take two Hershey's Kisses and turn them into a basketful of candy bars to feed the hungry, grumpy commuters. Some would accept his gifts with pleasure, while others would simply cast the candy onto the tracks as if it were poison. It didn't matter to Malchus whether they accepted his gifts. It didn't matter whether they smiled or cursed him to his face. He carried his books in a tiny suitcase filled with his mortal belongings and told the world how Peter had cut off his ear in the Garden of Gethsemane and how Jesus had healed it.

Malchus' strange behavior, even in the subways of New York City, was especially odd and troublesome. He looked weird, like something out of a book of medical anomalies. A doctor had told him that he was born without a brain; that his unusually large head was merely filled with spinal fluid and a thin membrane that contained a few brain cells, but nothing more. That Malchus walked, talked, and spoke with exquisite clarity was truly miraculous. His intense visions were an endless source of terror and ecstasy. He couldn't tell the difference between his benign mystical visions and his demonic hallucinations. Even his body seemed to exhibit various physical states. Some days Malchus would be solid and walk the streets of the city banging into people on the street just to see how they reacted. Other days he would be a liquid and slide between the cracks of doors and flow down pavement gutters. Sometimes he thought of himself as lubricating oil for the wheels on subway cars or even as mustard to be squeezed out on hot dogs. When Malchus was a gas, he was invisible and could go anywhere he wanted. He would stand on the subway platform or in the middle of the sidewalk and make grotesque faces at the people walking by. They didn't even notice him.

Malchus stood on the vacant subway platform and cursed God. "Why have you made me like this?" he screamed. "They told me I couldn't think, so I prayed. The doctors told me I'd never walk or talk either, and if I don't have a brain, how is it possible that I think?"

The poor little man was confused. He stuck his finger in the hole on the side of his head pushing it in as far as it could go so that he might feel his brain, or at least, touch the slippery fluid that supposedly sloshed in his cranium.

Malchus read books on his subway rides, especially large tomes on philosophy and theology. He demanded that God stop his visions and hallucinations. He didn't need a messenger from Satan to torment him. Malchus appealed to God hundreds of times, but God just sent back the same message written on the subway wall: "My grace is sufficient for you, for my power is made perfect in your weakness."

Malchus could have spent his entire life inside the walls of a New York City psychiatric hospital. He was a perfect specimen for long-term institutionalization: a ward of the state, destitute, psychiatrically disabled, physically disabled, and chronically ill. His thirty years as a patient were spent behind closed doors in the presence of clinical professionals, brutish guards, and severely impaired minds. But times were changing, and the mammoth institutions that housed thousands of mentally ill patients were now routinely sending them into the world and into the arms of a society that couldn't hold them. Science was changing, too, and the human mind was no longer considered just an ethereal construct, but a biochemical factory and physical entity just a bit more complex and interesting than the liver. Out of this scientific revolution came miracle drugs that helped put demons back in their holes. The quiet psychotic was now leaving his cell and wandering into the neighbor's backyard. Some would roam the landscape as helpless sheep, only to be slaughtered by hungry wolves. Others would burrow underground and be forgotten. Some would actually find homes and productive work in caring communities. For the most part, however, the world was just too busy for them. The institutions were shrinking or shutting down. The big mental hospitals were a casualty of the times, but nobody really cared.

Malchus was not one of the first to leave the confines of the psychiatric prison, but he was one of the last. He didn't know about the outside world because no outside world existed for him. His entire universe consisted of his hospital ward and his bed. Then one day, they opened the doors of the hospital and put him out with his bottle of pills, a few dollars, a child's suitcase filled with his books, a list of phone numbers to call, and a one-way ticket to an intermediate care rehabilitation facility in Brooklyn called the Brewery by its residents. They told him to take the subway, but he had never been on a train before. So they put him on a train, and he sat and rode it for nearly three days. The little man was told to go out and discover his new world, but he thought the subway was his new world. He slept in the cars, peed on the tracks, and ate stale candy bars from the vending machines. When he walked through the stations, he would hold his hat in front of him and people would throw in their loose change. This was Malchus' new home, and he was quite content to travel the city and meet the people beneath the streets of New York.

Occasionally, Malchus was arrested for disorderly conduct and they would bring him in to be observed by a psychiatric social worker. Most of the time, however, Malchus just needed to take his medication, which kept him calm and rational. When he didn't take it, he was a raving lunatic.

Once, after four days hallucinating in a lavatory in the South Bronx, he got into a subway car stark naked and swung from the overhead strap handles. When he was subdued and arrested, he told the magistrate that he was just making an aesthetic statement. He threatened to sue the city for defamation of character and for suppressing his right to free speech and expression.

Malchus' intelligence and rational behavior impressed the judge, but the social worker knew that Malchus had become a master of manipulation. So they took him back to the psychiatric hospital for a few days, filled him with medicine, and then sent him on his way back into the subway.

Human beings are not piles of refuse, but when enough of them get together in a drunken stupor or in a psychotic rage, society tends to treat them like garbage. Malchus was certainly not garbage. He was not filth, and as good fortune would have it, he was not a forgotten soul. By chance, a slovenly but good-natured social worker named Naphtali Ropshitz—Tali for short—shared a box of Goobers with Malchus at the Fulton Street station in Brooklyn. The two became good buddies.

Tali was a converted Hasidic Jew who embraced Taoism, but still had a deep craving for potato knishes and his mother's cooking. He spent two years as a member of the Hare Krishna in the late sixties and handed out flowers at airports. He shaved his head and danced in the streets. Tali was also a devotee of transcendental meditation and claimed to have spent time in India with the Beatles. When Tali had too much to drink, he believed that he was the reincarnation of Israel Baal Shem

Tov, the greatest of all Hasidic masters. There was nobody on the face of the earth that Tali didn't love. He even told people that if he and Adolf Hitler had been childhood friends, he would know how to make the devil into a saint! There was so much love in Naphtali Ropshitz's heart that he was fired by the city's Department of Social Services for being too compassionate.

Tali's father was a rabbi in the Williamsburg section of Brooklyn. He disowned his son, but still sent him a five hundred dollar gift during Hanukkah. Tali had good connections and became a self-styled street consultant working with the men in the rescue missions and in the flophouses. He roamed from one center to the next. He received free meals and a cot wherever he went. The mission workers loved him and were impressed by his abilities to motivate destitute men. He was a true twentieth century prophet on the streets of New York City. He got men jobs, picked them off the street when they were drunk, and said Kaddish for them when they died. He pointed to people with his big fat finger and told them that the messiah was coming on the train from Coney Island and that they'd better be ready. Now that the mental hospitals were unloading their patients by the thousands, he had his work cut out for him. Even the local parishes praised his street work and they made him an honorary Catholic.

Tali helped to keep Malchus sane and found a place for him at the Brewery, a rehabilitation center in the Greenpoint section of Brooklyn. He brought Malchus into the big facility and told the old-time residents that Malchus was an Aborigine from a south sea island in the Pacific. Malchus became something of a celebrity and entertained the men with his strange wit and physical acrobatics. He sorted rags and pulled out cotton cloth from hundreds of bags of home discards. The cotton was a source of revenue for the Brewery. It was bundled and compressed into huge bales and sold to foreign buyers. He worked in a thrift store for a while, but was too short to handle the cash register. He couldn't drive a truck because his feet didn't reach the pedals. He couldn't haul a sofa or a refrigerator, so they put him in the kitchen where he peeled potatoes, made salads, and baked cookies. He'd even feed some of the old sick men who were bedridden. Malchus became a successful human being despite himself.

CHAPTER 2

✠ ✠ ✠

JACOB KORETZ SAT ON THE FRONT STOOP of his apartment building, blood gushing from a fresh wound in his forehead. The old man cursed the assailant who had thrown a beer bottle at him from the welfare hotel across the street. Jacob was a good target and a big one at that, especially at seven o'clock in the morning when people were cranky and just getting out of bed. The old man was fond of walking up and down Washington Avenue, spewing blessings and curses upon his neighbors. The bleeding stopped. Daniel Aarons, Jacob's nephew, sat next to him and tugged lovingly at the old man's beard.

"Uncle, you need a shave. You'll be tripping over that damned beard in a few days. Why don't you get it trimmed?"

The old man nodded and grudgingly agreed to visit a barber. Jacob Koretz wasn't really an *old* man, but he had seen enough misery and suffering in his life of sixty-five years to fill a dozen novels. Most of the time, his mind was in exile beyond the Euphrates River, languishing in a medieval rabbinical yeshiva in Babylon. The sight of him on the street evoked reverence by some and disdain by others. He was the wandering prophet of the streets, the wild crazy man who talked to himself. His long beard had become a symbol of his suffering and a mark of his triumph. It had become an unkempt mass of knots, dried food, and insects. Daniel declared him a public health nuisance and demanded that he do something about the beard.

Daniel Aarons was a scholar and adjunct professor of psychology, sociology, and social work at Brooklyn College. That morning he told his uncle Jacob that he was going for a job interview that would change his life. Daniel assured Jacob that he was following a divine calling and listening to *a still small voice.*

In truth, Daniel Aarons was a mouse caught in an old trap, a trap that had been set behind the refrigerator many years ago and had not been noticed by the new tenants. The cheese was long gone, but Daniel stepped on this device and trapped himself. He was a live mouse with his neck not yet broken, but still very much a prisoner of a blind, mindless contraption that was not originally intended for him. The city was his trap. His mind was his trap. His uncle was his trap. His books, his science, his intellect were all his traps. He felt called by some higher power, but his tiny mouse legs just kicked the dark air behind the refrigerator.

"What a mind!" his uncle would say. "You could be a concert pianist, a great surgeon, a brilliant lawyer. But no, you just explore the anuses of fleas and then you ponder the dust that collects under the bed."

Daniel Aarons was an explorer of minutia, the spaces between letters on a page and the fine line that separates the wife from the lover. He was a creator of goals, sub-goals, sub-sets of objectives, and endless tasks. Daniel thought he was an explorer, but he set sail with Columbus only to discover that the world was actually flat and that he was living on the wrong side. His view was always from the underside, from the bottom up. He recognized people from the soles of their feet, from the warts on the underside of their chins, from the wrinkles on their elbows. But what do you expect from a man who was found on the top of a pile of corpses in a concentration camp—a newborn infant—by a couple of American GIs in 1945? Daniel Aarons was simply a miracle, but not a happy miracle. He wanted to be immersed in fire and be purified. He wanted to burn so brightly that the whole world would know that he was truly an instrument of a higher power, a tool of the Almighty!

Daniel looked at his uncle Jacob, his mother's only brother, and told him he'd be back in a few hours.

"Jacob, I'm going to my interview now. Please remember to take your medication and call Dr. Katz for an appointment. You know you need to get the prescription changed on your glasses. I've seen how you've been tripping over all the junk on the floor."

"I'd stop tripping over the junk if you'd pick up your damn books," Jacob said, defending his territory. He waved at his nephew as if to say, "Get lost. Don't bother coming back to my house with your crazy ideas. Get a real job."

Daniel thought about the anuses of fleas and specks of dust and cursed his uncle's creative metaphors.

He took the subway to Greenpoint and stepped off into a bleak landscape of warehouses, gray commercial buildings, and urban decay. The trapped mouse with the broken neck thought himself to be a sophisticated New Yorker, a man of high intellectual ability and strong moral character. He was a man of ability and action with the rod of the Almighty in his right hand and the knowledge of the universe tucked away in a dark, hidden cerebral cavity miles beneath the surface of his skull. He would take broken men and turn them into fine specimens of humanity. He would implement social policy to heal their mental afflictions. He would delve into the depths of their tormented souls and pull out their demons. A surge of energy suddenly came over him as he wound his way through this wretched part of the borough. He was coming to the Holy Land, like a crusader on his way to Jerusalem.

Daniel's head swelled until a sharp pain filled his skull. He felt as if his forehead was pressing against a solid wall of wind. His ears popped like windows in an airplane about to burst open after decompression. The back of his head was an overflowing Dumpster. He prayed and his head shrunk and shriveled like a spent balloon.

He stood on Ten Eyck Street searching for the Brewery. His anticipation was mixed with excitement and a twinge of anxiety. A rush of adrenaline went through his tense body as he approached the fortress by a stinking little canal called the English Kills.

Looming before him like a dark colossus was the Brewery. It occupied a full city block and had once churned out local beers with names like *Brook Brau* and *Huld's Original Lager*. The only thing this old brewery produced now was a steady stream of burned-out human beings. How ironic, this decrepit old building was now a rehabilitation center for alcoholics and chronically mentally ill men.

Daniel's head cleared. He could feel a cool breeze and the fresh scent of a garden. The sound of water from the nearby canal purified his mind. He walked onto a steep driveway that led to a loading dock filled with dilapidated trucks in various states of disrepair. The dead husks of old trucks cannibalized for their parts looked like long-dead corpses. A large hand-printed sign on a rusted chain-link fence simply read, **KEEP OUT!**

Two men on the loading dock stood like a tableau, their eyes focused on the intruding stranger. One of the men, a bearded cowboy, became violently animated, his hand and finger vigorously pointing to the trucks. The man wagged his finger at the uninvited stranger. Daniel stood behind the crumpled carcass of a dying truck that was moving slowly down the driveway in reverse with no red taillights and no horn. He was blocking commerce, inhibiting the vital business that was being carried out on the loading dock. The men were unloading the booty from the trucks.

Daniel hadn't made a good first impression, and he didn't know much about the collection of used household goods and bric-a-brac. If he were going to be successful, he'd have to learn this part of the rehabilitation business very quickly.

Daniel apologized to the men on the dock, but there was no verbal acknowledgment, just some rude body language. One of the men, the small fat one with the sneakers, spat a foul black wad of tobacco in Daniel's direction. The cowboy turned his head away from the stranger, scratched his crotch, and disappeared into the darkness of the warehouse. Daniel tripped and stepped on the lid of a garbage can.

Abandoned cars littered the old industrial area. Two burned-out stripped heaps sat like buffalo corpses, their hides eaten away to brown rust by the city's polluted air. They adorned the Brewery's main entrance like stone lions in front of a library. A large rusting Dumpster with flies and a slaughterhouse stench sat beneath the windows of the dormitories of the Brewery.

Daniel adjusted his tie. With his briefcase in hand, he walked through the grand entry assured of a warm and professional greeting from the highly trained staff. The inside foyer was poorly lit and smelled from mildew. A massive set of doors with iron fittings and brass knobs resembled the portals to a medieval castle. Above the filth and faded paint was an elegantly hand lettered sign: The Service Corps for the Religious Enlightenment and Rehabilitation of Alcoholic Men—a Christian Mission established in 1878 by the Reverend G. Walter Thurman.

Daniel reached out to turn the large brass knob on the door, but it wouldn't budge. His hand was covered in greasy soot. The knob, it seemed, had not been touched for years, and the great doors had not been opened for probably just as long. He wiped his hand on a sheet of paper and knocked with authority on the door. Through an interior window, Daniel could see a small light and several men talking and smoking. At the sound of Daniel's knocks, one of the men came to the door yelling, "Go to the loading dock entrance, this ain't a door no more." Daniel thanked the man who had given him the instructions, and he gave him a thumbs-up sign. Once again, he walked up the steep incline until he came to the loading dock, where, just as before, he encountered the two men—fat man with sneakers and the cowboy. Both were now smoking and squinting while pointing to the collected merchandise piled on the dock in a disorderly heap. The larger of the two men—the cowboy—wore a white T-shirt with a cigarette pack shoved up the sleeve. He sweated and wiped his dark brown forehead with a bright red bandanna. He kicked a large stuffed sofa that appeared to have lain in a tenement cellar since before the First World War. He spat on the forlorn object and cursed it.

"Piece of shit. I'm just going to have to take it to the dump and give it to the birds to piss on. Why don't the assholes in there tell them that we don't pick up shit like this? I'm gonna break my back carrying this piece of shit to the dump."

He kicked the sofa again as if it were a disobedient dog that had soiled the living room carpet. The third kick was fatal. Stuffing and its crumbling brown innards spewed out of the old, shabby body. He had punctured a vital organ. The sofa went over the side of the dock, presumably to its death. The other man on the dock was a small fat man with a shining, bald head. The two looked like a burlesque team. The little fat man told Daniel how to get into the building while the big man spat on the dock and continued to curse the sofa's corpse.

A heavy wooden ramp led from the loading dock to the entrance of the building and then to a suite of grimy, dimly lit offices. Daniel could see the movement of heads and the upward twisting of cigarette smoke. He heard a woman's hoarse laugh and then a round of heavy coughing. A door slammed and then the sound of footsteps came down a hallway. Daniel shook his head as if to get rid of his anxiety and he walked up the ramp. In front of the screen door sat a large, hideously deformed cat. The beast blocked his way and prevented him from opening the screen door. It refused to move and sat there like a security guard. Its fur was a dirty gray tinged with grease, soot, and automotive oil. Its left ear was flattened over its head. One long fang hung out of its mouth. The left eye was missing and the eye socket was sewn completely shut. Its front paws were flattened as if they had been run over by a truck. Its tail slapped the gray pavement like a metronome. This animal had been around the block a few times and it demanded respect. Daniel didn't attempt to pet the creature, but gingerly stepped over it and pulled the screen door open. The cat got the message, hissed, and walked down the ramp.

At last, Daniel Aarons entered the Service Corps for the Religious Enlightenment and Rehabilitation of Alcoholic Men. He walked into a small reception room. The stale smell of cigarette smoke made him queasy. He wiped his sweaty hands on his pants. The young woman at the front desk ignored him. Laughter arose from the office next to the reception room where a meeting was in progress. The screen door slammed shut. A small air conditioner grumbled and sputtered in one of the windows. It produced far more noise than cold air and dripped water into a pie pan on the floor.

On the walls of this little room, hung brown faded photographs of men who benefited from the programs of the Service Corps. Some of these men were in uniform and looked like doormen standing outside fancy apartment buildings with epaulets and medals. Some were toothless and shabby in T-shirts hauling furniture out of old trucks. There were gray, mousy women with hair pulled back in tight buns sitting at antique typewriters. A photo of a large preacher with a Bible and a huge tongue, pounding a pulpit, was the centerpiece.

Cheap and mismatched wood paneling hung on the walls of the office. A fluorescent fixture gave a yellowish light and buzzed in concert with the wheezing air conditioner.

Daniel sighed, took a deep breath, and prepared to be greeted by the young woman behind the desk. At that very moment, out of the conference room walked a short stocky man in a doorman's uniform. He didn't stop in his quick trot down a dark hallway to greet Daniel, who was still standing in the reception area. Quick footsteps could be heard down the hallway, followed by a metallic thud and then the shouting of several obscenities.

"Shoot fire! Croix, I thought I told you to put orange tape on this glass door and to put a bulb in the overhead socket. That was at least two months ago! I almost killed myself! Who the hell is in charge here? Shoot fire!"

The young woman behind the desk, who was apparently the Croix in mention, jumped up from her desk and briskly walked down the hall to meet the uniformed officer. The young woman, profoundly sorry at the incident, apologized profusely to the man, whom she addressed as Colonel Boyer. She shouted out to some other men in the building to tape the door and put in a new bulb in the overhead socket. Colonel Boyer, who was apparently on his way to the men's lavatory, soon returned through the doorway holding his hat in his hand and a handkerchief to a superficial wound on his forehead. His face was red, and beads of sweat rolled down from the top of his baldhead. He was angry and cursed under his breath as he made his way back to the conference room.

The young woman, now back at her desk, covered her mouth as if to stifle a laugh. She put her head down on the desk and sighed in exasperation into the blotter. Daniel took a seat and stared blankly at the screeching air conditioner. The young woman spoke to him in an unprofessional, familiar, and highly sarcastic manner.

"That's Colonel Boyer. He pronounces his name like the French actor, you know Charles Boyer. He's our executive regional officer and operations director, a very important person in the Service Corps." Her eyes rolled. "If you're Dr. Aarons, you'll be meeting with him and the board shortly."

As if he had just walked in the door and the incident with Boyer had never happened, Daniel spoke to the young woman with a traditional but stiff greeting.

"Good afternoon. I'm Dr. Aarons and I'm here to meet with Colonel Boyer and the board."

He sat across from Miss Croix's desk with his briefcase on his lap. He looked up and his eyes met hers.

"Hi, I'm Stephanie Croix," she said. "I run this place, or should I say it runs me."

She stuck out her hand, stood up, and made an obvious gesture to shake Daniel's hand.

He got up. "I'm very pleased to meet you," he said in a dry, business-like manner.

Stephanie told Daniel that she was not actually the center's director, but really the director's assistant, actually just a secretary with an art degree from a correspondence school. But since the center had not had an official director in more than nine months, Colonel Boyer made her the de facto director with no real authority, no official designation or rank, and no increase in salary.

"The real strings," she said, "were pulled from Biloxi, Mississippi, the national headquarters of The Service Corps for the Religious Enlightenment and Rehabilitation of Alcoholic Men. In other words, Colonel Boyer just comes up once every few months to see how things are going and they aren't going too well at all."

Stephanie Croix adjusted a form into her ancient Smith-Corona typewriter, which sat on her World War II vintage army surplus desk. One small flower sat in a Coke bottle next to her name plaque, which simply read, Lt. Stephanie Croix, Secretary.

Daniel was deep in meditation. Stephanie didn't look anything like the old prune-faced crones in photos on the walls. She had a freshly polished face with two large brown eyes that were frequently behind a pair of glasses. The glasses went on and came off three and four times a minute as she dashed from her typewriter to the desk blotter. She had a small mouth that she obviously amplified with bright red lipstick. The mouth grew substantially in size whenever she talked or smiled, exposing beautiful white teeth. From the red lips hung an occasional cigarette that dangled from the lower lip as if glued there. She didn't wear the female version of the doorman's uniform either, although she had the unofficial rank of lieutenant. Her slim body was covered with a pair of well-worn jeans and a faded blouse, which looked like it had come off a rack in one of the thrift stores. She wore a pair of very unstylish high-top sneakers. Her dark brown hair was very short and from behind, she almost looked like an adolescent boy. From the front, she looked like an adolescent boy with earrings and lipstick.

Stephanie instantly stopped her work as if a gong had gone off in her head, and she apologized to Daniel.

"Dr. Aarons, I'm truly sorry for the inconvenience. Nothing in this place works well or works at all for that matter. It's as if we're all in some sort of time warp where the clocks are all broken and we just keep making the same mistakes over and over again … like we're all in hell. But, I guess that's why you're here, to bring a little piece of heaven to this damned hell hole." Stephanie flattered Daniel. Her big eyes glowed and she tilted her head like a puppy.

"I'm really embarrassed," she said. "One of these days they're going to find my little shriveled-up body in some corner and throw me out with all the garbage." She laughed and pounded the keys on her typewriter. She apparently had no typing skills and used several sheets of paper to complete an application.

Daniel stared up at the ceiling and counted the water-stained tiles. The thought of throwing this girl out with the garbage, like so much refuse, brought back the depressing image of infants on tops of piles of corpses. Was she a bruised and damaged baby, too? Was she the child of alcoholic parents who beat her and hid her in a closet for weeks? Was she mortally wounded? Daniel Aarons wanted to touch her skin just to see how soft it was, even to see if it was real. Perhaps if he touched her she, too, would crumble like the buildings around him. Perhaps she was just another one of his sad visions, but at least she was a beautiful apparition.

"I know that your meeting was scheduled for two o'clock," she said. "You see, I've got it here marked on my calendar, but Dr. Jefferson, the woman who was scheduled to meet the board before you, just got here about a half hour ago and she should have been here at twelve-thirty. I'm sure they're going to want to talk with her for at least another thirty minutes."

Daniel's heart sank and he felt an uncomfortable pressure in his lower abdomen. He would be forced to ask Stephanie Croix for directions to the men's lavatory. The thought of sitting one additional minute in the hideous office with cramps or bladder pressure sent a cold chill down his already sweaty back.

Stephanie continued her monologue, and Daniel sat like the good listener.

"The sooner they get somebody in here who knows what to do with this place, the better I'll feel," she said with a cigarette in her mouth. "I'm not trained to deal with sixty drunks coming in and out, tearing the place apart, spitting, yelling, and threatening. I feel like a nursemaid half the time." She snuffed out the cigarette. "Don't get me wrong, there are a lot of good guys in here. It's just that when they get drunk, and believe me they get damn drunk, they come back, yell at me, and then tear the place apart. What am I supposed to do, pull their pants down and give them a spank? Just look at this place. You call this an office? It used to be part of the loading dock. They just put up a few walls, threw up some ugly paneling, and here I sit with a revolting view of a thousand worn out tires, a bunch of dead trucks, and an endless stream of bald, toothless men." She thought for a moment. "Well, some of them are cute. However, they're few and far between and they don't stay long. They're in for a week, getting bored or drunk, and then they're out the door never to be seen again. The old, ugly, fat ones, now, they're in it for life. Once they realize they can get some food, they settle down and become part of the woodwork, like the mice."

Daniel wanted to ask her why she stayed in this dump, why she didn't just find a better job. She was such a beautiful young woman, so why wasn't she on Madison Avenue making lots of money or having babies? He didn't open his mouth. Stephanie continued her confession and Daniel sat there like a good therapist with a talkative client, just listening and watching the clock.

"Oh, forgive me, I'm so rude," she said as she lit another cigarette. "Here I go talking on and on about this place, opening my soul to *you*. I'm sorry. It's just that sometimes I really don't have anybody who wants to listen to *me*." She continued her whining lament. "I listen to everybody else, but nobody wants to hear what I have to say."

She changed the conversation. "Oh, by the way, would you like something to drink? If you'd like to wash up, there's a lavatory right down the hall on the left. You'll be able to see it now. The men have just put in a new light bulb. You know, around here it really does take three guys to screw in a light bulb." She laughed.

Daniel was relieved that he wouldn't have to ask Stephanie for directions to the men's room. He placed his briefcase on the floor and thanked her for the advice. He walked down the dark hallway that was now dimly lit with a small yellow bulb, and opened a glass door that now had a large strip of orange safety tape running down the middle. Had Colonel Boyer not had his encounter with the door fifteen minutes before, Daniel would have been the one to bang his head and curse the darkness. He was grateful for that small turn of events and grateful for Stephanie Croix, a little flower growing out of a manure pile.

He entered the awful lavatory and looked into a small mirror that hung over the sink. His eyes were red and puffy. He washed his face and blew his nose. He wondered about the strange quaking that was going on inside of his body and why he wanted to be here in this place, in this mausoleum for the living. He thought of working with Stephanie, this creature they called Mutt. He could never call her Mutt, the dog. Could he actually work with her professionally or would he fall madly in love with this strange eccentric bird? He checked his fly and made sure the zipper was working. He left the grimy little lavatory and muttered under his breath that if he were hired as consultant, he would convert it into a broom closet.

Stephanie was at her desk peering out behind her big glasses. She had the phone to her ear and her right arm extended into the air as if she were stretching to touch the ceiling. She smiled as Daniel came back into the office and crinkled her nose. Daniel noticed for the first time that Stephanie had breasts. Not that he was surprised, it was just that her blouse was so unflattering that it took her stretching movements to reveal two small but nicely rounded mounds on her chest. She twisted in her chair with her arm outstretched; she seemed very uninhibited in her movements.

She hung up the phone. "I'd really like to talk some more, but I've got to get these invoices out today. The colonel will be out to look them over after this meeting and they had better be done right."

Stephanie continued her deskwork and ignored Daniel for the next ten minutes. Without the patter of her animated voice, Daniel was left with the monotonous drone of the air conditioner and the buzzing of the fluorescent fixture. To his left was a small room that looked like a truck dispatcher's office. A bare bulb hung between two men who were sitting and smoking cigarettes. They were silent and barely moved. A map of Brooklyn hung on a wall with concentric circles drawn around a dot, which was the location of the Brewery. The two men smoked incessantly and stared into the distance of their own private little worlds. The older of the two was an emaciated scarecrow with a pointy-head and tiny narrow-set eyes. His nose was a shiny pink beak that rested over a small pinhole mouth. The mouth held a cigarette that stuck straight out of the hole. Smoke drifted out of the beak and around the light bulb that hung from the ceiling. As if on cue, the man rose from his desk and walked into the waiting room. He then began his soliloquy to his audience of two, Daniel Aarons and Stephanie Croix.

"Look at me, I'm a disaster," his voice was like a squeaky wheel. "I'm a catastrophe. If you saw me on the street, you'd think I was a piece of dog shit and you'd walk the other way."

His eyes focused ahead on the air conditioning unit and not on Daniel or Stephanie.

"I've been in this place since nineteen fifty-two, sitting in this little room with Dixon. And look at me; I'm just a piece of dog shit."

Stephanie swiveled in her chair and interrupted the man's eloquent remarks.

"Ernie, that's enough. I know how you feel, but now is not the time for this. We'll talk about it later. Go back to your office. If you're that frustrated, see Chuck Conklin, he'll be happy to listen to you. Dr. Aarons is waiting to meet with Colonel Boyer, so please have some respect and courtesy for him and for the others who will be interviewed."

Stephanie treated him sternly, like a first-grade teacher would scold a misbehaving child. The man, in robot-like fashion, put the cigarette back in his mouth and retreated to the little dispatcher's office. He sat down and resumed his blank stare into the abyss of his life.

Stephanie looked at Daniel, raising her eyebrows in slight bewilderment.

"Looks like I've got to apologize again. That's Ernie Yeager," she said, fumbling with a pencil. "He's been here for an eternity. We've had to put him on the phones because he can't drive a truck anymore, and he can't lift anything more than ten pounds. He knows the city real well and he's a good dispatcher. But, most of the time, he just sits there and stares into space like a zombie. He doesn't belong here. He's going downhill fast, and I'm afraid he's just going to fade away. You know, I really have to talk to Colonel Boyer about him."

Her analysis was over. She shut up like a clam and resumed her work.

Daniel looked at Stephanie. He rubbed his chin. "That man needs medical attention. He's malnourished and suffers from dementia. When did he last have a complete physical?" Daniel asked with concern.

Stephanie just shrugged and rolled her big eyes.

Daniel sat in silence again as he watched Stephanie at her typewriter. He anxiously waited for her to yawn and to lift both her arms into the air so he could see her small round breasts beneath her tacky blouse. No such luck. She pounded a few more keys and lit another cigarette. She rummaged through a desk drawer and brought out a pair of scissors. She adjusted her seat and twisted her head as if to rid herself of a pain in the neck. She took a tissue from her desk and blew her nose loudly. The tender moment was lost.

Daniel Aarons had spent the last hour on a hard chair. A hot stone glued his pants to his legs. He wanted to get up and pull at the underwear that was now firmly stuck in his crotch. He twisted in his chair and fidgeted like a second grader at his desk on a warm spring afternoon. It was torture. He thought of running out of the building and screaming or maybe just tearing off all his clothes and ravishing Stephanie. His nervous bladder wouldn't let him rest. His frustration became anger, and he wanted to tell them all where they could stuff their damn consulting contract.

The phone rang in the little dispatcher's office and Ernie Yeager answered the phone. In a surprisingly firm and pleasant tone, he said, "Good afternoon, Service Corps for Men. God bless you, and how may we help you?"

The sound of the telephone's ring somehow reconnected a circuit in Ernie Yeager's addled brain. He came to life like an appliance that had just been plugged in.

Daniel looked at his watch. It was already three o'clock, and he had been waiting for more than an hour. Why were they taking so long? Was the candidate they were presently interviewing so magnificent and brilliant that they were already signing her up and measuring her for a uniform?

His eyes gazed upon the little dispatcher's office and on the face of the other man in the room. This man, he thought, surely must be a relative of the cat outside or at least they have some common genetic material. He was large and all that could be seen was a head and torso, but that head and torso were probably connected to massive tree-trunk legs. He looked like he was at least three hundred pounds of muscle and blubber. His giant square head was covered with a thin coating of slick black greasy hair and bushy eyebrows. On either side of the massive skull were rumpled cauliflower ears that shot out of his head like toadstools. Two large black eyes were bisected by a squashed mass that was his nose. Beneath the nose was a gaping black hole. When the hole opened, there could be seen three green teeth. From within that gaping hole came a large brownish organ, something like the liver of a cow. It was his tongue. The liver-like tongue moved in and out of the black hole like an eel going in and out of its cave. Beneath the mouth, connecting the whole work of art was a truly massive jaw that must have weighed twenty-five pounds. The man looks like the classic Neanderthal, but must have suffered from an advanced case of acromegaly. Or maybe he had been a prizefighter. It was apparent that he had taken terrible beatings, and his face was a road map of his many trials and defeats.

The phone rang and this man, whom Stephanie had called Dixon, lifted the receiver and sang with delicate tones, "Good afternoon and may God bless you. This is Service Corps for Men. How may we help you today?" There was a slight pause on the phone as Dixon listened.

"Well, how ya doin' Mrs. Freedman? Yes, this is Moby Dixon, and I'm still here with the corps. Yes, yes, they've been very good to me, and we sure appreciate all the support that you've given to the men all these years. Now, we'll be in your neighborhood on Thursday. Just like you usually do, put the papers in the grocery bag and the clothes in a plastic bag. And if you can spare a nice little check for the corps, we'll certainly be grateful. Well, we love you too and God bless you, Mrs. Freedman, and we'll see you on Thursday."

Dixon hung up the phone and resumed his position—huge brown tongue moving in and out of the dark hole.

Daniel smiled as he glanced at Dixon. He felt that grace was upon him, and he even thanked God for his wonderful creation. He was reinvigorated and ready for his meeting. He leaped from his chair and got up to use the lavatory one more time.

Moving quickly down the dark hallway, he stopped short of his destination as his eyes fell upon a little man—a dwarf with a large head and a floppy hat. The man looked like neither child nor adult. The yellow light in the hallway provided a strange and otherworldly shine to the dwarf's skin. He resembled an alien being from a bad science fiction movie. His eyes glowed like a cat's at night. He held the door open for Daniel with a small frog-like hand and introduced himself.

"Hi, I'm Malchus," the little man said with a slight smile and a tip of his hat.

"Hi, Malchus, my name is Daniel Aarons. Nice to meet you."

There was no subsequent handshake and Malchus proceeded down the hallway into the darkness of the building.

Daniel returned from the lavatory and went back to his seat in the receptionist's office. He wanted to ask Stephanie about this peculiar little person, but the door to the conference room burst open and out walked the last interviewee with Colonel Boyer right behind. The woman, tall and imposing with a large briefcase and several files, thanked Colonel Boyer for the interview and said to him in no uncertain terms, "I'll be seeing you in a couple of weeks."

As the woman walked toward the door, Stephanie stood up, thanked her for coming, and wished her the best of luck. The screen door shut. Colonel Boyer, noticing Daniel sitting in the office, broke into an endless litany of apologies for the delay. "Dr. Aarons, I'm truly sorry it took so long. We've gotten off to a late start today, and we've had endless personnel problems to deal with. The woman who just walked out of here is a deputy commissioner with the Department of Rehabilitation and Social Services. She's reviewing our accreditation status, certificates of occupancy, and city licenses."

Daniel knew exactly what Boyer was talking about.

Boyer continued to apologize. "We've had a few problems, but I think we can work them out. Dr. Aarons, please come into the conference room and meet the board."

Stephanie whispered, "Good luck." Daniel gave her a wink and walked into the conference room.

Colonel Claude Boyer, executive regional officer and operations director for the Northeast and Mid-Atlantic Region of The Service Corps for the Religious Enlightenment and Rehabilitation of Alcoholic Men, now officially called The Service Corps, welcomed Dr. Daniel Aarons to the Brewery with a vigorous handshake.

This was not the same Colonel Boyer—the buffoon—who Daniel had seen just an hour before, dashing out of the room, smashing his head into a glass door. This was a professional man in full control. Not even Stephanie, the de facto commander, was aware that the woman who had come in was a government official and not an interviewee for the consulting contract. Stephanie was in the dark, and Colonel Boyer made it clear that her role was merely peripheral. She was not management.

The Service Corps was a great and proud American institution, or at least it had been. It operated hospitals, psychiatric facilities, rehabilitation centers, and halfway houses for chronically mentally ill veterans. Its facilities were state-of-the-art medical centers, but also dilapidated buildings housing sick, dilapidated men. The Brewery was the laughing stock of the organization. It was deeply in debt and had recently lost its accreditation with the U.S. Veterans Administration. Its programs had been neglected for years and leadership was virtually nonexistent. An officer of the Service Corps assigned to the Brewery was sent, in essence, to Siberia or the dark side of the moon. If a new recruit could survive at the Brewery for at least one year, he would usually find himself sent to a modern rehabilitation facility or even to one of the hospitals. If he couldn't, he was unceremoniously drummed out or moved to an assistant position in some small city usually in a southern state. Sometimes he became a thrift store manager or a truck driver. Many Service Corps executives were burned-out hulks like the men they tried to help. They, too, became alcoholics or severely depressed. Some even took their own lives.

The Brewery had its own dark legends. During the past few years, the facility couldn't keep a director for more than nine months. The last one, a highly respected social worker from Milwaukee, was found hanging from the rafters in the warehouse. The one before him was taken away in a straitjacket, and he spent three years in a state psychiatric hospital. The Brewery in Greenpoint, Brooklyn, had become a condemned outpost by its own corporate structure. Even the honored grand leader and self-styled prophet of the Service Corps, General Malcolm Isaiah Thurman (grandson of the founder), hadn't visited the facility in more than twenty-five years. Such was the deplorable state of the operation.

Dr. Daniel Aarons walked into the long narrow conference room. At the end of a long table was a large desk used by past directors and was now the seat of power for Colonel Claude Boyer. The colonel escorted Daniel through the room and introduced him to four rather dour-looking professionals. The woman stood up and introduced herself as Dr. Myrtle McArdle, chair of the board of directors. She was gracious and apologized for the long delay.

"Dr. Aarons, it's a pleasure to meet you. I'd like to introduce to you some of the other members of our board. George Parnell, our attorney, serves as vice-chair, and this is Dr. Hyman Fleisig. Dr. Fleisig is a psychiatrist at Bellevue Hospital and his capacity here at the Brewery is to provide counsel to the mental health staff. Mr. Joseph Giotto has been on the board for over thirty years and is a local businessman."

Daniel performed the obligatory handshakes. His hands were cool and damp, but the shake was firm, and he looked each board member straight in the eyes. He did a quick internal analysis of the personalities in the room.

Myrtle McArdle, the psychologist and social worker, controlled the interaction in the room. Her eyes moved to the other members of the board like a chess player moving the pawns. She was a seasoned professional who had probably worked her way up the governmental ladder. She might be a department director or perhaps even an assistant commissioner.

Parnell, the attorney, was a weasel, a bottom-sucking invertebrate volunteering his time to the Brewery only because it put him into contact with potential clients and gave him access to the municipal bureaucrats in city hall. He knew nothing about rehabilitation, mental illness, or alcoholism; except that he himself was a drunken pervert who would probably sell his grandmother to make a buck.

Fleisig was a burned-out psychiatrist who looked like he had taken too much of his own medication. He couldn't keep the rich clients on Park Avenue, so he became a resident physician on a forensic unit at one of the large public psychiatric institutions in the city. He worked with serial murderers, child molesters, rapists, and the criminally insane. Some of his less offensive clients were deinstitutionalized and placed in rehabilitation facilities, such as the Brewery.

Giotto was a retired cop. He had been on the beat for twenty-five years until his knees gave out. A cigar hung in his mouth, and it cast a foul smell throughout the room. He knew all the tough guys in the neighborhood. His passion was a good pastrami sandwich and a cold beer. He owned a couple of pizza joints in Brooklyn and had connections to the Gambino crime family. His grandfather used to work in the Brewery, when it actually was a brewery. He said he had a spiritual connection to this place.

Colonel Boyer, the good old boy from Biloxi, Mississippi, hated New York City. He hated the people, hated the weather, hated the food, and especially hated this hellhole in Brooklyn. This was alien territory to Boyer, who was more at home with hogs and catfish. He was a southern boy who talked about the War of Northern Aggression and the atrocities of General Sherman. Boyer was no dummy, however. His slow talk and southern manners belied the fact that he had a PhD in organizational behavior and was a recognized expert in alcoholic rehabilitation. He avoided coming to New York City as much as possible, but this major facility in the biggest city in the nation was part of his territory. Because the facility could not keep a director for more than nine months, Boyer came up to New York to manage it himself until he could find a replacement. Boyer, however, didn't want to hire a new director. He wanted to hire a consultant to analyze the problem and develop a workable solution. This consultant would have considerable operating control over the facility during the contract period. Daniel was on the short list of consultants considered for the job.

There was a brief period of chitchat among the individuals in the room before the real technical questioning began.

"I hope you didn't have a long trip to the center, Dr. Aarons?" asked Myrtle McArdle.

"No, I only live a couple of miles from here," said Daniel. "I take the subway a few stops and I'm here, no problem at all. I'm very familiar with this area. I've lived in Brooklyn all of my life."

Fleisig, the psychiatrist was the next to speak. "Dr. Aarons, I'm very impressed with your résumé. I've actually read some of your papers in the professional journals and have found them quite inspired. Your reputation precedes you."

Myrtle McArdle looked at Daniel and shook her head in an affirmative motion as if to agree with Fleisig. The two professionals seemed to be on Daniel's side and liked what they saw.

Fleisig then gave a long dissertation on the benefits of deinstitutionalization and the improvement in psychotropic drugs to control the psychotic behavior of chronically mentally ill adults. He predicted the total elimination of major psychiatric hospitals within the next ten years, a savings of millions of dollars to taxpayers.

Parnell looked down at the thick pile of paper that was Daniel's curriculum vitae. He flipped through the pages and studied them as if they contained pornographic images. He doodled on a scrap of paper, picked his nose with a pencil, and yawned. He opened his mouth as if to ask a question, but no sound came out. His eyes went back to the scrap of paper and he finished his doodles.

Giotto sucked on his big stinking cigar and frowned. He gazed at the ceiling as if there was a giant pastrami sandwich hanging from the light fixture. He pulled the rotting weed with the slimy end out of his mouth and held it in his brown fingers.

"Dr. Aarons," Giotto asked with authority, "if there was a big fight in this place and the guys were killing one another, what would you do?"

What an incredibly stupid and pointless question, Daniel thought. Did he actually want an answer or was he just showing McArdle that he could do something with his mouth other than suck a cigar?

Boyer, obviously annoyed at the dumb question, rubbed his head.

"Joseph," said Boyer, "we have policies and procedures for dealing with violent behavior at the men's center. The staff knows what to do in every type of situation. Dr. Aarons would not have to deal with these issues. He's a consultant, not a damn cop." Boyer didn't have any patience with Giotto and it was obvious.

Myrtle McArdle looked at her watch and rolled her eyes. She glanced at Boyer, who gave a nod of approval.

"Dr. Aarons, you come highly recommended and your credentials are impeccable," said McArdle. "We're in a very difficult situation as you can plainly see. The members of the board and I are most impressed with your clinical skills and your experience in managing intermediate care residential facilities. You have obviously worked with volunteer boards in the past, and I believe your expertise would be highly prized by this facility as well as by the Service Corps. Colonel Boyer and this board would like to contract for your services. Would you be able to begin next week, say Monday?"

Daniel was caught completely off guard. He didn't expect to receive an offer in such a hasty manner. But, before he could analyze the situation in all its detail and evaluate the true motives of the board, he said, "Yes, Monday would be just fine."

CHAPTER 3

✠ ✠ ✠

JACOB KORETZ TUGGED AT HIS BEARD. HE scratched his leg. He fiddled with his ears. He gently patted the fresh wound on his forehead. His large mouth was soon to open and let forth with profound wisdom. He puffed on his cigar and then coughed loudly. He stood before his audience of one—his nephew, Daniel. The younger man chewed a pencil and looked bored. He was not in the mood to hear his uncle's latest tirade or to be a part of his latest and most obscure theatrical project. Uncle Jacob was a Renaissance man—the author of twelve plays, two thousand poems, eight novels, a sea of letters to the editor, a foray into abstract painting, and endless essays on every subject from Joe DiMaggio to the Kabbalah. A stained cat sat beneath a hanging plant panting and joined Jacob Koretz's audience.

"Now, Danny," said Jacob. "I want you to listen to this prologue very carefully and don't give me any of your bullshit. Just listen, and then I will ask questions." Jacob was intent on making his point whether or not his nephew even cared or listened.

The older man began with a flourish: "Is there anything as small as the mind of a man? And is there anything as pathetic as a grown man walking into a dark room with his hands covering his eyes? As soon as he is enveloped by the darkness, he experiences a bewildering terror, a feeling of utter abandonment …"

"Jacob, do we have any salami?" Daniel asked, his head in the refrigerator. "I could sure go for a salami sandwich right now. Any pickles?"

"I'm in the middle of an important speech," Jacob retorted, "and you ask me if we have any salami? Do I look like a fucking delicatessen?"

Jacob took a deep puff on his cigar and continued his prologue. "But he keeps his hands over his face to protect himself from the evil spirits that he thinks lurk within the shadows. I had always been told that there could be no truth found in darkness, but I did not realize that the darkness could sometimes be my friend. So, I remained a child and the darkness of the night still brings visions of strangers to my bedside, visitors who appear in the night and leave no message. They pull at my legs and tug at my feet, but I will not follow them. They—"

"Are you sure we don't have any salami?" Daniel asked again. "I thought I bought some last week. I can't find any in the refrigerator. Are you sure you didn't eat it, Jacob?"

"Daniel, for God's sake, at this very moment, I don't give a rat's ass about salami. Who the hell knows where it is? Have a little respect for your uncle's talent."

Again, Jacob continued the prologue. "When the door closes behind me, I am again paralyzed with fear because of what I might find in the darkness. So what do I do? I just stand there in the blackness, covering my face. That is my life until I die or until someone opens the door, drags me out of the darkness, and pulls my hands away from my eyes. We can learn so much from the darkness. It is not that it is dark, it is just that we are blind, and that is the blackest darkness that a man can experience. I tell you these things, my friends, because I have been dragged from the comfort of my darkness, kicking and screaming, and forced into a light that seared my eyes and caused me to lose every shred of sanity I thought I had. So bright was this light that I became transparent, but only for an instant. That instant, however, transformed my life. I can't tell you anymore because my words stick in my throat. So I ask you now, come with me through this door into the light and let us learn from our darkness."

Jacob halted his harangue, and the cigar immediately filled the gaping hole. He sucked in the smoke with a good healthy wheeze. The man threw back his head as if to ask the world, "This is good stuff, no?"

Daniel was cranky and he had no patience for his uncle's theatrics. "Twelve unfinished plays, which one is this?" Daniel asked. "Haven't I heard this prologue somewhere before? Isn't this from act two, scene three of *Becky's Backroom* or is it from *The Trough*? That bit about darkness, I could use it in some of my research."

Jacob was furious. He threw the cigar at Daniel. The cat ran out of the room.

"You damn son of a bitch," yelled Jacob. "Do you have to be so sarcastic about *my* work?" He grabbed a handful of small books from a pile of papers and magazines. "What do you call these, chicken shit?"

One by one, the old man showed the covers of his books to his nephew as if Daniel had never seen these books before. Six tiny volumes of surrealist poetry published in the 1950s by Sweet Sweat Press, now out of business. "I was no Communist, you know; I was just trying to make a living as a writer. I've supported you for too long." He spit tobacco out of his mouth.

Daniel stood in front of the open refrigerator, his fingers still searching for the salami.

"Jacob, I'm sorry, it's been a very long hard day. This was not the best time to entertain me."

The old man shot back. "What do you mean entertain you? I'm not here to entertain you or any other human being on this fucking planet! I'm here to spread the truth like warm butter on a piece of toast. What, you don't think there's any sin in this sick world?"

Jacob was indignant. He wanted to argue a point. He wanted to engage Daniel as a matador would engage a bull, but Daniel didn't have the patience or endurance to put up with his uncle. Jacob, however, would not let Daniel disengage. He taunted the young man and rolled up a newspaper as if he were going to strike a disobedient pet.

"What am I, a bad dog?" Daniel yelled. He put his hands in front of his face to block Jacob's blow. "Just calm down for a moment, goddamn it. Give me some time to breathe. I can't tell you how much shit I had to put up with today. Do you think you could put out the fucking cigar?"

Daniel turned his back on Jacob and stared out the third story window that looked over the trashcans on Washington Avenue. "What a hole, what a stinking hole! I've got to get some sleep."

Jacob was persistent. He was just getting his second wind.

"Being too smart is dangerous," Jacob said as he pointed his finger at his nephew. "Daniel, do you hear me? Too much cerebral matter is no good; it keeps you from seeing straight. A big brain squeezes your eyes until you can't see. Better to be a little stupid, but clever. At least if you're clever, you can make a good living. But if you're too smart, you have to spend too much time thinking about what the other guy's thinking, and that's a terrible waste of time. I know I'm smart, but not too smart. I learned from the real world, not from books."

Daniel opened a small bottle of sweet, red kosher wine. He poured it into a mug and gulped it down. Its thick, creamy texture coated his throat like cough syrup. He poured a little more into the mug and sat in Jacob's recliner.

"What the hell are you talking about?" asked Daniel, smugly. "How can a person be too smart? It's good to be smart, to have a good education. Why, do you think it's been bad for me?"

"Sure, just look at you," Jacob said. "You're an educated imbecile. You're the most brilliant dummy I've ever met. If you ate beans, you wouldn't know how to fart. So you've got a doctorate, what the hell good is it? You still get lost on the subway and you've lived in New York for thirty years. You have no girlfriend, no children, and you just sit in that damn stinking room with all those fancy books and journals. When are you going to get a real job?"

Jacob picked up his cigar and stuck it in his mouth again. A cloud of cigar smoke encircled Jacob's head like a halo.

"What do you mean by a *real* job?" asked Daniel. "I teach at a university, I do scientific research. I'm a visiting lecturer, adjunct faculty." The veins on Daniel's forehead were pulsating.

"Oh yea, *junk faculty* all right," said Jacob, and he pointed his finger at Daniel. "You visit that damn place once a week and they pay you minimum wage to talk to a bunch of shit heads just like you. What good is it being a fancy sociologist or whatever the hell they call you? You sit, think, and scheme all day and all that comes out of you is crap. It doesn't pay the rent and it doesn't buy the food. Danny, all that garbage in your head is making you a poor old man."

That was it! Daniel slammed his mug of wine on the side table. The red liquid sloshed upward like a volcanic eruption.

"Like you?" Daniel yelled. There was a long silent pause. The sound of a passing police cruiser was now plainly evident outside the building. The cat returned. Daniel bowed his head and knew he had said a terrible thing to his uncle.

"I'm sorry, I didn't mean that," Daniel said with his eyes down at the floor. "I didn't think you were against education. You went to the yeshiva for a few years, didn't you? You studied for the rabbinate, right? But the war ..."

"Yea, the war!" Jacob took a deep drag on his cigar. "I'm not against education, Daniel, but I knew plenty of educated people who were very smart. They destroyed people's lives and took their souls away. They were the worst kind of educated people. They sucked the life out of men and then pushed them into dark rooms. You know, I spent a lot of time in dark rooms and I learned to live like a blind man, taking small steps and keeping my hands in front of my face. I learned from the darkness and I survived to walk out into the light, but the light was a cold, icy white light that left me a living corpse. Look at me, Daniel, all I need is a shroud!" He closed his eyes and stiffened.

The two men stood at the open window in the front end of their apartment. Both were now silent, staring at the police cruiser as two cops were arresting a man in front of the welfare hotel across the street.

Jacob lamented, "The sound of the sirens and out appears another bare-chested young man with a cigarette hanging out of his mouth. They put him in the cruiser and off they go. They'll be back tomorrow. He'll be in jail for a day or two and then he'll be back to his old lady, punching her lights out and throwing beer bottles out of the window at depressed old men like me. The street is again silent. A cat hisses. End of act one."

Daniel sighed and turned to Jacob.

"Look, I'm sorry, I'm really sorry. I know you went through hell in the war—the concentration camps, the ugliness, the suffering. You've told me the stories a thousand times and I'm certainly not minimizing your pain, but the war's been over for a long time. Your medication has

helped you, and I've seen a great change in you over the past few years."
Daniel realized his mistake. His remarks were patronizing and certainly
not helping the situation.

Jacob responded, his voice like an arrow in a crossbow. "What do you
know, Mister Doctor? Have you ever been locked up like an animal in
a cage for three years, like some crazy son of a bitch monkey? After the
war, I came home from one cage and they put me right into another.
Those bastards sticking needles up my ass and tubes down my throat. I
don't know who was worse, the fucking Nazis or the devils at the state
hospital."

A deep blue mist seemed to hang in the room. The two men, both
survivors of the Nazi camps, stood in their temple, their shrine to sanity
and insanity. They became stone statues, sentinels gazing out across a
decaying urban landscape. Pigeons would sit on their heads, but they
would continue to stand there and peer out across their landscape of
time and space—an ocean, a desert, a planet in a far off galaxy. Beneath
them was the dirt and grime of a human-littered forest floor. They
tripped over the bones of long-dead dreams and picked at the scraps that
dangled from low branches. They could never reach the rich ripe fruit
that grew higher up. They could never taste the honey made at the top
of the trees. They could never live with the sweet young women who sat
in nests and pampered their eggs. They just sucked the smoke that came
from fat cigars. Their shrine was deep within the fog of exhaled days and
nights, and they knew they could always hide inside its walls.

Jacob would sit within his piles of books and stacks of newspapers.
The piles became his fortress and the words buried within became
his life. The stacks soon mirrored time and became archaeological
excavations. Jacob could proudly point to the beginning of the universe
at the bottom of one stack. At another level, he could find the extinction
of the dinosaurs. "Here's where the great asteroid pummeled the earth
and at the same moment I was born." His creations always seemed to
float to the top, like a valuable skim of high-grade petroleum. There was
a lot of energy in those creations, but it could never be harnessed. It
was always something quite ephemeral and short-lived, a million-degree
plasma that lasted for a nanosecond and then disappeared. Jacob would
sit for hours and look at his hands. He wanted them to play Chopin,

to paint, to write, but most often, he wanted them just to touch and heal.

The silence ended. The two stone monuments broke their gaze and stared at each other as they had always done for the past three decades. Two men: one was old, sarcastic, and burned out. The other was young, sarcastic, and burned out. Both, however, had been captives of Hitler's black box. One experienced the fury of the horrors of war like the memories of an intimate love affair and the other was oblivious to its darkness. One was a young man carrying corpses at Auschwitz and the other a tiny infant—just a seed—somehow surviving the engulfing fire. Uncle and nephew, forever connected at the hip, drinking from the same tainted well, sharing a common heart.

Daniel now looked at his uncle with compassion. "Jacob, I know it's the depression, but at least you can function in the world like a human being. You shop, you go out with your friends, and you see a movie. You know, for a guy sixty-five years old, you're not in such bad shape. You have women pounding on your door. They want to take care of you."

"Yea, Esther Cohen in 6B, she wants to make love to me. She'd just love to get her fat fingers into my pants. I teased her. I asked her if she wanted to come up to my place for a little salami. She blushed like a schoolgirl." He took a puff on his cigar. "Oh, yea, thank God for the pills, but can the pills give me back my life? Can they fill the emptiness that I feel every second of my life? Can they bring back your mother or Rachel? Daniel, I'm an old, empty aching vessel and God refuses to fill me. Why does He want me broken? Why doesn't He just kill me and get it over with? He keeps me alive so He can drop me off the shelf, like a thin vase. Every time He glues me back together, He drops me again so that I can break in new places. What kind of crazy God is this?" Jacob wiped the tears that began to fill his eyes.

"Ah, I hear the rabbi coming out in you again," said Daniel. "It's good to hear you say the word God without cursing Him. At least you still believe in Him."

"Does it make any difference whether I believe in Him or not? I'm here and in pain and He's not! On the other hand, if He is here, He's still hiding and playing some crazy game with me. You know, Daniel, for ten years God was gone, totally gone. I couldn't even pronounce the symbols that represented His name. Whenever I heard Adonai, Lord, it was like I was hearing some foreign word. He was ripped out of my mind, and I couldn't even imagine Him. His fire was extinguished in my soul. It was like seeing black holes and not knowing what was missing, but those holes were right in front of me all the time and they had no names or faces. The voices from within would only say, 'Hear O Israel ...' and then there was nothing but a shrill laugh. At least I don't hear the voices anymore, but those black holes still stare at me like the eye sockets in a skull." Jacob covered his face.

Daniel examined his hands as if to pull some magic potion out of his fingers. Perhaps the lines on his palm could tell Jacob his future.

"Jacob, I wish there were something I could do for you. I know you're in pain, but I feel so helpless around here. We just bounce off the walls in this crummy little apartment. I have my research and you have your books, your theater—"

"Daniel," Jacob interrupted, "when your mother was dying in the camp, I promised that I would look after you. I said, 'Sarah, don't worry, Daniel's in good hands.' She was always the healthy one, the sane one, the successful one, and the one carrying the healthy seed, but Hitler killed her. When they sent her back to the camp, she was literally half a woman—one arm, one leg, one eye—but pregnant with *you*. Imagine, pregnant and in that condition in a concentration camp, but her mind was always good and she was so beautiful, but they used her up to the end. She should have been a raving lunatic, like me. No, she stayed straight, focused, and then just dropped dead in the last days of the war. They even let her nurse you. It was a miracle that you survived at all those days after she died. No, God wouldn't let me drop dead. He needed me to take care of you, but He wouldn't let me have my mind. So I prayed and I cursed Him. I cursed Him for taking Sarah, I cursed Him for taking my Rachel, I cursed Him for Hitler, and I cursed Him because He would not bless me. I couldn't pray because all He left me were these damn black holes."

This story was not new to Daniel. It had become a regular theatrical production of Jacob's, complete with monologue and choreography. He had heard it many times before in every room of the apartment—during breakfast, lunch, and dinner—and when Jacob shouted at him while he was in the bathroom. It was a permanent mark, his mark of Cain. The curses became a daily litany and the litany became a sad, joyless mantra that did not bring peace.

The young man stared at the large head, the beard, and the stinking cigar. "I'm going to go out to Ho Fat's for some Chinese," he said. "You want some?"

"Yea, bring me back a hot and sour soup and an egg roll. No, change that to a cup of wonton and don't forget the noodles."

Daniel's mind suddenly changed gears, like a car inadvertently thrown into reverse. The higher primate mind turned off and a lower reptilian brain took control. The eyes darted and the head moved in lizard-like fashion to survey the mechanical contraptions that filled the small living room—the coffeepot, the electric blanket, the space heater.

"Oh, I'd better check the heater before I go out," he said, like a monotone one hears on a recorded telephone message.

"How many times do you have to check the fucking heater," Jacob retorted with obvious annoyance. "It's off. It's off. It's been off since six this morning. You've already checked it a dozen times. It's off! Did *you* forget to take your medication today, Daniel? And stop doing that with your beard, curling it between your fingers. You know how it drives me crazy. It's such a stupid habit whenever you get nervous and obsessive. You look like Shloyme, that little old man at the synagogue waiting for the janitor to open the door. He sits there and rocks like an idiot."

The two bearded men stared at each other looking like portraits on a cough drop box—the Smith Brothers.

"All right! All right! Calm down, Jacob, it's nothing to get upset about. I'll just go and check it one more time. You got any money? All I have is two dollars. I don't think that's going to cover the meal."

"Yea, yea, here's ten bucks." Jacob tossed the bill on a table. "Now don't forget the noodles, I can't eat wonton without noodles."

Daniel finished checking the heater. His reptilian brain searched out Jacob's territory. His lizard's tongue tasted the air looking for its next meal. He was combative and ready to strike.

"Why do you make fun of that old man at the synagogue?" Daniel asked. "He's praying to God and he's got some damned palsy, too. That's the only way he knows how to pray. It's very judgmental for you to say those things especially you, a Jew, who was going to be a rabbi."

"Oh, give me a break for crying out loud." Jacob blew smoke. "Shloyme wouldn't know God if the Almighty Himself pulled down his pants and crapped on his head. Besides, our inscrutable Creator stopped listening to him years ago. Shloyme's just angry and he doesn't know what else to do with himself. He really wants to curse God, because the Almighty always plays hide-and-seek with him and He always wins. He also expects the messiah to come every Friday like the milkman comes in the morning."

"Don't we all?" Daniel asked.

"For some, He's come and gone—those lucky goyim. For others, He's just gone. Some don't even give a damn. For the Jews, we just wait, but we're not sure what we're waiting for. Danny, I'm just going to sit here and wait until He walks through that door."

A quizzical look came over Daniel's face. The reptilian mind returned.

"Who walks through the door?"

"The messiah!" replied Jacob.

"What's his name, Jacob?"

"What's whose name?"

"The messiah, Jacob!"

"How the hell am I supposed to know? Maybe ..." Jacob paused for a moment. "John Doe. It certainly won't be Izzy Cohen. The goyim couldn't possibly have a messiah with a name like that. Even Jesus was a Jew, but they changed His name, too. That Jesus! He's like a sharp square block, and I don't think He can fit into the smooth round holes in my head. I bet you thought I never read the Christian Bible. I studied it years ago when I was struggling with a different demon. I'm not sure who won the battle, the demon, or me. Maybe I was just wrestling with the angel of God like my namesake, the great manipulator, Jacob. That's why I can't walk straight. He put my hip out of joint, too!" Jacob looked up at the ceiling. "Okay, God, you win! Now, Daniel, for God's sake, go and get me my wonton soup!"

Daniel left the dank depressing cell and vanished into the night searching for the perfect wonton.

Jacob Koretz sat in his recliner and lifted the stump of the cigar he had been smoking. He inhaled the smoke with both his mouth and his nose. A thick fog settled around his head, and his beard looked like a large brown clump of moss. His rotund body became a lump of soft malleable clay. It had been molded into many things, a brick, a graceful sculpture, and a vessel to carry holy water. Now, Jacob thought, he was just a paperweight, a circular blob of rock to be placed upon a meaningless heap of forgotten manuscripts.

He called for his cat. "Stain, get the hell over here." The cat was in grabbing distance and Jacob hoisted the furry oblong body of the cat into his lap. It purred and closed its eyes as Jacob stroked its fur.

"Vodka," Jacob said to the cat. "I need a shot of vodka before Daniel brings back the Chinese food. The vodka will help. It always helps."

He knew it didn't really help, but the clear liquid was just one of his few friends that seemed to be available at all times of the day and night. He reached for the small crystal decanter on the table next to his recliner and poured a small amount into a snifter. He drank it in one gulp and closed his eyes. The cigar followed the liquid, and both man and cat floated on a cloud to a small bungalow in the Catskill Mountains, a place of serenity where Jacob Koretz longed to be away from the filth and violence of the city, the incessantly crying infants, the drug dealers, and all the rest of the crap that cluttered his life. He sat under his own broom tree, like Jonah, and asked God that he might just die.

Jacob Koretz, however, could not disappear or die and he could not put the voice of God out of his mind. That still small voice, that ineffable whisper, those taps on the shoulder, would come to him and disturb his regular sessions of self-pity. He seemed to enjoy wallowing in his own muck, though he would never admit it. So the angel of the Lord would always put a little food by his head and say, "Jacob, get up and eat." Jacob Koretz opened his eyes and waited for wonton soup.

"Okay, God, here I am again," Jacob talked to the wall, "your obedient whipping boy, your dog. What is it with You? Isn't it enough that I limp like a cripple? Do I also have to be tortured by this damned bipolar depression, up and down like a yo-yo? One day I'm Superman on the subway racing to Manhattan to see friends and shows, the next day I'm dog crap on the bottom of a shoe. When I'm up and I think I have all the answers to all Your questions and all the pieces of the puzzle come together, You confound me and I come tumbling down like the Tower of Babel. All right, I'm a proud man; I've been arrogant. Do You want complete subjugation, complete submission? I'd gladly give it to

You, but You have made me into a fighter, a survivor, a rebel. I don't think You want me on my knees. No, You don't want a foot kisser, You have plenty of those. You want a debating partner. You want a Jeremiah. I'm sorry, Lord; I can't set foot in the synagogue like the other men. I can't mumble and humble myself. You know I've had my visions of You, but if I told others, they'd lock me up again. They already think I'm crazy, but I can't go back to the state hospital. You won't let it happen will You Lord? Please Lord, I'll get down on my hands and knees, but that's not what You want is it? You remember when my bed caught fire at the hospital. They said I was smoking in bed. No, that was You in my burning bush, and You were in the midst of the fire, but I was not consumed! You saved me from that fire. You saved me at the death camp, You got me out, and You followed me all the way to the halls of the state hospital. Bless You, Lord. Bless You, Lord. You even gave me the strength and sanity to take care of my nephew when his mother was gone. But when are You going to deliver me from my demons, these black holes in front of my face? How many times do I have to pray to remove these thorns from my flesh? Perhaps You could just come to me like a person and stroke my head. Maybe You can be my mother for just an hour, like when I was a little boy, stroking my head, and holding me in your arms, giving me a soft kiss on my cheek and tucking me into bed. Be a sweet beautiful woman and let me make love to you all night. Fill my bed with ecstasy, dear Lord. Why do You have to be such a stern old father and why am I so afraid of you? Be my personal messiah as You have promised our people for thousands of years. You gave the goyim their Messiah, why won't You give me mine? That's it! Lord, I demand that You send the messiah to me. You say, 'Ask and it shall be given.' Lord, I am asking and I expect to see the messiah by the Sabbath. Thank you for listening to me today. Amen."

The eternal flame went out in Jacob's head. The door closed. The angel of the Lord packed up his suitcase and left for Mount Horeb. The cat yawned.

Jacob Koretz was out of his trance, but he continued his soliloquy to the cat. "That's enough prayer for today. Let's see what's on TV and have a little Chinese food. Where's that brilliant nephew of mine? He's another one with his head up his ass. Insanity must run in our family, too much interbreeding in Eastern Europe. We should have intermarried with the goyim. I told him to study business or engineering or maybe even medicine. He has the brain; it's just upside down and backward. What does he study—philosophy, sociology, social work, psychology—useless, totally useless. What this world doesn't need is another philosopher with a PhD. Maybe if he was a medical doctor, we could both be in Florida by now, and I could be in the arms of some old yenta. Nah, who needs an old yenta. She'd just be a pain in the ass, nagging me to pick up my socks, lift the toilet seat, and take her shopping. Who the hell needs that? I'm hungry, where's Daniel?" Jacob snapped. The cat ran off. The real world of his private hell came hurtling back at his head at the speed of light. The room whirled around him and the pounding in his head became a knocking at the door.

"Yea, who is it?" Jacob screamed at the door.

The knock came again.

"Yea, yea, who is it? What do you want?"

The knock came again.

"For Christ's sake, who the hell is it?"

Jacob, annoyed and drunk, walked to the door and looked out through the peephole.

"Damn it, there's nobody there," he said to himself in his stupor. "Damn kids, they're probably peeing in the hall again."

He walked back to his chair. The knock came again.

"Shit!" he yelled at the door. "If I have to get up one more time, I'm going to break somebody's head open with my bare fist!"

Jacob heard a small voice coming from behind the closed door. He was still wondering if he was dreaming or having an auditory hallucination.

"I've already sent the angel of the Lord to Mount Horeb. If you want to find him, he's probably on the subway by now. Go away and let me die," Jacob shouted at the door.

Jacob's large head rested back on the recliner. The cat slithered out from beneath a curtain and jumped on the piano. Jacob hummed the strains of a Chopin nocturne.

"Can I use your phone? I need to call my agent," said the small voice from the other side of the door.

Jacob spoke to the cat. "Who the hell is this? He comes to my apartment so he can call his agent?"

Again, Jacob got up out of the sanctuary of his recliner and shuffled to the door. He stared out through the tiny peephole, but saw nothing. The dim hallway was vacant of all intelligent life.

"Please sir, I need to use your phone. It's important. I can assure you I'm no threat to your safety," the voice pleaded.

Jacob, in slow motion, opened two dead bolts and a police bar. Jacob saw the small visage for the first time and was not pleased.

"Go home kid, and stop peeing in the hallway," Jacob said to the little person at his door. He shut the door in the visitor's face.

Again there was a knock, but now Jacob opened the door and stood face-to-face (actually he had to look way down) to see the little man—a dwarf. A dwarf with a big head, one ear, and a floppy hat.

In perfect English and with the grace of a noble gentleman, the little man rephrased his request. "Pardon me, again, but I would really appreciate your letting me use your telephone so that I may call my agent."

Jacob wasn't sure if the effects of the vodka were now wearing off, or if the alcohol had opened up some new and unknown realm of consciousness in his brain. He was neither reclining in his chair nor talking to the little stranger. He found himself, for just an instant, floating at the top of the ceiling watching his body interact with the small man. He even noticed that the cat sitting on the piano stool was playing a Mozart sonata. Suddenly, Jacob was back in his body.

"Well, I … I'm sorry, but I …" Jacob stumbled and slurred his words. All thoughts were a slag pile of refuse. They poured out from the mouth and careened over the edge of his lips into the ocean below. His tongue was a useless organ, like a rock in his mouth.

"Thank you, where's your phone?" asked the dwarf.

Jacob could not believe that he had let this strange, small man into his home, into his sanctuary, into his womb!

"It's over there on the table next to the couch," Jacob said. "It's not long distance I hope?"

"No, I can assure you it's local, right here in Brooklyn," the little man answered.

Jacob saw the strange hand and the even stranger white, frog-like fingers dial a number. The receiver went up to the extremely strange, one-eared head.

"Hello, Tali? Yea, it's me, Malchus. I'm here at an apartment on Washington Avenue and I just wanted to let you know that I'll be home tomorrow. I should be here for a little while. I'm sorry I didn't call you earlier … Yes, I know you were worried, and I apologize for the inconvenience, but you know how I get. My medication was stolen, and I guess I wandered off. I've been at Penn Station since last Tuesday. But I'm straight and I've eaten, the sky is still blue, and all of that. I even went to a basketball game. All right, perhaps I'll make a visit to your place later in the week. How's two PM on Thursday? Tali, I don't know why I'm straight now, but I haven't taken a pill in days. I don't even know what I've eaten, but all I know is I'm feeling good. Maybe it's the exhaust from those new buses, full of a new brew of noxious chemicals that have beneficial effects on the brains of hydrocephalic dwarfs. Yes, I still have my hat—you don't have to worry about that. You're a good man, Tali. Yes, okay, I'll see you then. Bye. Ciao."

The alien hand placed the telephone receiver back in the cradle, and he handed the instrument to Jacob. The large bearded man received the device as if it was a radioactive nuclear weapon or a ray gun from outer space. He didn't touch the receiver, but slowly, carefully put the telephone back on the table next to the couch. Jacob looked at the cat and then looked for his decanter of vodka. He reached for his cigar and stuffed it in his mouth as if it was a pacifier.

Jacob's brain went into overdrive as he contemplated. What devilish monster had come into his holy temple? What demon from beyond the stars had entered his private domain? What instrument of Satan was this sent to devour his already boggled brain?

The little stranger smiled at the large bearded hulk and thanked him profusely.

"Jacob … Jacob Koretz," the old man replied. "The pleasure is all mine."

"Well, thank you, Jacob," said the dwarf. "I appreciate your kindness, hospitality, and well, at least let me pay for this call. Perhaps one dollar would cover it?"

"No, no, don't think of it," replied Jacob. "You said it was a local call, I believe you. You look like an honest man, a man of integrity and intelligence. Just one thing: this guy on the phone, he was your agent?"

Jacob couldn't believe that this strange creature could have an agent. A keeper perhaps, a nurse maybe, but an agent? Was the dwarf in the theater? Now that would seem a likely profession for such a weird little fellow. Yes, that's it! The circus is in town, Jacob thought, and this little man is one of its star entertainers: *Little Lazlo,* the dwarf from outer space. For sure! Perhaps, he is one of those tiny clowns who drive the little red car. Maybe he is a human cannonball. Better yet, he sweeps up the manure behind the elephants. What a sight, a little strange, one-eared deformed man with a broom cleaning up elephant shit. I have to go and see this show, thought Jacob.

"You called your agent?" inquired Jacob.

"Yes, my agent. I'm a professional basketball player," said the dwarf.

Jacob was not amused. The little man was obviously joking. No, Jacob thought, the poor soul standing in his living room was just another sick SOB who didn't know his ass from his elbow and was probably an escapee from a mental asylum or even the welfare hotel across the street.

"You play professional basketball?" asked Jacob incredulously. "Somehow, you don't quite fit the mold. Why do I get the feeling you're pulling my leg?"

"Perhaps I am," said the little man. "But I do love basketball, and I am certainly a professional at what I do."

"Just what is it that you do?"

"I'm a one-eared dwarf. However, your reaction is perfectly logical and quite appropriate. I'm not only the shortest basketball player in Brooklyn, but I also sing Italian opera. Sometimes, I'm the most brilliant mind on the face of the earth, and I don't even have a brain. I can move mountains and heal the sick, but I can barely walk up a short flight of stairs without collapsing in total exhaustion. Nevertheless, even with my clubfoot, I'm a superb dancer. Did you know that I've been alive for two thousand years?" The little man crossed his arms over his chest and looked defiant.

Jacob was now convinced that the vision in his living room was not a real man, not a human being at all, but an illusion, the simple result of indigestion. This hallucination was perhaps the product of his troubled, depressed mind, the vodka, and a poisoned cigar. The logic within Jacob's mind concluded that the mildew in his apartment, combined with the noxious fumes of the city, and the excesses of his alcohol consumption, led to the creation of this mental contrivance. He reached for his diagnostic manual of mental disorders to verify his conclusion.

Jacob took his index finger as if he were going to put it on a hot surface and touched the little man on his shoulder. The finger and arm recoiled as if burned on a stove.

"Wait a darn minute," Jacob said to the dwarf. "I thought you were just some sick little vision conjured up out of too much medication and too much vodka, but you're very solid!"

"Thank you, Mr. Koretz," said the little man. "I appreciate your hearty acknowledgment of my physical being. You know, I went from door to door in this tenement and something just told me that *you* would be the only one to open your door and your heart to me."

"And what did you say your name was, if I may ask?"

"Well, actually, Mr. Koretz, the official name on my birth certificate simply says Malchus, but I call myself Malchus One Ear." He pointed to his head, which obviously had only one ear. There was sarcasm in the dwarf's reply.

"I've always thought that Quasimodo would be more appropriate," said the little man. "Believe me, I have been called everything imaginable under the sun, but what else can you expect? Mr. Koretz, it would be an honor if you would just call me Malchus, simply Malchus."

Jacob rubbed his chin and searched the ceiling for a few answers and a few clues. All he could find were a thousand questions and puzzlements.

This was to be a very strange evening, Jacob thought. Perhaps, time had stood still. He checked his watch and noticed that the second hand had stopped moving, and his cat was still playing Mozart.

"That's a biblical name, too, if I recall, but it's not in the Hebrew Bible." Jacob was testing the little man.

"That's correct, Mr. Koretz, it's in the Gospel of John and Luke, too." Malchus recited his familiar story in a thoroughly dramatic way.

"While Jesus was praying in the garden, I was with my master, the Lord High Priest, Caiaphas. He instructed me to go with some of the officers of the temple to arrest Jesus. When we arrived, Jesus was deep in prayer. He was resigned to his death and there was nothing to be done. I was a strong young man then and a fierce warrior. When Peter saw me, he drew his sword and struck me on the right side of my face cutting off my ear."

The dwarf grabbed the right side of his head. "I stood there in terrible pain, holding my head and praying for God to heal me. The smell of blood filled my nostrils and the pounding of my heart was the only sound I heard. I could see that there was much yelling and screaming, but I couldn't hear a sound. Then I saw Jesus get up from His meditation and rush toward me with His open hands. He touched my head and immediately the bleeding stopped. He said I was healed."

Malchus took a bow as if he was on stage.

Jacob sweated and patted his forehead with a handkerchief. This strange little man spoke like a scholar with such eloquence and dignity. Could this person possibly be my alter ego, my long lost invisible playmate from my disturbing childhood? Jacob wondered.

"But you *don't* have a right ear!" exclaimed Jacob.

"That's correct," replied Malchus. "I don't have an external right ear, only this little flap of skin. But ever since that time in the Garden of Gethsemane, I've been able to hear the voice of God so clearly, it is as if there were a thousand angels singing to me. As Jesus said to the crowds, those who have ears let them hear. I have wonderful ears," the little man replied with a broad smile.

Jacob felt a kindred spirit. He wanted to reach out and hug the poor little deranged soul.

"Yes, yes, I hear voices singing to me, too," said Jacob. "But they drive me nuts. That's why I've been on medication for the past twenty years and in and out of psychiatric hospitals."

"Perhaps you are listening to the wrong voices," Malchus replied. "Perhaps you are listening to the voices with your *outer* ears. Maybe Peter needs to cut off your ears, too."

Jacob touched his own ears, which were now burning and virtually on fire. "Perhaps we're all a little crazy," Jacob said. "I think I'm going to sit down. This conversation is getting too much for me."

The old man sat in his recliner and once again held his lowered head in his hands hoping that when he lifted his eyes, the ghostly white vision would be gone. He raised his chin, but Malchus was still there, a faint smile on his face.

"Malchus, are you hungry, can I get you something to eat?" Jacob sounded like a Jewish mother. "Come on, eat something. My nephew's coming back with some Chinese food. I'd like for you to stay and meet him."

"I appreciate the kind offer, Mr. Koretz …"

"Please, call me Jacob," the old man insisted.

"… but I need to see a friend in the neighborhood. I know we'll be seeing each other again, and very soon. Maybe you can save an egg roll for me. Good-bye, Jacob."

A moment later, the little one-eared apparition with the big floppy hat was out the door. Jacob thought he would never see Malchus again. Perhaps the dwarf *was* only an illusion, the creation of a diseased mind and too much mildew in the bathroom. Jacob's mind had become an old piece of sponge cake that had lain on the kitchen table for too long and was now waiting for the cockroaches, but a cubic millimeter in his brain sparked with new life. The synapses between the nerve endings had never been busier.

Maybe I'm having a stroke, he thought. No, this feels too good.

Jacob Koretz sat in his recliner like an old man who had just made love to a beautiful young girl. His cigar lay burned out on the floor and the cat continued to play Mozart.

The sound of a key turning in a lock aroused Jacob from his reverie. He was back on earth, somewhere between Yonkers and Coney Island. His nephew, Daniel, walked into the dark, foul-smelling abode with a large greasy bag of Chinese food. The smell of chow mein filled the air. The cat stopped playing the piano and salivated on his owner's foot. Jacob was impatient and hungry.

"Danny, what the hell took you so long; I'm starving to death."

The aroma of Ho Fat's cooking was enough to break Jacob's deep spiritual mood. The egg rolls tumbled out of the slippery paper bag, the wonton soup sloshed on the table. The cat caught bits of chicken and shrimp as they fell to the floor.

"Danny, by the way, on your way up the stairs did you notice a little man with a big floppy hat? He's a dwarf with one ear and a big hydrocephalic head. His name is Malchus. He even plays professional basketball and sings Italian opera."

Daniel gave his uncle a strange look. Jacob sounded like a raving lunatic.

"What the hell are you talking about, Jacob? Are you all right? Are you sick or something? I've only been gone for five minutes, look at the clock. Have you been seeing little green men again and UFOs? You've been at the vodka, haven't you? You know you can't take medication and drink. It'll kill you. Don't you realize how dangerous it is?"

"No, Danny, no little green men," Jacob replied. "Just one little white one with a big round head and one ear."

Jacob let the subject drop and thought that perhaps Malchus was just an illusion.

Daniel had no patience with his uncle. "Jacob, here's your wonton soup with noodles. Eat."

The old man slurped his dinner. "So, Daniel, you still haven't told me how your interview went today with the ... what do they call it?"

His mouth full of noodles, Daniel replied. "The Service Corps for the Religious Enlightenment and Rehabilitation of Alcoholic Men, but these days they just call it The Service Corps."

Daniel continued to eat. He looked down at his plate and tried to spear a piece of broccoli with a soft plastic fork. He was not in the mood for discussion, but Jacob was curious.

"Come on, tell me already! Are we going to be rich with this lucrative deal and move to Long Island, or do we stay here and rot in this stinking dump 'til I die?"

"I got the contract," Daniel said matter-of-factly, his eyes still focused on the broccoli.

"Terrific, I can now retire!" Jacob shouted to the cat.

"Jacob, you don't even work, how can you retire?"

"I can retire from the world and you can support me," Jacob replied smugly.

"I already do that," Daniel said. "I start Monday." He wiped his mouth and threw a shrimp at the cat.

"Something's very wrong with the whole setup," Daniel said. "I went in there like a five-year-old on his first day of kindergarten, stumbling over everything. I was nervous, had to pee every five minutes. I was getting very bad vibrations from the whole rotten place. Jacob, the place is filled with alcoholics, seriously depressed guys, and schizophrenics. Nobody is on medication and some young girl, who doesn't have any education or experience, runs the place.

"This Colonel Boyer, a joker from Biloxi, Mississippi, who is the commanding general or whatever, wants to leave Brooklyn and get back to his catfish pond. I tell you, Jacob, there's something screwy about this whole deal. After I sat and waited for at least an hour, I met with four of the board members. The whole thing lasted for ten minutes and then they offered me the job. They offered me the job right there at the interview! No checking references, no discussion of operational or clinical procedures, nothing! 'Daniel Aarons, you're hired to be our new executive consultant. Oh, by the way, we four won't ever be seen again, and Boyer is already on his way to the airport.'" Sarcasm filled Daniel's voice as he stabbed a floret of broccoli with a knife.

"Sounds like you really stepped in it this time, my boy," Jacob said with a haughty attitude. A wonton fell from his beard and splashed in the soup. Daniel expected him to say something like I told you so. You should have been an accountant, or some other kernel of wisdom from his book of proverbs.

"You know, I'm going to need a lot of help if I'm ever going to get that place in shape, lots of money, and a good professional staff. There are sixty guys in there and not one of them has been evaluated in over a year! God knows what they have. The city just drops guys off at the curb and tells them to *go get rehabilitated*. I saw one guy who was almost totally blind fumbling around with automotive machinery. Another was so senile and feeble he should have been in a nursing home. Then there was this tiny dwarf with a big head and one ear."

Jacob jumped to his feet; Chinese food tumbled from his mouth.

"What? What did you say?" Jacob screamed. "A tiny dwarf with one ear!"

"Yea, why, what's the problem? He's one of the residents at the Brewery."

"Danny, there could only be one creature on the face of the earth who fits that description, and he was here in this very apartment just a few minutes ago. Remember, I asked you if you saw a little man?"

"Yea, but I thought you were just seeing things again. What are you trying to tell me?"

"Danny, either *both* of us had the same bad dream or we've both been visited by an alien being that has a plan for us. No, no, wait!" Jacob's face turned red. His arm swept across the table flinging Chinese food on the wall. "He's an angel, a messenger of God who has been sent to warn us of impending doom and disaster, perhaps a loathsome death!"

"Jacob, you're getting dramatic," Daniel protested. "I really think you're reading too much into this occurrence. He's a client at the center, just a poor soul. A little disabled guy. With a head like that, he probably has a host of psychiatric and physical disorders. He's no angel or extraterrestrial."

Nevertheless, this strange coincidence, this synchronicity, bothered Daniel. Something wasn't quite right. While there must have been a rational and logical explanation, Daniel was at a loss to explain it. A one-two punch caught Daniel in the head. His jaw hung open, exposing a mouthful of bok choy. His stomach tightened into a stiff hard knot. His brain wasn't able to deal with such inconsistencies.

"Oh, there's got to be a rational explanation, Jacob. I'll find out when I start work on Monday. It will all be clear and our minds will be at ease."

Both men sat at the table wrestling with the juxtaposition of disparate objects on an alien landscape. The cat played a Chopin nocturne. The roaches feasted on the moo goo gai pan that dribbled from the wall.

"Open your fortune cookie, Jacob." Daniel's voice was insistent. It was as if the answers to all their questions were to be found in the rolled-up crunchy morsel. "What does it say?"

Jacob's hands shook. He crumbled the cookie and pulled out the tiny paper locked inside. He unrolled it as if it were the holy Torah.

"Dear God! '*You will meet a tiny man with a big head and one ear who will change your life.*'"

CHAPTER 4

✠ ✠ ✠

STEPHANIE CROIX'S MIND WAS A SPONGE, NOT one of those soft pink things one finds in a bathtub slathered in soap or a flat dried-up relic under a kitchen sink. It was a living thing that reached out and grabbed minute particles of aesthetic and spiritual plankton. Its appetite was voracious, and it performed like an organism that had long outlived the dinosaurs, but remained essentially in its same form since the Cambrian era. Her mind and body were frequently going in opposite directions. This wasn't a bad thing since Stephanie had a very peculiar method of dealing with the universe.

The day after she met Daniel Aarons at the Brewery, Stephanie came home to her studio apartment to find one of her cats spread out on top of a canvas that had been stretched and was ready to prime. She couldn't get Daniel's face out of her mind. She wanted to recreate that face on a two-dimensional surface. She needed to dig deeper into its multitude of layers and expand it to produce a new image in three or perhaps even four dimensions. This was the essence of Stephanie's intellectual and creative processes. She could be nothing *but* creative in every sense of the word. When she wasn't creating something, she was depressed and felt invisible and without substance.

Daniel Aarons' flat face hung in a virtual mist between Stephanie and her canvas. The mist floated between her little kitchen and her living room and did not leave. She turned on her television to break the vision of Daniel's flapping lips and vacant stare.

"The Chinese diplomat lost face and took his life. It will not be known until the ambassador returns if there will be any international repercussions. It is hoped that a military operation will not take place," the newscaster reported on the TV.

Stephanie could not lose Daniel's face. She tried to connect his being with that of the Chinese diplomat, but no connection could be made. She stepped in front of her bathroom mirror and thought about *losing face*.

She gazed into the mirror and thought about the perplexing Oriental concept. She looked at the twenty-two-year-old face that had seen so much misery, especially in the faces of the old worn-out drunks. She studied the face as if it were a painting by Picasso. She twisted it and moved the eyes, placed the ears on one side. She saw it as a monstrosity with a gaping blood-red mouth. The face became a vagina, and she thought of how Picasso was so enamored with that part of the female anatomy. She removed her brain and placed it above her head as if it were a cloud. Her face became a long dead skull, its eye sockets containing small flames. She grabbed a crayon and wrote on the wall, the *Chinese diplomat lost face.*

The face in the mirror then became a perfectly round sphere, the eyes dribbled away down the cheeks. The nose was pulled off like putty. The mouth turned inward and vanished. The hair fell out. All that was left of Stephanie Croix's face was a shiny white featureless orb, a cue ball sitting on a pair of shoulders. She had finally gotten Daniel Aarons' face out of her mind, thanks to the suicide of the Chinese diplomat.

She blinked and the plankton in her sponge mind came together to form an entirely new being, a new creation.

"Yes, yes!" she said with supreme joy. She picked up the cat and passionately kissed its face as if it were her lover. The two embraced and danced around the room. The cat's eyes grew wide with terror, but Stephanie had received a divine communication and she wanted the cat to know it.

"Bamboo," she said, "it's an omen of great importance."

The cat was not impressed and failed to see the significance of the moment. She left Stephanie and joined her kittens, which were hiding beneath a table.

Stephanie beckoned to her muse. She stood on top of her celestial pyramid in the middle of her tiny studio apartment and asked for inspiration. The muse presented his heart to her in an echo, and then in a box of chocolate promises, which he put on her thigh. She was ready to paint!

A pain stabbed Stephanie's head—a familiar pain that she knew by name—a pain that bedeviled her and always arrived at the time she was about to create. It was like a floater in the eye that was always most apparent in the brightest sunlight, when everything seemed clear and full of color. It made her sweat and she banged her forehead with the palm of her hand as if to hammer it out. She and her pain were enemies, but also the best of friends. It tried to kill her every day, but it also gave her the visions she needed to paint. It encouraged her arms to stretch farther into the darkness of the waters that surrounded her. It enabled her to grasp the tiny one-celled animals she needed for her daily sustenance. She grudgingly invited her pain into her creative act and asked it if it wanted a drink.

Stephanie opened a bottle and she knew that if the brush worked, it would first have to be moistened with the spirit. She poured the clear liquid into a cup and drank. The small amount that remained at the bottom was left for the brush, which she named Amset.

"Amset," she cried, "son of Horus, protect my liver and those of all mortal men."

She hadn't been so drunk in weeks, but neither had Amset done such fine work.

Stephanie awoke the next morning lying naked on the floor beside her most recent creation and the sound of Bamboo's purring in her ear. She felt ashamed and disgusted with herself. She knew she was just like the men at the Brewery, except that they were old, decrepit, and sad. She was just sad. Her body was still fresh and alive. She could still fly through the air and pull colors out of the clouds. She could still be passionate, loving, and tender. She could still care for those old men who were still alive, and that was her very special calling. She was the goddess mother to all those men, this little twenty-two-year-old girl, mother to the world. Mother to Moby Dixon with his flattened face and cauliflower ears, mother to Ernie Yeager with his addled brain, mother to fifty-eight other guys who stunk like the street, mother to homeless cats, sad-looking rocks, and tarnished pennies. She was the mother to the world, so she called herself Mut, wife of Amun, mother of Khonsu, the moon god.

All those drunks at the Brewery, they were moon gods. Every month when the moon was full, they'd get drunk and sometimes not come home for weeks. They were creatures of the moon, pushed and pulled like the tides, always seeking their fortunes and always fighting the demons that came from the dark side. The men called her Mut, not because they knew who Mut was, but just because that was her spiritual name. Only special people could call her Mut, only those who became children or babies, only those who couldn't speak, only those who walked on four legs, or perhaps six or eight, and only those who sat in corners like stones. Plenty of life forms in the Brewery were qualified to call her Mut, but Daniel Aarons was not one of them. He couldn't see through her eyes or feel the liquid of space as she could. He couldn't see the colors she saw that were beyond the normal range of visible light in the spectrum. No, she saw beyond the ultraviolet, beneath the infrared. She would mix new colors and give them secret names. Only an alchemist could break her codes. The greenish-blues with a hint of orange and gold were *auramooth*. A fiery, silver black was called *celiszure*. The deepest black of depression was *corzhu* and the soft purple of death she called *sohoomwh*. The white of the blank canvas was simply *sootah*. All these secret names she would share only with those she loved.

Stephanie Croix gazed at her new creation, an abstract explosion of angular hard edges and sharp points that was Daniel Aarons' face. She did not like the face that she saw on her canvas. She wasn't sure if it was the painting or the man she didn't like. Two hours in a waiting room was certainly not enough time to appraise a human being. The angles and the points, however, were correct. Her judgment was right on target. This man of hard edges and sharp points would have to change if she was to tell him her name. She would not share with him the meaning of *auramooth* and she would certainly not allow him to see her when she was drunk or in her darkest depression.

Stephanie Croix lived her life as a surreal work of art. She experienced the world the way a steel strawberry kisses a cloud. Her apartment bore her unique view of life. Even her cat, Bamboo, was surreal, eating tomatoes and drinking wine. A mattress was bolted to her ceiling and a large mirror was on the floor. Sometimes she would sleep on the mirror staring up at the mattress, hoping to see lovers on fire.

Her phone rang.

"Hello, I'm not home. Go away," she said into the telephone. "I'm exhausted and hung over."

"Mut, is that you?" A small voice came from the receiver.

"No, it's not me. Me is like water filling ships. No lifeboats. Titanic mouth swelling, choking, sinking …"

"Mut, you've been drinking. I can smell it on your poetry," the phone voice said.

"Malchus?" Stephanie asked with surprise.

"Yea, it's me," Malchus said. "Have you been painting? I bet you've been up all night fighting with your face. Am I right?"

"Malchus, I'm scared. I'm scared again. The pain in my head … and that Daniel Aarons is nothing but hard edges and sharp points. I know he's going to hurt me. There's something about him, his big, stuffy mind."

Stephanie wasn't coherent. Her thought processes and patterns of logic, which were usually circular in nature, were giving her dangerous feedback. She was in a massive emotional overload.

"Mut, I met Aarons yesterday at the Brewery," said Malchus. "I know everything about him. I know where he lives and I spent some time with his uncle. Believe me, he's soft. Don't worry about his hard edges and sharp points." Malchus tried to be reassuring.

Stephanie, however, responded with a sense of urgency and despondency.

"It's not the *work* thing that bothers me so much, Malchus; it's him, his person, those deep blue eyes. Malchus, he's bittersweet chocolate, I know it. I feel it deep within me! He sat on his chair yesterday like a little schoolboy in the principal's office waiting to be scolded. I saw how vulnerable he is. He tried to look like a rock, but he was melting like a snow cone in July. Boyer told me how competent and educated he is, but that didn't matter. He's a baby, Malchus, and I know I'm going to have to share my colors with him one of these days."

"Mut, I really don't know exactly what's going on, but my gut tells me that something is going to break loose real soon, something cataclysmic, something that will change the universe. I think I'm going up again, but this time …"

"You mean another kidnapping?" Stephanie asked. She was familiar with all of Malchus' numerous alien abductions.

"No, not this time," Malchus replied. "No temporary visit or quickie physical. They're not going to stick tubes up my ass this time. There's going to be some kind of universal transformation! I can feel it!"

Malchus' voice drifted into silence. The line went dead. Stephanie was upset, but she knew that Malchus had had many visions and extraterrestrial visitations. The poor little man suffered greatly, but he loved Mut with a sincere but strange brotherly love.

Stephanie was perplexed. How did he know Daniel's uncle? Who is Daniel's uncle, anyway, and why did Malchus visit him?

Weird occurrences were no stranger to Stephanie. For her, oddness and mystery were natural. The sudden appearance of Malchus into her life a few months ago was no oddity or cause for concern. Although he was a severely deformed little man with one ear, his physical appearance was no cause for revulsion or even pity. Stephanie let him into her heart quickly and soon he was calling her Mut, too.

Stephanie's apartment was dead quiet. Bamboo and her kittens were hunting mice in a closet. She stood and looked at her damp creation sitting on the easel. She could still smell the faint aroma of vodka on the brush. She would hide the work of art until she could share it with Daniel. Perhaps she could never share it, and for an instant, she considered destroying the image. Nevertheless, it remained angular, jagged, and pointed.

Stephanie Croix sat on her floor and considered her world. No straight lines. No right angles. She hated nice, perfect, even things. She despised those pretty little jewel boxes that little girls kept because they were so precious. Nothing was precious. No *thing* was precious. Only living things were precious and none of them had straight lines or right angles.

"*Wabi-sabi!*" she screamed. "The world is *wabi-sabi.*"

All of her canvases were out of shape, trapezoids, truncated triangles, and twisted parallelograms. All were slightly askew and bent to rid them of their right angles. She tried to eliminate all straight edges. The results were not entirely satisfactory, but they provided a way for Stephanie to allow her creations to become just like her: sad, passionate, a little odd, a bit surreal, and always in a state of dissipation.

She went to her journal, a book of sketches, scratches, poems, and red wine stains. She treasured Bamboo's paw prints on one page. The cat stepped in some paint drippings and then walked across the open book. Even disgusting little roaches had their place in her book. A mother roach laid her eggs in the spine of the book and nibbled at the glue. There were no dates in the journal, just random thoughts, a doodle going in one direction, a thought going in another, poems written in circles, smeared charcoal sketches, a chocolate fingerprint, cartoons of strange little people with big eyes and bare feet. She opened the book to a blank page and wrote a poem.

> *Hot swirling melting oils came off her canvas*
> *to sear her eyes, to blind her blindness*
> *so that she could no longer just paint!*
> *With brushes and palate knife to smear images*
> *and spirit-embedded pictures, the canvas burned!*
> *The paint turned to dust.*
> *It was not enough for her just to be an artist!*

Stephanie stepped out of her mind and threw her body into her art and she dissolved in ecstasy! Who was this strange graceful creature? Why did God put her on this planet? She asked herself these questions as she gazed into the mirror. The mirror never lies, she thought, but it sometimes sends back slightly distorted light waves. That's because the Stephanie Croix on the other side of the mirror got out of bed a millisecond after I did. She's playing games with me today. The Stephanie Croix in the other universe is probably falling in love with her Daniel Aarons at this very moment, while this Stephanie Croix is still suffering with delusions of sharp edges and points.

There was a scratching sound at the foot of the bathroom door. One of Bamboo's kittens wanted to come in to use the litter box. Her train of thought came to an abrupt end and veered off its tracks into the paws of the tiny cat. She lifted him and held him close to her body and she dreamed of her life as a child, complete with other tiny kittens, a mother, a brother, a church, and incredibly icy winters.

Stephanie Croix was a complex being, a multi-layered creation of infinite depth. She was like a deep cave that contained precious metals and gems, but had not yet been mined. She had always been a spiritual child, a mystic, a dreamer, a sad lost orphan, and a drifter. She identified with lost dogs, stray cats, wild flowers, and frogs. They were all free and natural. She saw them as God's special creations with unique purposes. She hated the idea of pure breeds and despised the world's racism. She would proudly tell her classmates that she, like the dogs, was a mongrel, a mutt. She loved that word, mutt.

"I'm a mutt and I'm proud of it," she would say. "One of my grandfathers is French Canadian, and he married my grandmother who was Italian. On my mother's side, my grandfather was a Native American, and he married my grandmother who was Hungarian, and her parents were Gypsies!" Stephanie loved the romantic notion that she, too, was a Gypsy, a wanderer, a passionate but despised outsider.

Stephanie suffered from deep bouts of depression. Once, she cut her wrists and spent several months at Bellevue Hospital. She learned how to drink from her father, and she cursed the genes she had inherited from him. She was a textbook case, the daughter of an alcoholic and now a depressed alcoholic herself. She didn't know from which side she had inherited her depression, but it really didn't matter. Her father came and went and then was gone; she never saw him again. Perhaps, she thought, he might just show up one day at the Brewery. Every one of those guys was her father. Everyone loved her, but when they were drunk, they would push her, shove her, spit at her, or call her a damn whore.

The mystic and the Gypsy were always on the move and searching the heavens for the truth. She knew that the truth was there, probably right before her eyes, but she was still blind. She regarded all authentic spirituality as holy and she searched for God in many different fashions and varieties. She found it all confounding until she saw a moth emerge from its chrysalis. She dreamed that she was tied up in ropes. The more she struggled, the tighter the ropes became. She picked up a Bible and saw herself pouring fragrant perfume on Jesus' feet. She reached out to grab his resurrected body, but he told her that she could not touch him.

It was a new day. Stephanie Croix got dressed and went to work.

CHAPTER 5

✠ ✠ ✠

ONCE A MONTH, MALCHUS AND NAPHTALI ROPSHITZ (Tali) would go to the Metropolitan Opera at Lincoln Center. Malchus would wear his floppy hat and a long black cape that he had found in a bag of clothing that someone had dropped off at the Brewery. The cape dragged along the ground sweeping up trash and dog droppings. It would catch in subway doors, people would step on it, and tires of trucks were always leaving impressions. Still, it became just another one of his trademarks like his floppy hat. He'd carry a walking stick and wear dark glasses to shade his highly sensitive eyes.

In the grand plaza of Lincoln Center, Malchus would greet the crowds and tell them that he was the great impresario of the opera. He spoke Italian with an impeccable accent and gave autographs. Tali would wear a New York Yankees sweatshirt, jeans, and a pair of old, worn-out sneakers. The two would buy potato knishes and Cokes from a sidewalk vendor and saunter into the opera house like true connoisseurs of the art.

Once, during the intermission of *La Bohème*, Malchus and Tali entertained the patrons in the lobby by singing arias. They were still singing and having a wonderful time when a security guard unceremoniously escorted them out of the opera house. The two laughed as they ran across the grand plaza to the subway.

It was well past the rush hour and the trains were not especially crowded. The screeching of the steel wheels on the tracks excited

Malchus. He felt as if his body had been taken over and controlled by this mechanical female train. Each car was his lover's womb and he penetrated the doors that flung open with his masculine prowess. The two men rushed to the front of the train and peered through the window into the dark tunnel ahead.

Tali suddenly remembered that he had an appointment in Brooklyn.

"Malchus, I need to meet some men at Jay Street and take them to a rescue mission in Bushwick. You can change trains at Hoyt and Schermerhorn and take the G train to Greenpoint."

Tali had not mentioned his plans to Malchus during the day, and the little man was disappointed that they would not be eating together at the Brewery. The train came to a screeching halt at the Hoyt and Schermerhorn station and both Tali and Malchus left the train.

They stood on the vacant platform and Tali put his hand on Malchus' head. "Malchus, I'll see you Wednesday. Don't forget to take your meds and no booze. You hear me? No booze."

Malchus glanced up at his friend and smiled. Tali left the station leaving Malchus alone to wait for the G train to take him to Greenpoint.

A faint roar could be heard in the distance. The roar became louder and Malchus looked down the track and saw a strange old train with odd markings pull into the station. There were just two cars along with the pungent aroma of asphalt and oil. A generator hummed and brakes hissed. These looked like the old wooden cars from the Depression, complete with incandescent bulbs, rattan seats, and ceiling fans. There was no conductor or motorman and no passengers were visible. It rolled to a screeching stop in the station and Malchus entered the empty train.

What do you say to a man who has not only seen flying saucers, but has spent time vacationing on other planets? When that someone is also a one-eared dwarf, probably not much. When a man spends most of his life in a psychiatric hospital and talks incessantly about his travels to the other end of the galaxy, one just assumes that he's simply suffering from severe mental illness.

Malchus, like the prophets of old, was fond of gazing into the night sky and seeing glorious visions. These visions were not seen from mountaintops in the Holy Land, but from the solarium on the seventh floor of the Manhattan Psychiatric Hospital. They would not be seen on any other floor or from any other vantage point in the large facility. The solarium on the seventh floor faced the East River and Brooklyn. Malchus would rush into the hallway of the seventh floor ward, fall down on the floor, and clutch his head, throwing his arms up to heaven. He'd wail and scream like the prophet. "As I looked, behold, a stormy wind came out of the Bronx, and a great black cloud … and fire flashing forth … and from the middle of it came the likeness of four living creatures … under their arms on their four sides they had hands with seven fingers … and the living creatures darted back and forth … there were wheels all around, and wheels within wheels …."

The attendants on the ward had heard Malchus' description of his visions many times and they had no patience with his theatrics.

"Malchus, go back to the Garden of Eden and say hello to Adam and Eve," the attendants would say in their mocking tone.

"No, no, it wasn't the Garden of Eden, you dummies," Malchus replied. "I was never there. It was the Garden of Gethsemane where Simon Peter took out his sword and cut off my ear. But Jesus came to me and touched the side of my head and immediately the blood stopped flowing. I remember! He kissed me and said that I would be able to hear better than any man in Jerusalem. I would hear the voice of God in the whisper of the wind and the song of the bird. I would hear with my heart. I wouldn't need any ears. But Jesus turned to the high priest and told him that his ears had made him deaf to the voice of God."

It was usually at this time in his rant that Malchus became calm, but exhausted. The attendants didn't even have to carry him back to his room or tie him down. The dwarf simply walked back to his bed where he'd sleep for a full day. Malchus had experienced just about every kind of hallucination, vision, and apparition known to modern psychiatry.

The visions didn't cease, not even when Malchus was released from the hospital. They continued to be with him as sources of terror and amusement. But Tali helped him with his depression and his ecstasy. The two friends were an inseparable team, soothing each other's wounds and celebrating their victories. Together they could make it in this crazy world.

Malchus stood at the end of a subway car with a Milky Way bar in his hand. The doors shut and he was alone staring into the blackness of the tunnel. The train had moved so fast into the tunnel that he didn't notice the passing columns on the platform in the station. Hoyt and Schermerhorn seemed long gone, and he waited for the lights of the Nevins Street station. The lights in the car blinked off as they often did in old trains. Two men suddenly appeared at the opposite end of the car. Both looked pleasant, but were shabbily dressed in what looked like rags or sackcloth. They moved slowly toward Malchus in a very deliberate fashion, but not in a threatening way. One of them was short and walked with small shuffling steps. His eyes twinkled and his head was bald. He had a short goatee that accentuated his narrow triangular face. A smile appeared on this gnome-like man. The other one was quite a bit taller and very distinguished. He was handsome and had a full head of curly gray hair. He carried a large wide briefcase. Malchus wasn't quite sure what was going on or what to say to the two men. He felt awkward and out of place as the two men approached him.

"Would either of you two gentlemen like a bite of my Milky Way? It's a little stale, but I really don't like to eat alone."

The smaller of the two men greeted Malchus.

"Thanks for your kind offer, but chocolate irritates my stomach."

The taller man took a small piece, ate it, and smiled.

The short man spoke. "My dear son, Malchus, I am Raphael and this is Moshe. We are your guardian angels and we have a lot to tell you." Raphael clapped his hands and glanced at the ceiling of the train as if to see the approving face of God.

Moshe spoke. His voice was deep and elegant and his words came out as if they were sung by a great tenor on the stage of the opera. "A rabbi, a priest, and a minister were in a boat," said Moshe.

Raphael tapped Moshe on the shoulder. "For God's sake, Moshe, this is not the time for jokes. Let us first be serious with Malchus and give him his message." Raphael suggested that they sit down because this would probably be a long visit.

"I'm an angel, a messenger of God," Raphael said, "but my feet still hurt. Come, let's sit."

The two angels sat facing Malchus, studying the little man's face and hands.

"Good hands, good face," said Moshe to Raphael. "Could anybody possibly believe that he would be a great prophet, perhaps even a messiah?"

"Moshe, not so fast," warned Raphael. "The poor boy cannot possibly absorb such possibilities at this time. Let us be patient and proceed step-by-step, as it is written."

Raphael asked Moshe for the pile of papers that he was carrying in the briefcase. A great holy book, its spine now protruding from the open briefcase, remained a mystery to Malchus, and he stared at it as if it contained the very secrets of the universe.

"My child, the book you are gazing at contains all of the secrets of the universe, but you are not ready for that." Raphael seemed to have known what was on Malchus' mind.

"Shall we get down to business?" Moshe shuffled the papers. He glanced at Raphael who nodded affirmatively.

Raphael cleared his throat and began to speak, but Malchus immediately interrupted.

"Just hold it right there. Don't open your mouth and don't give me anymore of this angel crap. Excuse me, gentlemen, but it's not what I see that bothers me, it's what I'm *not* feeling. I might as well be taking the trash out. There's no passion here. There's no ecstasy. I'm not foaming at the mouth, and my head is not blasting apart! If this is a vision, I would know it, but I don't feel anything. Therefore, I must conclude that this event is not really happening to me. I'll just sit here and wait for the train to pull into Nevins Street. Thank you and good-bye."

Malchus sat on the rattan seat and stared through the two men as if they weren't there. He assumed that they were simply a part of a psychotic experience. This was not one of his Ezekiel-like visions, it was not like his two-week excursion in Roswell, New Mexico, with extraterrestrials, and it certainly wasn't a bit similar to his vacation on *Zardor*, the fourteenth planet in the *Kokoola* system.

"Do either of you gentlemen know what time it is?" asked Malchus. "I've got to be back at the Brewery by twelve or else they'll lock the door. I'll have to sleep out in the cold if I don't get back soon."

Raphael smiled warmly.

"Malchus, my child, my son, do not be worried about the time. Do not be worried about anything in this world. For you, at this very moment, the space-time continuum does not exist. While you are concerned about our reality and the reality of this situation, I can assure you that we are very real. In fact, the three of us are far more real than anything that exists on earth or in the entire created universe. And you, my son, are far more real than the time you need to get back to the Brewery."

Malchus was still not sure of what he was hearing or seeing.

"May I touch you?" Malchus asked.

"Of course, touch both of us," said Raphael. "We are very real and our bodies have been around for a very long time. That's why my feet hurt."

Raphael extended his hand for Malchus to touch. The hand was solid and warm. Malchus stood up and felt Moshe's large head of curly hair. He fondled it and combed it with his fingers. He knocked on top of Raphael's baldpate.

"Please come in, but take your shoes off," Raphael said with a grin. "You are on holy ground."

Malchus unlaced his sneakers and sat back down, his mouth and eyes wide open. The blackness in the tunnel soon gave way to a brilliant flashing light that filled the car and caused the faces of the two men to glow as if they were on fire. Malchus shielded his eyes from the painful light. A deep booming voice came through the windows and a powerful wind pushed its way through the cracks in the door. The voice was forceful and commanding, yet reassuring and loving. It cradled Malchus and penetrated his body to its very core.

"I am the God of your father, the God of Abraham, the God of Isaac, and the God of Jacob," the voice said.

Malchus hid his face. He was terrified and could not look at the piercing light.

The voice of God continued, "I have seen the affliction of my people who are enslaved in their bodies and minds and have heard their cry. I know their sufferings and I have come to deliver them out of the hands of their oppressors."

"Okay, Uriel, enough with the lights and sound," Raphael yelled to a man who appeared to be floating just outside the subway car. The man gave a thumbs-up signal and the lights and the booming voice were gone. Again, Malchus and the two angels sat in the silent car. The blackness returned and Malchus was utterly confused. His fear mixed with anger as if he had just been the butt of some heavenly practical joke. His alien abductors had never done anything like this. They were serious guys with no theatrics or shenanigans. When they crammed a tube down your throat, it was for authentic scientific research. Malchus was annoyed and grabbed his sneakers.

"Can I put my sneakers back on now or are we still on holy ground?" asked Malchus. "I think you two guys are just as crazy as I am and the three of us are having some kind of mutual hallucination. Where you guys in a state hospital, too?"

Moshe turned to Raphael, his voice expressing mild disgust. "I knew we shouldn't have started with the fancy light show and *vox Dei*. Look at Malchus; he's going through spiritual entropy. There will be nothing left of him to work with. We should have started with Elijah in the cave. I had a feeling that Moses and the burning bush would be just too much for him. Now we'll have to start from square one."

Raphael was not pleased at the turn of events. He had thought that Malchus would be much more receptive if he began his presentation with some commonly held image of God—booming voice, flashing lights, burning bush. Raphael looked at Moshe, "Perhaps you're right, let us try *Plan 33*."

Moshe took the massive book hidden in his briefcase and placed it on his lap. He spread his hands over the enormous tome and then clasped them together as if he were about to pray. His eyes flashed wide open and pierced Malchus with a burning stare. Moshe's voice was like rolling thunder.

"Malchus, there was a holy man who lived in Jerusalem after the Babylonians took the Jews into exile. His name was Benoni, which means son of my sorrow. After a long time, the holy city returned to normal, but it was destitute and without its temple. Benoni wandered the streets alone, walking almost naked and covered with filth. He pitied his deplorable condition and wailed in the alleyways. He had not been taken into exile because the Babylonians considered him worthless and one of the dead. When the merchants swept the streets at night, their brooms would push him into the gutter along with the excrement of the goats. Benoni continually prayed to God. He begged the Almighty to return to Jerusalem and rebuild the temple. He pleaded for God to bring peace and to restore his people in their holy land, but God never answered Benoni. God never even responded to his prayers.

One day, while Benoni was deep in prayer and not looking where he was going, he fell into a deep pit filled with stagnant water and the bones of dead animals. He cried out for help and prayed to God, but no answer came. The next day, around dawn, Benoni saw a face peering over the side of the pit. A man called to him, 'Are you down there, Benoni?' 'Yes,' Benoni answered. 'Please get me out of here, and I will be forever grateful for your act of mercy.' The man entered the pit, lost his balance, and fell headlong into the slimy water next to Benoni. He did not have a rope or any other tool to get out of the pit, so both of them were now at the bottom wading in the filth."

Moshe looked at Malchus and asked, "Is this making any sense yet?"

Malchus' face was as blank as an eggshell.

In exasperation, Raphael blurted into the silence. "Come on, Moshe, finish the story. Two men at the bottom of a filthy pit doesn't mean anything."

Moshe continued. "The man who had fallen into the pit with Benoni spoke, 'You know, my friend Benoni, God does not want us to live in a state of continual ecstasy and glory like the angels in heaven. No, he wants us to spend some time in the deep, filthy pit of our existence. When we stop feeling sorry for ourselves and repent of our error, we may rise through our condition to a higher level of being. Benoni, did you realize that when you move upward through your condition you could even carry the entire world with you? And God requires that in our love for our neighbor, we must go into the pit with him.' At that very moment, both Benoni and the man rose out of the pit. Benoni was on dry, solid ground, but the other man had disappeared. Benoni completely forgot about his dreadful situation and the desolation of Jerusalem and went about doing deeds of charity for those around him. Soon both the Jews and God returned to Jerusalem to rebuild the temple."

There was a thunderous round of applause. Raphael smiled and patted Moshe's hands, which were still resting on top of the massive book.

"Fine job, Moshe," Raphael said. "That was a beautiful story and so very true! You know, my dear Malchus, you will not find that story anywhere in the scriptures. That is because Benoni continued to remain anonymous and unknown for the rest of his life. All of his good deeds were done at night when darkness covered the land and the world was asleep. The poor people of Jerusalem would wake in the morning to find their wood chopped, their flocks tended, the candles in the prayer rooms lit, even their sick children had been made well! The scribes wanted to write about him, but they did not know who he was, so he became just another legend. But we know who he is and that is why Benoni is so special to us. He has a special place at this very moment, sitting at the right hand of God."

Malchus' eyes shined. A new insight was sprouting within him like a summer weed, but he wasn't quite sure what it was. He sat warm and contented like a tiny child who had just been told a bedtime story. He wasn't sure if he should drop off to sleep in the arms of Moshe or demand a further explanation. He decided to remain awake and wait for further revelations.

The two angels glanced at each other, proud of their accomplishment, and prepared to implement phase two of *Plan 33*. They knew their task was far from over.

"Moshe," said Raphael, "let us open the book now and show Malchus its full meaning."

Malchus' eyes flashed and glanced at the massive tome on Moshe's lap.

Moshe said to Raphael, "Are you ready?"

Raphael held the bottom of the book and Moshe held the front cover. In a glorious sweeping motion, the book flung open and instantly all time and space, matter and energy—including Malchus, Moshe, and Raphael—were sucked into an inky black vortex. Suspended in the darkness, the three held on to one another as they witnessed the formation of sparkling, white-diamond-like crystals far above them. The crystals changed to points of light, first billions, and then trillions, showering Malchus and his angels. Then the lights disappeared. The three men were left in utter blackness, suspended by nothing in the middle of nowhere. Malchus could not even see Moshe or Raphael, but he could feel their arms around him and he could hear the fluttering of what sounded like wings. A still, small voice came out of the blackness from every direction. It was as if the three men were immersed within the fluid of a womb and they were listening to the whispers of their mother.

The voice spoke. "The divine dark is the light where I dwell. Because I AM beyond the clarity of all human knowledge, I AM inaccessible. Unseeing and unknowing, you will attain the truth that is beyond all seeing and knowing except that I AM. Incomprehensible are my ways, inscrutable are my deeds, and indescribable are my gifts. Surpassing all understanding is my peace that I give to you. I tell you the truth if someone has seen me or has understood what he has seen and then he has not seen me. He has seen only his shadow."

The utterly black whirlwind gently and slowly carried the three beings out of the book and back into the subway car. Moshe's hair was sticking out in all directions. Raphael had lost one of his sandals. Malchus was speechless.

The three breathless men wiped sweat off their faces. Moshe smoothed down his hair.

"Malchus," said Raphael, "there remains one more thing to be done, the final task, the final joy! Moshe, do you have the seed, Malchus' seed?"

Moshe searched his briefcase for the seed, but he could not find it. He frantically looked in his pockets and discovered the precious object hidden within a matchbook. Moshe requested that he do the honors.

"No, Moshe, not this time. I am required to plant the seed. I have been waiting for this for a lifetime, a million lifetimes."

Raphael held a tiny seed in his hand, a seed no bigger than the head of a pin.

"Malchus, my son, do you know what this is?"

"Well, both of you have been talking about seeds, so I guess it's a seed."

"Malchus, remember that evening in the Garden of Gethsemane when Jesus came to you and touched your ear? Do you remember how he stopped the bleeding and told you that you would now hear in a different way?"

"Yes, of course, I've been telling that story to a lot of people for a long time."

"He left you without an ear so that Moshe and I could plant a new ear in your head. An ear that would allow you to hear the Word of God at all times. This tiny seed is like the mustard seed he spoke of. It is extremely powerful and can produce great works of charity and love. Now there's just one thing I must tell you. When we plant this seed in your head, you will forget everything that happened here today, but you will remember it in your heart and that is far more important. Sometimes the seed will disturb you, and it will be like a burning thorn in your flesh. It will push you to do things you wouldn't normally do, but it will also give you great powers to do miracles. Malchus, you have been chosen to be one of God's powerful prophets. Jesus promised that to you in the garden and His word is always true. Now come here and rest your head on my lap."

Malchus knelt on the floor of the subway car and put his head on Raphael's lap. His missing ear was obvious, just a small hole with a tiny flap of skin. Raphael dropped the seed into the hole in the side of Malchus' head and exclaimed, "It is done. Let us now celebrate!"

Moshe took a small flask of clear liquid out of his briefcase along with three cups. He gave each man a cup, but Malchus refused.

"I'm sorry, but I'm not allowed to drink this stuff. It really makes a mess of my head, especially in combination with my medication. No, thank you."

Moshe smiled. "No, Malchus, this isn't what you think it is. It is living water and once you drink from it, you will never be thirsty again."

The three held their glasses high and drank. Raphael said a short prayer of benediction and they packed up their books and papers.

The two men blessed Malchus and kissed him. Then they were gone.

The old train pulled into the Greenpoint station and Malchus calmly walked out of the car. The doors closed behind him and the train vanished from sight. As promised, Malchus remembered absolutely nothing.

CHAPTER 6

✠ ✠ ✠

"ROPSHITZ IS DEAD, LORD HELP US, ROPSHITZ is dead!" Moe Kutcher exclaimed. "Did you hear what I said? Ropshitz is dead. He walked with God and he was not, for God took him!"

Kutcher, a scrawny office clerk with a flare for the dramatic, couldn't break the terrible news of Naphtali Ropshitz' death in a more theatrical manner. He threw open the door to Daniel Aarons' office, only moments after the young man came into the Brewery for his first day of work, and made his pronouncement like a Greek chorus. Daniel's response was proper but very clinical.

"I'll call the police and the hospital," said Daniel. "Please make sure that no one touches the body until the authorities arrive. Who are his next of kin?"

Poor Daniel didn't have the foggiest idea who Naphtali Ropshitz was, but he was going to be on top of the situation and move according to established policy and procedures.

"Where's the body?" asked Daniel coldly.

"There isn't any body," Moe shrugged and scratched.

"What do you mean, there isn't any body?" Daniel asked incredulously. "I thought you just said that this Ropshitz guy just died?"

Daniel's response did not impress Kutcher. How could he be the new commander of the Brewery and not know the name Naphtali Ropshitz? How could he not know of the great deeds of charity of this blessed human being?

"Captain Aarons," Kutcher said, "Naphtali Ropshitz was not at the Brewery. He wasn't one of the men who worked here. He didn't drive a truck or work in a thrift store. Captain Aarons, Naphtali Ropshitz was one of the finest, most caring, most God-fearing, most beautiful guys that ever walked the face of this godforsaken planet." Moe's eyes filled with tears. He sighed and then regained his composure.

"He would give you the last penny he had if he thought you needed it to buy a piece of bread. He'd walk barefoot in the snow for twenty miles if he knew you needed a pair of shoes. He'd give you his last breath if he knew you were drowning. He'd scrape the dog shit off your shoes just to keep your floor clean!"

"Yes, Moe, I get the picture," Daniel said as he tapped on his desk.

Moe Kutcher continued his rant. "This man was a saint. No, a prophet and a savior all rolled into one. I remember when Sam Herring was sick and drunk for three weeks. Tali stayed in his room and took care of that buzzard until the old man finally died. Tali spoon-fed him and washed his clothes. He even dressed him like you'd dress a baby. Changed his underwear and took him for walks in the park. You know, when Sam died, Tali cleaned out his room and brought all his belongings back to his son in New Jersey. There was ten thousand dollars in cash hidden in Sam's mattress, and Tali didn't take a single dime. Such an honest man, that Tali. And did he ever ask for anything? No, he did it for free. He did it because he loved that old drunk, Sam, and because he loved all the guys in this place."

Moe Kutcher fell silent and Daniel spit a wad of gum into the trashcan. He looked at Moe and gave his first order. "Moe, please inform the men that we will have a meeting at ten o'clock to officially break the news of Mr. Ropshitz's death."

Moe didn't take the order well. He scratched both his thighs.

"No sir, don't do that," Moe replied. "I mean most of the men already know about it and they're grieving in their own particular way. I cried all night. Moby Dixon is still in a state of shock."

The large man, Dixon, whom Daniel had seen the week before, sat at his little desk, an inconsolable mountain of flesh, his eyes red from tears, and his mouth open to the wind.

"I see your point, Moe," said Daniel, shaking his head in the affirmative. "Perhaps the best thing to do would be to speak with each man on an individual basis. Let's allow the grieving process to proceed as needed and we'll take extra precautions. We need to be sensitive and caring at this difficult time."

Moe Kutcher nodded, his eyes closed, and his hands touched his heart.

"There's just one more thing, Captain Aarons, and I think I must be blunt. There is one man in the Brewery we haven't told. The news of Tali's death could be catastrophic for him."

Moe tugged at his crotch until he nearly pulled his pants off.

"He's a little strange man with a lot of problems. He's only been here at the Brewery for a few months, but in those few months, he's developed a very close relationship with Tali. He calls himself Malchus, and he goes around telling everybody that some guy named Peter cut his ear off or some kind of crap like that. Well, anyway, he and Tali became good friends, going everywhere together, sharing expenses. Tali helped Malchus get adjusted when he got out of the hospital. It was sort of a fatherly thing, you know. Captain, I really think that Miss Croix ought to be the one to tell him. She'll be able to break the news to him gently so that he won't go off the deep end."

"I've met Miss Croix," said Daniel, "and she seems like a very fine person. Perhaps she would be the best one to break the news to Malchus. I'll speak with her right away." Daniel stared at the top of his desk. "Oh, by the way, Moe, please don't call me Captain Aarons. I'm not an officer in the corps. I'm just a consultant to Colonel Boyer. You can call me Dr. Aarons or just Daniel would be fine."

"Sure thing, Doc," said Moe as he scratched his leg.

"Thanks very much, Moe, you've made the start of my first day here very special."

Daniel rolled his eyes as Moe left the office. He sighed and slumped into his wobbly desk chair. A stiff blast of wind blew in through a window and Daniel shivered even in the midst of the summer's heat. It was certainly not an auspicious way to begin one's first day on the job.

When Daniel walked into the Brewery that morning, no one bothered to say one word to him, let alone "hello or good morning" to the new boss. Maybe it was just too early. Maybe the men were already out on the trucks and in the warehouse. But where was his secretary, his executive assistant, Stephanie Croix? She certainly knew that he was starting work today, but she was conspicuously absent from her desk.

Daniel looked at his dilapidated desk, a discarded antique from the New York City Department of Education. It hadn't seen a dust rag in months, and its drawers had not seen the light of day since the last director opened it nine months before. Claude Boyer never used it. He liked to work at the large conference table used by the board of directors. Daniel didn't have time to straighten up his office and he certainly didn't have time to begin any paperwork. He needed to find his assistant and to deal with the immediate crisis that was overwhelming the Brewery: the death of Naphtali Ropshitz.

Daniel opened the door to his office, which was adjacent to the waiting room. Stephanie Croix's desk looked like a relic from a history museum, the ancient typewriter eagerly awaiting the slender fingers of its incompetent handler. A black rotary dial telephone with a twisted cord sat on top of a pile of unopened letters, presumably bills. An ashtray full of cigarette butts, the ends colored red with Stephanie's lipstick, adorned the doodle-laden blotter. A wobbly and mangled armless desk chair awaited her arrival.

Ernie Yeager and Moby Dixon sat in their dispatcher's booth like two shell-shocked pilots in the cockpit of a B-17. They had just been shot down. Daniel Aarons walked into the little smoke-filled office and talked to the flight crew.

"Gentlemen, I'm Dr. Aarons," Daniel said officiously. "Perhaps you've been informed that I would be starting my position today as executive consultant. I'm very pleased to be here and I am glad to meet both of you."

The two men were about to bail out of the stricken aircraft and leave Daniel to go down in flames inside enemy territory. Ernie Yeager, the copilot, put his earphones on and responded to a voice that might as well have come from General Eisenhower, himself.

"Mr. Aarons, this is a very black day," Ernie said. "We are all very sad by our dear friend's untimely death. I heard he was run over, crushed, and flattened by the wheels of a transit bus on his way to meet a couple of friends at Borough Hall. Poor Tali. Fortunately, he didn't know what hit him. He just smiled, waved, and stepped off the pavement into the arms of his Creator. Such a waste, it should have happened to

Ziggy Reynolds, that bastard, but not Ropshitz, certainly not Naphtali Ropshitz."

Ernie Yeager stared out into space as if looking for a bird or butterfly. He never looked anyone straight in the eye. He was a dreamy sort of guy who was in a constant state of agitation and despair.

Moby Dixon dabbed his eyes and talked about *Saint Ropshitz*. "He took me out for corned beef sandwiches and beer on Eastern Parkway. He even paid the subway. He bought food for my mother when she couldn't walk to the store and took her cat to the animal hospital on the East Side after a car hit it. But now he's gone and I'm sure he's in a better place."

The litany of eulogies was beginning to annoy Daniel, and he was feeling left out of something very personal and special. How could he have lived all these years without knowing this saint? How could he possibly attempt to fill the aching void? How could he ever get things back to normal in this fortress of desolation?

"Gentlemen, I know it's difficult, but could you please help me?" Daniel pleaded. "Could either of you tell me where Miss Croix is? Did she come to work today?"

"Yea, she's here today," said Dixon. "She's somewhere in the building, probably hiding."

"Hiding?" Daniel asked. "From what or from whom is she hiding?"

"Hiding from her pain, the men's pain," said Dixon with true insight. "Maybe she's even hiding from *you*."

"But I don't even know her," replied Daniel. "I haven't done anything to her. Why would she want to hide from me?"

"She just hides a lot. That's all," Yeager said.

Daniel was exasperated. Yeager and Dixon were not going to be of much help in this crisis. They were too immersed in their grief to be concerned with Daniel Aarons' professional problems.

"Thanks guys," said Daniel. "I think I'll just have a walk around the place and find her myself."

The new executive consultant for the Men's Rehabilitation Center was utterly alone and lost in his new headquarters. He was the commander of the Brewery, but he didn't have a clue as to who did what or where his assistant, Stephanie Croix, was hiding, if she was hiding at all. He ventured into the hall leading down to the disgusting little lavatory with the glass door and orange safety tape. Beyond that door was terra incognita. The Brewery was truly a surreal three-dimensional labyrinth of dark halls and stairways leading to blank walls. The shadows of men appeared on walls as if they were ghostly apparitions. Sounds came from all directions: the slam of a door, the flush of a toilet, a voice, and music from a radio. A light could be seen from under a door, a bright fluorescent light, and the low hum of an electrical appliance could be heard.

Daniel opened a door that took him to the upholstery workshop. The room was filled with chairs, sofas, and ottomans oozing stuffing and foam rubber. The skins were worn out and ripped. A slight, toothless man with a felt hat stood by a table stretching plastic over a kitchen chair. The radio played an AM station with music from the 1950s. He held an electric staple gun in his hand and used it like a weapon against the old furniture. On the table sat the hideous cat that had greeted him at the screen door just a few days earlier. The man and the cat were of one soul—both products and permanent residents of the Brewery. Both sprung to life as Daniel walked in the room. The toothless man felt threatened and showed his anger.

"Hey, fella, what you lookin' for?" asked the man with obvious annoyance. "Nobody's allowed back here except for the men. You want clothes, furniture? Go to the thrift store next door."

Daniel heard him murmur something that sounded like *sonofabitch*. This poor old guy didn't have a clue. He'd been sniffing adhesives and solvents for too long. For him it was 1933 and FDR had just been elected. Maybe it was December 7, 1941, a day of infamy. For Daniel Aarons, his first day at the Brewery was certainly a day of infamy that he would never forget.

Daniel introduced himself to the toothless man and his cat.

"Good morning, I'm Dr. Aarons, the new commanding executive. Have you seen Miss Croix?"

This man was not grieving for Naphtali Ropshitz, he had no red stains around his eyes, and he was not about to give a eulogy.

"Who?" The man retorted as if he had not heard the question.

"Miss Croix, Stephanie Croix," Daniel replied.

"Don't know anybody by that name," the man said. "You'd better check with Colonel Boyer up at the front desk."

The man was oblivious to all the changes and transitions at the Brewery, but Daniel attempted to make conversation.

"That's a nice piece of furniture you got there. Are you fixing the seat?" Daniel asked as if he were interested in that broken-down piece of furniture.

"This is a piece of shit!" the man said curtly. "I wouldn't put my ass on it if it was the last chair on earth. Would you want to sit on it?"

Daniel seemed to have hit a brick wall. He tried to pet the cat, but it growled and hissed just as it did on the loading dock.

Daniel was now more direct. "By the way, what's your name?"

"Seymour Zupnick," said the man, "but the guys around here just call me Potato because I'm a real masher." He laughed at his own joke and exposed a mouthful of rotten teeth.

"Well, Potato, it was nice meeting you," said Daniel with a dry smile. "And I'm sure we'll be seeing each other again soon."

Daniel left Potato and the hideous cat and ventured back out into the dark foreboding corridors of the Brewery searching for Croix. He needed her immediate assistance, her guidance, her lanky legs, and brown eyes, but at this very moment, he especially needed her directions around the maze of rooms and tunnels in the mammoth facility.

He opened door after door, discovering various broom closets and unkempt lavatories, uncovering dark cavernous workrooms and storage areas filled with bric-a-brac, trash, and treasures from unearthed tombs. Then he found Croix.

What sounded like the whimpering of a tiny child was actually the soft sobbing of Stephanie Croix. She sat on the floor of a tiny square room that had one window and a vase. The room was carpeted and smelled like flowers. It was a little sanctuary, a chapel filled with divine light and the delicate form of a young woman.

Stephanie was startled. Her big eyes blazed at the sight of her new boss. She jumped to her feet, shoeless, and wiped her eyes, apologizing like a child who had just missed the school bus. Her makeup was smeared, her lipstick a red mess, and her embarrassment profound. She had put on the official uniform of the Service Corps just for this occasion, Daniel's first day on the job, but she looked like an out-of-date flight attendant on a vintage DC-3.

Daniel smiled at Stephanie Croix and broke the silence.

"Am I glad to find *you*!" Daniel exclaimed.

CHAPTER 7

✠ ✠ ✠

NOT ONE SOUL HAD INFORMED POOR MALCHUS about Naphtali Ropshitz's death. Neither was there an official communiqué from the staff at the Brewery.

When Malchus reached his destination at the Greenpoint subway station, after his unforgettable (yet forgotten) encounter with Moshe and Raphael, he simply sat down on a bench in the middle of the station platform with his Milky Way bar and stared at the blank tile walls. Something, or someone, just told him to sit and be still. So he sat and waited on that bench and looked at the walls for almost two hours. Why was he sitting and what was he waiting for?

Later that morning, Malchus was still sitting on the bench when a train pulled into the station. A solitary man emerged from the train. It was Naphtali Ropshitz! Malchus wasn't expecting Tali, but he somehow knew that this encounter was predestined and part of some grand plan, something far bigger than the two men put together. Tali rushed out to greet his friend and they warmly embraced.

"My dear friend, Malchus," said Tali. "I knew you would be here waiting for me and you didn't disappoint me. Want a bite of my knish? Take, it is part of me."

Malchus took a bite of the soft warm potato pastry and then he touched Tali's face.

"You feel real, like flesh and blood," said Malchus with a confused expression.

"Of course, what do you think, I'm a ghost?" asked Tali. "Here Malchus, take a sip of my Coke, it's also part of me." Tali held the cup up to Malchus' mouth and he took a sip. "Good, let's walk."

The two men walked the long platform to the stairway and out into the open air of the grimy neighborhood. Neither said a word, but they knew that their time of true communion had come. Tali turned to his friend.

"Malchus, I'm taking you to the English Kills."

"English Kills, what's that?" Malchus asked, much confused. "Are you going to murder me?"

"No, silly, of course not." Tali slapped Malchus on the back. "The English Kills is a little waterway, a canal in this scenic section of Brooklyn. It's right behind the Brewery."

The two men walked in the night through dark alleyways behind warehouses and trucks. Nothing moved except for an occasional cat that passed in front of them.

"Tali, what's in the English Kills that's so important?" Malchus asked. "Can't you tell me?"

"No more games, my friend. Tonight the world will be turned on its ear. Tonight I must finish my work and go away."

Malchus was visibly agitated and nervous.

"What do you mean, finish your work?" Malchus asked. "You're going back to your father? He's decided to re-own you? I think you'd be a great rabbi. I'd come to your synagogue and I'd even learn how to put on the phylacteries."

Malchus stopped his chattering and looked deeply into Tali's eyes. Tali put his arm around Malchus' shoulder.

"Malchus, my dear friend, my brother, you must stay here, but God wants me to go to the ends of the earth."

Malchus panicked. "But, Tali, I don't want to leave you and I don't want you to leave me. Please take me to the ends of the earth, too."

Tali looked down into the little man's eyes and whispered, "Do you know that today the Lord must take Naphtali Ropshitz out of this world?"

The two men came to the bank of the feted canal called the English Kills and Tali put his hand on top of Malchus' head as if to bless him.

"Listen to me, Malchus, and listen to me very clearly. What I am about to tell you will be planted in your brain like a tiny seed, a mustard seed, but that seed will grow, blossom, and fill you with great wisdom and power. You will be called blessed, the prophet, and you will do miraculous work and good deeds. But for every good deed you do, for every sick person you heal, for every gift of love you bring to this lost world, God will empty you and you will forget your deeds and you will go about the world as an invisible man. He will make you so perfect and empty that He will be able to fill you exactly as He needs you. Malchus, you are now His chosen vessel on this planet!"

Malchus shivered in the night air, his tiny legs quivered, and he looked into the black murky water of the English Kills.

"Malchus," Tali said with the force of a powerful storm, "the world is a terrible, insane place. It's like a worn pair of pants full of holes, but with pockets of grace."

Tali took a tiny seed from one of the pockets in his pants. He got down on his knees and was now at eye level with Malchus. He removed the dwarf's hat.

"Put your head on my chest, my son," commanded Tali.

Malchus put his head on Tali's chest. The big man placed the tiny seed into the hole on the right side of Malchus' head and then kissed the top of his head.

"Tali, if you're going away, will you at least leave me a part of your Spirit?"

"You've asked for a very difficult thing, my son, because my Spirit belongs to God. But if you watch and see me leave this world, then you will know that you have received a double portion of my Spirit. The rest, you know, goes back to God."

Tali pulled off his New York Yankees sweatshirt, rolled it up, and threw it into the English Kills. The little canal immediately dried up.

"Go get it, Malchus, it's yours. It's your mantle, just like Elijah gave to Elisha."

Malchus picked up his mantle and put it over his head. The big baggy shirt hung down to his knees. He put his floppy hat back on his head.

As they walked, a light appeared in the sky, a furious bluish-golden light like a spaceship from another world. Its beam separated the two men and Tali was taken up in a whirlwind into the light.

Malchus watched and cried out, "Lord, Lord, I am your servant! God be with you, Naphtali Ropshitz!"

The light vanished. Malchus was alone on the bank of the English Kills wearing Naphtali Ropshitz's sweatshirt and not remembering a thing that had just happened.

CHAPTER 8

✠ ✠ ✠

SOME PEOPLE ARE NATURALLY LIKE STONES. SOON after reaching adulthood, they sink to the bottom of deep pools of water and they become dense, invisible, and lost. Others become a fine sheen of oil that floats on top of the water; their souls spread out for the world to see. When the sun shines on them, they become radiant rainbows reflecting the sky and all that passes over them. If a tiny speck of dust falls upon them or if the breeze should blow too hard, they become swirling eddies of color. They are never the same because they make themselves available to the world and the world is always acting upon them. They are beautiful but turbulent creatures forever in a state of flux and chaos.

Stephanie Croix, like the brilliant sheen on the water, was forever changing. Even in her despair and embarrassment in the tiny chapel, she moved with grace and knew that the tears she shed were healing tears used to wash the wounds of the men in the Brewery. Daniel had not yet tasted her tears, but he offered her his hand as she rose from the chapel floor. He drew her closer to himself and cherished this brief moment. He didn't know if she felt the same as he, but in an instant their relationship had changed and they both became a single sheen upon the surface of the water.

"Dr. Aarons," Stephanie said, staring at the floor fidgeting, "things are so mixed up around here today. The men are all over the city. Some are at other centers talking about what happened to Tali."

She dabbed her eyes and shrugged.

"Oh, I'm sorry," she apologized to Daniel. "You don't even know who I'm talking about. His name was Naphtali Ropshitz and he was the best thing that ever happened to these guys."

"Yes, I've heard all about him from several of the men whom I met this morning," said Daniel. "Moe Kutcher broke the news to me in his own unique way."

"Oh, so you've already met Moe?" She rolled her eyes. "He's been here since the end of the war. I think the *first* big one. He knows every guy here and all their secrets."

Stephanie smiled as she wiped her face.

"Miss Croix, I don't think I'd be able to find my way back to my office, not in this labyrinth of halls, rooms, and stairways," said Daniel.

"Yes, it's a very complicated place," she said. "It took me almost two months to find my way around here. There's a large natural spring beneath the building. They used it to brew the beer. The water filled enormous vats, but they sealed it off years ago. The rats still hide down there. Their little gray noses peek through the holes in the floor to sniff the fresh air. By the way, when you come into your office each morning, make sure you sweep the mouse droppings off your desk."

Daniel winced at the thought of working in a building filled with rats and mice.

"Do you *live* in this place?" asked Daniel grimacing.

"Oh, for goodness sakes, *no!*" replied Stephanie. "It's bad enough that I have to spend twelve hours a day here with these two-legged creatures. I have a little place on Adelphi Street. My lease will be up soon and I'd really love to move out of Brooklyn, maybe into some apartment on the Upper East Side." She was joking, of course. "My roommate moved out a few months ago, but she and I are still good friends. I'm alone now, but I do have my cat and she has her kittens and we all have the mice."

Daniel changed the subject. "Miss Croix, there's this little guy I met last week here at the Brewery. Moe said his name was Malchus. Apparently, he and Tali were close, sort of like father and son. He suggested that Malchus be told personally about Tali's death."

Stephanie broke down and slumped to the floor again. Daniel had touched a nerve and the floodgates of sorrow opened again.

The sound of heavy footsteps echoed in the room. Within moments, the dark hulking shapes of two men appeared. Daniel was suddenly nervous and apprehensive. The two men came closer to Daniel and Stephanie. Their footsteps were an ominous pounding cadence on the wood floor. Both were tall. One was extremely muscular and lean and the other was just big and heavy. The big man looked at Daniel and then spoke to Stephanie.

"Mut, you okay? Hey, baby, don't cry, John is here."

He took a roll of toilet paper out of his pocket, tore off a few sheets, and gently wiped her face. His enormous hand was as large as her head. He got down on his knees next to her and whispered something in her ear. She shook her head affirmatively and looked up at the mammoth gentle man.

"John, I just can't seem to control myself. I guess it's a combination of a lot of things: Tali's death, the changes here, the chaos and sadness all around, and I can't find Malchus anywhere. I looked in the big dorm and some of the small rooms, but he's nowhere. I hope he's okay. I'm worried about him. You know how he gets. Maybe he was run over with Tali and they didn't notice his body because he's so small."

Daniel watched the tender melodramatics between Stephanie and John and followed the toilet paper with his eyes as it rolled out the door of the chapel. He stood like a wooden Indian outside of a tobacco shop.

John lifted Stephanie from the floor as if she were made of balsa wood. Her body was limp and she rested her head on the big man's shoulder as he carried her off to the front offices, Daniel following behind like an obedient puppy. A cold sweat formed on his forehead as he searched his own pockets for useable wads of toilet paper, but found nothing but a threadbare handkerchief that he used to clean his glasses.

The four individuals (Stephanie in the arms of John) moved like a funeral procession toward the front of the Brewery. John kicked open the door to the waiting room and placed Stephanie on a love seat.

"John, I'm all right now," she said, flashing her eyes. "You're such a sweetheart." She touched his face and gave him a watery-eyed smile. The big man, with daggers in his eyes, pointed his big index finger at Daniel. "You be good to her, you hear me?"

The two big men left the waiting room. She and Daniel were alone again in their awkward, surreal positions: she lying on a love seat and he standing in the middle of the room reflecting the yellow tinge of the fluorescent lamp. She leaned her head back and soon regained her composure.

"Dr. Aarons, I'm the one who really needs to tell Malchus about Tali. He's a very sensitive little man and very few people know him the way I do. Did you know that Malchus writes poetry? He writes them, reads them to me, and then he throws them away. I've begged him to save them, but he says they're only for me."

"Why doesn't he just give them to you?"

"That's the way God works, he says. He doesn't save the things he creates, especially the things he really loves. He makes them, uses them, and then changes them into something else, something more beautiful. I have to find Malchus before something bad happens," she said. "I know he's out there. I know where he hides. He probably thinks I'm looking for him right now. Dr. Aarons, he needs me."

Daniel needed to get back to his office and try to bring some order out of the chaos. That's what they paid him to do and nothing was going to keep him from achieving his goals, not the chaos, not the death of Naphtali Ropshitz, not his growing affections for Stephanie, and certainly not the strange behavior of a one-eared hydrocephalic dwarf.

Daniel walked into his office. The high-backed chair at his desk swiveled around and seated on the cushion was Malchus wearing his floppy hat and Tali's New York Yankees sweatshirt.

"Daniel Aarons, I presume," said the dwarf. "Oh, by the way, Naphtali Ropshitz isn't dead."

The sight of the one-eared dwarf and his statement that Naphtali Ropshitz was not dead put Daniel into a temporary state of shock. It was as if he was in a time warp or trapped in some urban black hole. Daniel stared at the dwarf for nearly a minute, his eyes fixed on the tiny man's bulging head. Malchus didn't move from the chair, but continued to look Daniel straight in the eyes as if he were trying to hypnotize him. Daniel reached out to touch the little man just to make sure he was talking to flesh and blood, but Malchus took command of the situation.

"Dr. Aarons, I'm sorry for startling you," Malchus said. "It wasn't my intention to create a scene. I just came in here to contemplate the transition of my dear friend, Naphtali. I didn't even realize that you had come in this morning. I should have known that this was your briefcase and these were your papers. Please forgive me. I knew by the look on your face, when you walked in, that the news of Tali's death had been spread all over the building like some noxious rumor. That's why I wanted it known from the outset that I knew the truth!"

Daniel didn't say a word. He put his hand out and gestured for Malchus to remain seated in the big chair while he walked out of the conference room to apprise Stephanie of the situation. His voice was unsure and shaky.

"Stephanie, Miss Croix," Daniel yelled. "Please come into my office, I need you."

She reacted like a tightly wound spring and jumped to her feet. "Is there a problem?"

The still distraught girl trotted into the conference room, took one look at Malchus, and nearly fainted on the floor.

"Dr. Aarons," Malchus said sarcastically. "What did you do to this poor girl? Just look at her, she's a wreck. Do you usually work your employees to death? Are you nothing but an unfeeling taskmaster?"

An angry Daniel Aarons responded, "Okay, time out. Let's get to the bottom of this charade. Malchus, we don't know each other very well, but it seems that you've entered my life and taken up residence in a very sensitive part of my psyche. You've come into my home and put disturbing thoughts into the mind of my unbalanced uncle. And that's not all. You come into my office on my first day of work, sit at *my* desk, and scare the hell out of me. Not to mention that you've almost caused poor Miss Croix to have a nervous breakdown. Now, Malchus, or whatever the hell your name is, how can *you* be so insensitive?" Daniel smashed his fist on the desk causing an ashtray to bounce into the air and cockroaches to scamper.

Stephanie slowly walked to the desk and stood behind Malchus.

"Dr. Aarons," she said in a defiant way. "Excuse me, but I believe *you're* the one overreacting to this situation. I think *you* have misread Malchus' intentions and *you* don't understand the nature of his response to this terrible loss."

Before Daniel could open his mouth to say a word, the little man in the chair piped in.

"No, *he's* right, Stephanie," replied Malchus. "Dr. Aarons, I think you're right on target. If I were in your shoes, I'd be pissed off as hell! What kind of way is this to begin your first day on the job with all these strange people running all over the place and a one-eared dwarf taking over your office? If I were you, I'd be pissed off, too! There is one thing, however, that I must tell you, and I haven't a clue why I know this, but I am certain that Naphtali Ropshitz is *not* dead!"

Stephanie sighed. Daniel looked at the floor and seemed to say with his motions that Malchus was simply in denial.

"My dear friends," Malchus said, "and, Daniel, I now include you in that category even though we hardly know each other. This is not the time to grieve; it's time to celebrate. I'm not exactly sure what happened last night, but sometime after eight PM, after Tali left me to meet his friends at Jay Street, I experienced a high-grade, sub-space, hyperbolic, transverse event that modulated the synapses in my cerebral cortex. Now, because my hydrocephalic brain is squeezed around the inside of my skull, this space-time fabric anomaly caused the fluid within my cranium to vibrate at a very high frequency."

The dwarf's floppy hat popped off his head like a bottle cap under pressure. Malchus stopped for a moment and looked up at the ceiling. He took a deep breath and continued his odyssey.

"I had a similar experience about three years ago in the solarium at Bellevue when I was kidnapped by the *Favarians* and transported ten thousand light years to their planet. I spent two weeks there and ate wonderful blue food, like chitterlings. I was transported back to earth with a new pair of sneakers and a suitcase. I found myself in the subway munching on a warm potato knish and drinking beer. It was wonderful."

Daniel and Stephanie stood motionless like statues bombarded by bird droppings.

Malchus continued his tirade. "Now, what does this have to do with Naphtali Ropshitz, you may ask? Well, *I am* Naphtali Ropshitz! Although his body was crushed beneath the wheels of a city transit bus, he lives right here!" Malchus pointed to his head and then to his heart and showed off Tali's sweatshirt.

"I don't know how he did it, but that big fat wonderful man is eating knishes right up here in this swollen skull. And one of these days, he might just stick his head out of this hole in my head."

There was dead silence again. The ramblings of the dwarf ended and he waited for their response.

"Malchus, isn't that Tali's sweatshirt you're wearing?" asked Stephanie.

"Yes!" Malchus replied. "It was his and he wore it morning, noon, and night, every day, three hundred and sixty-five days a year. I cherish its stains, its holes and its stench—a fragrance that goes right up to heaven. No, I will never take it off either. I'm not sure how I came to receive this holy garment, but when I left the subway station in Greenpoint, I was wearing it and Tali was nowhere to be found. Somehow, it's like Tali gave me his power, his mantle, like Elijah gave his mantle to Elisha before he was taken up into the whirlwind. I wanted to follow Tali. I wanted to be one of his disciples. It would have given real meaning to my life, but he just said, 'Malchus, stay here, for the Lord has sent me to Flatbush.' Then I told him that I would not leave him, so I went with him to Flatbush. Then he said, 'Malchus, my son, stay here for the Lord has sent me to Brownsville.' Then I demanded to go with him, so I went to Brownsville. I don't remember much more than that."

Stephanie stood behind the chair and put her arms around Malchus' neck. She leaned over and kissed the top of his head.

"Malchus, I think you need to relax and rest. You're very tired and it's been an exhausting day. You need some sleep and a good meal. I'll help you up to your bed and hold your hand until you fall asleep. I won't leave you alone."

Malchus stood up. His glazed eyes stared into the black nothingness of space. Stephanie held his hand as she led him back to the big dormitory on the second floor. Daniel stood motionless in his office with his mouth open. It was only noon, the first day.

The following day was Tali's funeral. It was an extravagant affair. The famous, the infamous, and the anonymous attended. The synagogue in Williamsburg was packed. Underworld mob boss, Carmine "The Guillotine" Carbone from Red Hook, sat next to the bishop of Brooklyn. A gaggle of old, bedraggled men with sad blank faces sat behind the family and the important people. There were men in turbans, dashikis, and women in saris, long-bearded Hasidic Jews, cowboys, and a representative from the Hare Krishna. This wasn't some funeral with long eulogies and litanies of prayer. No, it was a free-for-all of screaming, crying, wailing, dancing, and a couple of fistfights. The little synagogue had never seen such a gathering, and the crowd poured out onto the sidewalk and into the street.

Naphtali Ropshitz's body lay in a simple casket as was required by Jewish law. Malchus, Daniel, Stephanie, and an entourage of loving souls from the Brewery came to pay their last respects to their beloved friend. Malchus wore Tali's sweatshirt. When he walked into the sanctuary where the great man's body was laid out, the solemn crowd gasped. Some were incensed that this deformed, one-eared dwarf would desecrate the holy garment of Naphtali Ropshitz. Others wept because they knew of the special relationship between the two men. Two elderly people approached Malchus and he immediately knew they were Tali's mother and father. The woman cried and the man sadly looked down into Malchus' face.

"You must be Malchus," said the mother, her voice choking. "Tali told me a lot about you. He said you were a very special person, almost like a son to him. It makes me very happy to see you and all his friends here today. My Tali was a very special person, you know. He didn't worship God like we do, but I'm sure that the Almighty will welcome him into heaven at the right time."

"Mrs. Ropshitz," Malchus said as he took her hand, "your son is in paradise at this very moment, I can assure you that. There was no man who loved God more than Naphtali Ropshitz. There was no man who served and sacrificed for others, as did your son. God takes back to Himself his own beloved creations and your son was His masterpiece."

Tali's mother cried and she knelt down to hug the little man. Malchus turned to the father and stared up at the big man's sad brown eyes.

"Rabbi," Malchus said, "I know how difficult this is for you and I couldn't possibly begin to comprehend your sorrow, but Tali was the most spiritually gifted man I've ever known. He talked to me about God as a friend who would lie down his life for the ones he loved. He talked about the messiah and the suffering servants who walk the earth, heal the wounded, and bring them closer to God. It was hard for him to be a religious man, but you loved him despite his inconsistencies. Rabbi Ropshitz, your son was truly a prophet like Elijah, who walked with man, but now he walks with God."

The rabbi could say nothing. He opened his mouth, but no words came out. He affectionately touched Malchus' head and slumped away.

Malchus talked to his friend in the casket.

"Tali, my friend, I don't know why I am talking to you like this. You're not here, you're in heaven, but I also feel that you are very much alive inside my head. Look, friend, I'm wearing your sweatshirt. It still smells and I'm never going to take it off. Well, I guess you'd want me to wash it every now and then. I feel powerful when I wear it and it always reminds me of you."

He stopped his soliloquy to Tali and turned to the crowd in the room.

"Ladies and gentlemen," Malchus' voice boomed, "dear and beloved friends. Naphtali Ropshitz is not dead. Naphtali Ropshitz is not dead. Naphtali Ropshitz is not dead!"

Malchus fainted. Daniel and a group of men from the Brewery rushed to him and carried the little body to a couch. They pressed a pouch of smelling salts to his nose and immediately his eyes opened wide and he spoke again.

"Naphtali Ropshitz is alive! Naphtali Ropshitz is alive!"

CHAPTER 9

✛ ✛ ✛

THE FIRST WEEK ON A NEW JOB is never easy, but for Daniel it was a harrowing experience. His emotions were raw. The men were just coming out of their funk over Tali's death with most of them remaining sober and taking their medication as prescribed. The trucks were working and Harry Fischer, the Brewery's crack mechanic, was back from a two-week drinking binge in Hoboken, New Jersey. Daniel was in control—a feeling he knew could leave him just as quickly as the drop of a mouse turd.

Speaking of mouse turds, Daniel's big accomplishment of the week was the elimination of fresh mouse droppings from the top of his desk. He filled his office with dozens of traps and sticky pads. The floorboards around the walls from one end of the room to the other were virtually covered with tiny execution devices. Moe Kutcher, the office clerk who lived in the residential apartments, had the unenviable job of removing the dead carcasses from the traps before Daniel came to work each morning. The cats were the benefactors of Daniel's ingenious plan. The operation worked beautifully. Not a single dropping was seen on Daniel's immaculate desk.

Stephanie sat at her desk pounding away at her miserable typewriter using correction fluid by the gallon. When she wasn't destroying the typewriter or cursing her mistakes, she'd sit at her desk humming or drawing doodles on her desk blotter. More often than not, she would be up and around the Brewery talking to the men who worked in the offices, workshops, or in the warehouse. When the men returned to the Brewery with their trucks and collected booty, Stephanie would go out to the loading dock and joke with them. They'd talk about all the junk they had collected and what items needed to be taken to the dump.

The phones were constantly ringing and Moby Dixon and Ernie Yeager were efficient operators, taking messages and passing them on to the drivers or to the clerks in offices.

Daniel walked into Stephanie's office hoping to find her at her desk. Instead, she was lounging on a worn-out leather couch on the loading dock that had just been unloaded from an incoming truck. Her body was draped across the tattered piece of furniture, her arm flung back over the side holding a cigarette. She laughed loudly with the cowboy who was hauling newspapers out of the back of the truck. He was telling her dirty jokes and sleazy stories. Daniel didn't like the cowboy and he hoped he wouldn't have to deal with him while the man was in a violent drunken stupor.

"Miss Croix," Daniel called to her from an open window. "I need to see you in my office. He looked away and under his breath mumbled, "Get your ass in here and stop talking to that dirt ball."

"Yes, Dr. Aarons," Stephanie shouted from the couch. "I'll be there in just a minute."

She took a long, last drag on the cigarette and flicked it into the driveway. She laughed at something the cowboy said and then walked back to the office adjusting her blouse into her pants. She had done nothing improper, but Daniel looked at her as if she had just committed a Cardinal sin with the devil himself. He also wanted to tell her something about the evils of smoking and carousing with the riffraff, but that was for another time.

"Stephanie, would you please prepare a memo to the executive staff," Daniel ordered. "I want to meet with them this afternoon. No, better yet, why don't you just tell them personally that I want to have a staff meeting."

She looked at her new boss in a quizzical manner and then raised an eyebrow. "And who do you want me to notify?" Stephanie asked in a snooty manner.

"The administrative, clinical, and operational staff," Daniel said mechanically.

Stephanie wasn't quite sure who these important-sounding individuals were.

"Well, we have the guys in the dispatcher's office, the warehouse manager, the residence manager, the office clerk, the fleet manager, the thrift store managers, at least fifty guys who drive trucks, bale clothes, work on trucks, work in stores, wash clothes, cook, or sweep floors. Then there's me and Malchus."

Daniel clearly didn't appreciate Stephanie's smart remarks.

"All right, Miss Croix, since we don't exactly have an organization chart of this institution, why don't you just make up your own list of men *you* think are important."

"Will do," she snapped back.

She sped off to her office and a half hour later came into Daniel's office with one sheet of paper containing the names of several men. The list, typed on yellowed onionskin paper, seemed to have been erased and revised numerous times. Daniel read the list that was still damp with correction fluid. He rolled his eyes.

"Let's see, we have Ernie Yeager and Moby Dixon, they're the dispatchers, and Moe Kutcher, our ever so subtle office clerk with that compulsive scratching."

Stephanie pointed her finger in Daniel's face and scolded him for his insensitivity.

"Don't make fun of Moe. He spent two years in Korea in a prisoner of war camp. He came back and said he was brainwashed. The army didn't believe him so they sent him to a VA hospital. He's been here at the Brewery since nineteen fifty-five. He scratches because he's always nervous." She began to scratch herself.

"He scratches his genitals because he's nervous?" Daniel asked.

"He's always nervous around other people, especially women," Stephanie said. "I don't intentionally make him nervous. In fact, I like him. I try to make him feel relaxed, and he doesn't always scratch when he's around me."

Daniel unintentionally scratched the top of his desk. "Yesterday, when he was in my office, I thought he was going to scratch right through his pants. I believe he needs some behavior therapy and some counseling. Perhaps a little calamine lotion wouldn't hurt either."

Stephanie sighed. "Oh, why don't you just give him a little time and be patient. He's very good at these little office jobs. Dr. Aarons, every man in the Brewery has been hurt by something or someone. They are all seriously ill, and we are here to help them. You should know that."

Psychology lesson number two from Sigmund Croix, Daniel thought. "Sorry, I'm just a little punchy these days," he said, "and I haven't been particularly patient or caring."

Stephanie smiled. "Sure, I know deep in that brilliant head, you're a good person, too."

"All right, who else? There's Chuck Conklin, our fastidious warehouse manager." Daniel was sarcastic. "John B. Waters in the dorms and apartments."

Stephanie interrupted. "He pronounces his first name like 'Jawn.' Remember, he's the big guy who carried me into the office last week after you found me in the chapel. He's our chaplain."

"Oh, him. Yes, I know who he is," Daniel continued. "Salvatore Cantucci on the trucks, Lemmy Alone in the stores, and Herby Croix in the kitchen."

Daniel was curious about the name. "Croix? Any relation?"

"He's my uncle and he's a drunk, too, but he hasn't had a drop in years. He came down here in nineteen sixty-three after he and my aunt split up. She's dead now. I don't want to talk about it."

Her family was obviously a sore subject. Daniel would have to be exceptionally delicate and sensitive about Stephanie's relatives and her apparently difficult childhood. He certainly wanted to meet Uncle Herby and requested that Stephanie include him on the list of staff to be present at the meeting.

"We haven't discussed Malchus. Just what does he do at the Brewery?" Daniel asked.

Stephanie smiled as if she had some very special secret information on the little man.

"Well, you know he is a very special person. He's not like one of the old guys. He's not a drunk. He can't drive a truck, bale clothes, or do much of anything that the other men can do. But he bakes wonderful cookies. He's very talented and artistically inclined. I should know; I'm an artist myself. Herby has even given him some special training and a chef's hat. Malchus looks so cute in the kitchen squeezing out chocolate cream into the pie shells, cutting up apples, and breaking eggs. He stands there on a stool at these big wooden tables mixing the batter, putting cherries on top of cakes. You know, when that little man is working and thinking rationally, he's an absolute miracle to behold! I've even seen him take his desserts to some of the men who are sick or to the real old guys who just sit around and mope. He's got a great bedside manner. I don't think you'll need to invite him to your staff meeting, he's not the administrative type. Besides, he's strictly a special services client placed here by the city's department of mental health. They could take him back to the hospital at any time and just about for any reason. But they don't really want him back."

"Okay, let's get these guys together in two hours. Can you do it?"

"Sure thing, Colonel." Stephanie snapped a military salute as she had always done for Colonel Boyer.

Daniel sat at his desk and pulled out his pipe. This was the first time he had had the opportunity to sit back in his wobbly desk chair and relax for a moment. The back of his chair tilted way back until he almost fell out of the seat. He filled the bowl of his pipe with a fine-smelling tobacco and lit it. The fragrance filled the air and the smoke drifted up to the ceiling. He watched the smoke rise and then lowered his sights on a tiny roach walking across his desk blotter. He didn't have the heart to smash it, so he just let it walk off the edge of the desk. He knew they'd meet again, perhaps later in the day. That little insignificant creature became something sacred, even to the hardened intellectual, Dr. Daniel Aarons. He sat for the next two hours, smoking and looking through his window at the small body of stagnant water known as the English Kills, and he waited for his men to show up for the staff meeting.

The Men's Rehabilitation Center was not your typical nonprofit business. For some unexplained reason, perhaps it was the grace of God, the Brewery remained open, provided marginal but basic services, and continued to receive philanthropic gifts of support, all without benefit of competent long-term leadership. Even so, the Brewery became deeper in debt each year and was on the verge of bankruptcy and closure. There were many rumors and allegations that former directors had skimmed cash from the thrift stores and that the rest went into somebody's pocket in Biloxi.

Daniel was going to get to the bottom of this. He was determined to have an effective operation that was in the black and one that was a model of service. He was not going to let this vessel go down under his watch. He would build a strong management team and convert the laughingstock of the Service Corps into its flagship. He would start with its current administration.

What was he thinking? At three o'clock that afternoon, he had requested that Stephanie round up the top brass and bring them in for his first staff meeting. At about four o'clock, his team arrived in various stages of disrepair and disgust. One by one, they entered the conference room, grumbled a few choice words at their new boss, and sat down at the long table.

Salvatore "Tooch" Cantucci arrived wearing a filthy T-shirt and smoking an equally filthy cigar. His hands were black and greasy. He managed the truck fleet and had a penchant for eggplant and garlic. Poor Tooch also suffered from excessive flatulence, which made him a pariah at group gatherings.

Lemmy Alone, director of thrift store operations, wore a bright red sport coat that he *borrowed* from one of the stores. Under the coat was a gaudy Hawaiian shirt open down to his navel. He wore a gold ring on each finger and several strands of love beads around his neck. His slicked-back receding hair was oily, but neat. A thin black moustache appeared to be painted under his large aquiline nose.

Chuck Conklin, the warehouse manager, was a small muscular man with an unpleasant scowl and bad teeth. His gray crew cut, large tattooed arms, and leathery skin made him look like Popeye the Sailor. Conklin was a former navy man, and his vocabulary reflected his preoccupation with human reproduction and various parts of the female anatomy.

Herby Croix, the Brewery's chef and director of food services, promenaded into the conference room with an air of savoir faire. His ridiculous-looking chef's hat floated on top of his big head like a cumulus cloud. He wore an apron covered with brown gravy and a veritable palette of food stains. Herby was a jolly man, slightly effeminate, and bore no resemblance whatsoever to his niece. Though he was said to be a highly competent chef and kitchen manager, he had spent most of his professional career behind the counters of greasy spoons in upstate New York and then several years behind bars at Auburn State Prison.

John B. Waters was the last man to enter the room. Jawn, as everybody called him, was an enormous hulk of a man. He was the only black man on Daniel's management team and ran the dormitories and apartments. He also served as the Brewery's chaplain. He wore a stocking cap on his head and a City College sweatshirt over his massive chest. He could lift a three hundred pound chest of drawers as if it were a box of matches.

The high-powered administrative management team of Dr. Daniel Aarons was now in session. Stephanie took the minutes. Daniel stood at the head of the table and spoke with an air of authority and assurance.

"Gentlemen, thank you for coming on such short notice to this inaugural staff meeting. You are the executive staff of this important organization—the president's cabinet, so to speak. Without you and your expertise, the Brewery would not function as a valued community service. No matter what we do here, however, the job of getting it done can be improved and that's where you come in." The men groaned. "That's where I need your full and total efforts. I need a one hundred percent commitment. Do I make myself clear?" They groaned again.

The smell of Tooch's gastrointestinal distress and rancid cigar filled the room. He covered his mouth as he belched, but the room still stank. Lemmy Alone smoked a cigarette and squinted as the smoke hit his eyes. He blinked continuously. Conklin sat with his face down, arms folded across his chest, and swore under his breath. Herby Croix smiled and sucked his teeth. John B. Waters looked at Daniel with eyes like sharpened, steel steak knives. Stephanie drew pictures on her stenographer's pad.

Daniel barked orders to his men in gestapo-like fashion, but failed to realize that his commands were going right out the window into the Dumpster on the loading dock. Every word was just another rotten potato or moldy piece of bread. The directives that remained in the room ricocheted between the walls until they fell like crumbs under the table. It wasn't that his words didn't make sense. No, his words, his commands, his plans were exceptionally brilliant and his speech was impeccable. The good doctor—as they say—was out of his league. He might as well have been talking Chinese to a tribe of Bolivian

Mountain Indians. This unfortunate monologue went on for nearly thirty minutes. Stephanie had long since ceased taking notes and was now daydreaming. John B. Waters finally broke the silence.

"Dr. Aarons, I have a few questions and several recommendations. Is this the appropriate time to comment?"

Daniel smiled. He was glad that at least one of the management team was listening. "Yes, Jawn, please respond, your comments are valued in this forum."

The large man rose from the table.

"First of all, Dr. Aarons, I would appreciate it if *you* would pronounce my name as John and not Jawn. My name is John B. Waters, but the ignorant folk around here," he looked at the others at the table, "still call me by that stupid name. Why? Because my former and now late friend, Benny Tolbert, used to follow me around like a little dog saying, 'Jawn, don't leave me hear alone. Jawn, can I work with you in the warehouse? Jawn, let's go get drunk and get laid.' So please, let's have a little dignity around here and call people by their real names or their chosen nicknames. The next person who calls me Jawn is going to have his vocal cords readjusted by John. Is that clear? And that goes for you, too, Tooch, Lemmy, Herby."

He pointed to each man with a large index finger. "Let me continue. Dr. Aarons, you are a highly educated man. You have excellent credentials. I have been told that you come with pages of references and that you have been published in numerous professional journals. You have received accolades from your peers and awards from the American Rehabilitation Association for your research on the deinstitutionalization of the chronically mentally ill. Dr. Aarons, it is truly an honor to be around such a scholar. I am very pleased that you have been hired by headquarters to run this important facility. But, Dr. Aarons, if you will excuse my French, you don't know shit about thrift stores, running a fleet of trucks, warehouse operations, or managing sixty chronic alcoholics, some of whom have dual diagnoses or are just plain psychotic most of the time."

A surprised Daniel Aarons, inflated by all the praise, was now punctured by John Waters' pin. Tooch farted, Conklin shook his head yes and cursed under his breath, Lemmy blew smoke like a chimney, and Herby Croix lost his smile. Stephanie's mouth opened with a faintly audible, "Oh, shit."

Daniel, his eyebrows arched and shaken by the cold facts of the truth, nervously brushed at the phantom mouse droppings appearing on the conference room table. He took his pipe from the holder on his desk and filled it with tobacco. This act occupied his time while he prepared for a dazzling repartee.

Daniel took the high road and did not become defensive. He knew his psychology and would not appear as a man with his back to the wall.

"John, my friend, my coworker, fellow employee of the Service Corps, you are a very perceptive person. I like that in a man. I don't want 'yes men' working for me. I don't want men talking behind my back, starting rumors, and causing trouble. I want men with good ideas who speak their minds and the truth when they feel it rising in their guts. I appreciate your honesty, and I can say to each one of you that I have much to learn, but you don't learn this business going to graduate school or by having a PhD. You don't learn this business by reading books or analyzing financial statements. You learn this business by getting involved, by riding in trucks, by picking up furniture, and by standing behind a counter in a thrift store. And that is exactly what I intend to do."

A cold sweat broke out on Daniel's face. He comprehended the reality of what he had just committed to do. He realized that he would have to spend the next few weeks sitting in filthy stinking trucks, breaking his back lifting mildewed furniture, sorting rotting underwear and socks, and standing behind a cash register at a store on Myrtle Avenue.

Stephanie applauded loudly, and the men at the table knew exactly where they had Daniel Aarons—over a big, wide, deep barrel. Conklin laughed under his breath and cursed, using his favorite body part. Lemmy squashed his cigarette butt on the table and blinked. Herby sucked his teeth. Tooch unsuccessfully squelched another fart, and John stared at Daniel with eyes as sharp as steak knives.

Daniel looked at his watch. The grand finale had come and gone and now it was time for the curtain to come down.

"Gentlemen, I thank you for your assistance, cooperation, and desire to make the Men's Rehabilitation Center a state-of-the-art facility, one that will make the entire Service Corps proud. Today is the first day of our glorious plan, and you are on the front line and the cutting edge. Together we will push the envelope. Together we will see our task as a military campaign and you, the officers, leading our men into battle. Now, let's go win the war!" Daniel's gut told him, however, that he was really like Napoleon at Waterloo.

The five members of the executive consultant's cabinet rose from their chairs and left the room. Tooch scratched his behind as he exited. John stopped and turned to Daniel, pointing his large index finger at the boss's forehead saying, "The battle has just begun."

The conference room was now empty except for Daniel, Stephanie, and the lingering olfactory remnants of Salvatore Cantucci's gastrointestinal distress. Daniel, feeling like a deflated balloon, looked at his assistant and realized that once more, he had lost control of the situation. He had prematurely ejaculated and would have to wait for the right moment to regain his virility, but Stephanie saw something appealing. She liked his vulnerability and his weaknesses, but she also liked his cleverness and willingness to bend to the needs and personalities of the men. Daniel Aarons wasn't all hard edges and points. He had a few soft buttons to press and she would push them soon. She also knew how to knead him like soft dough.

"You were wonderful," she said, batting her long dark eyelashes. "Those men have respect for you. You could have attacked John. You could have squashed him like a bug." She stomped her foot. "But you saw him coming from the start and played him like a fine hand of cards. The few weeks that you spend working with them behind the wheels of the trucks or in the warehouse will establish your credibility, and they'll begin to see you as their leader and mentor. Daniel … that was the finest meeting I have ever attended in this conference room and I've been to dozens."

She smiled and Daniel turned into melted butter. His head swelled like a melon, and he took a deep satisfying draw on his pipe. He sat down at his desk and thanked Stephanie for her honest comments and perceptions.

Someone pounded on the door of the conference room. Stephanie opened it and Malchus came in with an important message for Daniel.

"Daniel, it's your uncle, come quickly!"

CHAPTER 10

✠ ✠ ✠

DANIEL'S MOOD ABRUPTLY CHANGED WHEN HE HEARD Malchus' remark about his uncle. He rushed into the waiting room expecting to receive some bad news about Jacob Koretz. Had he, too, been crushed beneath the wheels of a city transit bus, or been beaten up by a gang of thugs? Had he finally decided to end it all by jumping off his pile of unpublished manuscripts? No, Jacob Koretz stood in the waiting room of the Men's Rehabilitation Center looking like he was about to recite a soliloquy from Hamlet. His beard was neatly trimmed, and he wore a fedora pulled low over his forehead. His suit and bright red tie were immaculate—no food stains, no roaches climbing out of the breast pocket, just a fine silk handkerchief impeccably folded.

"My dear children," Jacob eloquently addressed those in the room, "it is finished. My latest magnum opus is complete, and if I must say so myself, and I must, it is a brilliant literary work that will revolutionize the theater in New York. I'm even considering selling the movie rights to MGM."

Jacob presented his newly created jewel and held it above his head for the crowd to see as if it were the original Ten Commandments.

Daniel knew that his uncle had not just been with Moses on the top of Mount Sinai nor had he received a blinding revelation from the Almighty. He ascended into his manic state and was now a rocket traveling at the speed of light. These manic episodes were extremely creative times for Jacob Koretz. He would write incessantly and complete one manuscript after another. He would memorize lines from his plays and visit agents and producers. He could do more work in one month than most people could do in a year.

The old man continued, scene two: "Daniel, friends, this is by far my most inspired work, on par with the great Greek tragedies of Aeschylus, not to mention Shakespeare. It is called *The Stunt*. It's about ten brothers who commit the heinous crime, the dastardly deed, of murdering their father and then eating his body. It's not that they particularly hate their father. No, it's just that they believe that the act of drinking his blood and consuming his flesh will give them his power and his spirit. There are deep theological and sexual overtones in the play and this leads to extreme conflict among the siblings. Who, for instance, eats what part? Does Joseph eat the brain or must he be satisfied with the old man's liver? What of the genitalia? Do they divide it equally? Does Reuben, the eldest, or Irving, the strongest, receive the shaft of power? What becomes of the right testicle? Had it never descended or is it missing? Then there is the question of the mother's role in all of this. Was she actually the prime mover and instigator to the act and a willing participant or has she disowned her progeny? What of little Melvin who chooses only to consume one drop of his father's blood and to kiss the old man's buttocks?"

Jacob, emotionally exhausted, but delirious, took a seat on the couch in the waiting room and pulled out a handkerchief to wipe his eyes. He fanned himself with the manuscript. His presence filled the room and his audience of three, Daniel, Stephanie, and Malchus, were awestruck by his magnificent performance.

Daniel was rightly concerned about his uncle's mental stability. "Jacob, you look tired. Let me get you something to drink. You did take your medication today, didn't you?" The young man hovered over his uncle.

"Yes, I took my medication, Daniel, and stop sounding like an old yenta. This is a glorious day to be alive and to see the world through the eyes of God! I'm on my way to visit my dear friend, the genius, Julius Chomsky, and I thought that on my way to Manhattan, I'd stop by and see my favorite nephew in his new office. Is there something wrong with that?"

"No … it's … just that," Daniel stammered.

Jacob's eyes fell on Stephanie and saw the girl as if she had just descended from heaven.

"Who is this beautiful young creature, Daniel? Why aren't you introducing her to me?"

Jacob turned to Stephanie. "Have you ever done any acting? You have a particular grace that would be perfect on the stage. You are a willow tree in spring. You are a delicate beautiful flower. I used to know this girl in Budapest many years before the war. She was such a beauty, big black eyes just like yours, sleek and sexy and such a marvelous actress. Not just an actress, but a singer and an artist as well. She turned heads everywhere she went, and I was madly in love with her. For years, she wouldn't spit on the best part of me. She treated me like dirt. I was a maggot in her eyes and something you would scrape off the bottom of your shoe. But that was just her way to make me so hungry for her that I begged and pleaded like a starving dog for her to marry me. I wanted her to star in every one of my plays. I wanted to consume her body and soul. I wanted to make love to her morning, noon, and night and to fill my days with ecstasy. I wanted her to fill my house with beautiful children who would all look just like her."

Jacob stopped his melodramatic monologue. He dabbed his forehead with the handkerchief. He stood up, took Stephanie's hand, and stared directly into her face. His expression turned dour.

"But Hitler, that bastard, that devil, he killed her! Took her to Auschwitz and killed her. Put her on a damn cattle car and gassed her like a dog. That beautiful creature, she was so full of beauty and talent."

Jacob was in a sudden panic. He turned pale and looked at his nephew.

"Daniel, my son, don't ever let that happen to this child. Protect her from the evil that is in this crazy world. It lurks everywhere. It hides in cracks. It walks the streets like the insects. It even floats in the air like a noxious black cloud. And if you breathe it in, you get infected just like those Nazi bastards who killed my Leah and my Rachel and all my family."

Jacob ranted. He began to spin in the room, talking to the walls, pointing his fingers at God in the ceiling, cursing Hitler.

"But God saved me!" he screamed. "I don't know why, but He left me alone to look at this empty evil world. He gave me His gift, however. These black holes in front of my eyes. But he also saved Daniel, my child! Praise be to the glorious God and Creator of the universe! Praise be to the God who saves innocent infants and puts them on the tops of piles of dead corpses. Praise be to the God who has given me a son of my sorrow. Benoni! Benoni!"

Jacob collapsed on the couch and wept. Malchus ran to get Jacob a cup of water. Stephanie sat down next to him and stroked the man's head as if she had known him for years. Daniel stood in the middle of the room, motionless, stupefied, and simply sighed.

A tiny wink came from the old man's eye. Daniel knew his uncle's game and he wasn't going to allow Jacob to steal the show. He warned Stephanie directly.

"Stephanie, try not to take this too hard," Daniel said, staring at the ceiling. "He's played this scene from his personal tragedy many times before. It's all too true and he's played it to many a packed house. It's his safety valve when he gets manic. It's just one of his many ways to release the pressure that builds up inside of his head."

Malchus rushed in with the sloshing cup of water and sat next to Jacob. He held the cup to his lips while Stephanie continued to stroke his head. She dabbed his eyes with the handkerchief as her own eyes filled with tears.

Daniel shook his head and gave Jacob a dirty look from the corner of his eye that seemed to say: You old master of deceit. You manipulator. You have exactly what you want—a beautiful woman hanging on your arm stroking your head and a manservant feeding you.

Jacob looked at his nephew with a sly smile.

"Daniel, there isn't much in life that gives me pleasure anymore, but when Jacob Koretz is flying high, you might as well take advantage of my generosity and good looks."

Jacob looked at his watch. "Oh no, my appointment with Julius is in twenty minutes. I need to hop on a train and get over to Manhattan. If he doesn't like my play, I'm going to have to shove it up his fat ass like a suppository. Then, maybe, it'll sink in. But why am I so negative? He's going to love it and it's going to make him and me very rich and famous. Children, when I get back, I'm going to take you down to Sheepshead

Bay for a wonderful seafood dinner. Oh, what a glorious day it is to be Jacob Koretz."

The old man bounced back like a new pink rubber ball. He sauntered down the walkway like a twenty year old and briskly walked to the Greenpoint subway station with his work of art tucked beneath his arm.

Malchus rushed to the door and shouted at Jacob, "Good luck, Jacob, break a leg or whatever it is you need to break."

Jacob was on his way to fame and fortune. The three members of his supporting cast, however, were now seated on the couch, resuming their normal breathing.

"Malchus, I have a question for you," Daniel said. "You came to my home on Washington Avenue a couple of weeks ago and terrorized my uncle. He couldn't sleep for days. He was a nervous, depressed mass of human flesh sitting in a black funk, sucking a cigar. He blabbered for days about a dwarf from outer space who was a servant of the high priest and whose ear Simon Peter in the Garden of Gethsemane had cut off. Now, Malchus, I know it was you because I saw you here when I came for my interview. So, I know that my uncle was not just having a delusion. You are real and the person he talked to was *you* and not some alien vision. Am I correct?"

Malchus crossed his arms over his chest. "Dr. Aarons, not only are you very quick and intelligent, but you are also very perceptive and astute. I like that in a man, and that is precisely why I came to your home. I came not to visit your charming dear uncle, but to deal with you. You weren't home so I thought I'd make friends with Jacob. We had a wonderful time. By the way, who's your decorator?"

Daniel was confused. "I still don't get it," he said in exasperation.

The dwarf looked up into the eyes of his accuser. "Let me put it to you directly. A voice came to me in the middle of the night and said, 'Go see Daniel Aarons. He's going to be the next director of the Brewery.' I did exactly what the voice told me to do. I didn't know where you lived, so I went into Boyer's office after hours and rifled through the résumés—all two of them. I found your address and paid you a visit. Now is there anything so strange or evil about that? Don't you obey your voices, especially when they make reasonable requests?"

Daniel was at a loss for words. The little man told him the truth and there was nothing particularly sinister about his actions. Nothing sinister, perhaps, but definitely prophetic.

"Did the voice say anything else to you?" Daniel was fishing and Malchus knew it.

"Yes, the voice told me that not only would you be the next director of the Brewery, but that you would change the course of history and perhaps even bring humanity to its next level of spiritual evolution and psychic consciousness."

Daniel smiled. "Malchus, I think you're full of malarkey or something worse."

"Dr. Aarons, believe me, I've been filled with much worse."

Stephanie sat on the couch between the two men listening to their verbal dueling.

"Enough already," she yelled. "I see you two are developing a very special relationship, and I'm not sure I want to be around such cleverness and wit. Are we just going to sit here and waste our time talking about nonsense, or are we going to do our jobs and accomplish something great here today?"

Daniel got the message, but his sarcasm still flowed. "To the typewriter, Miss Croix! To the kitchen, Mr. Malchus One Ear. I will be out on the loading dock examining the precious cargo, and we will all wait for the return of the incomparable Jacob Koretz."

CHAPTER 11

✜ ✜ ✜

THERE'S NOTHING PARTICULARLY INTERESTING ABOUT A LOADING dock unless it's piled high with the discards and refuse of hundreds of families. This stuff isn't junk, it's history.

The cowboy, who greeted Daniel the week before with his tobacco spit, was now a smiling, weather-beaten young man with a surprisingly good set of teeth. He stood about six feet two inches tall with broad shoulders and a tiny waist. His short beard was scraggly, and more likely, he simply forgot to shave for a few days. He was muscular, lean, and didn't quite fit the stereotype of the old flabby toothless drunk. He was truly handsome enough to be a movie star. Perhaps he could do cigarette commercials. Woody Johnson was a truck driver and he knew his furniture.

"Hey, Doc, got a whole nice load of shit for you. Couple of walnut dressers, a laminated armoire, big stuffed chair, dinette set, few boxes of bric-a-brac. I tell you, some of this shit will bring a pretty penny at the stores. You know I'm one of the best in New York. No, *I am* the best." He smugly pulled on the brim of his hat.

"The best of what?" Daniel asked the cowboy.

"I just don't go out on these trucks to bring you back sacks full of rags and newspapers." He strutted on the loading dock like a rooster. "No, when Woody Johnson goes out in his wagon, he brings back treasures. There isn't a guy in this place who brings back better shit than me."

A muffled voice spoke. "Yea, what about me?" The fat man with the sneakers, the cowboy's sidekick, piped up from around the other side of the truck.

"Captain Aarons ... uh, Doc, let me tell you something," said the fat man. "If it wasn't for me, this phony cowboy would be sitting in Attica State Prison picking his nose and scratching his ass instead of picking up furniture."

Woody took off his hat as if to swat a fly, but smacked the fat man's head instead. "Turtle Man, why don't you just shut the fuck up? The captain's new on the job; he doesn't want to hear all about that prison shit. Now he probably thinks I'm some sort of rapist, serial murderer, or asshole like you. Man, when we get back to the dorm, I'm going to twist your head off and flush it down the toilet."

"Go jerk off your grandfather, Mr. Rodco," said the fat man.

The cowboy's hat found its mark again on the fat man's head.

"You little fat putz," Woody replied. "When's the last time your dick got some action? I saw you screwing that chicken in the kitchen yesterday, and now we're all going to have to eat that thing. You're disgusting, Turtle Head."

Daniel decided this comedy routine had gone just about far enough. "Gentleman, please, I don't want to hear about it."

The cowboy put on his aw-shucks smile. "Hey, Cap ... uh, Doc, whatever, we're only joking. We're just playing around. Turtle Brain and me are like brothers. Yea, we've been on this same truck for five years. You don't have to worry about us. I kid him. He kids me. Hey, who else is going to listen to us? I love this fat little creep."

He petted the fat man's head like a puppy. "So what if he smells like dog shit and spits tobacco juice? You know, he can even fart music through his asshole? Yea, he can do 'Happy Birthday' and 'The Star-Spangled Banner.'"

The two men laughed and Woody slapped Turtlebaum (his real name) on the head with his hat one more time. Daniel rolled his eyes. They were a unique pair, the comedy team of Woody Johnson and Sam Turtlebaum: the Cowboy and the Fat Man. Suddenly, this big attractive cowboy was just so much horse manure.

Daniel ran his hand along the top surface of the dresser as if to feel its fine grain. He wondered why someone would give away such a nice piece of furniture. Why didn't they hand it down to their children or even sell it? There must have been fifty years of history in that cabinet. He opened the drawers only to find them filled with neatly folded men's clothing.

"The old guy croaked and he didn't have any relatives," Turtlebaum said. He knew the whole story about the dresser. "He died three weeks ago and sat in his recliner until the neighbors couldn't stand the stink anymore. They called the cops and found him covered in roaches and maggots. Oh, by the way, we didn't take the recliner. He must have been some rich guy once. Poor jerk, he had all that nice stuff, silver, paintings, and walnut furniture in a little apartment on Eastern Parkway. He must have been there for forty years. His wife died last year, you know. I guess he just forgot that he was alive, sat down, turned on the TV, and croaked. Ain't so bad. Man, did that place ever stink!"

Woody added his two cents. "Yea, I almost puked on your fat head, Turtle Butt."

"Woody, every time I look at you I wanna puke," the fat man shot back.

The comedy team was at it again, and Daniel had had enough of their adolescent humor. He left them to continue their juvenile antics and to finish unloading the truck. He went back to his office and stared out the window, only to see Woody Johnson open his fly, pull out his "branding iron," and urinate off the side of the loading dock onto a helpless pile of mattresses awaiting shipment to the dump. Woody made it quite clear that he was quite proud of his instrument. Daniel hoped that Stephanie had not seen his gratuitous macho display. But it was too late. Stephanie stormed into Daniel's office, her face red with anger and embarrassment.

"That man is a filthy, disgusting animal. He does those things just to taunt me. He knows how I feel about that kind of behavior, but he keeps on doing it and nobody around here will talk to him. He knows my window faces the loading dock, and he does it every day just like a five-year-old child. Daniel, you're going to have to do something about that man. He's no drunk and I don't even know why he's here."

Daniel didn't want to confront Woody Johnson about his naughty toilet habits, but he knew that this type of behavior was serious and more than just childish mischief. It was aimed at Stephanie, and he would have to deal with the cowboy as soon as possible. He picked up the phone on his desk and called Tooch, the fleet manager.

"Tooch, this is Dr. Aarons," Daniel said. "I need to see you in my office right away."

Tooch was busy or so he said. "Can't it wait? I got six trucks to unload. I got three that are still somewhere in Brooklyn and one that's stuck in the Bronx." Tooch belched. "I'm waiting on a carburetor, too."

Daniel couldn't wait. "Tooch, I need to see you in my office now. This is an important personnel matter. You hear?"

There was silence on the other end and then Tooch covered the mouthpiece and cursed.

"Yea, yea," said Tooch. "Give me ten minutes and I'll be there." The phone slammed down.

Daniel waited for the fleet manager. He thought out all the various scenarios for dealing with Woody and how he would instruct Cantucci. He wasn't sure if the cowboy should be fired or just reprimanded, but he would discuss the options with the fleet manager.

A sharp knock came on the conference room door. Daniel expected to see Tooch.

"Yea, come on in Tooch," Daniel yelled.

"It's not Tooch, Daniel. It's Malchus and this is important."

Malchus didn't bother to wait for Daniel's reply to enter the room. He barged in waving his finger at his boss.

"I just have one word for you, just one word. *You* do it. *You* do it. Don't delegate the responsibility to Cantucci. Do you really think he gives a rat's ass about Woody Johnson peeing off the side of the loading dock? Do you think he cares about anything but filling his fat belly? Daniel, take that bull by the balls and tie him up yourself. That's all I'm going to say. Not one more word about this subject. I'm out of here."

Malchus stomped out and slammed the door.

How did he know about Woody Johnson? Daniel thought. Was he in the room with Stephanie? Was he listening in on some extension phone in the building?

Daniel had no answer, but he knew that Malchus was right. He would have to deal with Woody Johnson himself. He would have to protect Stephanie's honor. This was not something to delegate to some underling. Cantucci would do nothing but slap Woody on the wrist, if that much. He would need to make his decision, take action, and let Tooch know the results. He would have control and show the men that he meant business. Daniel was grateful that the little man came into his office at his hour of need. How prophetic. He picked up the phone and called Cantucci.

"Tooch, this is Aarons. I've taken control of the situation. I don't need to see you, but I will be talking with you later today or tomorrow."

Tooch slammed the phone receiver down without saying a word. Now it was left for Daniel to take charge, but he still wasn't quite sure what to do with Woody Johnson. This was not the time to consult Stephanie or anybody else in the Brewery. Daniel got his guidance from Malchus, and he would have to mete out the punishment with the Wisdom of Solomon. Daniel got up from his chair, walked out of the conference room into the waiting room, and saw Stephanie sitting at her desk. He didn't speak to her. He stopped at the screen door and cupped his hands around his mouth to call Woody Johnson, who was still unloading boxes from the back of his truck.

"Johnson, I want to see you in my office right now. It's important."

The truck engines roared and sputtered.

Johnson played deaf. "I can't hear you, what'd you say?"

"You heard me. I want you in my office this minute."

Daniel walked back to his office and did not look at Stephanie, but he wanted her approval.

Woody arrived at Daniel's office door. "Yea, what do you want, Captain?"

"Come in and sit down, Woody. I need to speak with you about something important."

Daniel lit his pipe and looked sternly at the young man who was not much younger than he was.

"First of all, don't address me as captain. I'm not a commissioned officer in the corps; I'm a paid consultant hired by Colonel Boyer. You may address me as Dr. Aarons."

Woody Johnson was not impressed, and a mean scowl appeared on his face. He looked like an eight-year-old who was about to be whipped with a strap.

"Okay, Doc, shoot." He folded his arms across his chest and pulled a cigarette from the pack that was stuck up his sleeve. He lit it and drew hard. He blew out the smoke with equal force. He was waiting to pounce.

"Woody, didn't your mother ever tell you that it was impolite to urinate on the furniture?"

The cowboy snorted, chuckled, turned his head to the wall, and muttered something like, "Shit, so that's what this is all about?"

"Captain, uh, Dr. Aarons," responded the cowboy, "I never had a mother. I never had anybody to tell me not to piss on the furniture. For that matter, I never had anybody to tell me where to piss at all. I grew up like a stray dog, and I learned to mark my territory like one, too."

Daniel sat straight up in his chair. "You know, Woody, that type of behavior is unacceptable here at the Brewery. I don't care how long you've been urinating off the loading dock, but today was your last piss. Is that clear?"

Woody took a long puff on his cigarette. He made a fist. He was preparing for a powerful comeback.

"Dr. Aarons, you seem like a reasonable guy, not like some of the other jerks they've had running this place. I want you to understand that I mean no disrespect. I don't drink, don't do drugs, and I've lived and worked in this place almost five years. Yea, Turtlebaum and me. We both came out of Attica. I spent ten years there for armed robbery."

His voice broke. "I was just a stupid kid when I went in, just seventeen. I don't mean to be making excuses, but I never had anybody give a shit about me, not from the day I was born. I was a foster kid, just bounced from one bad family to the next, and I pissed anywhere I felt like. So I ran around, drank, smoked, screwed, and robbed a little convenience store with an older dude. He's still in Attica. Anyway, we got caught. Simple as that. I held a gun. Never shot it. Never hurt nobody, but they sent me up to Attica for a long time. They told me where to piss and when to piss and how to hold it. Well, here I am now, a little older, but I guess you don't think I'm any wiser. You know, Dr. Aarons, you might say that I pissed my life away, but I'm proud of what I do here at the Brewery and I haven't been in trouble. I ain't perfect and I sure do love pretty women, but you won't find a better driver or expert in fine wood furniture."

The young man fiddled with the brim of his hat. He was silent for a moment. His lip curled in anger. He looked down at his hands and then snuffed out his cigarette. His grand finale was coming.

"Yea, okay, I was wrong, but I'm no disgusting slob and I ain't no animal. You can tell that to Miss Croix."

His voice was obviously loud so that Stephanie could hear him through the walls.

"I know she told you about what I did. She told Boyer and all the rest of the SOB bosses before you. They'd come out on the dock and shout at me, 'Johnson, you do that one more time and I'm gonna cut your dick off.' What did they expect me to do? But, Dr. Aarons, at least you listened to me and I thank you for doing that little thing. I promise you won't be seeing *Big Willy* on the loading dock anymore. Now don't you come roaming around the dormitory checking out for wayward winkies. We're not modest men around here. And you can be damned sure that I ain't gay either!"

The cowboy lit a new cigarette. "Is that all?"

Daniel was surprised and pleased by the turn of events. He looked at Woody and thought this man didn't need another beating; all he needed was somebody to lend him an ear. Tooch wouldn't have done it. Malchus was right. Daniel put his pipe down and extended his hand in a friendly yet professional manner.

"Woody, I'm really pleased we had this conversation. I think we're going to be doing a lot of work together. I'd like to spend some time with you and Turtle Face (Daniel grinned at the name he made) on your truck, just to get an idea of what it's all about. You know, driving, picking up the furniture, and that sort of stuff."

The cowboy beamed and smacked the brim of his hat.

"Yea, sure, Dr. Aarons, any time. Just name your day. I'll see ya."

Woody Johnson left the room as if he had just won a rodeo contest.

Daniel sighed in relief. This had been a good day, at least from the perspective of 5:30 in the afternoon. He walked into the Stephanie's small office and gave her a smiling glance and the thumbs-up sign.

CHAPTER 12

✠ ✠ ✠

THE OLD JACOB KORETZ DID NOT RETURN. He was dead. A new and improved version, however, was seen singing and dancing down Metropolitan Avenue in the Williamsburg section of Brooklyn. It was a polished, chrome-plated model filled with high-octane fuel. It sped up and down tenement hallways, flashed its gorgeous blue lights at old women, and ran over the trash and riffraff that lay on the sidewalk. Its gleaming white teeth and brilliant grille caused people to swoon. Its horn made them faint. Never before and perhaps never again would the world see such a dazzling Koretz! He visited three cousins, two business acquaintances, and one dead friend. Today Jacob Koretz not only broke the sound barrier, but he also climbed Mount Everest and won the World Series. None of this splendid, glorious, creative activity impressed Daniel, who waited for his uncle to return to the Brewery. It was already 7:30 in the evening and Daniel worried.

Where was his uncle? He should have returned hours ago. Jacob had promised to take them for dinner in Sheepshead Bay, but then no Koretz. Stephanie wanted to go home, but she stayed with Daniel and Malchus as they waited for the old man to return. Terrible thoughts went through their heads: he was dead; he was sitting in a dark alleyway with his head split open and blood gushing out; he was drunk and floating on a tire in the East River, he was ravished and spent by a gang of old Jewish yentas at the rest home. As Malchus paced the floor of the waiting room, a light went off in his head.

"What are we doing?" he yelled at Daniel and Stephanie. "Just look at us. We've become a pathetic collection of obsessive neurotics. All we need is a sink so we can wash our hands over and over. Friends, there is nothing to worry about. The great Koretz has won and he is celebrating. Give him another five minutes and he'll come bouncing through the doorway like a child coming home from school."

Sure enough, five minutes after Malchus' reassuring words, Jacob Koretz bounded across the threshold like a groom on his way to his honeymoon bed. The screen door burst open.

"Koretz the magnificent is now among you!" the old man said, flinging his arms open wide. Daniel was tired and in a bad mood. He didn't appreciate his uncle's lack of concern or consideration.

"You know, you could have called. I've been pacing the floor waiting for you, wondering if you were dead. Stephanie and Malchus were worried, too. We all sat here like Jewish grandmothers wringing our hands and searching the heavens for poor old Jacob Koretz."

"I'm so sorry, Daniel, but you know how I get when I'm in one of my moods, and brother, this is one of my moods!" He danced around the room with an imaginary partner. His euphoria was oozing out of his ears and pouring like torrents from his lips.

"This has been one of the greatest days of my life. Not only did that wonderful jerk, Julius Chomsky, love my play, but he also wants to produce it this year and convert it into a musical, an operetta, no less. Can you imagine that? Jacob Koretz, the author and librettist of an operetta. Move over Sigmund Romberg, get out of the way Victor Herbert."

Koretz continued to dance around the room throwing kisses in the air. He looked at his nephew.

"Daniel, beautiful Stephanie, dear friend Malchus, we must go and celebrate! Let's all go down to Sheepshead Bay. I'm famished."

Jacob Koretz was a volcano of emotion. Daniel knew it would be only a matter of weeks until his uncle would come crashing down and splatter into a thousand pieces. He was prepared for the disaster, but he also wanted to enjoy his uncle's enormous spurt of creative energy and life.

"Jacob, I'm very tired. It's getting late. Maybe we can do Sheepshead Bay some other time. How about if we just grab a bite here in the dining room?"

Koretz would have none of Daniel's old lady behavior.

"Daniel, you're about as much fun as a hemorrhoid. Why don't you consider what your friends would like to do? This poor girl looks like she could use a good meal and a good time. Malchus, have you ever been to Sheepshead Bay? The best seafood in New York. And after dinner, we'll go down to Coney Island and walk the boardwalk. I can smell that sea air now. Come on, let's go, it'll be great fun."

Daniel was thinking about Jacob's splendid idea. The thought of good seafood was appealing. The thought of walking around Coney Island late at night wasn't so appealing. Perhaps Jacob hadn't been there recently and seen how the old wonderland had become a depressing broken-down slum.

Daniel was about to make up his mind and give his decision when the sounds of an opening door down the hall broke his train of thought. John B. Waters and Chuck Conklin were about to bring him some news he didn't want to hear, especially at this time of the evening.

Waters, the spokesman, his face somber, his voice deep, spoke first. "Dr. Aarons, I'm afraid we have a problem. I didn't realize that you were still in the building. Chuck and I came down here to check some dormitory records, but since you're here, I better let you deal with this situation."

Daniel was drained. He had just climbed Mount Everest with Jacob, but now he felt that he would have to plumb the deepest depths of the ocean with Waters and Conklin. He was afraid to ask the nature of the problem, but braced himself for some bad news.

"I think you better come with us to Dormitory C. I really can't explain what's going on, and I think you'd better see this with your own two eyes."

Daniel stroked his beard. "Oh, come on John, can't you tell me anything down here? Do I have to go upstairs? Is somebody dead? Has there been a fight? By any chance, are you planning a surprise birthday party for me?"

The two men were dead serious. Their faces were like stones. Suddenly Coney Island became very appealing. Malchus, Stephanie, and Jacob awaited the news like an impending TV bulletin.

Conklin broke the news. "It's Peppler."

"Oh no, not again," Stephanie said. "It must be the third time this year!"

Stephanie was aware of the situation. Malchus rubbed his head and looked at Daniel for the answer. Daniel didn't have a clue what was going on. Now he just wanted to go to Coney Island.

"Would somebody please tell me what the hell is going on?" Daniel began to point his finger at Conklin and Waters. "Is this a game of twenty questions or are you all trying to drive me nuts?"

Waters responded clinically. "Dr. Aarons, you must see this aberration with objectivity and come to your own conclusion."

"Oh, bullshit!" Daniel responded.

Jacob would not let his mood be squashed by some aberration. His entire life was an aberration. "Can't this wait 'til tomorrow?" he pleaded. "I feel so good and I want to celebrate." He sighed and looked down at the floor.

John stared at Daniel and then at Jacob, frustration now beginning to appear in his voice. "Who is this man? Is he a new client? There's no room in the dormitories or the apartments, you know."

"No, John, this is my uncle Jacob. He's been visiting with us today and we were about to go out and celebrate the production of his new play."

Waters was now emphatic. "Dr. Aarons, I don't think you should be going anywhere tonight. The last time this thing happened, we lost three men. They went psychotic and we never saw them again. We can't afford another police investigation, and I certainly don't want all those priests hanging around the building with their holy water and rosary beads. And no more exorcisms! Besides, there is a full moon due in two days and you know what happens on full moon Mondays."

Stephanie's face became ghostly white. "Daniel, listen to John and do exactly what he says."

Daniel was exasperated, his voice filled with anger and frustration.

"All right, damn it, let's get the hell out of here, and go upstairs before this whole place goes to hell in a handbasket."

The entire entourage, Jacob, Malchus, and Stephanie included, left the office and proceeded through a series of long corridors and stairways that led up to Dormitory C.

An intense, hard-edged shaft of silver-blue light seemed to originate from both the floor and the ceiling of the corridor leading to the lower lounge. Its metallic structure, like a knife blade, contained diamond-like beads that slowly moved up and down the shaft. As the group approached the beam of light, the air became colder.

Jacob couldn't believe what he was seeing. "What the hell is this? Is somebody showing movies from the ceiling?"

It was apparent that only Daniel and Jacob had never seen this strange display of light before. Waters stayed at a safe distance and was not overly amazed or concerned by its eerie presence. He looked at Daniel as if to say, "You ain't seen nothin' yet."

Daniel stared at the hauntingly beautiful tube of metallic light.

"You mean this has happened here before? You know what this shaft of light is all about? Has it ever been investigated by scientific researchers? Have you called the FBI?" Daniel bombarded Waters with questions.

"Dr. Aarons, when any person comes to this place who ordinarily isn't a resident or a client, such as your friendly neighborhood police, the shaft of light conveniently vanishes. In other words, there's nothing to report and nothing to analyze or study. All they would naturally do is think that we're a bunch of drunks and crazies seeing things. And isn't that just what we are, a bunch of drunks and crazies seeing things? This is only the third time I've seen the light and this time it's brighter and much colder. Dr. Aarons, we need to go upstairs. This thing doesn't just begin and end here in this hallway."

The group of five climbed the steep narrow stairway that opened on to another corridor that led to Dormitory C. A terrified bunch of men in various states of undress stood at the top of the stairs. Panic was in their eyes. They shivered from the cold and from their fear.

Ernie Yeager wasn't wearing his dentures or much of anything else. "It's got Peppler in its jaws, Captain," he shouted in terror. "I think he's a gonner." The toothless man perceived the light to be a hideous monster, a beast that could tear and devour human flesh.

Woody Johnson, who was now peeing in his pants, had a more Hollywood version of the strange light.

"Captain, uh, Dr. Aarons, poor Peppler's been impaled on a stake of light just like he was Dracula or some kind of vampire. That thing's gone right through his heart and it's suckin' out all his blood!"

Each man had his own perception of the eerie aberration and each shared it in horrific detail with Daniel and the others.

It was time for Daniel to see this thing for himself. "There must be a logical, rational explanation for this phenomenon," he said, "just as there is a rational explanation for every physical thing and occurrence in the universe." He tried to be reassuring to the men, but his legs buckled within his pants.

Malchus had been pensive and quiet up to this point. He studied the men's expressions and their descriptions of the shaft of light. He analyzed the tumultuous situation and tried to understand its supernatural and psychic dimensions. As the entire group of clients, residents, and employees approached the door to Dormitory C, Malchus exploded in a frenzy of animated life and jumped to the head of the line holding his hands out, preventing Daniel from going into the large room. A virtual door opened in the dwarf's head and he, like some mechanical Oracle of Delphi, spewed reams of data and spiritual pronouncements. After ranting and raving for several minutes, he spoke in comprehensible sentences.

"My friends," said Malchus, "it is my great pleasure to inform you that I, too, like our compatriot Ron Peppler here, have personally experienced this same magnificent phenomenon. It happened to me on the seventh floor solarium at Bellevue Hospital."

The crowd shoved the little man aside like an annoying dog and stepped into the frigid room. They could not approach the light because of its intense cold, but at the same time, they felt a disturbingly strong attraction to it as it drew them nearer. A thick layer of frost covered the walls, floor, ceiling, and windows. The condensed vapor from their breath filled the room. They stood in awe, as the shaft of light appeared to be penetrating the body of Ron Peppler. The skinny one-handed veteran was in a seated position on the bed, but his body was actually about six inches above the surface of the mattress suspended in space. The brilliant shaft of blue light appeared to penetrate his head, go down through his spine, and exit through his buttocks. He was naked except for a skimpy pair of boxer shorts. The stump of his left arm rested on his lap. Not an eyelash moved. Not a breath taken. He was flash frozen and had been in that position for more than an hour. But slowly, imperceptibly, Ron Peppler was rising vertically through the room at a speed of, perhaps, one inch per hour. At ten o'clock, however, it was evident that the speed of ascent was accelerating, and Daniel calculated that Peppler would be at the ceiling by three o'clock in the morning.

Again, Malchus provided a source of insight, annoyance, and comic relief.

"Ladies and gentlemen, children of all ages, may I have your attention. I, too, have been through this exact same experience and I bring you good news. There is absolutely nothing to fear. In fact, what you are now observing is a blessing from the Almighty! Though it is not apparent to you at this moment, within the next twenty-four hours, we will all be celebrating. How do I know this? I, Malchus One Ear, like that great prophet Moses, was blinded by this same incredible light. It terrified me, but it also drew me near and told me that it had a message for me. And when the shaft pierced my heart, I knew that I had heard the voice of God. This happened not once, but at least three times in the solarium on the seventh floor of Bellevue Hospital at precisely seven thirty-three in the evening. That's exactly the same time that this shaft of light appeared in this dormitory and pierced Ron Peppler."

The crowd was angry, disturbed, and didn't want to listen to the deranged ravings of the one-eared dwarf. They yelled at him and pushed him away.

"Moonface, you're just a little crazy son of a bitch. Go back to Bellevue."

"Yea, midget, you're full of shit, and I'm gonna flatten that big stupid head of yours with my fist if you don't shut the hell up."

Stephanie couldn't bear to listen to the insults heaped upon her distraught friend. She had heard enough from the rowdy bunch.

"Shut up, you idiots," she yelled. "I want to listen to Malchus."

The room was a frigid meat cooler. Stephanie huddled behind Daniel to try to get some of his body heat. Jacob stood like a round snowman with a gray beard. The room became deadly silent as all watched the petrified body of Ron Peppler slowly rise to the ceiling. Intrigued by Malchus' comments, Daniel wanted to hear more.

"Well, Malchus, is there anything else you want to say?" Daniel asked.

"No, that's it," Malchus replied. "All we have to do is wait."

"Wait for what?" Daniel asked.

"The message," Malchus replied.

"What kind of message?" Daniel insisted.

"I have no idea and it would be foolish to second guess the Creator by assuming the nature of the message," Malchus replied. "My suggestion is that we all go downstairs, have a nice cup of hot chocolate, and see what happens. I don't know about you, but I'm freezing my ass off."

Malchus left the room.

The rest of the group maintained its vigil until, as Daniel predicted, at three o'clock in the morning, Ron Peppler rose through the ceiling and vanished into thin air. The shaft of light, too, was gone and the room began to warm. The men returned to their beds, but there was no sleep that night.

CHAPTER 13

✠ ✠ ✠

DORMITORY C WAS EMPTY. AT PRECISELY 7:33 PM, exactly twenty-four hours after the magnificent shaft of frigid, silver-blue light appeared in that room of the Brewery, Ron Peppler returned to his bed.

There was no shaft of light; there was no frost, only the body of Ron Peppler very much alive sitting on his bed in his boxer shorts and wearing a New York Yankees sweatshirt. Scattered around him on his bed were dozens of fragrant rose petals. The delicate aroma of the flowers filled the dormitory and wafted into all parts of the Brewery, including the offices and the warehouse. Even the men on the loading dock commented about how fresh the air smelled.

Stephanie, especially taken by the stimulating smell, searched out its origin. In bloodhound fashion, she followed her nose and within minutes was at the entrance to Dormitory C. A moment later, Stephanie was on her knees, her hands clasped in prayer, eyes pointing to the sky, tears pouring down her face. The scrawny little veteran sat on his bed admiring his new hand and the five new fingers that were now a permanent part of his body. He gazed at the digits like an infant who had just made a new discovery. He said nothing, but continued to smile.

Stephanie rose to her feet, screaming at the top of her lungs, "Daniel, Malchus, Jesus Christ, I need you. Get in here now!" The sound of her cries filled the warehouse and the dormitories. In minutes, men filled

Dormitory C and each received the startling vision of Ron Peppler and his new hand. And each man received the vision in a unique way.

Ernie Yeager lost his teeth and blabbered like a baby. Moby Dixon cried, his big brown tongue hanging out of his mouth, "I told you they were angels. I knew it, I just knew it."

All Woody Johnson could say was, "Holy shit, holy shit, it must've been aliens from outer space. I knew it was a UFO!"

Stephanie cried and crossed herself repeatedly while saying the rosary.

Daniel was speechless. He was shaking, curling his beard, and staring at the fully rehabilitated man, convincing himself that he was just dreaming. "This is a dream. It can't be real. These things don't happen. There must be a logical explanation for all of this. I must be going mad. God, help me."

Jacob, who spent the night at the Brewery sleeping on the couch, was now in an even higher paradise. He still didn't know whether it was his manic mood or the miracle that manifested itself before him. He recited a psalm and praised the Lord.

Malchus walked smugly into the room, a broad smile on his face. "I told you we'd all be celebrating today, didn't I?"

The dwarf strolled over to Peppler's bed and stared at the man. "Hey, where did you get that sweatshirt?" he asked. "It's nice. Look, I got one just like it." Malchus was wearing the sweatshirt that Tali had given him. He had never taken it off.

Peppler didn't respond. He just smiled in a childish way and stared at his new hand.

"Well," Malchus said to Peppler, "I guess there's not much to say at a time like this. You know the same thing happened to me when I was in the Garden of Gethsemane. Got my ear cut off and then Jesus healed it back up. It doesn't look as nice as your hand, though."

Malchus picked up a handful of rose petals and threw them around the dormitory. Stephanie picked them up and clutched them to her chest. She continued to kneel on the floor and cry, prayers cascading from her mouth. Malchus came to her and caressed her head. Daniel didn't know who or what to worship, so he just stood there looking at the man and his new hand.

The next day, Ron Peppler left the Brewery. He was never seen again.

A strange calm filled the Brewery in the days following Ron Peppler's disappearance, reappearance, and re-disappearance. Strangely, this calm bothered Daniel. He knew in his gut that chaos was just a heartbeat away and that the Miracle in Dormitory C, as it was now called, would soon be a fond but confounding memory.

Daniel needed spiritual guidance so he called on John B. Waters. Waters was the only man in the Brewery who had a genuine military ranking from the corps—a captain. On special occasions or when the brass from Biloxi visited the Brewery, John would wear his doorman's uniform. He also received his commission as an evangelical minister licensed by the corps to preach the gospel, conduct weddings, funerals, and serve communion. He acted as the Service Corps's chaplain and spiritual counselor in addition to his duties as manager of the dormitories and residential apartments.

The residential apartments, where Waters lived, were actually small private rooms, essentially cells, for commissioned officers, managers, and long-term clients who had established their reputation and loyalty with the Service Corps. There was also an apartment set aside for the center's director. Rarely did Daniel stay at the Brewery at night. He preferred to go home to make sure his uncle was all right—at least that was one of his excuses. He needed to get away from the daily pressures of running a large rehabilitation facility and dealing with sixty men and all the problems that went along with them. He felt confident that John could handle most of the nightly incidents and turmoil such as fistfights or the occasional drunken brawl.

Daniel treated Waters not just as a good manager, but also as a friend and confidant who could be trusted. Waters' loyalty, however, was to the Service Corps, and he acknowledged Colonel Claude Boyer as his superior officer. Daniel rarely needed to give John direct orders; he knew what to do and he did it with skill and competence. Like most of the men, his weakness was alcohol, but he hadn't touched a drop in years. He was dry, but continued to fight the battle as if he had had his last drink just the day before. John's temper was legendary and God help the man who crossed his path when he was angry. Many a wall bore the signs of his powerful fists.

The day after Ron Peppler reappeared with two hands, Daniel was still in a state of shock and denial. He was so shaken that he got drunk—of all things—and slept in the director's apartment for nearly twenty-four hours. When he awoke, Peppler was gone and so were some of the answers to the mystery. Daniel couldn't get this supernatural event out of his mind. It shadowed his every thought and action for days. It was as if God inserted his finger through the natural membrane of space and time and fiddled with the inward parts. But isn't that the definition of a miracle?

Daniel even distanced himself from Stephanie because she was in a state of pure elation and joy. He avoided Malchus as much as possible. That enigmatic little man was saying and doing incredible things. His flashing brilliance one moment and spastic raving lunacy the next were a constant source of enlightenment and revulsion. Daniel needed to talk to a trained counselor who had both feet planted on terra firma. He considered visiting a friend who was a psychiatrist, but was afraid that she might consider him paranoid schizophrenic based on the visions he had experienced. There was only one person who could possibly understand what he was going through at this time in his life, and that was John B. Waters.

Waters, while astute and sensitive, didn't mince words, and he was not known for his tact.

"Daniel, you look like day-old shit," said John. "Why don't you get the hell out of this dump and take a day off. Go for a walk in Prospect Park or just get on the Staten Island Ferry. The Brewery can survive without your ugly face for one day. It's been here for a hundred years and it will be here for a hundred years after you're gone. You aren't doing us or yourself any good by hanging around and acting like some sick bastard from the VA hospital."

Daniel hadn't shaved. His eyes were bloodshot. His formerly neatly trimmed beard was a scraggly, knotted mess. He hadn't bathed and he smelled bad.

"John, you're probably right," Daniel said. "You know, I haven't been here long enough to get burned out, but after last week's revelations I feel like I've been here ten years. I appreciate your taking the time to talk to me."

"Sure, Daniel, that's what I'm here for. When I'm not kickin' ass or punching holes in walls, I am the Lord's servant and His man alone."

Daniel sat on a torn-up, stained couch in John's small apartment. John sat on a straight-backed chair. He looked like a large black bull, snorting and ready to charge. The thin flimsy chair creaked and could barely hold his massive frame.

The patient didn't talk. He looked around the room and felt at home. The walls were covered in homemade bookcases, cinder blocks, and boards from floor to ceiling. There must have been a thousand books in the room; some piled on top of one another.

"Yea, I love my books," John said. "They're my true lovers. You know, Daniel, a lot of people throw out their books just because they get old and dusty or because the pages crumble and fall out. But it's not the bindings or the pages that matter, it's those words. Each one can be a magnificent picture and when they're put together on a string, there's magic."

John reached out to a special shelf that had a glass covering and removed a book.

"Look at this." He held it out for Daniel to see. "It's a Bible from 1812, thrown out like it was a burned-out toaster. How can people do that to a beautiful piece of art? Look, Daniel, it has names in it, the names of a family, people who came and went, got married, and died. Now why would a family dispose of a treasure like this? Well, it's mine now, and I'm the keeper of this family jewel. It's never going to see the light of a thrift store, at least not in my lifetime."

He stroked the cover of the book with his large hand and gently placed it back on the shelf behind the glass. He waited for the discussion to proceed, but Daniel continued to look around the fascinating room that reminded him so much of his own personal treasures, the ideas, the thoughts, the logic. So many books on theology, philosophy, psychology, great works of literature, but also a pile of yellowed pornographic magazines from the fifties and a box full of records, old forty-fives, and seventy-eights. On the far wall above one of the bookcases hung a wooden plaque filled with several army medallions and ribbons, including a Purple Heart.

"I see you were in the war," Daniel said. "Korea?"

"Yea, I spent some time over there, got a little shot up. Almost lost the use of my right leg for a while. Sat in a VA hospital in Richmond for two years getting rehabilitated. I was just a young kid, full of myself."

"How'd you get to New York City?" Daniel asked.

"I killed a man," John said in a matter-of-fact way.

Daniel took a deep breath. Perhaps this was not the right time to pursue this line of questioning.

"Don't you want to know why I killed a man and how I got to this godforsaken place?" John pointed his big finger in Daniel's face. The ball was now back in his court.

"All right, tell me the whole story, all the horrible violent facts, the months in the courtroom, the years behind prison walls, and your innocence."

"You make it sound so romantic, Daniel, like I was some poor dumb black man caught in the jaws of a white man's racist system of justice." John looked up at the ceiling searching for words. "No, the plain fact was I got drunk, we played cards, he cheated, and I shot him. End of story. I was up for murder two, but my lawyer plea-bargained for manslaughter. I spent ten years in the state penitentiary in Richmond and then they let me out. I got drunk and stayed drunk for two years until the Service Corps scraped me off the sidewalk and got me into a good program. I worked in a warehouse, sorted rags, baled paper, hauled furniture, cooked slop, screwed broads, and stayed sober. I repeat, I stayed sober and I am still sober."

The big man stood up. "If it were not for the Service Corps, I'd either be dead or rotting in prison. Daniel, I could go on for hours about how these good, down-to-earth folk in their silly uniforms made a man out of me and showed me a God who loves and cares for sick, stinking drunks and burned-out street bums, but I'm not going to tell you anymore. You know the story. It's just that I've lived it."

John's sincerity and honest talk impressed Daniel. This man was no saint, but he was a solid rock with a strong mind. In different circumstances, he could easily have become a professor, a physician, or certainly a pastor. His speech was sometimes eloquent and poetic. His intellectual abilities were probably just as good. He just didn't have the schooling or the credentials.

John touched a particularly important photograph that hung in the center of his wall.

"Daniel, the corps has been my entire life for a long time now. I don't have a family, except for these men. I've got a good job here managing the dormitories, I have the opportunity to preach God's word on Sundays, and I can minister to them and help them keep off the booze and the pills. Now it hasn't exactly been paradise around here, you know and the brass in Biloxi hasn't been much help either. Actually, some of those stupid SOB's down there would like to see this place go up in flames so they could shut it down and collect the insurance money. I think they'd like to open some neat little rehab center for rich outpatients. Daniel, Claude Boyer's all right, he just hates New York. He's a smart man, but he gets lost on the subway. You know he got on the wrong train once and wound up on 125th Street in Harlem. He was terrified, nearly shit in his pants. But none of the passengers picked on him because they thought he was just a poor slob doorman. When he came back to the Brewery, he was so pissed-off he kicked his foot right through a glass door. He had to have thirty stitches."

The two men laughed. John provided a good release valve for Daniel. They both felt relaxed, and Daniel could now lean back on the couch and discuss some of his own gnawing questions.

"John, I just don't get it. What happened to Ron Peppler a few days ago is either an outright miracle or it just plain didn't happen. Shafts of icy blue light don't just suddenly appear, men don't float up to the ceiling and then vanish into thin air, and people don't grow new hands. Am I damn crazy or what?"

John laughed and slapped Daniel's knee. "Perhaps you are crazy; maybe I'm crazy, too. Maybe all this was a hallucination. Maybe this place is actually a secret government research center and we're testing new psychedelic drugs. Maybe I'm actually General John B. Waters, United States Army!" John roared.

Daniel's frustration rose to the surface. He didn't appreciate John's sarcasm.

"Waters, you're not helping me one bit. I'm just getting more confused. I can't live with this uncertainty, these irrational presuppositions, and conclusions. I can't get a handle on it. There's nothing to observe, nothing to analyze. The damn guy is gone and all I have left is my memory and my imagination and it's driving me nuts."

There was a moment of silence. John looked out the window of his room onto the black rooftops of the surrounding warehouses. The toot of a boat whistle broke his reverie.

"You believe in God, don't you?" asked John.

"Now don't start evangelizing me, John. I'm a Jew and I have a difficult enough time dealing with an angry, vengeful God who demands justice and mercy and then rains down torture and disaster on his faithful subjects. I got tired of wrestling with Job. Every one of my bones is out of joint, and I've been scratching my boils for thirty years. All I need is sackcloth and ashes."

John smiled and straightened up. He leaned over and looked Daniel in the eyes. "The struggle is good. The wrestling is good. It just means that God wants *you* and He's not going to let *you* go. Let me ask you another question. Do you easily let go of a lover? Do you give up your child to a stranger? Wouldn't you do illogical and crazy things if it meant maintaining a relationship with someone you loved? Wouldn't you even give your life if it meant that your entire family could be saved? Daniel, friend, I read my Bible not because it provides me with easy pat answers about God. I read it because God is continually challenging me with questions and I like a good contest. The more I wrestle, the stronger I get, and I demand that God bless me, just like Jacob demanded of God in the Bible! And what does God do? He blesses me and continues to confound me and show me miracles. I should be dead right now, but I'm not. Here I am sober and smart and giving directions to a half-assed PhD who looks like he just fell in a pile of dog shit. I am a miracle! I repeat, I am a miracle!"

The preacher looked up at the ceiling, clapped his hands, and yelled, "Alleluia!"

Daniel expected him to start singing "Amazing Grace."

"John," Daniel said, "I'm glad you know which end is up, but I need logic and numbers. I need to measure things and verify results. I'm a scientist."

"You need logic and numbers, Dr. PhD? Count your fingers."

"That's the problem, John. Ron Peppler had five on Thursday, and then he went through the ceiling and came back with ten on Friday.

Where's the logic in that?" Daniel put his head between his legs as if he was going to faint.

John scratched his head. "Okay, that was a bad illustration. Daniel, let me tell it to you simply. There is no logic in this world, period. Numbers lie and what you see with your own two eyes isn't necessarily the truth. Newton had it only part right and Einstein corrected him. Now, somebody's going to come along and correct Einstein, it's only a matter of time. Daniel Aarons, smart man that you are, you can make yourself sick and miserable by straining at gnats, or you can celebrate and be happy by acknowledging that miracles do happen. I choose to celebrate miracles and to thank God for His lovely illogical ways. Now get the hell out of here and go to work."

Daniel rubbed his hands through his greasy hair. He had just received a personal sermon from Brother John B. Waters. No questions were answered, but he did feel a little better. He got up from the couch and prepared to leave John's room.

"John, just one more question."

"Shoot."

"What do you make of that little man, Malchus?"

John laughed.

"Malchus? That crazy one-eared dwarf who sees visions from the solarium on the seventh floor of Bellevue Hospital? Daniel, he's probably *your* personal messiah!" John roared.

CHAPTER 14

✠ ✠ ✠

SOME MESSIAHS ARE MADE AND SOME MESSIAHS are born. Some appear out of nowhere and save their people or drive them to the edge of their doom.

As for Malchus One Ear, he was a messiah, or more specifically, an anointed one of God. He was sure of this fact because Herby Croix anointed him in the kitchen of the Brewery. When a large tin of olive oil the chef was pulling off a shelf tipped over and poured out on top of Malchus' head, he knew that it was an authentic sign from God. Malchus took this sign to be a calling that God was directing him in a special mission. This wasn't some weird vision or alien abduction, it was a genuine historical event witnessed by at least three men in the kitchen. For days, Malchus smelled like a Greek salad complete with anchovies and feta cheese. He didn't wash off the fragrant oil, but wore it as a visible symbol of his anointing. After thirty days, Malchus proclaimed that it was no longer necessary to wear his anointing and he bathed. Actually, the men couldn't stand the stench of rancid cooking oil and they threw him in the shower, clothes, and all.

Being a messiah is a wonderful joyous thing. It's also an awesome burden. Some messiahs have big jobs and others have small ones, but in the eyes of God, every job, no matter the size, has the potential for saving the entire universe. A true messiah never knows how important he or she is. He only knows that he is a messiah and that he has work to do for God. The smallest, simplest act of giving a drink of cool water to a thirsty person can change the course of history and perhaps even prevent a war or other great catastrophe. It's not the exploits of great leaders that make the difference; it's all those little acts of love and charity that move the universe along. You don't even have to be Jewish to be a messiah, but it can't hurt.

God continues to anoint messiahs to carry the true message throughout the world and it is often accomplished most sublimely through the weakest, smallest, and most oppressed of persons. Malchus One Ear fit that description quite adequately. Malchus was anointed to be one of those messengers, and he did his best to fill that role despite himself.

The Brewery had always had its share of messiahs, both true and false ones. What happens when two messiahs, one true and one false, are in the same room? Do they cancel each other out? Do they annihilate each other like matter and anti-matter, or do they have a friendly theological discussion?

Daniel had his hands full dealing with one messiah, but tonight he had two messiahs sitting in the dining hall of the Brewery. The little one with the New York Yankees sweatshirt was quite familiar. The other, who resembled a circus giant, was a startling addition to the personnel.

One evening, the new messiah and his entourage paraded into the Brewery's dining hall as if they were royalty. A handful of scowling disciples announced his coming like prophets of doom in the desert.

"I am the voice of one crying in the wilderness: prepare the way of the Lord, make His paths straight. Every valley shall be filled, and every mountain shall be brought low, and the crooked shall be made straight, and the rough shall be made smooth."

The magnificent messiah walked into the dining hall and his presence was breathtaking. The huge thin figure was messiah-like in every detail—purple garment, sandals, beard, a sad long face with piercing black eyes that looked up toward heaven. Malchus wasn't impressed and knew that the stranger and his brood were about as authentic as the plastic flowers on the dining hall tables. The bearded messiah spread his long arms open wide preparing to give a magnificent invocation to the men before they ate. The tall man proceeded to walk to the tables and turn each glass of water into a fine-smelling purple liquid, presumably wine. The men were terrified. Some screamed and were moved to tears. Some cursed and spat like cats. Some prayed or spoke in tongues.

"Jesus has returned; we're saved!" said Ernie Yeager as he lost his teeth. Moe Kutcher scratched himself with urgency heretofore unseen at the Brewery. Some of the men drank the liquid and convinced themselves that it was a fine Merlot or Cabernet, while others merely stared at their glasses in amazed silence. The dining hall lights flickered and the sound of rolling thunder was heard. A sudden gust of air rushed in through the open windows and blew napkins and cigarette smoke around the room in a whirlwind. Tongues of fire appeared to lap at the ceiling fixtures. Dishes and glasses smashed to the floor as tablecloths ripped in half. A dense black cloud formed at the foot of the tall messiah, and the room began to shake as if an earthquake had hit Brooklyn. Then there was silence, an absolute silence that virtually sucked the sound out of each man's ears. For a moment, it was as if the earth had come to a screeching halt and then the sound of clapping hands and the voice of John B. Waters. "Fantastic, man! That was absolutely fantastic!"

John B. Waters stood up, beamed, and continued to clap. He walked over to the messiah, put his arm around his neck, and hugged him as if they had been good buddies for years.

"Guys, I got a surprise for you," John said with a broad smile. "This is my good friend, Jonah Vaark, the Flying Dutchman from Schenectady. We spent some time together in Korea and at the VA hospital in Richmond. He's without a doubt the best magician I've ever seen."

John turned to Jonah. "Man, what a performance; that was your best entrance yet. You got these guys shitting in their pants."

The lights came back on. The sounds of thunder and quaking earth were gone. The smoke cleared. Ernie Yeager searched for his teeth beneath the tables and Moe Kutcher continued to scratch with wild abandon. Daniel groaned and pulled a small tin of aspirin out of his breast pocket. He gobbled down several tablets.

Malchus was still unimpressed and pointed his little finger at the tall imposing man. "I knew you were a phony the minute I laid eyes on you," the dwarf said. "You know it's not nice going around telling people you're the messiah when you're actually nothing but a two-bit trickster and a mediocre magician. You didn't have me fooled for one minute. You know, I used to have this roommate at Bellevue. One day he was Jesus Christ, the next day Genghis Khan. He could change water into wine, too, but his was a delicate Pinot Noir, not this cheap purple shit."

He took a sip and spit it out. "Not only that, but I saw him walk across the East River. Now, can you do that? You know, I liked him better when he was Genghis Khan, he was much funnier."

The towering man looked down at Malchus and didn't say a word. There was a look of pity on the big man's face.

Malchus walked out of the dining hall; he wouldn't be a further part of this charade. The rest of the men resumed normal body functions and finished their *wine*. Jonah Vaark continued his magic act and pulled twelve cats out of a hat. He sang favorite hits from Rodgers and Hammerstein shows and danced with members of his entourage. As a grand finale, he vanished into thin air in a blaze of glory. He was never seen again. It was by far the greatest floorshow ever presented at the Brewery and the last time a messiah danced in the dining hall.

CHAPTER 15

✠ ✠ ✠

NOBODY EVER ACCUSED MALCHUS OF NOT HAVING a sense of humor. One could never tell when the little man was actually miffed, playing jokes, or just putting on airs. He was a born entertainer, telling the most incredible stories about his adventures on the planet *Schnipichuck* or his numerous alien abductions. Angels, demons, otherworldly humanoids, and the spirit of Naphtali Ropshitz frequently visited him. Once, he actually took a group of men on a visit to the solarium on the seventh floor of Bellevue Hospital to show them exactly where many of his most famous abductions and visions had taken place.

On most days, Malchus would sing Puccini in the kitchen and bake his wonderful little cookies—delicate, fluffy, sweet pastries with a dot of vanilla cream on top. He baked them by the dozens and brought them out to the men working on the loading docks and in the warehouse. He'd send them off with the men on the trucks, and they were always part of the evening meal's dessert. The cookies satisfied a particular hunger in the men, and they consumed them like communion bread. Perhaps that's exactly what they were made of—manna from heaven. The men at the Brewery begged Malchus to bake more cookies; they just couldn't get enough of them. He always gave them what they wanted, but responded in his enigmatic way, "Man doesn't live by cookies alone, but by every word that comes from the mouth of God."

When Malchus wasn't baking cookies or making desserts, he was serving food. One of his favorite jobs was to carry sandwiches and cookies to the men who were sick in bed and to the older men who were feeble or incapacitated. Some of these men had transferred to the city-run nursing home adjacent to the big city hospital in Greenpoint, a couple of blocks down from the Brewery.

The Ten Eyck Street Nursing Center was a dismal, dingy municipal facility built during the Depression years. The building hadn't seen a fresh coat of paint since 1934. Malchus went to the nursing home every week to see Benny Lieberman to bring him a small cup of homemade chicken soup and a box of his now famous cookies. He'd put the meal in a child's metal lunch box and rush out the door like a kid chasing after a school bus.

A sinister group of young boys soon noticed his regular weekly routine. At first, they just taunted him. "Hey, Moon Face, hey Dough Boy, what planet are you from?"

Then they got physical and pushed Malchus into the street and stole his lunch box. These incidents didn't deter the little man from his appointed rounds. There was always an ample supply of old metal lunch boxes in the warehouse, and he was always baking cookies. So Malchus just kept on coming. His cookies, too, became a favorite with the sinister gang and Malchus decided that he would *buy protection* and give them a dozen each week on his way to the nursing home. In addition, he entertained the young boys with his incredible stories of alien abductions and visits from angels. Eventually, he became an honorary member of the gang and their spiritual leader. They stopped robbing convenience stores and beating up old women and most of them even went back to school.

Benny Lieberman was a small toothless man, almost blind, and deaf in one ear. He served his country well during World War I and then went to work for the Service Corps in Philadelphia in 1922. He stayed with the corps for fifty years, mainly as a store manager, but his health began to fail. At seventy-five, he was now a permanent resident of the Ten Eyck Street Nursing Center.

The relationship between Benny and Malchus was strong, and Malchus became Benny's de facto grandson and next of kin. When the old man talked, it was mostly about those events that were in the distant past: his exploits during the Great War, his women and wasteful ways during the twenties, and then his long service with the corps. That was Benny Lieberman's life and not much else. When he was lucid, the stories flowed like torrents of rushing water, but much of the time all he said was "yea and okay." A couple of bad strokes left Benny a bedridden invalid, but that didn't deter Malchus. He provided Benny a few happy hours before the old guy just slumped over and died one evening during one of his visits. Three people came to Benny's funeral, including Malchus and the rabbi. The third was his nurse, Sarah, who worked at Ten Eyck. Benny Lieberman passed into history, now just a fond memory to just two caring souls.

Sarah was a young nursing assistant who had a great bedside manner with the patients at Ten Eyck. She thought Malchus was very amusing, and she introduced him to many of her patients on the floor. What most of these folks needed was a lot of touching and personal communication with other human beings. Many of them were so isolated and lonely that they slipped into comas and just faded away. The city didn't have the money to provide for adequate therapy or recreation, so Ten Eyck became a mausoleum for the living.

Malchus was familiar with institutional life and living in cold, faceless facilities. He had always lived in the margins of society and on the edge of sanity. For him, Ten Eyck was another mission field, and he spent virtually all his time either baking cookies at the Brewery or serving at Ten Eyck.

Sarah introduced Malchus to Sylvia, a young, chronically ill woman on her floor. Sylvia had been wheelchair-bound for almost ten years and suffered from various neurological disabilities. What she lacked in physical strength, she more than made up for in her hopeful attitude. Though she had difficulty speaking, she had a marvelous sense of humor and a great reservoir of faith. How Sylvia survived so long at Ten Eyck with her sanity in tact was a miracle in itself. Malchus brought her a box of his cookies and then took her up to the balcony on the third floor where they could watch the sunset and then look at the stars.

"Oh, Malchus, look at the sun!" Sylvia would exclaim.

She had a hard time getting the words out. Who would think that seeing the sunset could be such a wonderful experience? Well, very simply, nobody had ever thought of taking Sylvia up to the balcony on the third floor. Her room faced north, and for all she knew, she could have been on Mars. Malchus was an expert on the movements of the sun, and he told Sylvia of his exploits in the solarium on the seventh floor at Bellevue Hospital. In fact, he told her she could even see that solarium from the third floor balcony of the Ten Eyck Center. He pointed to a large brick building overlooking the East River.

"Sylvia, you see that big old brick building? Now count seven stories and move your eyes over to the right. There it is—the solarium, my launching pad into the unknown, my stepping stone to the stars."

He was dramatic and pointed to the sky. "It was there that I was first abducted by a family of amphibious *Zenubians* that took me to their planet on a scientific expedition to a moon covered by a shoreless ocean. I thought they were vacationing because they were having such a good time. They brought me such wonderful food from under the sea, and they taught me how to swim and not to be afraid of water. I used to be so afraid of water that I was even scared to wash."

Sylvia laughed.

"Even when I was thirsty, I'd have to close my eyes before I drank a glass of water," he told her.

Malchus walked over to Sylvia, his eyes meeting hers. "You know, at the hospital, the doctors told me that when I was an infant, some lady found me floating in a garbage can in the East River. I guess that's why I used to be so terrified of water. Now, I can even take a bath without complaining and flushing the toilet is a pure joy."

Sylvia laughed so hard she nearly fell out of her wheelchair. Her scrawny, birdlike body twitched and shook as she became emotionally agitated, but she enjoyed every minute being with Malchus.

The two sat on the balcony awaiting the arrival of the stars like excited children anticipating a display of fireworks on the Fourth of July.

"Look, Sylvia, there's Betelgeuse and Rigel, and those three stars in a row make up Orion's belt. Did you know that the ancient Egyptians used Orion's belt to help them align the pyramids? It's true; I was there. I was one of Pharaoh's surveyors. He didn't know which way the pyramids should point, so I suggested that he look up into the night sky for some guidance. After that, I became his chief surveyor. Of course, I had two ears then and I was much taller."

The clear night sky was black and the stars twinkled. The lights of the city blazed on the Manhattan skyline. Suddenly, a beam of light from the seventh floor of Bellevue Hospital appeared from across the East River at just the spot where Malchus had pointed to earlier. It was coming from the solarium. The beam grew brighter and seemed to extend across the river, coming toward the Ten Eyck Nursing Center. In less than a second, the intense beam reached the third floor balcony and both Malchus and Sylvia were bathed in a powerful bluish gold light. Malchus became agitated, and he ran around Sylvia's wheelchair several times.

"I know this light, Sylvia," Malchus said. "It's come here to tell us something wonderful."

The intensity of the light temporarily blinded the two. Sylvia was terrified and cried out to Malchus. "I can't see you, Malchus, where are you?" Malchus reassured her that nothing bad would happen.

"Don't be afraid, this is a good light. It wants to help you. Maybe it's a whole flock of angels. I'm right here with you, Sylvia."

He tried to grab the arm of her wheelchair, but before his fingers could touch it, the little man was lifted off the balcony like a feather in a tornado. He lost track of Sylvia and couldn't hear her voice. He spun around in the ferocious whirlwind, calling out her name until he blacked out.

When Malchus regained consciousness, he was lying on the floor of the balcony gazing up at the sky. The patterns of stars he had viewed just minutes before were long gone and had traveled down below the horizon. Orion's belt was nowhere to be seen, only the red star Betelgeuse just over the skyline of Manhattan.

"Sylvia, are you all right?" Malchus cried out. "I can't see you. I guess I'm still in a daze; everything is spinning. Oh, my head. I think I'm going to throw up. Did aliens abduct us? What's that wonderful smell? Is that you, Sylvia?" He was completely bewildered.

"Malchus, I'm over here on the other side of the balcony. Just turn your head and you'll see me."

He turned and there she was, still sitting in her wheelchair holding a strange square object.

The two stared at the strange object on Sylvia's lap.

"What's that in your lap?" asked Malchus. "It smells great."

"I'm not sure what it is, but it's warm," said Sylvia.

Malchus touched it and shrieked. "Oh my, it's a knish! It's one of Naphtali Ropshitz's potato knishes."

Sylvia didn't have any idea what Malchus was talking about. He looked up into the heavens and clapped his hands.

"Sylvia, you were with Tali, my dear departed, yet very much alive, dead old friend. He must have taken you up to his starship and transported you to another dimension."

Sylvia was still very much confused. "I don't remember a thing."

"Sylvia, listen to your voice. Listen how clearly and easily you're speaking!" exclaimed Malchus. "And your hands, they aren't shaking! And you're not trembling or twitching! Sylvia, do you feel any sensation in your legs?"

"Malchus, I don't know what I feel right now. But it just feels warm and wonderful."

The scrawny little chicken girl was smiling broadly as Malchus quickly wheeled her down the hallway and into her room. She was humming and the expression on her face was one of ecstatic bewilderment.

"Malchus, I've changed," she said with a laugh in her voice. "I feel this strength and power that I haven't experienced in such a long time. It's like I've gone back at least ten years to when I could talk and walk without trembling or falling down. Malchus, what did you do to me?"

"Sylvia, I haven't done anything to you. I was up there being blown around by that beam of light and hit on the head by all those soft light bulbs."

Sylvia slowly stood and walked under her own power from the wheelchair to the bed, the holy knish still in her hand. She sat on the bed and burst out in hysterical laughter. She looked down at the knish and petted it like a kitten.

"Should I eat it, Malchus?"

The little man was speechless and merely shrugged his shoulders. He stared at Naphtali Ropshitz's wonderful gift.

"Yes! Let's both have a piece of the miracle knish."

The two of them finished the knish and sat there in utter joy and amazement until the break of dawn.

CHAPTER 16

✠ ✠ ✠

MALCHUS HAD A WAY WITH WOMEN; THEY found him irresistible. He was both child and man, tiny cuddly infant and old philosopher, raving lunatic and mystic poet. The more Malchus gave to women, the more they came back and begged for another helping. He just couldn't stop himself. He had this unlimited supply of gifts to satisfy the needs of hungry and lonely women. His giving nature was also his greatest source of satisfaction. He was simply a jug of water that continually poured out, but at the same time being filled by a higher source. Consequently, he was never empty and could always satisfy the needs of a thirsty person.

Unfortunately, his relationships never seemed to last very long and that distressed him. Just as he was getting to know somebody, they'd change and become something else or move on. Parting was always a sad time, but Malchus knew that person was going on to something far better. His friendships with Naphtali Ropshitz, Ron Peppler, and Benny Leiberman were perfect examples of this principle. Tali became an archangel and traveled the universe in a beam of light. Ron Peppler grew another hand and became a jazz pianist, and Benny Leiberman just died and went to heaven.

Scrawny little Sylvia, the chicken girl from Ten Eyck, became an eagle and flew away. She just walked out of the nursing center one day and joined The Little Happy Sisters of the Poor, a convent of nuns in

Flatbush. Although they were a cloistered order, Malchus would visit the convent and bring them his cookies.

Malchus wasn't a boastful man, but he was cocky. Women loved this trait, but men were more likely to ignore him and simply push him out of the way. His self-assured, know-it-all attitude was especially grating on Daniel.

One day shortly after Daniel came to work, Malchus barged into his office with a spate of complaints and his own plan for correcting the problems.

"Daniel, in conclusion, I just have one word for you. Keep your finger on the pulse. Keep your finger on the pulse."

"Malchus, that's six words," Daniel replied sarcastically.

"Okay, Dr. Aarons, executive consultant, let me put it to you bluntly and a little bit less delicately. You've got to have your fingers up the men's asses at all times. You've got to take their temperature. Do you get my drift?" He slammed his fist down on Daniel's desk.

The picture was clear, but revolting. Daniel got the message. "Malchus, are you saying that I am not keeping in close contact with the men and that I don't understand their psychic and emotional needs?"

"Bingo, bull's-eye, boss." Again, he slammed his fist down on the desk.

"What do you suggest I do? Tuck them into bed and tell them a good night story? For one thing, it's not my nature to get too close to these guys, and secondly, it's important that I maintain a professional distance, both for my sake and especially for the sake of the men. I can't be seen as a buddy or pal. Malchus, if they knew for one minute that they could get close to me, they'd take advantage of every situation. I'm not going to let that happen. The way I maintain control is through proper professional separation and state-of-the-art treatment programs. If I had my fingers up their rear ends, they'd consider me nothing more than their mommy. Just look at the way they treat Stephanie. I'm surprised she's not wiping their asses and blowing their noses. They call her pet names and she takes it like a dog. I wouldn't call her Mutt, but I've noticed that you have taken to calling her that stupid name, just like the rest of the guys."

Malchus paced around the room. He wasn't making any headway. Daniel was a stubborn, hardheaded scientist who thought he could manipulate people into rehabilitation.

"Daniel, you have no idea what you're saying. They don't call her Mutt because they think she's a dog; they call her Mut, M-U-T, because that's her personal name. She's the mother of the moon god; it's her identification. Only those people who become like little children can call her by her special name. When they open up to her, she can love them with all her heart. I know it sounds ridiculous, but that's the way she works. You won't find her in any of your psychology textbooks."

Daniel got up from his chair and rubbed his fingers through his hair. He lit his pipe and stared out the window at the little polluted English Kills.

"Do you think I could call her Mut?" Daniel asked.

"No!" Malchus was emphatic. "You have no right to call her Mut. Only *she* can tell you to call her by that name and only when she's good and ready. She'll let you know."

Daniel sighed and opened the iron door in his heart. "You know, she's a very special girl. I was immediately attracted to her the moment I saw her. You remember, the day I came for my interview. She was so disorganized and scattered. I thought she'd come apart at the seams right before my eyes, but the way she handled those men was really amazing. She has very strong powers of persuasion and an intensity of spirit that one finds only in older, mature women. It's as if she has experienced many past lives."

"She has, Daniel, she's a very old soul in a child's body," Malchus replied. "She's incredibly wise and sensitive. She just doesn't know how to fully utilize her power. She's blessed, Daniel. God has blessed her, and you are going to have to help her achieve her full potential."

He looked at Malchus with surprise. "Me? What can I do? I can't even touch her. I mean it would be improper to develop a relationship with her that was anything but professional. We have to work here together in the same office to accomplish the mission of the Service Corps, but there are times that I just want to kiss her and take her out of this hole and stare into her big dark eyes and hold her close." Daniel was dreaming. A soft smile appeared on his face. "But she's such an enigma, a terrified child and a wise old woman, a beautiful girl and a silly mixed-up school kid." He slapped the top of his head.

The two men stared out of the window and gazed upon the golden light of the setting sun that reflected off the English Kills. It shimmered and somehow transformed into a magic river that was no longer the fetid, polluted canal. Malchus seemed to float off into a purple haze. His eyes glazed over.

"Daniel, I once knew a girl just like Stephanie, many, many years ago when I was a wood-carver in France."

"Oh, no. Is this another one of your fantasies from the netherworld," Daniel asked.

"This was during the time of the Black Death, 1347, I think. I was sick as a dog, puking up everything I ate. My tongue got big, fat, and hairy. Pus covered my eyes. I had boils and scabs all over my body. This beautiful girl came to visit me. She was very distraught and afraid. She had been condemned as a witch and a demon and was running from church authorities. Oh, and she was Jewish, too, and they accused her of bringing the plague into the city. She asked me if she could stay and hide for the night. Of course, I couldn't refuse her. Why would I want to? Well, just to look at her was a sheer joy and an absolute pleasure. She had long golden hair and sad green eyes. For some strange reason, she touched me with her gentle soft hands and my sores began to heal. When I awoke the next morning, I was well. The fever left and I could eat again. But she was gone. She was like some wonderful dream, a beautiful mist that slipped under my door and then drifted out the window. The church authorities never found her, and I survived the plague to live another few years with the vision of that girl in my mind. Daniel, Stephanie is that girl! I know it. She's here to bring beauty into the world and to heal sick men. I think she's here to heal you, too."

Suddenly, Daniel began to feel a heavy weight in his body. He felt strange and ill as if he was carrying an entire sick civilization on his shoulders. He sat down and thought about his own deep dark bouts with depression. His angst sprouted from the ashtray on the desk and a rain cloud appeared over his head. All those terrible visual impressions of death camps came into his mind. He felt like cursing Malchus for bringing up his illness. What did the dwarf know of Auschwitz? Had he been there? Daniel looked at the little man with deep compassion.

Both men were essentially orphans. Neither had ever been blessed with a father or a mother. Sure, Daniel had his uncle Jacob, but he was denied his natural parents because of the sinister behavior of evil men. He covered his eyes.

"I'm sorry, Daniel. This discussion has gotten a little out of hand. You look like you need to be alone. I'll go now."

"Wait, Malchus, what's going to happen now?" Daniel asked.

"With who?" Malchus responded as if he had just walked in the room.

"With Stephanie and me."

"Oh, everything is going to be just fine," Malchus said. "I'm absolutely sure of it, but first I have to go upstairs and bake some cookies for Stephanie. She's invited me over to have dinner with her tomorrow at her apartment. She's going to teach me how to paint and then I'm going to tell her some exciting stories from beyond the galaxy. I hope we still have some of that wine left over from Jonah Vaark's performance. See ya."

Malchus' mind switched into reverse and he reverted to a little boy. He skipped out of Daniel's office singing a child's song in falsetto voice. He was already on another planet, and he completely forgot the preceding conversation. Daniel sat motionless in his chair and waited for the clock to strike five. He would spend another difficult weekend with his uncle Jacob, who was now quickly coming down from his manic state.

The next evening, Malchus dressed in his finest New York Yankees sweatshirt and put on his hat. He grabbed a basketful of his cookies, a bottle of cheap red wine, and was off to the subway. As was his habit, he went to the front of the first car in the train and pressed his nose against the window glass. The train started with a jolt and quickly passed into the darkness of the tunnel. He thought about beautiful colors and paints, the unique mixtures and textures that only Stephanie could create. The tunnel became a tube of paint and he became pure color squeezed out through the opening. He felt as if he were being born again. His body was spread over a canvas by Stephanie's fingers into the delicate figures of lovers and saints. He felt warm and loved. The train pulled into the Clinton-Washington station and he walked several blocks to Stephanie's place on Adelphi Street. The bottom floor of her tenement had been converted into a local community office. Students, teachers, and neighborhood activists were going in and out of the building at all times of the day and night. It became a meeting hall and an art studio for students who lived on the upper floors. Stephanie was alone now in her apartment, her roommate had left months ago. Now her roommates were just the cats and the mice.

The door to her apartment was painted a deep mauve with a burgundy rose in the middle. A sweet, highly erotic aroma, like an exotic perfume, filled his head. He grinned nervously like a teenager on his first date. He knocked and Stephanie opened the door. She looked sultry, like liquid fire, and Malchus' heart raced.

"Come into my parlor said the spider to the fly." She laughed and Malchus gladly walked into her web.

Stephanie was lovely. She wore a long, silk robe that tied with a thin belt. It was very Oriental with swirling colors and arabesque designs. She was barefoot, wore long heavy earrings, and looked like a Gypsy. Her dark brown eyes penetrated his soul and he became a small puddle of mush on the floor. She took off his floppy hat, flung it on a mattress, and kissed the top of his head.

"Take your shoes off," she demanded. Stephanie was already half drunk and Malchus was under her spell. She moved like a young cat and her scent was like sweet smoke. It wound its way through the deep recesses of his body and penetrated all of him. If she had gobbled him up that very moment, he would have been forever grateful.

There were no lights in the room, only the flickering of a dozen red candles. Malchus felt that he, too, was one of those candles with his head on fire.

They sat on the floor opposite each other, a small tablecloth spread out covered with a collection of weird and exotic-looking vegetables and fruits, brown bread, and tall glasses for wine.

"What's this thing?" Malchus asked. He picked up a bright red, fleshy fruit with a pinkish orange skin.

"This, my darling, Malchus, is a Samoan passion pod," she whispered in a sultry voice. "Just one bite of it and you will be able to make wild crazy love for three days straight without need for sleep or food. Only the kings on certain south Pacific islands are allowed to eat it. Did you know that in one year, King Kamuamua of Tannatua sired over five hundred children?"

Malchus squeezed and petted the fruit with delight.

"Wow, his wife must have been exhausted," Malchus replied. "Does this one have a name? It's a rather wicked-looking fruit." Malchus pointed to a long squash-like vegetable with a strange smooth purple skin and yellow circles on each end. It resembled a snake.

"That is the heavenly *Taznovsoy*," said Stephanie as she lasciviously fondled the fruit. "It grows only in the Transylvanian mountains on the border between Romania and Hungary and only during the month of April. My grandmother gave me the seeds on my thirteenth birthday, and she showed me how to plant them in special pots. It is said that it is a favorite of vampires and lonely, loveless women like me. Its flower lasts for only one day and then it withers. If the speckled turtle moth does not fertilize the plant during that day, the entire plant dries up and dies within minutes. It's very sad and tragic. An ancient ceremony is said to enhance the growing of the fruit and to increase its fertility. Young men and women take off their clothes, and in pairs, eat the fruit—the man at one end, the woman at the other. When they get to the middle … well, you know what happens." She laughed.

Malchus' heart beat wildly. He knew that Stephanie was only teasing him, but he encouraged her vivid imagination and wildly inventive stories.

"Give me your glass," she said. "I want to fill it with this incredible warm nectar from *Noozykoozy*. It will absolutely light up your head." Malchus' head was already so light he could float up to the ceiling.

"Is that nectar also a gift from your Hungarian grandmother?"

"No, silly." She touched his face with the end of her finger. "I got it from an extremely handsome alien when his ship crash-landed on the roof of my tenement. I'm the only one who heard the craft land, and I ran up to the roof to see what happened. He stood there, his space suit in shreds, his arms bleeding a deep purple blood. I brought him to my apartment and bandaged his wounds. He was so light and delicate, but so very beautiful. His voice was like a soft song, and he spoke to me in the poetry of his home planet, but I understood every word he said. He fell asleep in my arms and was with me the entire night. When I awoke, he was gone and so too was his space ship. All he left me was this wonderful bottle of nectar from his home and some wonderful memories. When I drink it, it reminds me of his gentle touch and his poetry. Sometimes I miss him so much. He said that he was searching for his family. They had been taken by an evil race of carnivores, and he didn't know whether they were still alive. He'd been searching the galaxy for hundreds of our earth years. I cried for many days after he left. I even did a painting of him. Do you want to see it?"

"Yes, of course," Malchus replied. "What was his name by the way?"

"Oh, it wasn't just a single name. It was more like a line of poetry, a string of audio pearls, a puff of soap bubbles. I just called him *Muananananaoobuabooba* for short."

Malchus was excited. He, too, had had similar experiences with aliens.

"Did you and, uh, Mani … booba make love?"

Stephanie looked at him with surprise.

"Malchus, of course not. He was a married man and I a virgin. That is, of course, until I see the face of my husband in a vision on Saint Agnes's Eve. We slept together, but he never touched me in a sexual way. He was the perfect extraterrestrial gentleman, even if he was an alien from another planet."

Stephanie rummaged through a pile of canvases looking for the painting. "Where are you, Manibooboo? Ah, here you are."

She brought the twisted, trapezoidal canvas to Malchus and held it before a line of candles. The red paint glistened. The blues and greens swirled around a strangely familiar face.

"Mut," Malchus said, "Manibooboo sort of resembles a nice fellow we both know. Don't you think?"

"Well, yes. There is a resemblance between him and the great Dr. Aarons, but Mani is so much softer and he speaks in poetry. Daniel wouldn't know a poem if it hit him between the eyes. He's all theory and calculations. I wish he'd just let up a little and stop being so damned efficient."

Malchus came to Daniel's defense. "He is doing a good job, you know. He tries so hard and he really does have the welfare of the men as his first consideration. Well, maybe he's not the most sensitive person, but he's learning. I talked with him today about changing his management style." Malchus picked up another vegetable. "Hey, why are we talking about Daniel Aarons? You invited me over to eat, drink, be merry, and to teach me how to paint!"

The two friends sat on the floor and finished consuming the funny fruits and voluptuous vegetables. The wine, or nectar, flowed freely and both could hardly stand, let alone hold a paintbrush.

Stephanie was drunk. "Malchus, I can't show you how to paint."

"Why not, Mut? Have you had too much to drink?"

"No, Malchus, I can't show you how to paint because I don't have anymore canvases. Where am I going to put the paint?"

Malchus thought for a moment. "Mut, I have the absolute perfect solution to your problem." He pulled off his sweatshirt and presented to Stephanie two smooth white surfaces—a front and a back. She was surprised but quite pleased.

"You want me to paint *you*?" Stephanie asked in surprise.

Malchus just smiled.

The concept was unique, and she examined her new primed soft white canvases.

"Malchus, you only have one nipple!" she exclaimed.

The little man looked down at his chest as if his manhood had been stolen.

"Do you want to hear the long sad story?" he asked.

"Please, keep it short. I just want to paint."

"You know, when I was just a baby, they had to do some serious surgery on my heart, you know, repair valves, and give me some new plumbing. I guess when they closed me up they forgot about the nipple. It was just too small and insignificant a body part, especially for a boy. I guess they figured I'd really never need it anyway."

Stephanie laughed and looked at Malchus with her sad brown eyes. She reached out and caressed his chest, searching for the missing nipple.

"Malchus, my little darling, tonight you shall have two nipples."

The beautiful drunken Gypsy artist threw off her exotic robe, exposing a long paint-stained T-shirt. It came down to her knees. She wore nothing else. Her long legs made Malchus dizzy, and he waited to be touched by her brush and covered by her paint. Beneath the light of the flickering candles, she mixed the paint on her arms with her fingers.

She moaned and sighed as if some invisible man was caressing her body. She took a dab of raw sienna, mixed it with a hint of cerise and mauve, and applied it lovingly to his bare chest. Within a moment, the dwarf had two nipples. She had completed the surgery botched so many years before. She turned him around, massaged her canvas, and warmed it with her fingers. She applied a fine linseed oil and began to paint his back. Her tender brush strokes tickled his white flesh and she applied delicate, almost transparent, layers of paint. She sighed, hummed, and fondled his single ear. A tiny, fine brush and black paint were used to create intricate patterns, and her creation was beginning to take on the look of a superbly crafted tattoo. After nearly four hours of painstaking work, Stephanie completed her masterpiece on the back of her friend. Malchus was overjoyed and in ecstasy. He tingled with delight.

"Don't move. Just lie there on your stomach for at least another three hours. The paint has to dry," she insisted.

"Can't I look at it?" Malchus was impatient. He expected to see the Mona Lisa permanently emblazoned on his body. The candles had long since burned down and Stephanie began to turn on various lights in the apartment.

"Here, look at yourself," she said. "You're absolutely gorgeous." She stood up and held a mirror so that Malchus could look at her canvas.

"I can't believe it. It's fantastic. My God, I am beautiful," he shouted.

His entire back was covered with flowing wings and bodies of angels, clouds, and beams of light. He could have been the Sistine Chapel. There was the stairway to heaven, twelve cherubim, and the faces of Michael and Gabriel, the archangels. He thought their faces looked familiar as if he had met them on the subway.

As the sun rose, the two were exhausted, but elated. Stephanie was still drunk, and she took off her T-shirt and danced naked before his eyes. For an instant, Malchus glanced at her body before she walked into the bathroom to bathe.

This was truly a special and holy night. Malchus, in a crazed, drunken frenzy, threw open the window and yelled to the crowd below, "Look at me! I am a work of art and I have two nipples!"

Stephanie emerged from the bathroom wearing a fresh clean T-shirt, her face dripping with water.

Malchus grabbed her, pulled her to the floor, and passionately kissed her on the lips, thanking her for what she had done to him. She held him close and sobbed.

"Stephanie, my darling, you have made me beautiful. How can I ever thank you for this wonderful gift?"

"Malchus," Stephanie responded with tears in her eyes, "You were always beautiful. You didn't need any artwork. I just helped out a little."

Malchus was raving and prancing around the apartment like a child. "I love you, I love you, I love everybody! The world is beautiful. Thank you, God for creating me. Thank you, God for Stephanie."

She was afraid that the little man was going to explode in his wild frenzy.

"I must go my darling, Stephanie, but I'll be back soon." He ran shirtless out of the apartment on to the street yelling at the top of his lungs, "Look at me, I'm a work of art, and I have two nipples!" He entered the subway entrance. Stephanie could still hear him yelling as he ran to catch his train.

CHAPTER 17

✠ ✠ ✠

DANIEL SLAMMED THE PHONE RECEIVER INTO THE cradle and cursed the party on the other end.

"That nasty, irritating son of a bitch," he mumbled to himself. "He's going to make my life miserable. No, my life is already miserable and he's just going to make it worse. I don't need to take his shit! Just who the hell does he think he is?"

That *who* on the other end of the line was none other than Manasseh Cain, chief controller and bean counter for the Service Corps. His call, all the way from national headquarters, informed Daniel that the brass from Biloxi would be making a quickie inspection of the facility sometime early next week. No specific date or time was given, but he needed to be ready at a moment's notice. Daniel felt pressured and squeezed by a bunch of do-nothing social bureaucrats and pseudo-military types who looked and sounded important, but didn't know their asses from their elbows. He'd speak with his supervisor and get to the bottom of this. He picked up the phone and called Colonel Claude Boyer, executive regional officer for the service corps. A slow, nasally voice answered.

"Hello, this is the Service Corps and may God bless you. How may I direct your call?"

"Yes, this is Dr. Daniel Aarons, executive consultant at the Brooklyn Brewery. May I please speak with Colonel Boyer?"

The nasally voice responded, "I'm sorry, sir, Colonel Boyer is not in."

"Do you expect him in shortly?" Daniel asked with impatience.

"No, sir."

"Do you know when he will be in?"

"No, sir. But I don't expect him to be in for a long time," said the nasally voice.

Daniel was uneasy with the automatic robotic response of the girl on the other end.

"Is there anybody at headquarters who could tell me when Colonel Boyer will be in his office?"

"Yes, sir, I will connect you to him immediately."

The phone rang twice and a familiar voice answered.

"Yea, this is Manasseh Cain, can I help you?"

Daniel was furious. The last person he wanted to speak with was Cain.

"Mr. Cain, this is Dr. Aarons. I was trying to get Colonel Boyer, but they apparently transferred me to your office. Can you get me to Boyer?"

"Sorry, Aarons, that is impossible," Cain said as if he were talking to a stranger.

"What do you mean? Is there a problem about my speaking to my direct supervisor at national headquarters?"

"Aarons, you *are* speaking to your direct supervisor."

Daniel huffed into the receiver. "Cain, what the hell are you talking about? I report to Boyer."

"Boyer doesn't work here anymore. He's gone, finished, and now I'm in charge."

Daniel smacked the top of his desk.

"What the hell happened?" Daniel demanded. He couldn't believe the words of this scoundrel. "He hired me to run this facility and to make the needed changes. Nobody informed me that Claude quit."

"He didn't quit, Aarons," Cain said. "He was *eased* out."

"Well, where is he? I need to speak to him. It's urgent."

"I think you'll find him living nicely on his daddy's hog farm in North Carolina. He's got a fine job sizing cucumbers for a big pickle company near Goldsboro. But I don't think he'll be of any help to you now. Poor Claude just sort of freaked out and went berserk. After a particularly stressful meeting with General Thurman, Claude simply pulled down his pants and pissed all over the great man's desk. Then, he took a dump on the floor and threw it in the general's face. We had to fumigate the whole office. We didn't press charges, poor fellow. We just put him up in one of our mental facilities for a few weeks and then sent him home to his daddy. Aarons, we didn't need him here in Biloxi, you see. We have high moral standards and this incident could have caused us a lot of embarrassment. Don't worry about Claude; we'll take care of him."

Daniel stared out into space. He felt his blood pressure soar. His hand choked the phone receiver as if it was Cain's neck.

"You'll take care of him, all right," Daniel retorted in anger. "You'll probably give him a lobotomy and rip out his vocal cords so he can't say anything to the press about those kickbacks and mismanagement at the national headquarters."

Cain was smooth and the pitch of his voice had not changed.

"Daniel, I don't recommend that you mention this situation to your men. There is some sensitivity that we have to deal with and it would be better if I tell them myself when I'm visiting for my inspection. And please, for God's sake, don't tell that loony string bean secretary, Crux."

"That's Croix," Daniel responded. "What's the problem with telling her about Boyer?"

"Well, I heard that she and Boyer were an item. You know, balling on the rag bales, humping on the hassocks, tricks in the trucks."

Daniel's skull was about to explode. He didn't believe a word that came out of this scumbag. Stephanie was not that kind of girl and he knew it in his heart. Cain was just testing his loyalties by creating rumors and vicious lies. Perhaps Boyer had not committed those supposed atrocities after all, but actually quit the corps in frustration and disgust. Daniel Aarons would find the truth.

"Cain?" demanded Daniel.

"Call me Manny, all my employees do."

"I don't believe a word you said about Boyer or Stephanie Croix. They're fine people and you're slandering their good names. I won't allow you to do that to them, and I expect an apology to Miss Croix when you come. Have I made myself clear?" Daniel was hot.

"Hey, Danny, you sound mighty pissed off. She's never heard a word out of my mouth. Does that mean that you're screwing her, too? I've heard that every son of a bitch in that place has given her a piece of his manhood. I just want to let you know, my fine Dr. Aarons, that *I* am now running this entire show from the Atlantic to the Pacific, from the Canadian border to the Gulf of Mexico, from my office in beautiful downtown Biloxi, Mississippi. General Malcolm Isaiah Thurman is only here in body with his bottle of Southern Comfort. His mind left years ago. I'm not going to let this noble organization turn into a shit hole. There's a lot of money to be made in this business, as you know. I got big government contracts with the feds and every one of them could go on for years. *Comprende*, Doc?"

Daniel dropped the receiver as if he was holding on to a dead rat. He clenched his teeth and was about to spit blood.

"Danny, you still there on the phone?" Cain asked.

Daniel picked up the receiver and cursed under his breath.

"My friend," continued Cain, "you could make some good money on this deal, if you're smart, and I know you're damn smart. But if you give me trouble, if you even fart in the wrong direction, I'm going to pull the plug on that crap house you run and send you and sixty drunks out on the street. I can make life very difficult for you. I can even make homeless men and loony-tune secretaries disappear. Or, and I believe you will prefer this option; I can make Daniel Aarons, PhD, a wealthy man. I'll give you a break, my friend, Daniel. I'll be at your office next Wednesday at ten AM. I want to meet with you and your key staff. No bullshit and no problems. See you then. Oh, by the way, I do not intend to eat in your dining hall. The last time I was there, I almost died of food poisoning, so don't think of giving me another case of ptomaine. Bye, Danny."

For the second time that morning, Daniel Aarons slammed down the phone receiver. But this time, the machine broke into little pieces. He picked up what remained of the unit and hurled it against the wall, smashing it into smithereens. He ranted, raved, and cursed the damn Service Corps and all the filthy bastards who now ran the place.

"That damn son of a bitch! That bastard!" shouted Daniel. "That lying, stinking pile of rancid rat shit! I'm going to kill him when he gets here. I'm going to put my fingers around his throat, choke him, and then tear his guts out with my bare hands. I'm going to kick him in the balls and then shove his head up his ass!" There was no one in the room to hear his tirade except for the roaches and a single mouse hiding in a corner.

Daniel cleared all the papers from his desk with a single swoop of his arm and then he threw his books and an ashtray at the wall. He broke a window with a paperweight and even dumped out all his good pipe tobacco. He was pissed off and everybody in the Brewery was going to know about it.

Stephanie ran into Daniel's office. The place was a disaster. Broken glass and paper everywhere. Daniel sat hunched in his chair; his eyes stared out into space.

Stephanie trembled. "What's going on here? Daniel, what happened? You look like you just sat on a bomb."

He looked up at the girl. He couldn't believe the filthy things that he heard from the mouth of Manasseh Cain, but he wasn't going to interrogate Stephanie, at least not at this moment.

"Surprise, surprise, surprise." Daniel's sarcasm was at its peak. "Cain from Biloxi is coming on Wednesday." He literally spit out the words.

"Oh, is that why you're so mad?" she asked, her question soft and timid.

"Is that why I'm so mad?" He repeated the question. "Is that why I'm so mad? Yes, that's why I'm so mad! That bastard is now the grand high pooh-bah of the Service Corps. Did you know that Boyer was now sizing cucumbers in a pickle plant and living on his daddy's hog farm in North Carolina? Did you know that the great and noble General Malcolm Isaiah Thurman is an addle-brained, senile old drunk? Did you know that he thinks you and Boyer …?"

He stopped himself before the foul words came out. "Stephanie, this man is an evil menace. His motives are sinister, and he will take one hundred years of honest, benevolent work and turn it into dust!"

At that very moment, Malchus knocked at Daniel's door. He was holding a broom and dustpan.

"Hey, did we have some minor war or a little tornado in here?" Malchus asked. "I brought my broom. Do you want me to start sweeping up all the shit?"

Daniel kicked the trashcan.

"Yea sure, go ahead and clean up."

Malchus began to sweep the floor and pick up the broken pieces of the phone while listening to Daniel and Stephanie discuss the arrival of Manasseh Cain. He broke into their conversation.

"Excuse me," Malchus said, "but I couldn't help but overhear your discussion about this incredibly vile character from national. Daniel, let me ask you a question. Do you know how big the devil is?"

Daniel couldn't be bothered with Malchus' nonsense, he was too angry.

"Malchus, what the hell does the devil have to do with Manasseh Cain?"

"Absolutely everything," the dwarf replied sincerely. "Perhaps you are making Cain out to be a greater threat than he actually is. The simple point of my question is that the devil can be as big or as small as you want him to be. If he is perceived to be small potatoes, then he can be easily mashed, fried, boiled, or even made into chips. Daniel, we create such big demons that we lose all perspective of their ability to do us harm. Usually by that time, it's too late and they've already done their dirty work, wars, pestilence, disease, crime, you know the rest. We have personified them, glorified them, and given them life. If we kill them early and nip them in the bud when they're teeny tiny little spuds, we can live in a world of peace. It's that simple. I've killed numerous demons … and made a lot of chips. The problem is that they just keep coming back, like weeds or roaches." He stomped on the floor. "Daniel, I can absolutely assure you that Manasseh Cain will leave here in peace. There will be no conflict and the Brewery will continue to flourish under your glorious and gifted leadership." He went back to sweeping up the mess on the floor.

"Well, Malchus, I'm glad you've got things so well organized," said Daniel. "As far as I'm concerned, everything seems to be coming apart at the seams."

Malchus dropped his broom and walked over to Daniel's side.

"Relax, Daniel, why don't you and Stephanie go out for a walk. Cool down. Go have yourselves an ice cream cone. You'll feel much better. I'll clean up your office, and when you get back, everything will be picked up and you'll both get back to work as if nothing ever happened. I'll take care of your demons."

Stephanie sighed. "Malchus, you're such a sweetheart. You just want people to be happy." She looked at her boss with a smile. "Come on, Daniel, let's do as the doctor says and get ourselves a good stiff ice cream."

Daniel took a deep breath and rubbed his fingers through his hair. "Thanks for cleaning up. I'm sorry it's such a mess."

"Don't mention it, boss. Believe me; I've cleaned up much bigger messes."

The two left the office and Malchus continued to sweep the floor. He talked to himself and to his guardian angels.

"Guys, this is a big one. I feel a lot of evil is coming to Brooklyn. I can feel it in my bones. I don't know if I can handle it all by myself. Let's see, I'll need about a gallon of holy water and at least ten dozen cookies."

The little man cleaned until the office was spotless. Daniel's tobacco was back in the humidor and the papers were back on the desk. Only the broken window gave a clue as to the chaos that had invaded Daniel Aarons' mind. A new phone was brought in from the warehouse and the lines of communication were restored. Daniel and Stephanie returned from the ice cream parlor looking like beaming teenagers on their first date. Malchus waited in the front office with broom in hand. His plan was beginning to work. There would be peace.

Manasseh Cain flew in from Biloxi as planned and arrived at the Brewery on Wednesday at precisely ten o'clock in the morning. He was not alone. Along with the new chief was his small entourage of three gray, mousy bean counters. Each man was a pitiful, faceless gnome with green complexion and bony fingers. They tapped endlessly on their calculators and sharpened pencils by sticking them in their ears.

Cain was aptly named; he looked evil. His small wiry body, sharp pointed nose, and buckteeth provided the perfect caricature. A large, hairy, purple mole grew on his forehead. His claw-like fingers were always moving and pointing. It was as if he scratched at dirt looking for insects to eat. He wore a ragged, threadbare gray suit and a thin black tie. No doorman's uniform for Cain. He smoked incessantly and his body reeked of stale tobacco. He was vulgar, slimy, and the epitome of bad taste. He sent cold chills down Stephanie's spine. She avoided his leering stare and kept her distance. Daniel greeted his new boss and assistants with the perfunctory handshakes, but felt defiled by touching the man and he wanted to wash. He invited them into the administrative offices.

"Gentlemen, why don't we go into the conference room? My crack staff will be waiting for us."

Cain and the three vermin followed Daniel into the large room. Seated at the long table were Chuck Conklin, Salvatore Cantucci, Lemmy Alone, Herby Croix, and John B. Waters. Each man had a long scowling face that expressed loathing and disgust. Stephanie sat at the corner seat of the table and Cain made a beeline to the seat next to hers. Her revulsion was obvious, but Cain would not let it deter his advances. She tried to take notes.

This was Cain's meeting and he took control. Daniel sat at the other end of the table, his arms folded tightly across his chest.

"Men, for those of you who don't know me, I'm Manasseh Cain, formerly chief controller for the Service Corps. As of last week, however, I became the chief operating officer, COO for short. General Thurman is still President and CEO, as well as Chairman of the Board, and, of course, he is still in full control, but the day-to-day responsibilities for operating the corps and its facilities are now in these hands." He held out his bluish, skeletal, claw-like appendages to the men sitting at the table. Stephanie looked away and shivered.

"Colonel Claude Boyer is no longer with us. He is gone, out, eliminated, terminated, *finito!*"

Cain's voice became more emphatic and shrill.

"Claude Boyer never existed, and it would be better if you erased him from your memory. Don't even think of finding him or calling him. He cannot help you now. The poor man had a nervous breakdown and his mind is completely gone. It's as if a hole had been drilled in his forehead and his brain had been sucked out. He can't even recognize his own face. But rest assured poor Claude is being taken care of and he enjoys the pickle business."

The fear and disgust that was first apparent at the table now included a quaking terror. The pupils of the eyes of Daniel's men grew wide and their mouths hung open. Cain's three mice sat expressionless. Stephanie took out a handkerchief and dabbed her eyes. That was exactly what Cain had expected to see from the girl. Yes, he thought, there was a romantic relationship between Croix and Boyer and he, Manasseh Cain, would take up where Claude Boyer had left off.

Daniel sat virtually motionless, his eyes and face taut as a stretched wire, his teeth clenched, his arms and hands ready to grab the throat of the Nazi bastard sitting at the opposite end of the table. Suddenly it was clear; Manasseh Cain had become the reincarnation of Adolf Hitler. All Cain needed was the moustache. The voice took on a staccato tone and the pronouncements became orders coming from the mouth of *der Führer* himself. Was Daniel making this petty demon into a full-blown devil? Was Satan incarnate really sitting at the table with him? Daniel looked under the table just to check and see if Cain had cloven hooves. Daniel got a grip on himself and mentally slapped himself in the face. Cain reverted to the small vile little man from Biloxi.

Cain gave his commands. "Aarons, I want to take a full walking tour of the building this morning. My men will be going over the books. They can use the conference table. Please have your assistant bring in the ledgers and the journals."

Daniel called in Moe Kutcher. "Moe, this is Mr. Cain. His men will be doing a partial audit. Will you please bring in this year's books?"

Poor Moe Kutcher was already terrified and he scratched until his pants began to smoke. Cain looked at him in disgust.

"Man, have you got crabs?" Cain asked Moe in disgust. "You know the best thing for that condition is gas. We used to gas our livestock to get rid of the bugs. Stopped their itching and scratching for weeks."

The picture of Cain as a Nazi exterminator came racing back into Daniel's mind. Kutcher, panic on his face, ran out of the room to fetch the books.

"Aarons, I'd like you to stay in the conference room and help my staff go over the books while I take the guided tour. Miss Croix can be my personal guide." He gave her a sly wink. "I'm sure she knows every little nook and cranny in this big place, don't you Miss Croix?"

Stephanie was repulsed by the thought of being alone with Cain. The last thing she wanted to do was to go anywhere with this beast. She tried to get out of the assignment.

"Oh, but Mr. Cain, I have so much paperwork to do, and I've got a week's worth of invoices to deal with and phone calls to make ..."

Cain would not let her out of her assigned duty. "All that business can wait. Your assistance to me is vital at this time."

Stephanie looked at Daniel. Her eyes asked for help, but none was available.

The two walked down the hallway that led to the warehouse and the huge cotton baling machines. Soon, the sound of tiny little feet, like that of a house pet, was heard coming from behind Cain and Stephanie. Cain turned around to see Malchus shuffling behind him like a little scruffy puppy. Malchus didn't speak a word. His facial expressions, however, spoke volumes of coded messages to Stephanie.

Cain was startled and jumped back, "What the ... who the hell is that?"

Stephanie played the game. "Oh, that's just little Malchus. He's just one of our more severely disabled clients. He only has one ear as you can see, and he's kind of dumb."

She looked at Malchus and he gave her a wink. "Actually, I think he's completely deaf. He doesn't ever talk and I believe he's quite mentally disabled. He's a friendly little man, however."

Stephanie patted him on the head like a good little dog. Malchus stuck his tongue out and panted.

"He likes to follow the men as they go about their work in the warehouse," she said. "He's harmless. Come on, Malchus; let's go with the nice Mr. Cain to see the warehouse and all the secret parts of the building."

Malchus, a silly stupid grin on his face, followed the two into the big open spaces of the warehouse. The vile lecher tried to stay as close to Stephanie as possible.

The warehouse was a huge, open, cavernous building outfitted with several powerful baling machines to compress clothing, rags, and newspapers. Each bale weighed nearly a thousand pounds and lifted into place by a forklift. Ellis McCoy, a wizened navy mechanic, had worked the baling machines for nearly twenty years. He named the machines after his dead wives. Margo was a newspaper baler and Blanche was used for old clothing and rags. Ellis oiled Blanche's *big screw* and cleaned the bushings in her motor. Her pit was empty, but he would have her filled up and tight in a matter of hours. Cain tried to strike up a conversation.

"That's a mighty powerful baler you got there."

"Yea," said McCoy as he spat a wad of tobacco on the floor. He wasn't in the mood to talk to anybody.

"Do you get two cents a pound for the rags?" Cain asked.

"I dunno," McCoy said.

"Mind if I give her a try?" Cain wanted to put on a show for Stephanie.

"You know what you're doin'?" asked McCoy, who then spat on the floor again.

"Sure, I used to manage an industrial site for the Service Corps in Toledo, Ohio. I had ten balers. We'd send out at least three semitrailers of baled rags every week. I'm an expert in this business, made the corps millions on exports to Hong Kong."

Cain attempted to impress Stephanie with his knowledge of the rag business and the operations of a baling machine. He threw a pile of rags into the baler pit and started the motor. The metal plate moved and compressed the small load. That same operation done numerous times would create a massive, wire-bound cubic bale. Stephanie wasn't impressed. She had seen it done a hundred times before and with greater finesse. Ellis McCoy wasn't impressed either. He blew his nose and spit tobacco juice into the pit. Cain wasn't making any points with anybody. That didn't really matter as he was now in full command.

He pointed to a doorway that led to a small storage room.

"What's in there, Miss Croix? It looks like a cozy little room."

Stephanie didn't like the tone of his voice.

"Oh, just some old rotten mattresses and bedding," she said. "We have to spray them down, you know, before we can tag and sell them. It's the law."

"Yea, I know the dam law," he said angrily. "Let's go and see it."

The two walked into the mattress spraying room with Malchus following closely behind in puppy-like fashion. No sooner had Cain and Stephanie entered the room than he grabbed her around the waist and threw her down on a mattress. He slobbered on her and tried to kiss her.

"Come on babe, make me feel good. Let's suck face," Cain demanded. He tried to pull her pants off. "I can make you very rich and happy," he said as he continued to slobber on her. She pushed him away and kicked him as hard as she could in his groin.

Cain barked and let out a mammoth wolf-like groan. He growled and grabbed his crotch.

Stephanie spit in his face. "You filthy, disgusting pig." She slapped him and ran out of the room.

Malchus grabbed Cain's leg, bit as hard as he could, and then kicked him in the behind. As he tried to grab Malchus, Cain's smashed his head into a metal bucket that hung on the wall of the mattress spraying room.

"You little deformed bastard! I'll tear your fucking guts out!" shouted Cain.

Stephanie ran past the baler and out of the warehouse, followed by Malchus. Cain came out cursing, yelling, and still holding his sore crotch. "You bitch!" Cain yelled. "You've screwed every bastard in this damn place. I'm not going to let you off so easy. I'll kill you!"

Ellis McCoy turned around and heard Cain's ugly threats and shouts, but he just kept on working and filling the baler pit. Stephanie and Malchus ran back to Daniel's office. Daniel and the three mice were busy at the conference table poring over ledgers and spreadsheets.

"That filthy pig, Cain, tried to rape me!" Stephanie cried. She adjusted her blouse and pants. Daniel looked up at the frightened girl. Her words were like a knife. Daniel had blood in his eyes and clenched his fists. Even the three mice rose from the table and came to her rescue. One even brought her a glass of water.

Malchus corroborated her story, but Daniel didn't have time to listen to the details. He dropped everything and ran into the warehouse looking for Cain.

"Cain, you son of a bitch, where are you?" Daniel yelled.

Daniel saw Ellis McCoy at the baler throwing heaps of rags into the pit. His first load was about ready for compression.

"Ellis, did you see Cain?" asked Daniel.

"Yea, I seen him, and I seen what he did to Mut, that son of a bitch. If I get my hands on him, he's dead meat, that son of a bitch."

"Is he still in the building?" Daniel asked. "Do you know where he went?"

"The last time I seen him he was yellin' at Mut from the mattress room. Son of a bitch was holdin' his balls and screaming. Looks like she kicked him real hard. Hope his pecker fell off. He deserved it. Son of a bitch. I'd slit his throat."

Daniel searched the warehouse, the loading dock, and the various workshops looking for Cain. No trace of the greasy slimeball could be found. He went back to the conference room cursing under his breath.

"I couldn't find the dirtbag; looked all over," Daniel said. "When I get my hands on him, I'll wring his neck like a chicken and send him back to Biloxi in a box." Daniel's face turned beet red. He pounded his hand with a fist.

The mice were huddled around Stephanie, still trying to help her regain her composure. She was crying. One of the mice was on the phone with headquarters complaining to a supervisor about Cain's inexcusable behavior. One was taking copious notes as Stephanie gave her story. The other held a glass of water and lovingly looked into her eyes. The one on the phone hung up and apologized.

"Dr. Aarons, Miss Croix, I am so sorry for this totally unforgivable incident," said the mouse. "This is not the first time this type of thing has happened. We've been traveling throughout the northeast region for the past three weeks. At every facility we audit, Cain finds a secretary, a store worker, a client and then tries to molest her. It's disgusting and we're not going to be a part of it any longer."

The other two mice shook their heads in agreement. One made a feeble attempt at making a fist and hitting the table.

"We're going to take care of him and rid this demon from our midst," the mouse said. "I've taken care of the official calls and Ralph, here, has taken Miss Croix's statement. We'll find Cain and deal with him in an appropriate way. He's not going to stain the reputation of the Service Corps."

The mouse completed his remarks. The three mice suddenly become handsome princes with names and gentle, caring faces.

Malchus was still trying to catch his breath. The little man was furious and stomped around the room. "When I catch that bastard, I'm going to tear him to shreds and rip out his knee caps. Nobody is going to treat my Mut like that."

The five angry men and one harassed woman squawked and stammered in their fits of rage. Hands were wringing and fists were pounding walls. Cigarette smoke bathed the room in a foul gray cloud. Eventually, the room grew quiet and there was some semblance of peace.

Cain did not return nor could anyone find him.

That evening, the three mice, Ralph, Bernard, and Irving, decided they would go to the dining hall and have some dinner. Later, they'd go into Manhattan for a few hours and then come back to the Brewery and stay in the guest rooms prepared for them. Daniel also decided to stay at the Brewery that night.

The next morning, everything appeared normal. The men went to the loading docks, trucks began to move, and rags and paper were brought into the warehouse. Ellis McCoy had completed the bale he started the day before and was mechanically lifting it out of the pit. Hank Riley, the forklift driver, got his machine in place to lift the bale when he noticed something strange.

"Hey, Ellis, you dumb asshole. What the hell is this?"

The bale was lowered and the two men stared at the vaguely human appendages barely protruding from the tightly compressed bale of rags. It appeared to be the ends of five claw-like fingers, which could only belong to a vile animal like Manasseh Cain.

Both men were scared and spat tobacco juice on the cement floor.

"Shit!" Riley said as he stood on the warehouse floor shaking. "We better call Dr. Aarons right away."

McCoy looked at the blue fingers and talked to himself. "Son of a bitch, bastard. Now the cops are going to blame it on me. Son of a bitch. Hope his pecker fell off."

Daniel, sleepy, mean, and exhausted from the previous day's events, came into the warehouse prepared for the worst. The three men stood before the large bale like veterans before the tomb of the Unknown Soldier. Daniel took a pen out of his pocket and gingerly uncurled the bluish fingers of the hand surrounded by tightly compressed shreds of men's underwear and socks. The fingers still flexed and rigor mortis had not yet set in.

"It's Cain all right," Daniel said. "I'd know that rat's claws anywhere. His body's still warm. This must have happened just a couple of hours ago."

He looked at the two scared men who were contemplating the terrible event unfurling before their very eyes. They looked at each other, looked at Daniel, and then said one word, "murder."

"You know, I've got to call the cops," Daniel said to the two men.

"I didn't do it, Dr. Aarons, I didn't do it! I swear," McCoy replied in fear. He was now dribbling tobacco juice on his shirt. "I was upstairs all night. Waters can vouch for me. I was puking last night after dinner and went to bed. Something made me real sick. Go ask Herby Croix. I almost cracked him on the head because of the bad shit he served last night. No, no, you ain't gonna' pin no murder on me."

"Ellis, nobody said it was murder and nobody is blaming you," said Daniel reassuringly. "I realize it looks circumstantial, but there are scientific ways to show whether it was murder or not."

Daniel thought to himself, however, that it sure did look like murder and Ellis would be a prime suspect.

Riley looked at the fingers. "Poor bastard," he said with a slight grin. He got back on his forklift and drove to the other end of the warehouse.

"Hey, Riley," Daniel called out, "be available to answer questions from the police. Don't go anywhere today. Understand?" Daniel looked at Ellis and took a deep breath.

"Ellis, you need to hang around, too, but don't touch anything. Forget the bales today and just go sit in the game room and wait until I call you. The police will probably have a lot of questions, but don't worry, I believe you. You have no motive for killing Cain."

McCoy was in a panic. "I saw what he did to Mut. I wanted to put my hands around his neck and—"

"Shut up, McCoy, I don't want to hear about it. Just keep your mouth shut and keep cool. This is going to be a long day."

Daniel went to his office and called the police. Within fifteen minutes, three officers, two detectives, and a technician arrived. They carried boxes filled with cameras, equipment, and rolls of yellow tape to rope off the alleged murder site. Within minutes of their arrival, the center was buzzing with the restless, nervous chatter of men smoking. The uniformed officers roped off the warehouse and the detectives began to make their lists. Slowly, like archaeologists uncovering a dig, the baling wire was cut and the compressed rags were delicately removed from around the body of Manasseh Cain. The body was fully clothed and intact, except for a pair of socks that was either inserted into the mouth by the killer or pushed in by the force of the compression of the baler. The body was lying face up on the rags, a crushed cigarette in the mouth. The eyes were wide open and staring up into the warehouse rafters. Cain's other hand appeared to be clutching his chest.

The police technician photographed the body from various angles and one of the detectives dusted for fingerprints. The body was superficially explored for bullet holes and knife wounds, but none found. It was the standard perfunctory police examination. The real work, however, would be done in the laboratories and in the coroner's office.

Cain was put in a body bag and taken away. Interviews were conducted throughout the day. By 5:00 PM, everybody who needed to be interviewed met with the detectives and gave their stories. No charges were pressed and there were no arrests, pending further investigation.

Daniel, Malchus, and Stephanie sat on the sofa in the waiting room, dazed and exhausted after a day of police interrogation. The three mice, Ralph, Irving, and Bernard, nervously twitched and coughed at the conference room table. Irving had a nosebleed and held his head back with a handkerchief to his nose attempting to stem a flow of blood.

Each person in the administrative offices loathed Manasseh Cain and each had a perfectly good reason for wanting to see the insect squashed dead, or at least, retired to the dark side of the moon.

During the next few days, the three mice remained in Brooklyn awaiting the coroner's inquest and the results of the autopsy. They worked in utter silence and secrecy at the conference room table and barely said a word to Daniel or Stephanie. They came and went as a trio. They ate together and even slept in one guest room. Daniel was convinced that they were the perpetrators of the crime, but he had no evidence. He knew their dislike of Cain was only surpassed by Stephanie's visceral hatred, but she wouldn't hurt a fly.

Ralph, Irving, and Bernard were still busy at the audit. The day-to-day activities of the Brewery continued as usual.

About a week after Cain's death, Malchus came running into Daniel's office.

"I've got it solved. The mystery is over. I know who killed Manasseh Cain!"

Daniel sat and didn't say a word.

"It was about four o'clock in the morning," Malchus said. "I couldn't sleep because I had this light shining in my eyes. It came from outside the building right above the warehouse. I ran downstairs into the warehouse and saw Cain standing by the baling machine looking up at the beautiful strange light. The beam surrounded his body, just like what happened to Ron Peppler, and then it lifted him off the ground. I saw him grab his chest and then the beam vanished. It simply disappeared while Cain was in the air. He dropped about ten feet right down into the pit of the baling machine. I ran to the pit, but it was so dark that I couldn't see him. All I saw were underwear and socks. He must have sunk below the surface of the rags. Well, as usual, I just forgot everything and went back up to bed. It was only this morning, when I was putting on my socks that this vision came back to me."

Daniel, skeptical as usual, thanked Malchus for his insight and told him directly to say nothing about his visions. Ralph, Irving, and Bernard, however, heard the entire vivid account and glared at one another suspiciously. They, too, had discussed a strange light in the sky, but then dismissed it as just the effects of eating unwholesome dining hall food.

The next day the police arrived at the Brewery—two uniformed officers and one detective. They looked dreadfully serious. All activity at the Brewery came to a screeching halt. Some men hid for fear of being arrested on trumped-up charges. Others hid in the assumption that they would be framed for Cain's murder.

The detective walked in and asked to speak with Dr. Aarons.

"I've got the coroner's report," the detective said.

"Well, did you find the murder weapon?" asked Daniel. "Do you have any suspects? Are there any arrests pending?"

"No," replied the detective in a matter-of-fact way. "Looks like Cain simply died of a heart attack and fell into the baling machine pit. He was a real heavy smoker, you know. At least, that's what the autopsy said. Guess it was just his time to say *sayonara*."

Daniel felt a wave of relief pass over him like a cool tropical breeze. No arrests. No murder. No foul play. Just natural causes.

"There was *one* thing, however," said the detective. "Very strange. His anklebones and tendons were severely bruised. It was as if he had been dropped from a height of at least ten to fifteen feet above the baling pit. He must have sustained that injury somewhere else, possibly in a fall not too long ago. It's obvious that it couldn't have happened here. There's nothing above the pit but open space."

Daniel broke out into a cold sweat and loosened his collar.

The detective closed his notebook and shook hands with Daniel. "Well, Dr. Aarons, that about wraps it up. I appreciate your assistance and the help all your men have provided during the investigation. Call me again when you need me."

The officer left. Daniel took out his pipe and sucked heartily. Malchus walked in and smiled.

CHAPTER 18

✠ ✠ ✠

DANIEL WALKED INTO THE MIDDLE OF THE warehouse to the site of the infamous baler where Manasseh Cain met his sudden death. Some said it was very timely and none too soon. The cold steel pit was now empty, except for one tiny baby sock that somehow avoided being crushed and baled along with all the other discarded underclothes.

Daniel looked up into the ceiling of the vast hangar-like building hoping to find some remnant of the light beam or evidence that alien forces had been at work. There was no indication of anything strange or unusual in the emptiness. Daniel thought of this agglomeration of steel, bricks, and flesh as a living thing, a breathing and strangely conscious biophysical entity, a black hole sitting in the Greenpoint section of Brooklyn distorting space and warping time. There was nothing normal or usual about this place. It was filled with an intoxicating brew of benevolent and malevolent spirits. Some were invisible and ghostly; others came with flesh and blood. Some even crossed the line between animal and vegetable, the living and the dead.

Miracles occurred in the kitchen, and limbs appeared on amputees at the same time men were brushing their teeth or taking showers. Miserably ill men simply vanished from sight one day and returned the next day feeling like spry teenagers. Mice, rats, and roaches crawled across filthy floors in some rooms, while others, like the little chapel, were perpetually bathed in the delicate sweet fragrance of roses.

Some men came to the Brewery simply to die. They were drawn to it like elephants to a secret burial ground. Rooms and corridors appeared and disappeared. Stairways climbed to blank walls. The sound of running water could be heard in areas far removed from plumbing. Odd voices, peculiar smells, squeaks, screeches, lights, shadows, apparitions, and changes in temperature were all a part of the Brewery's ambience. But even with all of this paranormal activity, Daniel still didn't believe that the building was haunted.

Stephanie believed the place was infested with an extended family of angels whose job was to communicate with destitute men. Malchus simply believed that all his visitors from other galaxies had just changed residence from the seventh floor solarium at Bellevue to the Brewery. Daniel was convinced that there was some very real and measurable psychic energy at work, creating spaces and opening and closing portals to other dimensions, but he didn't know where to begin his research. Besides, he had a rehabilitation facility to operate and sixty men to manage. The answers would come slowly in time, whatever time that might be.

Today, however, Daniel determined to talk to the men at their jobs in various places in the warehouse, the shops, and in the residential area. He left the warehouse and stepped into the upholstery shop where Seymour "Potato" Zupnick was busy removing torn seats from a kitchen chair. He reupholstered the seats with a brightly colored vinyl, polished the chrome, and sent them off to the stores. His cat sat on the counter in his usual sphinx-like position licking a crushed paw.

"Good morning, Potato," Daniel said smiling. "I see you've got a lot of work ahead of you. Did all this stuff come off yesterday's haul?"

"Yea, I got about four sets in here," Potato said. "Must be at least twenty chairs. Should keep me busy for a month if I don't get sick or die. But, hell, if I get sick, one of those gorgeous nurses might come to sit by my bed. Maybe even take my temperature and give me a back rub."

Daniel looked hard at Potato.

"Nurses? Since when do we have visiting nurses coming into the building to give massages?"

"Well, Captain, do you remember last week when Larry Morshinski had the flu? He was shivering and sweating. Puked up everything he ate. There was this tall woman in a white nurse's uniform. She had a nurse's cap on and she was rubbing his head, just like a mother would do for her kid. When he fell asleep, she left. I haven't seen her since. Larry's better, but he doesn't even remember anybody visiting him. You know, she sort of reminds me of a nurse who took care of me in France after D-day. That's how I got the name, Potato. It all started in August of forty-four in a little town just outside of ..."

Daniel was no longer paying attention to Potato's old war story. His mind was on Potato's sighting of a ghost, angel, alien being, or whatever. Were all the men having visions and visitations?

Daniel had experienced some of these same types of visions. He, too, saw Ron Peppler rise through the ceiling and come back with a new hand. Was he just as crazy as everybody else was in the Brewery? How long had all this been going on? Was it only since Malchus became a resident several months before?

Potato finished his story. "And that's how I got my name, Potato. Simple as that and it's stuck with me since nineteen forty-four."

"That's really interesting, Potato, thanks for sharing."

Daniel put his hand on Potato's shoulder and tried to rub the rough fur of the cat, but it only growled.

"Potato, how long have you been here at the Brewery?" Daniel asked.

"Gee, I guess ever since the end of World War Two. All I know is that it's been a long time. I've probably upholstered ten thousand chairs since then."

"Have you been seeing nurses and other strange people around here since then?"

"Well, Captain, I've seen a lot of strange folks around here. Sometimes I'm drunk, so I don't really know if they're real or not. I guess it don't matter. Sometimes I see pretty, naked girls running up and down the halls. I even had one stick her boobs in my face. I sure did like that. I've seen bulls with men's heads, barbecued pigs, lots of different colored elephants, plenty of mice and bugs crawlin' all over my arms. Oh, and I've even seen Franklin D. Roosevelt taking a dump in the crapper down the hall. Now that was special."

Daniel left Potato, the cat, and World War II under a long roll of avocado-colored vinyl and wandered into Walter Schiller's radio and

TV repair shop. He greeted the man as if they were friends from the old country.

"Hey, Walter, what's on TV?" Daniel asked.

"Oh, the same old shit; nothing but Vietnam and that son of a bitch liar Nixon. You know, I never trusted him. He always looks green on TV, even on black and white sets."

"Bet you're an old FDR man, right?"

"You bet. He was a son of a bitch, too, but a good son of a bitch. I learned radio because of him, got me through the Depression and then they put me on a Liberty ship. I know my stuff. I can fix any radio or TV they bring me. I got every tube known to modern man. Soon the TVs aren't going to have tubes. No, just these little transistors, you know, solid-state stuff. Then you won't need me. Well, if I can't work, you might as well shoot me."

Walter fiddled with his TV. The tall, lanky electrician looked like a strange concoction of basketball player and accountant. His thick glasses rested on his narrow nose that had long hairs growing out of it. He wore a green eyeshade and squinted as he turned tiny screws and twisted wires.

Daniel was searching for answers to questions he had not yet asked. Nuggets of data and information seemed to pour forth from the men with whom he spoke even before he began his pointed interrogatories.

"You know, Dr. Aarons," Walter said, "you asked me about what's on TV? Well, let me tell you. This is sure going to blow you away. I'm standing here, I guess it must have been last Tuesday around three. I'm working on this old Emerson radio, when all of a sudden every damn TV and radio in this shop turns on. Every damn one, even the ones that aren't plugged in! The busted ones, too, without tubes! Now, how could that happen? Well, I sit down, take a blood pressure pill, and watch what's going on. It's Harry Truman on the TV and the radio. He's telling the world about how we dropped the A-bomb on the Japs! I nearly shit in my pants. This goes on for about five minutes and then the whole place goes dead. Nothing works, not even the TV's that I fixed. I left and went upstairs to go to bed. The next day, it was like nothing happened. The same old thing, Nixon's ugly mug and the body count in Vietnam. You know, Captain, I've been here for almost ten years and every year things get stranger. You got crazy guys, you got criminals, you got guys who have wings, and you got that little one-eared dwarf from Mars or wherever he's from. Sweet Jesus, I don't know how I stay sane in this loony bin." Walter shrugged and scratched his head.

"Walter," Daniel asked, "did you say that there are men here in the Brewery with wings?"

"Yea, damn wings. I seen them myself with my own two good eyes." He took off his thick glasses and pointed to his extremely nearsighted eyes. "You don't think I'm crazy, do you? They don't actually fly around the building like birds, you know. They just sort of walk around and talk to the guys. I don't know where they work. I guess they're on the trucks or in the stores."

Daniel breathed deeply and curled his beard, hoping that this conversation was just an auditory hallucination, but Walter continued to talk.

"And let me tell you something else. These guys with the wings, they put their arms around some of the men like they was some kind of queer boys. And then there's a lot of soft talking and even crying. It really spooks me."

Then Daniel asked the big question. "Do these guys with wings look like angels?"

"Shit, no. Angels don't wear dungarees or cowboy boots. They don't hold men like they was holding a girl. Captain, you better get to the bottom of this fast. I don't want to see Harry Truman on the TV again, and I sure don't want to have one of those guys with wings lookin' for me!"

Daniel smiled at Walter and left the radio repair room. He walked down a corridor, made a few zigzag turns and landed in a spot in the Brewery that he had never seen before. He opened a door and found a room that resembled a small classroom. The farther he walked inside of the room, the clearer and sharper the furniture and objects seemed to appear. It now resembled a small synagogue. At the end of the room was the Holy Ark holding a Torah. A candelabra held two lit candles on a table in front of the ark. There was a small bookcase with tattered prayer books and various worn wooden benches. The room was similar in size to the other chapel in the Brewery, except that this room appeared to be much older and in a part of the original brewery structure.

No electrical wires or lights were visible, but the brilliant light of the sun shone through a tiny window near the ceiling. Another small narrow door was located to the right of the Holy Ark. Daniel heard a cough and then a sneeze. A young bearded man was sweeping the floor. Daniel introduced himself in his usual formal manner.

"Hello, I'm Dr. Daniel Aarons. I don't believe we've ever met, and I don't think I've ever been in this room before."

The young man smiled and stopped sweeping. "That doesn't surprise me. This place is so big I often get lost in it myself. I've lived here for quite some time, you know. I'm surprised you haven't noticed me before. I'm part of the janitorial staff. All I do is clean and wipe and get rid of the garbage. It's amazing how much filth collects in a place like this. As soon as I get one corner clean, another gets filled up with dust and trash. The men around here are no help either."

"I didn't get your name," Daniel said.

"Oh, I'm sorry, it's Pinchas Koretz, but everybody just calls me Pinky."

Daniel was intrigued and very surprised.

"Did you say your name was Koretz?"

"Yes. You know like the famous Hasidic master. I was named after him," Pinchas said.

"My uncle's name is Koretz, too. Jacob Koretz. What a coincidence!" Daniel replied, his eyes now wide open in amazement.

The young man didn't seem surprised at all.

"Well, perhaps you and I are distant relatives, cousins, maybe. You know we do look very much alike."

Daniel walked closer to Pinky and the closer he came, the more the two resembled each other until they were virtually identical, except for their clothing. Both had dark curly hair with short beards, fair skin, and piercing blue eyes. They could have been twins. Perhaps they *were* twins.

Daniel was fascinated and disturbed by his double, his mirror image. It was as if a part of him had vanished at some point in his past and had now returned from a different space and time. Daniel shivered and stared at his twin. There was definitely something extraordinary about this seemingly supernatural encounter.

"Who are you, Pinky Koretz?" demanded Daniel.

The young man put aside his broom and touched Daniel's shoulder.

"I'm your brother. Isn't it obvious? Your long dead twin brother, and here we are in this magnificent house of worship." Pinky laughed.

The young man smiled and now put both hands on Daniel's shoulders.

"Look, Daniel, there is the Torah, here are the prayer books, the volumes of Talmud sit on the benches. There is a world that is crying out for God. What are you doing about it?"

Pinky's question was profound, but Daniel wasn't ready to think about God, let alone do anything about a world crying out for the Almighty.

"I don't have a brother, let alone a twin brother," Daniel said. "Uncle Jacob never said anything to me about having a twin. What's this game you're playing?"

The two men sat on benches and stared into each other's eyes.

"Daniel," said Pinky, "Jacob tells you the story of how he finds you on top of a pile of corpses in the death camp of Auschwitz. Isn't that correct?"

"Yes, but how do you know ..."

"I'm your brother, Daniel, remember? We were both on top of that pile, two little pieces of flesh torn from a dying woman's womb and thrown on a heap of human bodies. You were breathing and I wasn't. Jacob picked us both up and held us in his arms. An American soldier told him that I was dead. I remember the look on Jacob's face as he placed me back on the pile. He wanted so much to take me with him. He trembled, cried, and screamed about the black holes that were forming in front of his eyes. He knew those piles of corpses so well that he virtually became a part of them."

The two brothers clutched each other's hands and tears welled up in their eyes.

"Daniel, there is something else I must tell you because it will enable you to heal Jacob."

There was a pregnant pause, and it was as if the world had stood still.

"Daniel, Jacob is not your uncle. He's your father. After Rachel, his first wife, died in the camp, Jacob met Leah. She, too, was a very beautiful woman, and somehow in the misery, filth, and death of the camp, they fell in love and were determined to find a way to create new life. The thought of bringing a child into that horrible world was both a wonderful and an awful act. How could they choose to create a life that would certainly die in the camp? They knew it was a selfish act, but also one that God had ordained. What a terrible choice, what a terrible burden! So God gave them two children, one to die, and one to live. That is the burden and the guilt that Jacob Koretz lives with each and every day."

An avalanche of emotions overwhelmed Daniel. His hands quivered, his voice trembled. "But what happened to my, *our* mother?"

"She died in childbirth," Pinchas said. "Again, one to die and one to live. Jacob has always felt responsible for her death. Perhaps if she had not gotten pregnant, the two of them could have walked out of the concentration camp together when the Allied soldiers came to deliver them from their suffering. But she was dead only hours before they arrived. He has always blamed himself for my death and the death of our mother. Daniel, he loves you very much, but at the same time, he has never been able to deal with his guilt and the agonizing experiences in the camp. He tried to distance himself from the horror by distancing himself from you. The pain was just too great. And so he became your uncle and not your father. He blessed you with his sister's family name, Aarons, because he wanted to dedicate you to God to be a high priest and rabbi. Every aspect of your life was to be holy and consecrated. Every act of your life was to be in the service of God and humanity. That is why we are here together at this instant in God's creation. The whole universe has stopped for this very moment. God is waiting."

Daniel was confused. "God is waiting? Waiting for what?"

"He's waiting for your decision. Have you chosen to consecrate your life and to be in His service?"

Daniel's mind was reeling. How could he answer such a question in an instant?

"I don't know what to do, Pinky. I've never been a religious man. I've always found our religion to be so illogical and irrational, so full of superstition and myth. How could I accept a faith with a jealous God who abandoned his people in the death camps? I'm a scientist. I need logic; I need things to fall into place and to make sense. I don't understand God's love. It's so inconsistent and capricious. If He is a merciful God, why does He allow injustice to continue? Why does He allow infants to die of disease and starvation?"

Pinchas was silent for a moment and seemed to search the ceiling of the synagogue for answers to the difficult questions.

"Daniel, He created the universe with its own free will, but we are His eyes, His ears, and His hands empowered to change the course of the universe. He has given us the capacity to move mountains if we must. He has given us the power to heal the sick, prevent disease, and to show the world His love. But all that power can be used for selfishness and destruction. We must choose and the choice is always ours."

Daniel shrugged and then reached out to touch his brother's face.

"Pinky, I feel so weak and powerless. All I have is my science and logic to fall back on. It's my foundation and my peace. It keeps me sane."

"Daniel, God is with you all the time. He infuses you with His power and spirit, but only if you choose to accept it. Very often—more often than people realize—God comes into this world through a person so that He can show His love to His creation. Humanity is like the sad wife who waits for her husband to come back from the war. She doesn't realize that she has the power to end all wars and to keep her husband by her side. And we don't realize that we also have the power to bring God back anytime we choose. But we timidly wait and expect miracles to happen by themselves. Daniel, *we* make miracles happen."

"Then what must I do, Pinky?" Daniel pleaded.

"Good, that was the question I was waiting for. You must simply sacrifice your life and walk through that door." Pinky pointed to the narrow door next to the ark.

"God wants me to kill myself for him?" Daniel asked.

"No, of course not. God doesn't need any dead martyrs. He wants you as a living sacrifice. You're no good to Him as a corpse. That is why He spared you and that is why He continues to wait for your decision."

"If I sacrifice my life for Him, what reward can I expect?" asked Daniel.

"Now I know you are testing me. What reward do you expect?" replied Pinky.

"Heaven?"

"You already have heaven. Daniel, heaven is not something you inherit or a place you move into when you die. Heaven is a state of being in complete harmony and accord with the Almighty right here and now. It begins as soon as a person makes the decision to turn to God. But now, Daniel, you know the secrets of the universe and you must choose. If you do not choose, the knowledge you now have will be turned against you."

"How can this beautiful knowledge be turned against me?"

"This kind of knowledge in the world of the living is like ripe fruit. It must be eaten and consumed while the fruit is fresh. If it is not eaten, the fruit will rot on the branch and attract flies. The flies will produce maggots that will infest other fruit. Before you know it, all the fruit is gone and the people starve."

The mystical discussion between Daniel and Pinchas was suddenly broken by a moan coming from the other side of the room. Daniel turned around. Sitting in a dark corner was a small man. He beckoned to Daniel to come near him, but Pinchas grabbed Daniel's arm and held him back. Daniel looked deeply into the darkness until he saw who was sitting there.

"Cain, is that you?" Daniel asked. "I thought you died in the warehouse. What are you doing here?"

There was no answer from the man in the dark corner.

"Daniel," Pinky said, "Cain who sits in his dark corner of the universe is the hinderer. He is a very disagreeable person, but for many people, he appears as a very handsome and charming young man. Some people see him with horns and call him Satan, but I am glad that you just see him as a little evil man. As long as you keep him small, he can never harm you. But remember, if you do choose God, you will see more of that evil little man than you may care to. His mission in life is to hinder people and trip them up. He wants to confound people like you, Daniel, who have been offered the knowledge of the ripe fruit. He will try to infest your life like a fly and its maggots. So you must always be vigilant and put him in his place. Daniel, have you made your decision yet? There is the door you must walk through if you have chosen God."

Daniel heard a knock from the other side of the narrow door. A man dressed in a Service Corps uniform stood at the threshold. He looked like one of the doormen in the old photographs, and he waited for Daniel.

"Pinky," Daniel asked, "can't I just go out the way I came in?"

"Yes, of course you can. That is your decision, but I, as your brother, am here to help you and to give you the guidance you need to make your decision. Not everyone who is in this situation is so fortunate."

Daniel was confused. "Pinky, will I ever see you again?"

"Yes, Daniel, of course. We are one."

Daniel turned to look at the narrow door and at the man who was standing and waiting. When he turned back to say good-bye to Pinchas, the room had become empty and barren. The Torah and the Holy Ark were gone. His brother had vanished. The only thing evident was the delicate fragrance of roses. Cain quickly left through the wide door that led to the hallway, but Daniel, greeted by the man in uniform, was escorted through the narrow door.

On the other side of the door, Daniel found himself once again in the corridor of the Brewery. He walked to the door he had originally entered expecting to find a sanctuary, but instead found just another broom closet.

Malchus stood at the end of the hallway staring at his friend Daniel.

"Malchus," Daniel asked, "how big did you say the devil was?"

CHAPTER 19

✠ ✠ ✠

THE MONTHS FOLLOWING DANIEL'S ENCOUNTER WITH PINCHAS were a time of great transformation. The universe, he concluded, was not necessarily a logical or ordered place. The irrefutable laws of physics and the inscrutable dynamics of the Almighty were in constant tension, but that was part of the Creator's nature as well as His sense of humor. God would not be a puppet master, but would give His children free will to create. Scientific investigation and experiment could not explain everything in the universe.

Consequently, Daniel began to accept the paranormal activity in the Brewery as a normal and stable state of being. He deduced that the Brewery was more than just a rehabilitation facility, it was a virtual giant nerve synapse—a conduit or junction box—through which passed the great power of the universe. Anyone or anything that transversed through the synapse was transformed. The transformation, however, depended upon the cognitive attitude, emotional stability, and spiritual maturity of the person. Because the synapse was a point of entrance, exit, and attraction of both good and evil souls, the Brewery became a virtual hub for beings both physical and spiritual to move from one parallel universal plane to another. Daniel calculated that since there were at least 500 trillion synapses per cubic centimeter of biological cortex in the human brain, the number of parallel unversal planes could exceed 333 quintillion at any particular moment, but more so on Tuesdays. It was as simple as that.

The great synapse took its toll on the professional relationship between Daniel and Stephanie. As Daniel became less rigid in his thinking and more tolerant in his attitudes toward the supernatural, Stephanie became more organized and even a better typist. As a result, these two highly attractive beings were about to meet in the space/time continuum and either change the course of the universe through some cataclysmic event, or fall in love. Neither situation, however, was a satisfactory option at this time.

Malchus, in his inimitable way, would have to play the role of catalyst and maintain a state of equilibrium in this extremely volatile psychochemical reaction, or else all hell would break out. In other words, it wasn't yet time for Daniel and Stephanie to go running off to get married and have babies. There was still too much work to be done at the Brewery and both of them were indispensable components of the equation. But the challenge for Malchus would be extremely difficult at best.

Daniel sat at his desk, which was covered in files, smoking pipes, and a humidor of wonderful-smelling vanilla tobacco. The aroma of the burning tobacco was a sign of security for Stephanie and whenever she inhaled it, she came slinking into Daniel's office just to get a whiff and to be close to him. Just the sound of his flicking lighter was enough to entice her into his office under the pretense of delivering important information. The hypnotic smoke became an aphrodisiac and Daniel became aware of its delightful but dangerous power. Even the pipe tobacco, he thought, had been transformed into a powerful spiritual tool and Malchus was aware of the whole game.

"I see how you look at her," Malchus said to Daniel. "It's dangerous and you're going to get into trouble."

Daniel was defensive and postured like a teenager. "Hey, don't tell me how to look at her. What about you? You fawn all over her like a sick, driveling fool. Is she still painting frescoes on your back? How many times have you gone back to her apartment for a little art restoration?"

"Daniel, there's nothing sexual about what she does to my back," Malchus responded abruptly. "It just feels so wonderful when she rubs that warm oil in with her fingers and coats my body with soft, fragrant-smelling paint. She sits there under the light of candles, dressed only in a T-shirt, and we drink wine and talk all night." Malchus closed his eyes and painted the air with his finger.

Daniel shot back. "Nothing romantic or erotic, like hell! She's never painted *my* back."

"Daniel, believe me, we're just good friends. She never touches me in a sexual way. Besides, I could never give her what she really wants or needs. I know that and she knows that and, because we both know that, our relationship doesn't have a sexual component. It does, however, have a wonderfully unique physical aspect and that's something very special between the two of us. And even more than that, we can talk with each other for hours on end. She's a very deep and old soul, you know. She's been around for tens of thousands of years and sometimes she sounds like an ancient sage. You know, I think she once was the Oracle at Delphi. All that wisdom packed into that gorgeous, skinny body."

Daniel threw a pencil at the little man. He knew he was sinking into a quagmire of muddy emotions and becoming a swirling concoction of conflicting passions. His physical and emotional attraction to Stephanie was growing geometrically as each day passed. But his intellectual needs and requirement to maintain a professional distance with his subordinate made him irritable and testy. Just the sound of her voice on the phone or the patter of her footsteps on the floor in the next room caused him to lose his train of thought.

His good friend, Malchus, was a constant source of irritation as well. Of course, that was part of Malchus's plan. Daniel knew that Malchus was no real romantic threat and there would be no contest, but he was still terribly envious of the little man's intimacy with Stephanie. Her fingers were caressing Malchus's body, not his. She was spending her nights with Malchus and not with him. Both men needed and desired her touch and her affections, but both would have to receive it in different ways. This was the only way it could be at this particular point in time in the history of the universe.

Malchus knew, as well, that he could not prevent their relationship from developing nor would he want to stop it altogether. He just needed to inhibit it slightly so that the work of the Brewery could be completed. The only question that remained was: What was the final work to be done and when would it be accomplished? In the meantime, he would enjoy Stephanie's company and pursue the vague mission established for him by God. It was as simple as that.

Daniel didn't want to be left out of Stephanie's life. He wanted to be part of her inner circle of confidants and to know her secrets, at least some of them. She, like many of the men at the Brewery, was eccentric and enigmatic. Daniel would have to be creative to get what he wanted.

Stephanie walked into Daniel's office with an armload of unpaid bills and dropped them on his desk. She bent down over the desk, her nose just inches from his. He could smell a faint hint of the wildly exotic perfume that drove him mad. He could see a faint hint of her breasts through her blouse.

"If we don't pay these bills by Friday, they're going to turn off the electricity and the phones," she said. "Do you want to sit here in the dark?"

Daniel glanced into the large brown eyes and thought about sitting with her in the dark all day and all night. He wondered if that was a leading question. He pressed on in a totally different direction.

"Stephanie, may I ask you a personal question?"

She stood up straight like a soldier. "No, of course you may not. This is a business and superiors don't ask personal questions of their subordinates." She paused and got in his face again. This time she whispered in his ear.

"What deep dark secrets do you want to know? Because if I tell you my secrets, I may have to kill you, too. But since you're such a respectable human being, I would have no fear in welcoming you to my apartment tomorrow evening for dinner. You can bring the wine."

Daniel choked on his saliva. She had read his mind.

"Yes, I'd love to," he blurted out.

The next day at nine in the morning, Stephanie came into Daniel's office, her eyes wild, her hair a mess. She looked sad, tired, like she had been up all night sulking or worrying about the problems of the world. Or maybe she'd just been drinking too much.

"Daniel, I need to change our dinner date," she said. "I can't tell you why, but can we postpone it for a while?"

Before he could think about her proposition and get a word out of his mouth, she was on her way out the door. Hardly one word had passed between the two of them. Daniel was troubled about the incident. His mind and his guts were giving him conflicting information. His irritation and just plain bad temper were apparent and his uncharacteristic disinterest in the men was evident. His staff avoided him. Poor Daniel Aarons was in love and it showed badly.

Stephanie called in sick the next day. The following morning she arrived at the Brewery and sat slumped in her chair for the better part of the day, talking to herself and scribbling on the desk blotter. It was time for remediation and action. Daniel needed to talk with her, but he was in no position to be a good counselor. He needed a little therapy himself so he called Malchus into his office.

Malchus sat at the end of the long conference table and attempted to look dignified and important.

"This is not a good situation, Daniel," said Malchus. "The two of you are acting like lovesick adolescents, but I think there's a lot more under the surface. I know she's really conflicted between what she feels and what she knows she must do. She's just that type of girl. And I know you're experiencing some of those same feelings. I'll talk with her this morning as her friend, not as her therapist."

Daniel wanted to get on with the business of the day. It was quite apparent that he had been neglecting the men.

"Thanks, Malchus. I need to get to work paying these invoices or we're all going to be sitting on the sidewalk by next week."

Malchus left the conference room and walked back into Stephanie's office. She was gone. A note left on her desk read: To whom it may concern, I've left for the day. I don't know when I'll be back. Please don't call. Love, mut.

The note was meant to be seen by Malchus. It was really a cry for help. He called her apartment number from her desk phone, but there was no answer. He called every half hour until it was nearly five in the afternoon. Finally, Stephanie answered the phone. She had been drinking heavily.

"Mut, I got your note," Malchus said. "I want to help. Please talk to me. I'm your spiritual buddy, and I don't want to see you hurting like this."

"Malchus, I knew you'd call, but I don't think there's anything you can do for me right now," said Stephanie with a cry in her voice.

"Why not? I've always been there when you needed me. Is this a new problem? There's always a remedy."

The line was silent for several moments. Stephanie began to sob on the other end.

"Malchus, you really couldn't begin to understand."

Malchus was frustrated.

"Understand what?" he asked.

"He's back," she said.

Without saying good-bye, she hung up the phone. Stephanie couldn't possibly share this experience with Malchus or with any other human being. It was so personal, so intimate, so real and unreal that she could barely understand it or express it in words. She dreaded the nights and the pleasures of the Stranger's visits. She drank pots of coffee just to keep herself awake so that she could postpone the intense delights and keep him away. But she could no longer keep her eyes open, and she fell into a deep sleep on a hard chair.

As was his habit, the Stranger came after midnight, lightly tapping at her door. At first she refused to get up from her chair.

"Go away, please go away," she shouted. "I can't be with you tonight. Don't you realize what you're doing to me?"

Her words were like feathers thrown at a mountain. The tapping on the door continued and it would not let up. She crawled off her chair and went to the door on her knees. She grabbed the knob, but did not turn it. A deep powerful voice came from the other side of the door.

"Stephanie," the voice said, "I know you are there just on the other side. You must let me in. You have no choice and I have no choice. We must do what we must do."

"No, I do have a choice," she said. "Go away and leave me alone!"

"Don't you want me?" the Stranger whispered. "Don't you want me to touch you? Can you deny that I give you incredible pleasure? Open the door, Stephanie. I want to take you in my arms and kiss you throughout the night. I want to caress your thighs, your breasts, and make love to you 'til dawn. I want to come into you and fill you with every part of my being. You know you are mine, all mine, and I am yours, all yours. There is no one else but you. Haven't I been a faithful lover? Do I spend my nights with anyone else? I could easily open this door myself, but I know that you want to open it for me."

The Stranger's deep voice was now quiet. Stephanie could no longer help herself. Her craving and her unquenchable desire for his body and his tender words proved an impossible obstacle to overcome. She turned the knob and threw open the door to let her Stranger in. He stood there naked, a massive, powerful hulk with flaming blue eyes and black hair. She remained on her knees as he walked toward her and he pressed her head to his thighs. He picked her up as if she were a single delicate flower and carried her over to the awaiting mattress that lay in the middle of the floor.

She was no longer in control, but now gave herself totally and completely to her Stranger. She could not move, and it was as if she were embedded in his flesh and he was breathing for the both of them. She felt him fill her and his essence moved up through her body like the sap in a tree. How could this incredible pleasure last for so many hours, she thought. But then time had no meaning. The hours of ecstasy were like minutes, and she craved more of him as the night went by. His deep moans and endless tender words were like the soft dabs of paint that she would apply to her canvases. His fingers, like fine brushes that penetrated her skin, added to her exquisite sensations. She was a deep blue tropical sea, and he knew where all her treasures were hidden. He returned night after night to search her secrets and keep them secure just for himself.

When the sun came up, her Stranger was gone. She didn't see him leave. She never saw him leave. It was as if he had never been there. Not even a tiny lingering fragrance of his body remained, only the utter and complete emptiness of a hollow woman. He had taken a full and complete drink of her, and she was now dry and desolate as a desert wilderness aching for a few drops of rain. She lay naked on her mattress like a worn and tattered garment. She felt exhausted, old, ashamed, but still craving his body. She knew that she could not withstand these nightly visits for long and that she might try to end her life. She had tried once before and failed. He had been a part of her life years ago, and now he was back to take his pound of flesh. How could something so wonderful, beautiful, and fulfilling leave her so completely empty and wasted? Why was the Stranger coming back now at this time in her life when she was beginning to find purpose and meaning? Why did he choose this moment to give her endless sexual pleasures when she was beginning to have strong feelings for Daniel? Was this a testing of God or of the devil? Was she wrestling nightly with an angel of the Lord or with Satan himself?

Whether her Stranger was flesh and blood or simply spirit, she was not quite sure. He breathed, he sweated, his lips were hot and moist, and his body was firm and strong, but she remained intact. This gave her a small sense of relief that perhaps he was not real, at least in the physical sense. He could not defile her, and she would remain a virgin as she had vowed until she married. But her emotional and spiritual energy were waning and she feared that she would be dead before long.

Stephanie cried and tried to get dressed. She put on her makeup and left for work.

CHAPTER 20

✠ ✠ ✠

THERE ARE TIMES IN A MAN'S CAREER when even the best things become tasteless and stale, when the daily chores that once brought joy now just bring boredom. Everything in the world operates in cycles, and nothing goes in a straight line for very long. The forces of entropy and decay balance the forces of structure and design. This is good and in God's way, because there could be no organization without entropy, no life without death, no hope without despair.

Relationships, too, suffer from the inexorable passage of time and move through their cycles. People, like planets in a solar system, circle a central point of gravity. They are held in their orbits by their own centrifugal forces and the intrinsic energies that prevent them from being sucked up by the great central force. In their orbits, they frequently encounter other planets, moons, asteroids, and comets that come near to them. Sometimes, planets seem to ride together through space on their journeys around the sun, but that is only an illusion. The inner planet always travels faster and soon leaves the outer planet behind. Eventually, they find themselves on opposite sides of the sun. Occasionally, there are collisions between bodies where one dies and the other receives the full mass of the other during impact. Neither matter nor energy is ever lost, however, and the entities are transformed into something new and different.

Daniel and Stephanie were two planets in orbit around a great central force. Malchus was a speeding comet traveling in and out of the solar system, spending much of his time in the Oort cloud or penetrating deep within the orbits of Daniel and Stephanie. He avoided collisions only through the grace of God. Jacob Koretz was a giant asteroid whose orbit had not yet been determined. He could vaporize at any moment. All the other men in the Brewery were moons, meteors, comets, and various bits of interplanetary flotsam and jetsam that made navigating in the universe so dangerous and such an exciting challenge.

Daniel lost his bearings, his galactic compass seemed to be pointing in the wrong direction, and he could feel it in his heart. When he looked up at the stars, he could no longer find Orion's belt or even the North Star.

Stephanie Croix was in a distant orbit, her axis pointing away from Daniel and at apogee with his planet. It had been nine months since Daniel first walked into the waiting room of the Brewery and set eyes upon Stephanie. It had been nine months since he became its leader, and it had been nine months since he had first encountered the enigmatic dwarf who was slowly but surely changing the course of the world. Good things were supposed to happen during periods of nine months. Human gestation was nine months, and the birth of new life was a gloriously anticipated event.

Not so for Daniel Aarons. He felt that he had miscarried an opportunity or that he had never even been impregnated. His home life became even more troubling as Jacob continued to struggle with his mental illness, his bipolar disease, and the black holes that plagued his physical and spiritual vision. Daniel still couldn't discuss his visit with Pinchas, and he was terrified by the prospect of disclosing such an event to his agitated uncle, who was in reality his biological father.

Jacob had to be hospitalized twice during that nine-month period, once for his depression and once for getting into such a fight with Esther Cohen in apartment 6B that they both fainted and had to be taken away by ambulance. To make matters worse, his triumphant musical comedy, The Stunt, was canceled after just one week. As it turned out, people who went to see the play lost their appetites and didn't patronize the restaurants in the adjacent area. The merchants put up such a big stink that they boycotted the theater and put up a picket line.

Potential customers wouldn't cross the picket line and couldn't buy tickets. Julius Chomsky decided to close the production before he was sued. Daniel had never seen Jacob so depressed and despondent. Jacob just sat in his big recliner for weeks on end staring out into space, smoking his cigars. He wouldn't eat or take his medication. He claimed that the black holes were getting bigger and that within a month he would be totally blind.

Stephanie was also sliding down a steep slope leading to a seemingly dark, bottomless pit. She called in sick so often that she used up all of her sick days and vacation time. The paper work wasn't being done and what she typed was completely unreadable. Had she not been the Stephanie Croix whom Daniel loved and cared for, she would have been fired and out the door long ago. She became a liability to the Brewery, but Daniel just couldn't dismiss the girl, and he didn't know what to do with her. She wouldn't confide in him and continued to play her strange cat and mouse game.

Daniel's frustration was evident in his sour moods and bad temper. He'd sit in his office and smoke his pipe all day, or he would just go out on the loading dock and talk to the men on the trucks. He would look at her as she walked into the office and notice that she wasn't wearing makeup or that her clothes were mismatched and disheveled. He wanted to slap her in the face and demand to know her problem, or maybe just grab her and kiss her. Why do things always seem to fall apart just when they appear to be getting better?

So what did Daniel Aarons, this great mind and leader, finally decide to do? He called a meeting of his spiritual staff, John B. Waters and Malchus One Ear, and ordered a mammoth banquet of Chinese food.

The three men, against all good judgment and propriety, ate nine courses of various types of Cantonese and Szechuan food and drank copious amounts of vodka and other alcoholic sprits. The three wise men were drunk.

"Gentlemen and good friends," Daniel said in his stupor. "A word from the great Oriental sage, Suk Wang: Life is like a shit sandwich, some days you just take bigger bites."

The men applauded and continued to stuff their faces. Malchus, too, was inebriated, and it didn't take much for the little man to be flying into a very erratic orbit. With an egg roll hanging out of his mouth, he addressed his friends.

"Comrades in arms, attention." Pieces of cooked cabbage spewed from his mouth. "I used to have a friend at Bellevue who, when he became scared or troubled, could actually stick his entire head up his ass. You know, sort of like when an ostrich gets scared and sticks his head in the sand. He'd run up and down the hallways in that position for days until the attendants caught him and gave him a shot. They'd actually have to anesthetize the guy to remove his head."

Daniel and John rolled on the floor in hysterics. Waters was drunk, too, but he could hold his liquor. He knew that his conduct was way out of line and that he could be fired, but he was with the boss and desperately needed to let off some steam.

"You know, you stupid sons of bitches," John said with blood in his eye. "What we're doing is wrong. What kind of example are we setting for the men here at the Brewery? This is the first time in five years that I've had a drink, and here I am with the boss and this little one-nippled Martian, and look at us, we're a damn, sorry disgrace." John slammed his fist on the table and food bounced into the air.

"Waters," Daniel said, now cross-eyed, and slobbering. "What did you say about a one-nippled Martian?"

"Yea," John replied as he pointed to Malchus. "This little melon-headed pigmy only has one nipple."

Daniel looked at Malchus and belched loudly.

"Malchus, my dear little friend, my bosom buddy; you never told me that you only had one nipple. Was it shot off in the war? Did some gorgeous babe bite it off while you were screwing?"

Malchus, even in his drunken stupor, looked menacingly at Waters. "Why did you have to go tell him about my secret? I thought you were a spiritual counselor and that everything I told you was confidential?"

"Malchus, my man," John replied. "You run up and down the hallway with your shirt off every night. Every guy in this fucking place knows that you only have one nipple. My God, the entire world, except Captain Aarons here, knows that you only have one nipple. My cat knows that you only have one nipple. That cockroach crawling out of the chow mein knows that you only have one nipple. Have I made myself clear?"

There was a moment of silence before the three men regained their drunken composure and resumed their disjointed repartee.

Daniel put down his glass of vodka and threw away his chopsticks for which he no longer had any manual dexterity.

"Captain Waters, I have an important theological question for you. Are you ready?"

"As ready as I'll be tonight, Boss. In five minutes, you might find me sleeping under this table."

"Why does God make us suffer so?" Daniel asked.

"Oh, brother," Malchus interrupted. "Do you have to be so depressing?"

"That's an easy one," said John, "but I'd rather you ask me how many commandments God gave to Moses on Mount Sinai."

"John, you're avoiding my question," Daniel said angrily.

John was pissed off and picked his teeth. "Daniel, I am stoned drunk and you are stoned drunk and little One Ear is booze-saturated and you want to ask about why God makes us suffer? Man, lighten up and enjoy the juice. We won't be enjoying it tomorrow, believe me. You'll probably be kissing the commode and feeling so guilty that you'll be asking to be shot for your sins."

Daniel looked at Malchus for an answer. The little man was trying to be straight and give a reasonable response, but his eyes glazed over and he slurred his words.

"Guys, it's simple," Malchus said. "God does not make us suffer." He picked up a fried wonton. "You see, our lives are like this wonton. God gives us the container, this nice flaky pastry, just like my cookies. We can fill it with a savory blend of meat or we can fill it with crap. Now, Dr. Daniel Aarons, which wonton would you rather eat?" Malchus stuffed the entire pastry into his mouth and chewed it with relish.

"You know," Waters said, "for a little white midget with one nipple and no brain, you sure do say some good stuff." He slapped Malchus on the back and half of a wonton flew out of his mouth.

"Hey, where's the fortune cookies?" asked Daniel.

The three men broke open their cookies and read their fortunes.

"Daniel, what does yours say?" asked Waters.

"Tribulation!" replied Daniel.

"Whoa, that sounds bad. What about yours, Malchus?"

"Tribulation!" Malchus dropped his cookie.

"Okay, John, how about you?" asked Daniel.

"Oh my God!" Waters' mouth hung open. "Tribulation!" he replied.

"Well, gentlemen, it looks like we all got tribulation ahead," said Daniel with a smirk.

The three men attempted to regain some semblance of sobriety, their eyes staring down at the food mess and spilled vodka that littered the table. Their heads were beginning to hurt. It was now nearly midnight and each would have to be ready to go back to work by eight the next morning. Malchus and John tried to mop up, but it was no use. They simply conked out at the table. Daniel grabbed his pipe, walked out into the darkness of night, and tried to clear his head. He sat down on a weather-beaten leather sofa and didn't realize that he was *not* alone on the stuffed piece of furniture.

A voice came from within the darkness.

"Good evening, Dr. Aarons. I see that you and your friends have thoroughly enjoyed yourselves tonight. I'm glad you had such a good time and that you had the opportunity to discuss some deep theological issues. I just love deep theological issues, too. It makes me feel right at home. I'm always present in spirit when men of true faith get together."

Daniel didn't know who was speaking. It was too dark, but the voice sounded vaguely familiar. He lit a match and held it in front of the man's face.

"Oh, my God, Cain, it's you!" Daniel exclaimed.

"Cain, yes it is. My God? Well, now, that's your choice."

Daniel jumped off the sofa.

"I see you received my little fortune cookies. Are you prepared?" A sinister grin covered Cain's face.

"Prepared for what?" Daniel demanded.

"Well, what did the cookies say?" yelled Cain.

"Tribulation!" replied Daniel, his voice now shaking.

"Good. Then you know what to expect, and I will be waiting for you at every door, at every turn of your head, whenever you look at the beautiful Miss Croix, whenever you go home to your *father* Jacob, and whenever you deal with that obnoxious one-eared dwarf."

Daniel puffed on his pipe, closed his eyes, and hoped that this, too, was just a hallucination, an apparition, that would pass with the alcohol.

CHAPTER 21

✠ ✠ ✠

MONDAYS ARE GENERALLY BAD DAYS, NOT BECAUSE the day is intrinsically evil, but because modern man just doesn't like the thought of stopping the weekend's pleasures and returning to the toil of the salt mine. The blessedness and peace of Sunday is suddenly thwarted at twelve o'clock midnight by this most gray and terrifying second day of the week. It approaches not as a gentle young girl with flowers in her hair or as a holy Sabbath intended for meditation and prayer, but as a speeding freight train at full throttle laden with anxiety, dread, and endless responsibilities. It belches forth the black smoke of *to do* lists from its monstrous steam engine and compels you to lie upon the tracks.

Monday hits you in the face as you open your eyes and stare up at the ceiling waiting for *the bowling balls from heaven.*

Yes, Moby Dixon was not only a prizefighter, but he was a poet, too. And every Monday morning like clockwork, he greeted Daniel at the door of the Brewery with the reassuring question, "Hey, Boss, are you ready for the bowling balls from heaven?"

At first, Daniel would just say in an automatic way, "Of course, let'm come," and then he'd make a silly motion as if he was throwing a ball down the alley. "Ah, strike!"

After about four weeks of this nonsense, he finally asked Dixon, "What the hell are the bowling balls from heaven?"

Moby Dixon was pleased to respond, and he gave Daniel a sampling of his personal theology that he learned from the seminary of hard knocks.

"Dr. Aarons, we receive gifts from God all the time," Moby said in preacher-like fashion. "Sometimes these gifts are like cute, sweet kittens. They're gentle and pretty and they give us lots of pleasure. Sometimes His gifts are like marshmallow cream pies that slowly drift out of the clouds and into our mouths. They taste good. He also gives us brussels sprouts. But most of the time, God just gives us bowling balls from heaven—big, heavy, dark things that come down fast. If we're not ready, they crash down on our heads and kill us, but if we're ready and have our eyes looking up to God at all times, we can be ready to catch them as they come down. Then we can go bowling! Some people are always looking down expecting terrible things to smash into their heads, but I just keep my eyes wide open and my hands outstretched ready to grab God's balls."

Moby Dixon completed his sermon and stood at his pulpit more like an old ex-boxer just clobbered by a good left hook than a Sunday schoolteacher.

The thought of grabbing God by the balls was a new and intriguing theological concept for Daniel. It made Mondays a little bit more humorous, but not much.

Not only was this a Monday, but it was also a *full moon Monday*. A full moon Monday came, thanks to the laws of nature, only on occasion, but when it did arrive, the very fabric of space and time could be transformed forever. Men at alcoholic rehabilitation facilities were very aware of this stellar event and the ancient myth that surrounded it.

Consequently, they took full advantage of its powers to wreak havoc on persons, institutions, and especially on mechanical devices such as trucks. On full moon Mondays, entire fleets of trucks would cease to operate because their engines malfunctioned or because the human operators that gave them life and spirit were nowhere to be found. When this situation occurred, the whole facility suffered. The men in the warehouse didn't have anything to do and were more apt to get into trouble. There was also no money coming in, which caused real headaches.

An able administrator, like Daniel Aarons, needed to learn from these debilitating situations and not repeat the same mistakes over and over. At the outbreak of Daniel's first full moon Monday, he decided it wasn't necessary to wait for the drivers to return to their trucks. Rather, Ernie Yeager, Malchus, and Daniel became the crew for one of the vehicles and drove a route to pick up bags of clothing and a few sticks of furniture. This was a dumb decision, since neither Ernie nor Daniel could drive a manual shift and Malchus couldn't reach the clutch or accelerator pedals.

The unfortunate conclusion to the day's efforts was one stalled truck on the Brooklyn-Queens Expressway and a stolen load of good furniture from the back of the truck. It wasn't because the three had not somehow learned to crudely operate the vehicle. No, it was simply because Daniel forgot to put gasoline in the tank before leaving the loading dock. At ten o'clock in the morning, the day was shot for the three men, and when they got back to the warehouse, they found a situation of utter chaos and confusion.

At least thirty men were shouting, cursing, crawling, or fighting on the sidewalk in front of the Brewery as a giant plume of black smoke poured from a truck sitting in the driveway on the loading dock. Several firefighting units were on the scene, including a couple of police cars and a camera crew from a TV station. It appeared as if Daniel had deserted his ship while it was burning at sea. The reporters rushed up to him, stuck their cameras into his sweaty, distorted face, and asked him probing questions about the safety of the facility and the mass drunkenness and general disorder of the men. Daniel mumbled a few choice words and then made a complete ass of himself in front of the camera and eight million New Yorkers.

"Get this goddamn thing out of my face or I'll kick your ass from here to the Bronx," he yelled.

His comments were not those of a seasoned PhD with expertise in psychiatric rehabilitation. The entire incoherent and disjointed diatribe was seen on the six o'clock news that night. Poor Daniel was mortified. Calls came in from Biloxi wanting to know the sordid details. Daniel wondered how they got the news so fast, unless, of course, someone from the Brewery called it in. He received threats from the insurance company, from the Department of Rehabilitative Services, and from the

Department of Environmental Control, the last of which informed him that there would be a substantial clean-up fee for the oil and gasoline that spilled into the English Kills. Both the fire department and the police did their investigations to determine whether it was just an accident or arson. To make matters worse, Malchus was highly agitated and blabbered to all the strangers and investigators at the facility about his extraterrestrial adventures and alien visitations.

A strange notion came into Daniel's head from a source that could only be described as heavenly. He saw Stephanie in her office nonchalantly arranging flowers as if there were no chaos or disorder in the world, as if her life were a sunny suburban bed of roses and she the contented mother of six children. She looked perfectly at peace, and he wondered if she had been drinking or had taken tranquilizers. As he came closer to her, he could smell her warm perfume and hear her gently humming. She turned and smiled at her boss. Her face beamed and all she could say was, "He's gone."

At that very moment, Lemmy Alone blasted into the front office like a torpedo heading for an oil tanker. Daniel was an easy mark and he would be sinking fast. Lemmy put his bony hand on Daniel's shoulder like a slick thief who was about to sell him the Brooklyn Bridge.

"Danny, I need to speak with you. I know this isn't the best time, but I have an immediate crisis to deal with."

Daniel was up to his neck in alligators, investigators, and the press and Lemmy had a crisis?

"Lemmy, can't this wait?" Daniel's eyes darted from one chaotic scene to the next. "I've got fifteen phone calls to make and I'll probably be seeing the mayor of New York City walk in the door in the next five minutes. My office stinks like smoke, and we have two feet of water in the warehouse."

Lemmy looked down at the floor, his eyes filled with crocodile tears. "Daniel, my aunt Gertie just died, suddenly, like that." He snapped his fingers. "My mom's a wreck; she doesn't know what to do. Gertie didn't have any insurance, not even enough to bury her or even to take her to the cemetery. We just can't leave her in her room and wait for the sanitation department to pick her up. She's not a piece of garbage, you know."

Daniel's patience was wearing thin. Lemmy wanted something, and he knew that Daniel had more important things on his plate.

"Danny, friend, you know that fifty-nine Cadillac hearse we got in last week from Murphy's Mortuary? I'd like to use it to take Gertie to her final resting place. How's about a hundred dollars for the whole thing? It'll be out of your hair by three o'clock. Here, look, I even have the title to it in my pocket. Just sign it over and I'll drive it away. You'll never have to see that ugly monstrosity again and Gertie will be so happy."

Daniel was fascinated by Lemmy's clumsy manipulation of the situation. He could have come to him days before to buy the old hearse. Why was *now* such an opportune time, why at this terrible moment of confusion and disorder?

"I'll let you have the car under one condition," Daniel said.

"You want two hundred dollars for it?" Lemmy asked.

"No, I want to know what motivated you to ask for the car right now when all hell is breaking loose around me and things are coming apart at the seams."

There was a long period of silence as if Lemmy was arguing with himself. He pulled out a cigarette, got up to walk around the room, sat down again, and scratched his head.

"Gee, Danny, I don't know exactly. I'm a born finagler you know that. That's why I'm the manager of the stores. I've always been a good retailer. People are more likely to buy or sell things when they're under pressure, when they can't think straight. I guess I'm just taking advantage of the situation to get a good deal."

Daniel was satisfied. "Thank you for being honest," he said, patting Lemmy on the shoulder.

Daniel took the title and signed it over to Lemmy. "Here, take your hearse and give your aunt Gertie a decent ride."

Of course, there was no Aunt Gertie, or if there was, she wasn't dead yet.

Daniel thought about his response to Lemmy's request to buy the broken-down old hearse. Did he win or lose the game? He could have lost his temper and thrown Lemmy out of his office. This day should have driven him berserk. Nobody would have blamed him if he slugged the TV reporter in the face or quit his job. He felt that he was in control for a brief instant in time. He thought about Stephanie and her strange remarks about the man who was now gone. *Who* had been there in the first place? A nagging feeling returned and he went back to Stephanie's office. Moe Kutcher came running in, his right hand compulsively brushing the crotch of his pants.

"Dr. Aarons, I think we have a dead man upstairs in the big room. Looks like somebody took a toilet seat to his head. Blood all over the floor."

Daniel responded in his usual professional manner.

"Moe, get those emergency technicians upstairs before they leave the warehouse. I'm going upstairs. Are you sure he's dead?"

"Well, he's not talking and—"

"Never mind, just go get those technicians."

Daniel ran out of the office, down the hall, and upstairs to the big dormitory. The stairwells were poorly lit and Daniel tripped over what appeared to be a man sitting in the middle of the stairs blocking his way.

"What the hell are you doing sitting here?" Daniel demanded. "Get out of my way. There's a man up there dead or dying."

The man on the stairs spoke in a calm, reassuring voice. "The man isn't dead or dying, he's just bleeding profusely. But they'll have him fixed up in no time."

Daniel's nemesis, the ghostly visage of Manasseh Cain, made his appearance again and was doing his best to create havoc and to hinder Daniel's progress. The man looked much larger than he had appeared a few nights before sitting on the sofa on the loading dock.

"I told you I'd be back," Cain said. "Well, here I am."

"Cain, what the hell do you want?" Daniel demanded.

"I have all the hell I need," Cain responded. "I have all the hell I could possibly want. There are things, however, that I desperately desire and those things that I desire I must have and have completely."

"Do you want to be executive consultant of the Brewery?" Daniel said with exasperation. "Because if you do, you can have the whole stinking place, lock, stock, and barrel. I'm sick of this damned job. Everything I do here turns to shit and nobody gives a damn!"

Daniel's frustration was evident, and he began to shrink before the looming evil of the man sitting on the stairway.

"That's wonderful, Dr. Aarons. I'm so glad that I've had the opportunity to speak with you this afternoon and, by the way, it's not your job that I want. Heaven forbid, it's not even *you* that I want! You're too holy, too honest, such a perfect pain in the ass. You're nothing but tasteless oatmeal and soluble fiber. What I want is sweet and juicy, something to melt in my mouth and you can believe me, Daniel Aarons, I've had quite a taste of her these past few weeks. What an utter joy to come to her apartment at midnight and caress those soft breasts, those thighs." Cain licked his lips. "But I've given her a little vacation. I haven't seen her in days, and she probably thinks I'm out of her life. I'm sure she will miss me. She loves the way I give her pleasure. She just can't seem to get enough of me."

Daniel suddenly realized whom Stephanie had been talking about. Her Stranger was none other than Manasseh Cain, the personification of evil, the devil himself! The man on the stairs grew even larger until his entire body filled the stairway. There was no light coming from above. Daniel felt cold and weak, his energy draining from his body.

A small voice came from above the ballooning body of Manasseh Cain.

"Daniel, how big is the devil?"

It was Malchus calling to Daniel from the top of the stairs. Daniel remembered that Malchus had asked him that question before.

"He's as big as I want him to be," Daniel replied.

The bloated body of the satanic figure shrunk back to human size, but remained fixed to the stairway.

Cain turned his head and stared at the dwarf.

"Very smart, little man, but your remedy is just temporary. Now I know your game. I have declared my intentions to both of you, and it will no longer be necessary for me to deal with either of you in my present form. Stephanie Croix is not a strong girl, but her soul is old and very wise. I want it and I will take it. Her body will give it to me."

Cain pushed Daniel aside and ran down the stairway into the darkness. Malchus waited at the top of the stairs.

Nervous, fidgety men filled the big dormitory. A scared young man sat on his bed holding a towel to his throbbing head. The blood on the floor was mopped up. The emergency medical technician was putting away his equipment. No dead man.

CHAPTER 22

✠ ✠ ✠

THE FIGHT IN THE DORMITORY WAS NO big deal. The young man with the bruised head only needed a few stitches and the old oak floor simply soaked up the blood. The young man's armor-plated skull was no match for Emmett Riley's toilet seat. Emmett didn't believe in placing his tender, delicate buttocks on a toilet seat that was used by thirty drunken men, some of whom couldn't piss off the side of a boat and hit the water. As a skilled woodworker who fixed furniture in the shops, Emmett fashioned his own personal toilet seat to protect him from filth and disease. He even monogrammed it with his name engraved in gold letters. The thing weighed about eight pounds and it had become a useful weapon as well. Emmett often carried it around his neck like a security blanket. When it wasn't in use, it hung on a large hook over his bed surrounding a picture of a very large-busted woman. Since the toilet seat had been used in several dorm fights, Daniel confiscated the device and assigned Riley to do daily lavatory cleanup. Consequently, the toilets, showers, and porcelain fixtures were virtually spotless. They were so clean, so to speak, you could eat off them. Eventually, Emmett Riley was cured of his need to have a personal hygiene toilet seat. Since he was now *Commodore Commode* (as the men called him), he took control of his own affairs and became a model worker at the Brewery. Daniel had at least one success story of which to boast.

The smoky aroma of the truck fire still filled the downstairs administrative offices. The burned-out hulk still sat near the loading dock, its blackened body and tireless wheel rims made it look like an animal carcass that had been in the sun too long. A few parts were still salvageable and Tooch cannibalized the remains until there was virtually nothing left. The fire wasn't arson, but it was no accident either. It was simply a lit cigarette carelessly thrown into a volatile pile of oily cotton rags.

Stephanie was a happy worker, at least for this minute. Her moods were as erratic as the movement of a housefly. She changed her looks and expressions so often that you could be talking to her one moment and believing that you were talking to someone else the next. She'd come into the office in the morning with her short dark brown hair combed in bangs over her forehead. A few minutes later, her hair would have a hint of orange and brushed straight back. She'd go from bright red lipstick to dark purple between 10:00 AM and noon. Two earrings at 3:00 PM became a nose ring by quitting time. She'd change her outfit just as often with clothing pulled out of bins in the thrift store. Poor Daniel never knew whom she was or to whom he was talking. Even the color and texture of her voice changed. One minute she'd be deep and sexy and the next she'd sound like a three-year-old with nasal congestion. Stephanie Croix had become a chameleon that could virtually change before his eyes!

Daniel, who was getting used to the unending turmoil in the Brewery, could not deal with Stephanie's Jekyll and Hyde transformations. He wanted some stable vantage point, and he hoped that Stephanie would be his star on the horizon from which to navigate. In a terrible moment of anxiety and frustration, he grabbed her by the arm and shook her like a rag doll. He screamed in her face.

"What the fuck is going on Stephanie? You've been in and out the bathroom fifteen times today changing clothes, hair, shoes, makeup. What gives?"

His behavior was very unprofessional and she pulled herself away from him. He was like the crazy father of the teenage girl who had just been told that the daughter was running off with the soda jerk from the corner drugstore. She would have none of his anxieties or impulsive physicality.

"Don't you ever touch me like that! No one touches Mut, mother to the world, wife of Amun, mother of Khonsu the moon god."

She continued to rant, placed curses on him, and waved her arms as if they were magic wands. Moby and Ernie ran out of the dispatcher's office to see what the ruckus was about, but Stephanie continued her chants and spewed ancient curses.

"Amset, Amset," she said, "son of Horus, mummified man that you are, protect me. Save me from his evil grip."

She spun around like a top, her arms going in all directions. Smoke appeared to pour from the top of her head like a chimney. She looked as if she would either bore a hole in the floor or take off like a helicopter and go through the ceiling. An ear-piercing screech came from her mouth like the sound of a thousand fingernails on a blackboard. Her breath was like that of a thousand dogs.

Men came from all over the Brewery to see what was going on. Malchus ran from the kitchen and tried to rescue her from her wild destructive frenzy, but the field of energy that surrounded her was just too powerful. She picked up the little man and threw him against the wall. The windows in the front office shattered and glass flew everywhere. This terrifying scene went on for at least five minutes and then it was suddenly over. It was as if she had been unplugged from an electrical socket. The office was devastated. The forces, the sounds, the smoke, and fury were all gone in an instant, and Stephanie came crashing down like an egg dropped from the roof of a ten-story building. Daniel ran to her, scooped her off the ground, and placed her gently on the couch. She was unconscious and barely breathing.

"Call nine-one-one," Daniel demanded.

Her body quivered and shook; she foamed at the mouth and then sighed. Her breathing started and within moments, she opened her eyes and gazed upon the terrified face of Daniel, the man who loved her, and the man who seemed to have precipitated this terrible episode.

"Daniel, Daniel, sweet Daniel," she whispered.

She reached up with one finger to touch the tear rolling down his cheek.

"Daniel, I thought he was gone forever. He stopped coming to my apartment to make love to me and to torment me, but now he's here to stay. I can't ..." She fainted again.

The ambulance arrived and Stephanie was taken to a hospital only a few blocks from the Brewery. Daniel, Malchus, and John followed behind in one of the trucks. She remained in intensive care until she regained consciousness a few hours later. The three men stayed at the hospital and waited for news of her condition.

Daniel was beside himself with guilt. He blamed himself for everything that went wrong and was feeling sorry for himself and his miserable attempts at running the Brewery.

"I've had it," he said with a sigh. "I just can't stand another minute more working in that insane place. I used to be a nice quiet intellectual, reading books and teaching a few classes, but now look at me! I see ghosts, have visions of extraterrestrials, and talk to Satan on old couches in the warehouse." He looked up toward the ceiling of the waiting room in the hospital. "Are you testing me, God?" he asked angrily.

The question was rhetorical, of course, but Malchus, in true rabbinical fashion, answered the question with a further series of questions.

"Daniel," Malchus asked, "are you a blind, quivering mass of self-pity wallowing in a fetid pool of putrid human waste?"

"No, of course not," replied Daniel. "I'm not the type of man who feels sorry for himself."

Malchus rolled his eyes.

"I've had considerable experience with a wide variety of difficult, interpersonal relationships," continued Daniel in his usual arrogant manner. "Much of what I see and hear at the Brewery is nothing more than the result of intense emotional disturbance and the power of the psyche on the delicate matrix of space and time. It's like the warping power of gravity, just more subtle and inconsistent."

"Good," said Malchus. "Daniel, do you believe in the devil?"

"Well, no. I mean, yes," Daniel replied with an evident arching brow. "Well, I do believe in the personification of evil. How can evil exist in anything but a rational thinking mind and who else on this planet is capable of rational thinking? A tree that falls on a house is not evil and neither is an earthquake that kills thousands. Evil is always premeditated and presents itself in human form, like a Hitler or a Stalin."

"Good," said Malchus. "Daniel, how big is the devil?"

"As big as I want him to be," Daniel responded like a schoolboy.

"Exactly!" said Malchus. "And for some ridiculous reason, you want him to be so big that you will consent to losing control of the Brewery just so you won't feel responsible for the consequences. In other words, my friend, you have given Satan exactly what he wants because you think you are powerless and incompetent to change your life. Daniel, you have the power to move mountains, but you resign yourself to being moved by external forces like a feather in the wind."

"But what about Stephanie?" Daniel asked. "She's lying there unconscious."

"Daniel, Stephanie's been battling Satan for millennia. She was at war long before you came to the Brewery. Remember, she's a very old soul in a young, weak body. She craves release and the final ascent to God. There's a lot of power and wisdom sitting in that delicate earthen vessel, but she's an easy target for the evil one who will grab her and imprison her as long as she allows him into her world. Daniel, she told me her secret. Every night, her Stranger came to her in the person of a beautiful man, and he gave her physical pleasures that were beyond anything imaginable. At the same time, he was taking life from her and digging a pit within her soul like an animal that digs in the soil to make its home. I'm afraid he's made his home in her and we will have to get him out. She no longer has the power to do it herself, and Daniel, I don't have the foggiest idea how we're going to do it. I'm wrestling with my own demons and just trying to stay out of alien spacecraft."

Suddenly, Malchus' eyes rolled to the back of his head. He stammered and then began to talk like a blithering idiot. "Maybe she'd like some of my cookies. I've got a great idea; she and I could take a trip to *Bachooch* in the Andromeda galaxy."

Malchus was digressing rapidly and his monologue was now nothing more than incoherent gibberish. He deflated like a balloon and simply sputtered onto the floor. Whatever energy and focus Malchus had was now lost but was resurfacing in Daniel. He now had the full picture of Stephanie's condition and her lingering illness. But was it a physical disease, a mental illness, or an actual possession of her soul by the devil? Malchus opened a small door into Stephanie's problems, but it would require Daniel to tear down the walls and pull out her demons.

The door to the waiting room opened and an ER nurse somberly asked to see Stephanie's next of kin. Daniel followed the nurse to a small adjacent room where Stephanie was hooked up to a full array of tubes and monitors. Her eyes were wide open and her cheeks were flushed.

"Well, don't look so happy to see me," she said sarcastically.

Daniel couldn't believe his eyes. Just thirty minutes before, she was a raving psychotic, spinning out of control and swallowing her tongue, and now she looked like a happy young mother who had just given birth to her first child.

"You look perfectly ... beautiful, like nothing happened," Daniel said in amazement.

"I feel just fine," Stephanie replied. "Why am I here in the hospital? What happened to me at the Brewery? The last thing I remember is getting up from my desk to go to the bathroom and then ... Nothing!"

Daniel didn't remind her about his aggressive behavior or her remarks about the beautiful Stranger who came to her bed each night. He'd deal with that problem later.

"You just fainted and we called the rescue squad," he said.

"Well, when can I get out of this place? I'm really not sick, you know."

"The doctor says he'll keep you overnight just to make sure nothing else happens. It's just for precautions. I'll come tomorrow morning and take you home. Now you better get some rest." He delicately kissed her cheek and Stephanie smiled.

CHAPTER 23

✠ ✠ ✠

DANIEL AARONS WAS A RESPONSIBLE MAN. HE was responsible for the safety and well-being of sixty alcoholic and chronically mentally ill men. He was also responsible for one depressed uncle (who also happened to be his biological father); one very disturbed girl whom he deeply loved, but who was now possessed by the devil, and one highly inconsistent one-eared dwarf with great wisdom and supernatural powers when he wasn't blabbering gibberish or baking cookies.

The great leader of the Brewery sat on a subway train headed for Greenpoint. He tried to make some sense of his crazy life, but came to the conclusion that everything was simply senseless and without meaning. There was no rhyme or reason for anything. Shit just happened. If Daniel had never been born, life would still be meaningless because it wouldn't matter. He thought how the world might be if Pinchas, his brother, had lived and been saved from on top of the pile of corpses in the concentration camp. He thought about Jacob, his father! He still hadn't told Jacob about his visitation from Pinchas and as far as Jacob was concerned, they were still uncle and nephew. Daniel felt that his life was hanging by a thread and at any moment, it could break, tumbling him into the abyss of oblivion. But at the same moment, he felt that he had reached a point of no return and that in a very short time all the loose ends would be tied together into one strong unbreakable cord. The tug-of-war within his soul sapped his energy and blurred his focus.

He traveled through the dark tunnel to his destination, Greenpoint Hospital, where he'd pick up Stephanie and take her home.

Greenpoint Hospital was a massive municipal facility and Stephanie was somewhere inside that medical machine being treated, processed, or simply ignored. Daniel walked to the front desk and spoke to the volunteer.

"I'm here to pick up Stephanie Croix," he said. "She's being discharged this morning. She was brought into the ER yesterday, and I'm not sure where she is today."

The elderly woman behind the desk flipped through a clipboard of hospital patients.

"No Stephanie Croix here now. She was discharged about an hour ago," the woman said in a clipped, curt manner.

"Are you sure?" Daniel asked. "I was supposed to come get her. Is there someone here who might have seen her leave, perhaps a nurse on her floor?"

The woman called the nurse's station on the seventh floor and told Daniel to go see the nurse on duty. She had seen Stephanie leave. When Daniel arrived at the station, the nurse told him that she left with a tall man who claimed to be her husband.

"Damn!" He slapped his head as if he knew there was tribulation ahead.

"Did she put up any kind of struggle? Was she on medication when he came for her?" Daniel asked in exasperation.

"Nope, she just left the hospital. No meds. Looked fine to me. I wheeled her down to the car myself."

"The car? She went with the man in a *car*?"

The nurse looked at Daniel as if the word *car* was not part of his vocabulary.

"Yes, her husband had some nice fancy car," the nurse said. "But, I don't know anything about cars. It looked new. Bright red. Hey, are you a relative or something?"

"Yea, something," replied Daniel dejectedly.

The nurse simply shrugged and got on with her business.

Daniel called the Brewery, hoping that Stephanie and her *husband* might have called. There had been no phone calls and no messages. In desperation, he went to her apartment on Adelphi Street. He banged on the apartment door, but there was no answer. He turned the knob and the door opened. Her apartment was empty—no sign of furniture, clothing, cats, or food. It looked like it had been scrubbed down, cleaned, and painted just days before, awaiting the arrival of a new tenant. He left the apartment and spoke with one of her neighbors just leaving the building, an older woman carrying a grocery bag.

"Excuse me, do you know Stephanie Croix?" Daniel asked the woman. He was polite, yet frantic on the inside.

The woman spoke with a heavy accent. "Don't know her good. She go in and out all day. I say hello in hall."

"Have you seen her recently?"

"Who you?" The woman was mistrustful of Daniel's questioning. "I don't give no personal information. You a cop?"

"No, she works for me and she's been in the hospital," Daniel said gently. "She was discharged from Greenpoint this morning, and I don't know where she is. She might be really sick."

"You her pimp, huh? Nah, you don't look like pimp. You look like nice man. Sorry, it's just that she go in and out all the time and these dirty guys come and go all night. They leave in the morning. I see her crawl out of her apartment like a cat. She a secretary?" The old woman laughed.

Daniel stiffened. "She's a nice girl. She just has problems and she's depressed … and a few other things. I'm concerned that she might hurt herself."

"Let me tell you something … What's your name?" the woman asked.

"Dr. Aarons."

"I knew you were a good man, a doctor, too. Dr. Aarons, she left the building last week. She moved out with this good-looking guy in a flashy red car. She said he was her husband. What was I to know? I thought he was her pimp. She looked so happy, not like when she slinked out of her apartment in the morning. A truck came by after she left and cleaned out the place. I don't know where she went, sorry. I can't help you no more." The old woman threw up her hands and said, "Poof."

Daniel left the tenement and slumped down on the stoop. He blamed himself for the miserable way things turned out. Perhaps he should have shown his true feelings to Stephanie, although that wouldn't have been the professional thing to do. He loved her and that was the most important thing in his life, certainly more important than his damned career.

He walked the streets for hours thinking of what to do and where she might be. He decided not to go back to the Brewery, but to walk home. The disorder he left yesterday would still be waiting for him tomorrow morning. He climbed the three flights of stairs to his apartment and entered the small living room that contained Jacob's library and the piles of decaying newspapers and magazines. Jacob Koretz sat in his recliner and smoked a cigar. Malchus, the unexpected guest, sat across from him reading aloud from one of Jacob's earlier volumes of poetry. Daniel closed the door and looked at the two occupants. He knew he was going to have an interesting evening.

CHAPTER 24

✞ ✞ ✞

JACOB BLEW A PUFF OF SMOKE IN Daniel's direction as if to attract his attention to the metaphors pouring from Malchus' mouth. Jacob always loved to read his poetry to audiences, but when another individual was gracious enough to read it aloud to him, he felt truly honored. The old man got up from his recliner with an unexpected surge of energy and pointed to a pot simmering on the stove in the kitchen.

"Danny, I've made a delicious pot of beef stew today, and we're all going to have a nice dinner tonight and talk about poetry, philosophy, beautiful women, and get a little drunk."

Daniel was not in the mood for poetry or any of his uncle's crazy, mixed-up philosophy. His head churned and his heart ached. He brought home with him several laundry bags filled with guilt, responsibility, and remorse, and he'd have to launder each of them before he went back to work tomorrow. He threw up his hands like a man who just had a gun stuck in his back and looked at the two men in the smoky living room.

"Stephanie's gone, vanished!" Daniel exclaimed. "She got picked up by some guy at the hospital, and he took her off to the Catskills to get married. She's probably rolling in the sack right now. He drives a red Mercedes and has two homes, one in Manhattan, and the other in Palm Beach. I bet he has his hands all over her body right now. What the hell, she doesn't need a stinkin' job at a rescue mission for old drunks when she can live the life of Riley with some rich, fancy dude. She doesn't need to put up with the likes of a moody, self-pitying, neurotic like me. I bet they've made love ten times in the last five minutes, probably did it in the back of his limousine. I'll call the employment commission tomorrow, maybe they can send over a temp, fast. She couldn't type to save her life anyway. Used enough *white out* to cover a billboard."

Jacob and Malchus sat patiently as Daniel continued his weary lament. Jacob blew smoke, and Malchus took small sips of Jacob's wine.

"She was such a sweet girl, though," Daniel said as if he were delivering her eulogy. "A little screwy and wild, but she really had the heart and she cared so much. I was in love with her the moment I saw her banging away at that old typewriter. And what about those big floppy sneakers? Damn!"

Malchus put his drink down and stood up. He had heard enough from Daniel and the endless chorus of guilt.

"Daniel, you talk about her like she was already dead and buried and you were responsible for killing her. Get a grip, man! The fight has just begun. You haven't lost your love to some flashy, rich, sex-hungry stud. The woman is under the power of the Angel of Death, Satan himself, and *you* are her only salvation. It was so obvious. I should have seen it earlier. All those signs, all that weird behavior."

Daniel banged his head against the wall three times.

"I think I see now!" he said with a gleam in his eyes. "All those guys coming to her apartment in the middle of the night; they weren't different guys, they were the same guy! But I thought the devil looked like Manasseh Cain, ugly, scrawny, creepy, with clawed fingers."

"Daniel," Malchus said, "the devil makes himself look just the way you expect him to look. If you expect a big guy with horns and a tail, you got it. If your devil is a dashing young stud who can give you orgasms all night, he's the one knocking at your door. Some guys, as you know, can even find him right here in this bottle." Malchus pointed to the vodka. "Gentlemen, I see the devil every night, but he's never the same twice. He's always sneaking up behind me. Sometimes, he's an innocent-looking alien taking me to another planet, but then he gives me an ice water enema and smiles with his four pairs of lips! Other times, he's a kindly old woman who invites me up to her apartment for tea and then ties me up in a garbage bag and throws me into a Dumpster."

Jacob sprung to life as if he had experienced a jolt of an electric current.

"Daniel, the ancient rabbis even go as far as to represent the devil as the greatest benefactor in the whole universe. Can you believe that? Because of the devil, the Law of God was given to us as a protection against him and as light to guide our way."

He picked up an old decaying book and read, "Before Adam sinned, he obeyed only the wisdom whose light shines from above; he had not yet descended to the ground from the tree of life. But when he yielded to desire to know the things here below and to descend to them, he became acquainted with evil and forgot the good. He separated himself from the tree of life. Before Adam and Eve committed their first sin, they heard God's voice from above. But after they sinned, they couldn't understand even the voice of Satan from below."

"You mean we don't even understand what Satan is saying to us because of our sin?" Daniel asked, sounding like a young boy questioning his rabbi.

"Precisely," said Jacob. "We are deaf to all things spiritual, the virtuous spirits, as well as the evil ones. The good ones have to guide us and push us around like wooden dummies, while the evil ones lure us to certain destruction through their beautiful seductions and temptations. Unless your ears have been cut off, you remain deaf. It's only when your natural ears have been cut off that you can receive the spiritual ears that God intended for you. And that's exactly what happened to our dear friend, Malchus. He was deaf to all things spiritual as the servant of the high priest, but when Peter cut his ear off in the garden, he allowed God to heal his ear and to give him a new sense of hearing."

Daniel and Malchus looked at the old man and pondered his words of wisdom. Koretz, himself, couldn't even fully comprehend the depth of his new understanding, but he continued to speak.

"Evil comes to fruition through spiritual deafness. When Adam and Eve saw the fruit of the tree, they liked what they saw, but they couldn't hear the warnings of God, and the words of Satan made no sense to them either. So they took the fruit, ate it, and it became a part of their very soul. That is what has happened to Stephanie, she has seen the fruit of the devil, and she has found it pleasing to look at. She climbed down from the tree and set foot upon the earth where she could no longer hear the voice of God."

Koretz grabbed a knife from the kitchen table. "Daniel, Malchus, which one of you is going to cut off her ear?"

All three touched the sides of their heads as if to ponder the consequences of cutting off an ear. Only Malchus knew the reality of the act and its consequences. All three men experienced a new and deeper insight and wisdom. As had been the case so many times before, Malchus had been the catalyst for God's action. Either he was the example pointed to by others or he himself was unwittingly bringing about miraculous changes in the world.

Within minutes, through the divine utterances of Jacob Koretz, Malchus' entire life was taking a new turn. The seeds that had been planted in his head by his guardian angels were now beginning to germinate. As if pulled by a heavenly tide, Malchus walked to the window of Daniel's apartment and climbed out onto the roof of the lower section of the building. The sun was beginning to set, and a beam of silver blue light came from across the East River to exactly the spot where Malchus was standing. Immediately, his body began to glow and he became translucent. Daniel and Jacob ran to the window and observed the beautiful, eerie light and the glowing form of the dwarf.

Three men now appeared with Malchus on the roof as if the light had beamed them down. Naphtali Ropshitz was on one side, Raphael and Moshe on the other. The three angels and Malchus were suspended in a glowing sphere of light that floated over the roof like a cloud. A face became visible over the sphere and two arms appeared to hold it and support it above the roof. A soft voice came from the great sphere of dazzling light.

"This is Malchus," the voice said, "my good and beloved servant. I have chosen him to perform miracles and to change the course of the universe. Many years ago, I gave him the ears to hear the voice of God. Yesterday, I sent him angels who planted seeds of love in his head. Today, I give him the power to heal the sick and to destroy the evil in the world."

Daniel and Jacob stood frozen in amazement as they saw the heavenly vision and heard the divine voice. Jacob was confused and didn't know how to respond to this incredible sight.

"Daniel, let's invite them all in for dinner, they look a little hungry. You know it's a long way from where they have come," Jacob said.

Daniel had seen this light before, first when it took Ron Peppler and gave him a new hand. Daniel got down on his knees and covered his face because he was afraid to look at the face in the light. But somehow, he knew this face. It was the same face that had given Malchus his new ears in the Garden of Gethsemane and the same face that held open the narrow door at the Brewery during his meeting with Pinchas. Perhaps it was the face of his messiah.

Jacob knew in his heart that it was the face of God, and he cried out a prayer from the psalms. A stream of light poured out from the hands that surrounded the sphere, hit Jacob squarely in the face, and knocked him to the floor. The flash temporarily blinded Daniel, who rushed to Jacob's side. The old man screamed in pain.

"Daniel, I can't see, I'm blind!" the old man yelled. "The whole world is gone! I'm blind. I'm blind!"

Several moments passed in utter silence and then Jacob screamed again. "No, wait a minute, I'm not blind, I can see! But now I can't see those damn black holes anymore. Daniel, those black holes that were in front of my face, they're gone. It's a miracle! I've been healed. I can see!"

Daniel hovered over Jacob and hugged his neck as the old man continued to shout his praises to God. The brilliant sphere of light filled the entire room and now surrounded Daniel and Jacob. A heavenly apparition stood before the two men, it was Pinchas Koretz. This time he was not the young janitor sweeping up the synagogue or the dead infant on the pile of corpses in the concentration camp. He was a majestic angel, a being of pure light who radiated a stream of love to the two men in the room. He spoke in words and gestures that only Jacob and Daniel could comprehend. He spread out their entire lives in front of them in an instant, and before they could take their next breath, Jacob Koretz was holding both of his sons in his arms.

CHAPTER 25

✠ ✠ ✠

HUMAN BEINGS ARE IN A CONSTANT STATE of physical, mental, and spiritual evolution, which is what the Creator intended. Growth and change are inevitable. The Almighty is forever forming his creatures, kneading them like dough, and then pushing them through a series of dies until they are finished products, like pasta. Some become angel hair—capellini—and are a delight to eat with a light white sauce and a fine wine. Others are simply ravioli stuffed with meat. Sometimes the dies are wide, and the product passes through easily, but other times the die is extremely narrow and the passage is long and arduous.

God kneaded Malchus One Ear and sent him through a long series of dies until he was extruded in to a virtually perfect product. Not quite capellini, but perhaps vermicelli. The little man had become aware of his new role as one of God's prophets, but that didn't stop the devil from tempting him day and night or tormenting his small, sickly body. No, on the contrary, Malchus continued to be perfected through a multitude of trials: floods, isolation, loneliness, and finally fire.

Malchus still stood less than three feet tall and had practically no brain to speak of, just a big jug head filled with water. He proudly wore his floppy hat like a crown and sported Naphtali Ropshitz's New York Yankees sweatshirt, which had become his mantle.

The angelic fresco that Stephanie had painted on his back had long since faded, and he missed his friend very much. He knew Stephanie was still in the hands of Satan, and it was still a mystery to him how he would get her back. God had given him power, but he did not know how to use it against the forces of evil. He was given the creative power to heal both the body and broken relationships, but was he also given the power to destroy the personification of evil, the devil himself?

Malchus could now experience the Creator's universe through a clear and open mind. Many memories flooded back to him, especially the good memories of the gifts given to him by Tali, Raphael, and Moshe, his three guardian angels. His delusions and hallucinations ceased, but his visions of angels and extraterrestrial beings continued. Eventually, he concluded that they were all the same. He traveled through the vast expanses of the universe through time warps, wormholes, and black holes. He made sense of the intricate matrix of infinite parallel universes that connected the physical worlds with the spiritual realm.

The great dazzling beam of light that transformed him in Daniel's apartment would now call to him when he climbed to the roof of the Brewery. Everything Malchus accomplished, however, was still in the guise of the one-eared dwarf with the floppy hat. He could have asked God to give him a handsome new body with powerful arms and long legs, and he could have had a deep, robust voice to declare the Word of the Lord. Malchus knew, however, that God wanted him to continue to do his work in anonymity and without the praise of people. He would receive his praise directly from God.

Nobody noticed any changes in Malchus, not even Daniel who witnessed the transformation first hand. For the sake of the world, Malchus persisted in telling his wild crazy stories and baking his cookies in the Brewery's kitchen. Each day, he would take a dozen to the Ten Eyck Nursing Center and feed his friends. The old ones laughed and left the world with smiles on their faces. Some of the young ones actually threw off their diseases and disabilities like old clothes and walked out of Ten Eyck forever. Malchus' touch was a healing touch, and he cared for his friends like a loving brother. The days brought peace and fulfillment to Malchus the prophet, but his nights were still filled with torment and temptation. But isn't that where the devil works his best, in the dark?

Seven weeks after his transformation on the roof of Jacob's tenement, Malchus felt great pangs of loneliness as if he were a small child craving the warmth and affection of his mother. He had never known such affection, since the real intention of his mother was to send him away to be saved by a more able and caring world.

That night, Malchus dreamed of floating on the wide, open sea. He cried out to the fish and the birds, but he received no response. For forty consecutive nights, he had the same dream, waking exhausted and very depressed. His strength was ebbing, and he felt that he could no longer serve his friends at Ten Eyck. His prayers were to no avail, and he was beginning to think that God had abandoned him once more. On the forty-first night, however, he found himself again on the sea, but a voice was calling to him from a distant island.

"Malchus, I'm your mother," the voice cried. "Come to me, child, I want to give you the love you never had. I'm sorry for casting you adrift on the wild sea. I've been here on this desolate island all by myself for so many years and I'm so lonely. Do you forgive me, Malchus?"

Malchus cried out to the voice, "Yes, Mother, I forgive you. I'm coming to rescue you. I'll take you off that island and we'll go home."

He reached the shore of the island and saw a small, thin, gray woman dressed in rags sitting on the beach. He leaped out of his boat and ran to her open arms and she began to caress him. She kissed his cheek, but then began to kiss his lips like a lover. Her soft caress became a powerful embrace and Malchus could feel that her heart was beating wildly. The gray, haggard woman became a beautiful young girl with long, golden hair. She threw off her rags and tightly pressed her naked body next to his. She took his head, placed it on one of her breasts, and begged him to become the infant she never suckled. Malchus had never experienced true warmth or intimacy with a woman, not with his mother as an infant nor with a lover. The beautiful girl's legs wrapped around his small body, and she begged him to come into her. She kissed him ravenously and pressed her fingers into his back. He became a part of her body. His ecstasy continued for what seemed hours, but Malchus was beginning to realize that his strength was waning. He felt his body get smaller and smaller as she squeezed and pressed him inside of her. He wondered now if this glorious experience wasn't just some illusion, a temptation from Satan to seduce him and steal his power. He pushed the girl away and she cried.

"Malchus," she pleaded, "I can give you the pleasures you need and desire. We can live on this beautiful island together for eternity, and I will be forever young and beautiful. Malchus, I was created for you and you alone. Let my body be your refuge, let my breasts feed you, let my lips caress your face, and I will make you happy."

Malchus continued to push her away, but as he pushed she persisted in her pleas. He touched her face for one last time and then turned away from her and ran down the beach. He looked back and saw that she was again the thin, gray woman in rags pleading for him to return.

"Malchus," she said, "if you will not return for a beautiful woman, won't you return for your dying mother? If you do not come back to me, Satan will claim my soul, and I will be forever damned."

She reached out her hand and Malchus came back to touch it, but in a moment of strength he continued to push on in the opposite direction. When he turned his eyes back to the vision of his mother, she had vanished. No trace of her was left. He knew then that this beautiful apparition was nothing more than a trick of the tempter.

Malchus searched the beach for the tiny boat that brought him to the island. It was nowhere in sight, and he thought that it must have floated away. Fine, white sand covered the shore. Palm trees filled with coconuts and other exotic fruits lined the beach, and sweet-smelling flowering bushes were all around him. He stopped to pick some red ripe fruit that hung over his head and heard the strong voice of a young man.

"Go ahead," the voice said. "Eat all you want, there's plenty more where that came from."

Malchus turned around and behind him stood a young, very handsome man with bronze-colored skin and light brown hair. He smiled. His eyes were dark blue, and he held a couple of the large red melons.

"I guess you suppose I'm the devil, or Satan, or whatever his name happens to be today," he said to Malchus. "Well, maybe you're right and maybe you're wrong. You seem to be lost and running from something, but I'm right at home. Oh, by the way, your boat is over there."

He pointed to Malchus' little boat anchored just a few feet from where the two men were standing.

"You know, Malchus, people make me out to be such a bad fellow, such a wicked bastard."

"How do you know my name?" Malchus asked.

The young man looked surprised.

"This is *your* dream, isn't it? This is your island. Whom else would I be talking to? You must understand, I don't do this for my health. This is my job and I'm damn good at it. I only visit people on their personal islands, and I don't invite them to spend a weekend in hell either. I haven't been to hell in a long time—it's no fun. I prefer the real world. It's so unpredictable and exciting, just the way the Almighty created it. I wish people showed me a little more gratitude. Without me, they'd still be climbing that damned tree like monkeys, not knowing who was speaking to them either from above or below. When I coaxed that sweet little couple, Adam and Eve, down from their safety and security and gave them some of my fruit, it certainly did open their eyes. They've been drunk and happy ever since, but they've also learned how to walk on two legs instead of climbing around on those branches with their dumb ears pointing up to heaven. Their brains have gotten so big that the Almighty had to make their skulls larger. I see you have a pretty big head yourself. What a shame that it's only filled with water. Poor little guy doesn't have a brain to think with. I tell you, I have absolutely no intention of sending you to hell. In fact, in my entire existence of several hundred trillion years, I have never sent any poor soul to hell. Honest to God. The truth is, my good friend, people choose to go to hell and I only provide the hand basket. I don't even have a big neon sign on the place anymore. I took the big, wide doors off years ago, because people wore out the hinges. Folks just seem to know how to get in even if they're groping around in the dark. Every so often, I get mobs of them just clambering to get in as if I'm running a sale on souls. But I guess you're just not interested. I don't know why I'm even wasting my time with you. Am I wasting my time?"

"Yes," Malchus said emphatically. "I have no interest in your fruit, your place of abode, or anything else you have to give away."

"Oh, that's really too bad," Satan replied. "I saw how you enjoyed that beautiful, luscious young thing on the beach. Bet you never had so much fun. You can't tell me it didn't feel good, can you?"

Malchus hesitated. "Well, yes, it was very pleasant while it lasted. But I was also very conscious of her ability to drain my energy and sap my strength."

"Hey, I can get you one that'll keep you happy all the time and she won't take anything from you." Satan took out a catalog with photographs of beautiful women and showed it to Malchus. "I just wanted you to come down here and talk with me. You could have stayed there for all eternity, if I let you. Let me ask you a question, little man. You've been living in that shrunken, misshapen body for thirty years. It's ridiculous. You even have to aim up to take a piss in the toilet. Do women ever look at you with yearning? Do men take you seriously? Does anybody ever see you as anything but a circus freak in a big stupid hat?"

Malchus was speechless and hurt. He looked at his tiny body and sighed.

The young man continued. "You got water in your head, dwarf, and you really believe you've been all over the galaxy visiting planets. Well, I'll tell you something, prophet of the Lord, it's all a pack of lies and a pile of crap, and you are the chief bird sitting on that pile of shit chirping at a deaf world. So why don't you just give it up? Now, I'm not asking you to sell your soul. I don't know where people get the idea of having to sell their souls. We don't have that type of economy here. We sort of work on the simple barter system, and people usually come out with the good end of the deal. I have guys in beautiful mansions with blonde babes up to their armpits. There are fancy women smothered in furs and diamonds. They can lounge around at their own private pools to their hearts' content, but Malchus, I know you want something more than just the *things* of life. That's not important to you, I know that. You're a smart man with a high sense of purpose and mission. I'm very impressed, and I wish you a lot of luck in your new position. Now, because of your new title and heavy workload, I'm sure that you'll find that little awkward distorted body not particularly conducive to working miracles, healing the sick or stopping buses before they run over little children. I bet the last time you healed somebody you had to stand on a New York City telephone book. Am I correct?"

Malchus nodded.

"Well, have I got a deal for you. For absolutely nothing down, no soul, no body, I can let you have one of these gorgeous new physiques complete with well-developed musculature, high IQ brain, non-clogging colon, and equine-caliber genitalia."

Five very attractive young men came out of the bushes to present themselves before Malchus. Each was a perfect specimen any man would be proud to own. The thought of being six feet tall and urinating *down* into a toilet was very appealing to Malchus. He remembered the wonderful feelings he had with the girl on the beach. He dreamed of a clear, calm, fully functioning brain that would only complement his God-given powers and divine mission.

"I'm intrigued by your offer," Malchus said. "And I would be lying if I told you it didn't interest me. Believe me, I've felt jealous of most men who take their good strong bodies for granted. They go out and have sex with beautiful women, drive fast cars, wear attractive clothes. I can't do any of that. I've also seen those good bodies filled with poisons. And I've seen those men do violence to other men. They've also hurt and destroyed the bodies of women and children. Thank goodness, I can't do any of that with this little body. No, Satan, I have no need for your attractive enticements. This peculiar little vessel has done me good, and I guess it's exactly what God wants me to have."

"You're a mighty strong man, little Malchus," said the devil. "I knew you'd be a hard sell. Well, if you won't do it for yourself, how about if you do it for somebody you love? Isn't sacrifice something that you're all about?"

"What are you talking about now?" Malchus asked the devil.

Satan pointed down the beach. "See that little girl over there. Why don't you go over to her and see what she wants."

Malchus walked along the sand to the young child who was sitting on a stone with her eyes toward the sea. She looked to be about twelve years old.

Malchus gasped. "Stephanie, is that you?"

The little girl was crying.

"Yes, Malchus, it's me," the little girl responded. "He's got me here on his island and he won't let me go."

"But, Stephanie, this is *my* island and my dream. I can throw him off whenever I feel like, and I can take you home with me."

"No, Malchus, I'm afraid it's not that easy. I did a real stupid thing and ran away with him. I made all kinds of dumb trades and deals and now he owns me. He likes little girls, too. Malchus, you have to help me. You have to get me away from him or else I will be spending eternity with Satan."

"Don't worry, Mut, I'll do something. I won't let him have you." He kissed her cheek and walked back to the evil wheeler-dealer.

When he looked back at the rock where Stephanie had been sitting, she was gone. Malchus was furious and punched the devil's kneecaps, but it was like punching the air.

"You're a sly bastard, Satan. What do you really want? Do you want me? Do you want my soul, too?"

"You're really slow, my little friend," said Satan. "I don't want *you*. I don't even want that scrawny little girl over there. I have enough souls to last me for the next ten zillion eons. I simply want you to stop doing your miracles and retire from your work as the Almighty's anointed one! Go back to your little hole on the seventh floor of Bellevue Hospital and never be seen again. I want you to completely lose your mind because *you* are hindering my operations."

Malchus laughed. "I'll make a deal with you, Satan. I'll stop hindering your operations if you'll stop hindering mine."

"It's not so easy, Malchus. I've been in this profession for a long time. I just can't up and leave. I don't have any progeny to take over the business." He paused. "Unless you want to be my partner."

"Forget it, Satan, I'll never be in league with the devil, and I'll never forsake my mission."

"Suit yourself," the devil said. "It's not going to be easy; I can assure you of that. I hope you can swim and put out fires. As for that darling little girl sitting on the rock, she will just be one of many whom I will torment for eternity and eventually destroy. But you have your mission and I have my work. You know, I'm really getting tired of starting all these world wars, famines, and diseases. You sure you're still not interested?"

"No," barked Malchus. "And for that matter, you can go to hell!"

"Oh, but hell is such a boring place," said Satan. "Good-bye, Malchus!"

The devil picked up the little man by the scruff of his neck and threw him as far as he could into the sea. Malchus couldn't swim, but he paddled the water like a dog. He screamed, but there was no one to help him. His arms were heavy and tired, and he sank into the blackness of the deep waters. But as he sank, he felt a warm hand beneath him, and he rose to the surface of the sea in a bubble. The bubble burst and he awakened from his dream covered in sea foam and sweat.

Malchus sat on his bed in the dormitory and contemplated what he had just experienced until the morning sun streamed through the window. As the first rays of sunlight struck Malchus on his bed, Moby Dixon walked past the dwarf still in reverie.

"Hey, bubblehead, did you just take a bath?" asked Moby and then gave out a roaring laugh. "You're covered in suds. The bathroom is over there."

Malchus glanced at his hands and legs, which were covered in white foam. He lifted his right hand, blew at the suds, and a thousand bubbles drifted up to the ceiling. The sun shone through each little sphere and a rainbow of colors appeared on the wall behind his head. Within seconds, they had all burst and disappeared.

Malchus rose to his feet and screamed to the men in the dormitory, "I have the answer. I know the truth. There is only *one* spirit! There are no good spirits or evil spirits; there is only the Spirit of God! Evil is only the absence of that spirit and our job is to clear the way for that spirit and open all of the empty vessels and let that spirit flow in!"

The men looked at one another and then at the little foam-covered dwarf. They were confused.

CHAPTER 26

✠ ✠ ✠

STEPHANIE HAD BEEN GONE FOR SEVERAL WEEKS, and there had been no sign of her except for the vision in Malchus' nightmare. While Daniel now believed in the reality of the dreamworld, he was convinced that what Malchus had seen was just a fantastic lie concocted by the devil.

As for Jacob, the transfiguration that occurred on the roof of the tenement was a major turning point in his life. He was a changed man with a mission and a new sense of urgency. His powerful personality was now focused and clear. His interminable mood shifts of depression and manic behavior were gone. The black holes that had plagued his vision for nearly thirty years had disappeared, and he could appreciate the beauty and grace of creation.

He filled the apartment with flowers, threw out mounds of moldy old newspapers, and even vacuumed the rug. His greatest pleasures were when he visited the synagogue and prayed with joy and enthusiasm to a newfound God. He took delight in visiting with Malchus and the patients at the Ten Eyck Nursing Center. At the center, he'd read to them, feed them chicken soup, and give them hope and the message of a loving God.

Jacob's terrible burden of guilt had been removed from his mind. He was at peace with Daniel. His relationship with the Almighty became powerful and personal, and he saw the face of the Lord in everyone he met. Like the Hasidic masters of old, he was able to call upon his God to heal the sick, bring joy to the hearts of the depressed, and even save lost souls. Jacob Koretz had become such a new man that even his son, Daniel, had a difficult time recognizing him. But Daniel realized that his father was simply a remarkable example of the radical transformation of human beings by God!

Daniel, too, was changed by the divine event on the roof of the tenement, but his transformation was still only an intellectual ascent. What he had seen had not yet moved him to act. His heart was heavy and he was still depressed about Stephanie's disappearance. He had done everything possible, morally and legally, to find the girl, but there was no trace of her.

Daniel walked through the corridors of the Brewery and spoke with the men asking them if they had seen her or if they might know what had happened to her, but they were just as confounded by her sudden departure. Their Mut was becoming a fond memory. Some of the men even asked Daniel when he was going to hire a new secretary to take Stephanie's place. The paperwork piled up on her vacant desk, and Moe Kutcher was asked to fill the position of office clerk and part-time secretary. He was no better a typist than she was and he cursed the stuck keys as he nervously scratched his body.

Another week went by. Malchus and Jacob were busy at Ten Eyck while Daniel moped around his office. He became an absentee leader who rarely went out on the floor of the warehouse or watched the trucks come in with their loads at the end of the day. He'd frequently come to the Brewery late in the morning and not leave until midnight.

One evening after the trucks came in and the men were up in the dormitories, Daniel lit his pipe and walked through the lonely deserted warehouse to the alleyway that divided the original building from the newer section. He gently tapped his pipe against the brick wall to loosen the spent tobacco. The ash drifted out of the bowl and landed on a large pile of ashes and cinders several feet down the alley. A man, whom Daniel had never seen before, perhaps one of the newer residents, was sweeping the refuse into a metal trashcan. Daniel flicked his lighter to get a closer look at the man's face. He was gaunt, plain, and had short red hair. He stopped his work and rested his chin on the broom handle.

"What are you doing sweeping ashes at this time of the night?" Daniel asked, surprised by the man's presence. "I can hardly see my hand in front of my face. Can't that wait 'til tomorrow? Those ashes aren't going anywhere."

"Oh, I'm not so sure of that," the man replied.

As Daniel walked closer to the man, the ashes seemed to glow faintly as if they had been burning. A whispering sound arose from the pile.

"What's this pile of ashes doing here?" Daniel asked. "Did one of the men set a fire earlier? I've told the guys never to burn trash so close to the building. This place could go up like a matchbox."

The man scooped up a handful of glowing ashes and held it before Daniel's face.

"What the hell are you doing?" Daniel demanded. "You're going to burn the skin off your damned hands. Put those ashes down."

The man spoke, feeling no apparent pain from the burning embers. "No, Daniel, I hold these ashes because they are *my* ashes. Here, look at my arms."

His arm was tattooed with numbers. It resembled Jacob's arm, which had been tattooed by the Nazis at the concentration camp.

"You're just an apparition," Daniel said, as if the comment would make the man vanish into thin air.

"Touch my arm, Daniel," requested the man. "I am real flesh and blood and I am also spirit."

Daniel reached out and gently touched the man's arm and then he lightly touched his face.

"Real?" asked the man with a smile.

"Yes, very real," Daniel replied.

"This pile of ashes is not only me; it is also all of humanity that has come and gone and all of humanity that waits to be born again. Look, Daniel!" demanded the man.

He took the handful of ashes and gently blew on them. Immediately, the embers swirled in the air and became tiny crying infants caught by waiting mothers. The vision disappeared. He took another handful of ashes and threw them high into the air. This time, they became men and women with beautiful strong bodies and glorious voices. Again, the vision disappeared. The man looked at Daniel and asked, "Do you want to see more?"

"Yes, of course," he said, "but I'm not sure of what I've already seen."

The man took a third pile of ashes in his hand and gently stirred it with his fingers. He blew on it but nothing happened. He softly exhaled on the pile again but nothing happened. Finally, he held the pile of ashes up to his face and let a tear drop into his hand. He blew stronger but again nothing. At last, he dropped the pile of ashes on the ground and they remained cold and lifeless.

"What does it all mean?" Daniel demanded.

The man looked at Daniel and then walked closer to him. "Daniel, God gives us the choice of life or death. These ashes are dead because they have chosen not to live again. The Creator can turn this pile of ashes into a living, breathing soul, but that soul must choose life and it must simply respond to the breath of the Almighty. And that breath simply comes from the face of God."

Immediately, Daniel realized what this demonstration meant and at that very instant the man's face began to glow, and the space around him became a dazzling blue-white sphere. Daniel knew that the man was an angel sent to bring him a message.

"Daniel, God desires for all of us to live and to have everlasting life, but we must choose," the angel said. "Not even God's tears can change a heart that does not choose life. But you have chosen wisely and so has your father, Jacob."

Daniel felt a sudden call to action. His heart beat wildly, and he knew that the angel would have an important task for him to accomplish.

"Then what must I do?"

"You have already done the first part; you have walked through the narrow door. But now I give to you *your* pile of ashes."

The angel picked up a pile of ashes and placed them in Daniel's hand. Daniel touched them and then blew them into the air. In an instant, the ashes were gone and so was the angel. He was alone again in the cold, dark alleyway, his eyes not yet adjusted to the night. He was disappointed because he expected the ashes to come to life and sing or become little infants, but there was no life. He stood waiting for another vision, but nothing came.

Daniel slowly walked to the end of the alleyway and heard the soft whimpering of what sounded like a child. The sound grew louder, and within the deep recess of a door to the warehouse, sat a young person crying. He bent down and lit a match to see who the child was. The face turned toward him. It was Stephanie!

CHAPTER 27

✠ ✠ ✠

COINCIDENCE, PREMONITION, SYNCHRONICITY, DIVINE PLAN, THESE WERE all the things that went through Daniel's mind as he gazed upon the frightened face of the young woman crouched in the recess of the door. Was this actually Stephanie Croix, the wildly erratic girl who had so thoroughly penetrated Daniel's soul, or was this just a vision of wishful thinking covering the face of some old alcoholic?

The girl whimpered and sobbed as Daniel touched her thin and battered face. The eyes that were once so big and bright were now sunken and black. The skin that had glowed rosy was now pale, even under the light of a hot flame. Her short-cropped dark hair, which had once been her trademark, was nearly shaved to her scalp. She crouched in the corner of the recess with her knees up to her chin, and when Daniel looked into her eyes, he knew that this was the Stephanie Croix whom he loved and not just another fleeting apparition.

Daniel got down on his knees, his face just inches from hers, and cupped her face in his hands, just like he had cupped the pile of ashes given to him moments before by the angel.

"Stephanie?" he whispered with a slight hint of a question. His breath covered her face, and she seemed to come alive again, her eyes meeting his in the faint glow of the small flame. He gently kissed her mouth and then held her close to his chest. He could feel her deep sobs within his body. He held her firmly and prayed that she would not vanish into thin air.

They did not speak as he lifted her from the pavement. She was emaciated and he could feel her ribs. Her wasted appearance reminded him of those pictures of Holocaust survivors who stood behind barbed wire waiting for their liberators. Her clothes had become rags and a smell of soot and burned fabric permeated the air around her. It was as if she had been in a fiery hell and the flames had almost consumed her. Daniel noticed long scratches on her arms, and the palms of her hands were so sore that she could not let him hold them. She was so light that Daniel lifted her up as a father would lift a small child. He carried her back to the front office in the Brewery where he placed her on the couch. He turned on the overhead light. She winced and hid her eyes. Daniel could now see the full extent of the damage that had been done to her. He was livid and punched the walls with his fists.

"How could he do this to you?" Daniel asked with a cry in his voice. "What kind of beast is this man?" He didn't expect any answers from her.

Stephanie needed immediate attention, but this time he would not leave her side. This time he would claim to be her husband. He would guard the doors of the hospital. She could not escape or be abducted by some satanic being. Then, he thought, how would he explain her wounds, her bruises, the vast extent of her scratches and burns? Hospital personnel would think he was responsible for battering his wife. He was not in the frame of mind to conjure up any stories, she needed help quickly, and that was all that mattered.

Daniel called 9-1-1, but then dropped the receiver when he noticed that the inside of her forearm had been tattooed with numbers, just like Jacob's and the angel's forearms. He felt sick to his stomach and searched his memory for some logical explanation to this additional atrocity. His anger at Stephanie's tormentor and his desire for revenge was only tempered by his gratefulness that she was now with him. He ran up to the dormitories to awaken John and Malchus and tell them of Stephanie's return.

At the hospital, Daniel protested to the staff. He wanted to be by her side at all times and not let her out of his sight. Malchus wisely advised him that Satan would not touch her any longer. The devil had taken all he wanted from her and disposed of what was left. She was now in the hands of God and the people who loved her.

For a week, Stephanie remained at the hospital in a state of shock and began to regain her physical strength. She didn't speak except for tiny whimpers and sobs. Her sleep was fitful and at night, she would thrash the air and scream. The medical team told Daniel that while she was physically recovering, she had experienced a severe mental trauma that would require long-term psychiatric care.

Stephanie was moved to a psychiatric ward of the hospital. When Jacob visited her one evening, the true nature of her ordeal in hell came forth like molten lava from a volcano. She sat in a corner of one of the larger visiting rooms, her hair had begun to grow in, and color was returning to her face. Though still thin, she had lost the sickly, emaciated look. Her eyes, however, were still vacant and she stared out into deep space. When Jacob saw the girl sitting on her chair, stiff, immobile, and terrified, it brought back those terrible memories of the concentration camp. He held her two small, cold hands, bowed his head, and prayed. As the tears fell, she lifted one of her hands and touched his face. She began to speak in sentences for the first time since Daniel found her, but her words were not in English. She spoke in Yiddish, and Jacob understood what she was saying.

Malchus and Daniel stood beside Jacob as she spoke to him. She lifted her eyes to the sky and began to speak.

"Jacob, it is you! I never thought I'd see you again. You look so much older and you have a beard and glasses. They've tortured you."

The pupils in her eyes grew wide, and for the first time since Daniel found her, she focused on a person's face—the face of Jacob Koretz. The old man was puzzled and confounded, but her voice, her mannerisms, and even her looks now reminded him of his beloved Leah who had been his lover in the death camp, the woman who gave birth to his two sons, Daniel and Pinchas.

She grabbed Jacob's arms and her fingers pressed into his flesh, her eyes became wild, and the words poured from her mouth in the native tongue of the Jews of Warsaw.

"Jacob, I've missed you so much, but now you're back with me. They forced me to carry the bodies, to drag them along the ground, and pile them up. I saw you. You carried bodies, too. You pushed them, picked up pieces of them, and placed them in piles for the crematorium. I begged the SS officer to leave me alone for just a few days. He knew I was sick. I think he even knew that I was pregnant. Perhaps he thought it was *his* child. Jacob, I'm so sorry. He raped me so many times, I'm not even sure if the baby inside of me was yours."

Her words were inconceivable to Jacob. He looked at Daniel and spoke with a cry in his voice. "How could this girl possibly know of my deepest and most horrendous experiences? How could she express the torment of my Leah in such a personal way? It is as if she really did experience the hell of the camp."

Stephanie continued to speak into Jacob's very soul as if Daniel and Malchus were not in the room.

"Jacob, do you remember the last days? Those terrible last days when I was so delirious with fever and pain? I think they already knew that the allies would be tearing down the gates in just a matter of hours to set the condemned souls free. But Jacob, I was alone, hidden away in some awful dark room when the labor pains began and there was nobody in this entire world to help me give birth to my baby. At the moments of my greatest pain, I could also feel my greatest joy because I knew that a new life would be coming out of me. But at that same time, I didn't want anything new, beautiful, and alive to be brought into such a horrible, evil world.

"When I pushed, I screamed until I almost passed out, but I knew that I had to continue to give birth. When the tiny body finally emerged from the darkness of my womb into the darkness of the world, I lifted the child, but he was not breathing and he did not cry. For an instant, I was glad that he would not have to suffer by living even one second in the death camp. I screamed and cried and asked God to kill me, too, but he kept me alive because there was still another child inside of my body. I did not know it before, but I had been carrying twins. The intense pain began again, and God gave me the strength to give birth to another child. But this time, the baby cried and I laid him on my breast. And that was the last time I saw my children. Jacob, I hemorrhaged and died soon afterward."

Jacob cupped his hand around her face. He wanted to speak to her, but he couldn't find the words. She continued to tell her story.

"Another woman from the camp found me a few hours later just as the American soldiers were coming into the camp. She discovered the two infants on my chest, took them out into the yard, and held them like dolls. She was sick and dazed out of her mind. One of the babies was still alive and crying, demanding to be fed. The other was limp and dead. I, too, was now gone, but a part of me lingered on in the death camp, hovering over my babies and the corpses waiting to be burned. She carried the babies in her arms until a man came to her and told her that the babies were dead. Even the one who was alive could hardly cry. In a mindless daze, he took them from her and placed them in a cart. As if he were piling tiny logs of wood, he took the two infants and neatly placed them on top of the pile of corpses."

She stopped for a moment and then placed her hand on the side of Jacob's face. She touched his beard.

"Jacob, that man was you, and when that one tiny infant on the pile began to whimper, you arose from the dead and picked up both of the little bodies, the dead one, and the one who was crying. His cries awakened your soul, and you just stood in the darkness looking up to heaven and screaming psalms at the Almighty. The American soldiers could not believe what they were seeing when they walked through the death camp. Some of them cried, some were angry, but most were just in shock and could not believe the magnitude of the suffering and torment.

"After months of battle, they had finally walked through the gates of hell. An American soldier found you and your sons. He told you that one of the babies was dead. For you, the pile of corpses had become a sacred mountain with your sons at the summit. When I knew you and Daniel were safe, my guardian angel called me to join the rest of those who had died in the camps. I whispered to you the names of your sons. The one in your arms was Daniel. You could not remember much more than his name because of all the pain and the guilt that you carried.

"Jacob, I knew that some day we would be together, and that I would be able to communicate to you the truth that happened in the camp. I thought it would be only in heaven, but your pain was so intense that I needed some way to come to you while you were still alive and while you could still do something magnificent for humanity. I needed to help you heal, Jacob, that is how strong my love is. So I asked the angels if I could return to this world, and through this girl, have Satan take me back to the camp. I pleaded with them." Leah closed her eyes and sighed deeply. The girl's body went limp.

Leah was gone, but Stephanie had returned. She looked into the eyes of Jacob and Daniel and spoke for the first time since she had returned.

"I knew that both of you loved me very much and that your love would save me from Satan and the evils of the world. Your prayers saved me. God opened the narrow door and you walked through."

She turned to Malchus, smiled, and touched his face.

"Malchus, servant of the Lord, your time is coming."

She said nothing more and then fainted into Jacob's arms.

CHAPTER 28

✛ ✛ ✛

RECONCILIATION, KNOWLEDGE, AND WISDOM—THESE THINGS BRING TRUE peace and understanding to people. They transform the heart and transfigure the soul. They bind relationships, bring peace to disturbed minds, and even heal broken bodies. Only God knows the workings of the process and He does not share all of His knowledge with His creation. However, He does provide sufficient revelation so that imperfect men and women can do miracles. The Almighty even uses the forces of darkness, evil, and destruction to bring faith, hope, and love into an empty and hungry world. While the Creator remains transcendent and beyond the comprehension of mere mortals, He provides a narrow door for entry to His kingdom, a smiling face and open arms, and a doorman who knocks and shows the way. The door is never a great golden gate with heavy iron locks, but merely a simple wooden door with a big, easily turned knob. In fact, the moment a person touches the knob, the door springs open and the doorman waits on the other side.

Malchus always had a difficult time opening doors. Most of the doors were just too big and heavy and the knobs too high and difficult to turn. His hands were small like a child's, and the large steel doors in the Brewery were always a challenge for him. Stephanie had often been there when he needed a door opened and now, after several months away from the Brewery recovering from her journey to hell, the young girl returned a transformed person. The color in her face had returned and her dark hair had grown in. She even gained a little weight, though she could still pass for a scarecrow. She had not forgotten anything about her harrowing experience, but her mind was now able to sort things out, and she began to write down her deepest thoughts and feelings in a journal. Her words were elegant and she combined them with imaginative drawings. Gone were the sharp edges and the grotesque distortions. She was now seeing the world through new eyes and with a new heart. The little frightened girl was now a woman and she cherished the life of Leah, who now lived within her heart. The two women were now one and inseparable, and Stephanie became a new stronger woman with profound insight and power.

As she walked into the waiting room of the Brewery, a host of men greeted her with hugs and flowers. Their long lost Mut had returned. She stood by Daniel's side and it was now apparent that the two of them would be intertwined both emotionally and spiritually for the rest of their lives. She touched Daniel's face and kissed him on the cheek.

She went to her desk and sat down behind a dusty pile of papers that had been neglected, but somehow this was not to be her calling. She was never good at punching keys on a typewriter and her new powers were certainly not directed toward the management of an office. Daniel understood that the Stephanie he once knew was gone and that she was a new creation. He now fully accepted the fact that Stephanie could leave him forever and follow her dream and her calling. For now, he would just let her discover what she was to be in this world. This would be a time of healing, growing, and maturing. Daniel loved Stephanie and would do anything to bring her to wholeness, but he also wanted to be close to her, to talk with her, and touch her.

She touched the towering stack of papers on her desk with her two hands. She looked up at Daniel. "You want me to do all this paperwork today?" she asked and then laughed. It was the first time in many weeks that Daniel had seen a real smile. It was pure joy to see her face light up just as it had done so many times before.

The weeks that followed Stephanie's return were marked by a calm peace and even a comforting monotony. Daniel managed the Brewery and got some new contracts from the city department of corrections. Stephanie spent most of her time counseling the men and opening doors for Malchus. She still had that ability to listen to the pain in men's souls even when their mouths were saying something entirely different. There was one thing that she requested of the men: that they no longer call her Mut.

"Mut is gone," she said. "She died while I was away. Please, just call me Stephanie." She did not share her deep secrets with them, of course, but they knew of her transformation. She was no longer the strange, moody, chain-smoking girl in the front office.

The winter months at the Brewery were especially difficult and uncomfortable. The trucks wouldn't start, the heating system in the dormitories broke down, and many of the men kept warm by staying drunk or finding alternative sources of warmth, like using kerosene heaters. Daniel had his hands full with stubborn machinery and frustrated, ornery men. He stood on the loading dock listening to the gripes of Salvatore Cantucci, and he shivered as the cold blasts of air swirled around the paralyzed trucks. Stephanie ran out of the office with Daniel's long winter coat hanging on her arms. She was already dressed for a cold January day in New York City.

She pushed the coat toward him. "Here, put this on before you freeze to death. I need to talk with you, it's important."

Daniel was preoccupied. "Stephanie, I've got five dead trucks just sitting here. I need to get them moving today or we'll be at least a week behind schedule. I might as well close the place down if I can't get them going."

Stephanie was insistent; everything else could wait. "Daniel, this is more important than the trucks, or the schedules, or all the stuff we have in the warehouse. Button up your coat and take a walk with me down to the Kills, now!"

She grabbed him by the sleeve and tugged him like a stubborn child who didn't want to follow his mother's instructions. They walked down the long, gray dead end street, passed the alleyway where Daniel had found Stephanie several months before, and then stopped at the concrete abutment of the Kills. She held his arms tightly and looked deeply into his eyes.

"Daniel, do you love me?" she asked. Her words were sharp and to the point. There was nothing vague or mysterious about her question.

Daniel was surprised and a little annoyed. "You took me all the way out here to ask me if I love you?"

"Daniel, do you love me?" she asked insistently.

Without hesitation Daniel replied, "Yes, Stephanie, I love you. I've loved you for a long time. Don't you know that?"

"No, I don't know that because you've never said it to my face. You've done every wonderful thing for me except tell me that you loved me. Now, say it for me one more time."

"Stephanie, I love you with all my heart and soul," Daniel said with conviction.

Stephanie was prepared with her next but very confounding question. "Daniel, do you know what today is?"

He looked up at the sky as if there was a giant calendar floating over his head. "I think it's January twenty-first. Why?"

"I had a dream about you last night or perhaps it was a vision," she said. "It was a beautiful vision, and we were surrounded by children and family, and there were many others around us wishing us well. It was such a sweet dream that when I awoke, I felt so wonderful. Daniel, last night was the Eve of Saint Agnes. A young woman is likely to dream about her future husband on Saint Agnes' Eve and I dreamt about you. Daniel, will you marry me?"

Daniel was caught off guard and seemed to lose his balance. He shivered in the frosty air and their breath condensed like a cloud around their heads.

"Yes, yes, of course I'll marry you," Daniel said at the top of his voice. He looked up at the sky again as if to get a nod from some higher power.

They embraced and kissed, but Daniel still didn't know what had hit him. Stephanie, however, knew exactly what she was doing because she was following the guidance of her spiritual eyes. She held him tight and looked into his eyes. They both glanced into the murky waters of the English Kills and saw the reflection of a black, smoky cloud moving over their heads. The Brewery was on fire!

CHAPTER 29

✠ ✠ ✠

IT WAS BOUND TO HAPPEN. NO, PREORDAINED! The insurance company's risk managers warned Daniel about all those inappropriate space heaters and unattended kerosene stoves. Keeping the Brewery warm during the cold New York winters was like heating the Arctic. Every calorie of heat either went through the roof or out the windows. Even the dormitories were like refrigerators. To make matters worse, some of the men took to drinking just to forget the discomfort of the cold. When they got drunk, they were more inclined to accidentally trip over a kerosene heater or deliberately kick over anything that got in their way.

As the thick, black smoke poured out of the upper stories of the warehouse, Daniel and Stephanie ran back to the massive facility. When they arrived, they found a horde of men standing around on the sidewalk shivering and in various states of undress. The men who had been in the living quarters were now safely out, as well as those on the loading dock and in the administrative offices. By the time the fire department arrived, the large building was fully engulfed in flames. The whereabouts of perhaps twenty men, including Malchus, were unknown.

The icy, cold winds played havoc with the firefighters' attempt to douse the flames, and the spray from their hoses blew back into their faces. The warehouse was a literal fuel depot, filled with baled cotton rags and greasy newspapers. The old timbers of the building were as dry as kindling. Nothing could survive the ravages of the monstrous flames that leaped out from every window.

Stephanie counted the men who stood outside watching the great Brewery turn to ashes. There were still thirteen men unaccounted for. They could be anywhere inside the burning inferno, or now simply wandering the streets.

Malchus was nowhere. Stephanie knew that he would find it especially difficult to make it through the labyrinth of rooms and corridors in the massive building.

Several engine companies and a hook and ladder unit were on hand to fight the ever-increasing blaze. The warehouse was now totally involved, and it would be a miracle if anything or anyone survived the great conflagration.

A deafening explosion came from the far side of the warehouse adjacent to the English Kills. The east wall collapsed, sending tons of brick and rubble into the little canal. A radio message from the firefighting unit on the east side said that they had survivors and needed ambulances immediately.

Daniel and Stephanie ran to the back of the building facing the Kills. Amid the thickening smoke and dust of the collapsing rubble, a small group of men ran as if on top of the water to the other side of the English Kills. They stood shouting to the crowd on the other side, and in front and center was Malchus waving his hat at the firefighters and emergency crews.

Stephanie, who was just barely visible through the dense haze, screamed at Malchus. The men were coughing and covered with cinders and ash, but were unharmed.

Suddenly, another loud, roaring explosion came from deep within the warehouse section of the Brewery. The sidewalks trembled, and within moments, hundreds of people surrounding the building witnessed a truly unbelievable phenomenon. A mammoth geyser of water from the natural spring beneath the Brewery burst forth from the lower basement and spewed a gigantic column of water nearly two hundred feet into the frigid January air. Within minutes, the water from the geyser had doused the enormous fire and quenched the destructive flames. The massive column of water, like a huge liquid tongue, then receded back into the earth.

The fire was out, but the warehouse was a total loss. Thankfully, not one life was lost. All the men were eventually accounted for, including three who had been on a drinking binge in Hoboken, New Jersey. Even Potato's cat strolled, soot-covered, down the street as if nothing had happened.

The thirteen men who managed to get out of the warehouse alive had been guided through the flames by Malchus.

Daniel was grateful for all Malchus had done, but then he knew that Malchus was blessed to do special things. When asked how he managed to save all those men, Malchus told them in a matter-of-fact way.

"We were all in that blazing warehouse and the thick, black smoke covered the ceiling. I could hear the men choking and screaming, but I'm so much shorter, so it was easy for me to find my way around in the fresh air down near the floor. Besides, I had Naphtali Ropshitz with me to guide the way. When the east wall collapsed, Tali just told me to walk on the water over the English Kills like it was dry land. All I did was follow his directions."

CHAPTER 30

✟ ✟ ✟

DANIEL AND STEPHANIE STOOD AT THE EDGE of the large, water-filled crater that formed during the Great Conflagration when the natural spring beneath the Brewery burst forth with a glorious column of water and put out the fire. The appearance of the spring was no surprise; it had been there since the beginning of time—well, at least since the end of the last Ice Age. It was the reason the Brewery was built in Greenpoint in the first place.

For more than one hundred years, the companies that made beer at the Brewery took advantage of the virtually endless supply of pure sparkling water. When the Brewery was shut down during the era of Prohibition and purchased by the Service Corps, the spring was virtually forgotten. Nobody needed or wanted pure, pristine water. They got all they needed from reservoirs in upstate New York. The new owners of the Brewery, who would have nothing to do with alcoholic beverages of any kind, covered up all the cisterns, closed off all the tanks and pipes, and put a new concrete floor over top the whole works, virtually entombing the natural spring. And there it stayed, this magnificent, deep well, covered over for forty years until the fire brought forth its glory.

As it turned out, Malchus was the unwitting instigator of the Great Conflagration. While carrying a dozen homemade cookies to his coworkers in the freezing cold warehouse, he inadvertently kicked over a kerosene space heater placed too near a bale of old newspapers. Consequently, the whole place went up in flames in just a matter of minutes, but who is to say that this incident was really the fault of just one person? Perhaps it was the divine intervention of the Almighty Himself, who just happened to use Malchus as his catalyst just as he had used the little man so many times before.

Some people are like natural springs filled with pure, sparkling water. Some are even filled with living water, the kind you need drink only once to quench a lifetime of spiritual thirst. Malchus was one of those filled with living water. God was always filling him up and never leaving him dry. Malchus offered his water freely to anyone who would drink and offered more if they became thirsty.

As it turned out, the Great Conflagration and the destruction of the warehouse were just possibly the best things that ever happened to the Service Corps in New York City. Not only was the natural spring an abundant source of pure water for drinking, but it also contained highly beneficial minerals known to prevent a host of ailments and diseases. As a result, the water became a valuable commodity purchased by the manufacturers of medicines, cosmetics, and soft drinks.

Within two years following the destruction of the warehouse, the Brewery was rebuilt and converted into an efficient bottling plant. It generated millions of dollars in revenue for the Service Corps and provided hundreds of jobs for the people in the community, including the men who had previously worked in the Brewery. It became one of the most effective rehabilitation centers in the nation and a model for the Service Corps. A new housing community was built across the street, which was named the Waterworks, and the dilapidated neighborhood came back to life like a long dormant flower. Some simply called it the miracle in Greenpoint.

Daniel Aarons, known as the father of the miracle, prospered. He formed a new nonprofit corporation, of which he became president, and used the revenue generated to establish a foundation for the improvement of rehabilitation and mental health services in Greenpoint. Stephanie Croix, now Mrs. Daniel Aarons, attended City College of New York where she completed her Master's degree in Art Therapy.

Jacob Koretz, even at his advanced age of seventy, went back to seminary to finish his rabbinical training and to help the patients at the Ten Eyck Nursing Center. He lived by himself in a new apartment at the Waterworks. He continued to write his long, voluminous poetry and produced several off-off Broadway plays.

The age of miracles and visions seemed to have ceased for Daniel and Jacob, but that suited both of them just fine. They knew their missions and they no longer needed the coaxing of apparitions or painful memories from the past. But what of Malchus One Ear?

EPILOGUE

✠ ✠ ✠

EACH YEAR FOLLOWING THE GREAT CONFLAGRATION, JACOB
Koretz had a Passover Seder in his small apartment in the Waterworks.
Jacob would naturally ask the youngest child at the table to participate
in the traditional rite by asking the *four questions*. This year, Jacob
chose Malchus to be the youngest child since most of the guests were
elderly patients of the Ten Eyck Nursing Center. One was a woman in a
wheelchair, named Rebecca, who was a new resident. Neither Jacob nor
Malchus had ever met this woman before. Following the ancient ritual,
Malchus stood at the head of the table and asked, "Why is this night
different from all other nights?" He expected the standard response from
Jacob as it had been repeated to children for generations. At that instant,
the woman seated in the wheelchair answered Malchus' question. She
closed her eyes and recited some strange biblical-sounding verses.

"The woman conceived and gave birth to a son," she said. "And when
she saw that he was a strange baby, she hid him three months in a paper
sack and kept him in the cold dark cellar of her tenement. When she could
hide him no longer, she took a garbage can and filled it with newspapers
and a tin of evaporated milk. She put the child in it and placed it among the
flotsam on the bank of the East River. His sister stood at a distance to see
what would happen to him. A woman came down to gaze upon the river.
She saw the garbage can among the floating debris and sent her assistant to
bring it in. When she opened the garbage can, she saw the child. He was
crying and she took pity on him. He was a special child like none that had
ever been seen upon the earth. The woman took the child, nursed it, and

delivered it to the sanctuary of Bellevue Hospital. Because he had only one ear, they named him Malchus."

There was silence in the room. No one at the table understood the woman's story, but Malchus heard it before and knew the woman was talking about him. As if nothing had happened, Malchus repeated the question.

"Why is this night different from all other nights?"

Again, the woman responded.

"Malchus, I am the little girl who stood at a distance on the bank of the river. I'm your sister, Rebecca."

Again, there was silence. Nobody knew what to say. Was this woman actually Malchus' sister? Malchus looked at Jacob and simply shrugged his shoulders. For an instant, time seemed to stand still and the finger of the Almighty was writing on the wall in Jacob's apartment. Jacob, in his wisdom, seemed to see the entire vision before him and responded to the helpless stare of the dwarf.

"Malchus, why don't we take Rebecca into the living room so that you can talk with her and then later on we'll all invite the prophet Elijah to join us at the table for a glass of wine."

Malchus and his sister sat alone in Jacob's small living room and didn't speak for several minutes. Then he broke the silence.

"Nobody ever told me that I had a sister," he said. "I just thought I was thrown out like trash and landed in a garbage can in the East River. At least, that's what they told me. But, how do you *know* that I'm your brother?"

Rebecca turned to Malchus and requested that he hold her hand. Malchus reached out, and for the first time in his thirty-three years, he held the hand of his only known relative.

"Malchus, I didn't come looking for you, but when I saw you at the nursing center, I knew you were my brother. I could never forget that day on the bank of the river when our mother sent you away. She was a very sick woman. She was just a child herself when you were born, and I was barely ten years old. Several weeks later, she took you down to the river and cast you adrift like Moses in the River Nile. She read her Bible and she knew the story. She actually thought that somebody would hear your cries and find you. She hid you away in the cellar because she thought that *she* had been cursed, but that *you* were actually a blessing in disguise. She continued to feed you, but she was so disturbed and troubled that she didn't know what she was doing. It wasn't long after you were found that they found her, too, and took her away. I never saw her again, but everyone said she died in a state hospital. I became a ward of the state and because of my chronic illnesses I, too, lived in institutions for a long time. Now I need intensive nursing care. I guess that's why God sent me to Ten Eyck because He knew that I'd find you."

All the pieces of Malchus' life were beginning to come together. He knew there was no deception and that Rebecca was truly his sister, his flesh and blood. The vague resemblance, especially in the eyes, the big, sad eyes spoke volumes.

"Rebecca, what was our mother's name?" Malchus asked.

"Her name was Maria," said Rebecca. "She was a Gypsy."

Malchus suddenly became dizzy. A flood of memories came back to him, including the visions of his guardian angels and the night that Naphtali Ropshitz died.

"Please tell me more about Maria," Malchus said. "Why was she so troubled? What could have led her to do such strange things?"

Tears welled in Rebecca's eyes and for a moment, she turned away from Malchus.

"She was a survivor of the most terrible hell that any person could possibly experience, the hell of Auschwitz," Rebecca said with a soft, quivering voice.

Malchus' eyes filled with tears. He had heard of that terrible place so many times before from the lips of Jacob Koretz and now his own mother, too, had been a captive of the terrible death camp.

"For two years she survived only to see her entire family wiped off the face of the earth. She was depressed, hopeless, and stayed that way until the day she died. At least, that's what they told me."

Malchus took a tissue and wiped the tears from her eyes, but continued to ask Rebecca painful questions about their mother's past.

"But Maria came to America and started a family, didn't she?" asked Malchus.

"No, she didn't start a family," Rebecca said. "Malchus, we may have come out of the same womb, but we didn't have the same father. Our mother sadly gave her body to any man who wanted it. That's what happened to her in the death camp and that's how she survived. Her soul was closed shut and buried deep within the cold rocks of hell."

"What about *my* father?" Malchus asked. "Did you know him?"

"Malchus, your father is not of this world, at least that's what Maria claimed."

Rebecca had a difficult time speaking of this, but she opened her mouth and strained to find the appropriate words.

"I was just a little girl. A strange man appeared one night in our mother's apartment. I heard a crashing sound on the roof of the tenement and we ran to see what had happened. A small glowing sphere seemed to have landed on the roof. A man stood by the sphere. His clothes were in shreds and his arms were bleeding. Maria brought him to the apartment and bandaged his wounds. He was so full of light, delicate, and very beautiful. His skin was milky-white and almost transparent, like *yours*. His voice was like a soft song and he spoke to us in the poetry of a strange world, but we understood every word he said! He fell asleep in my mother's arms, and he stayed with her the entire night. When I awoke the next morning, he was gone and so was the sphere. I had never seen Mother so happy. She said that the strange man had given her a gift, a special seed that would grow, mature, and fill the world with blessings. The seed, she said, was planted in her womb."

Rebecca took a long breath. "Malchus, *you* are that seed and that strange man was your father! When you were born, the doctors said that you wouldn't survive because of your severe deformities. They wanted to take you away even before Maria could see you. She thought that God had cursed her again for all the evil she had committed in the death camp. But she took you, and in her madness, hid you away from the world until she could set you free. No one could save her, but she thought that she could save you—a tiny deformed infant who would become a blessing to the entire world!"

Malchus stared into Rebecca's eyes then put his head in her lap and cried.

Shortly afterward, he wheeled Rebecca into Jacob's dining room where they continued to celebrate the Passover. Jacob welcomed Elijah the prophet into the Seder.

Funny, he looked just like Naphtali Ropshitz!

The End